BLOOD HUNT

BLOOD & SHADOWS BOOK 4

BOOKS BY ALIANNE DONNELLY

BLOOD AND SHADOWS
Blood Moons
Blood Trails
Blood Debts
Blood Hunt
Shadow Hawk

DAWN OF RAGNAROK
The Royal Wizard
Dragonblood
Prince of Deceit

THE BEAST
Bastien
The Beast

OTHER TITLES
Wolfen
Virtual
Function: L1VE

ALIANNE DONNELLY

BLOOD HUNT

BLOOD & SHADOWS BOOK 4

For my readers.

The teachings of history are clear on this matter: those who do not prepare for the future get trampled in its wake. I don't intend to be a footnote to a footnote—I will carve my legacy into the skeleton of the human race. If not with light, then with Shadows.

-Sen. Matthew Griffith (A Memoire)

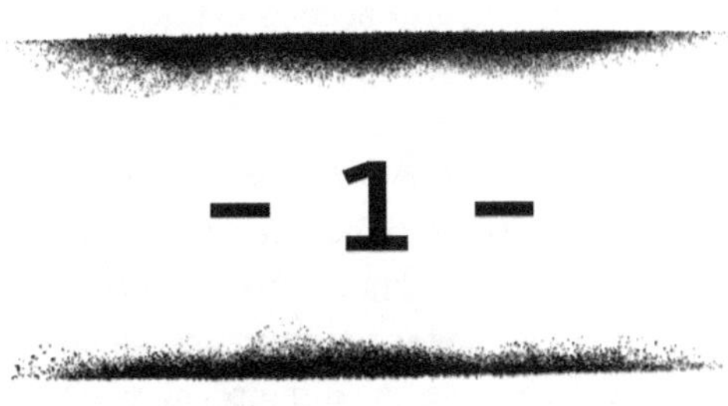

– 1 –

December 24, 3035 – Resphera, Mars 2

"Put it down," Pixie said quietly.

The man didn't hear her.

She slammed her hand down onto the bar right in front of him, and repeated, "Put. It. Down."

"Problem?" the bartender asked warily, already reaching for the hidden alarm underneath the edge of the bar. Everyone was twitchy these days.

Pixie sent the drink mixer away with half a thought, then focused back on the man swilling his whiskey.

The drunkard shrugged her off. "Get lost, little girl."

Not so little anymore. Old enough to be on her own, to have traveled light years to this place, found a job, and made friends, made something of herself—all on her own. Something she'd been proud of, until tonight.

Pixie hadn't crossed any lines yet; she could still turn back. Heaven knew if—no, *when*—the Special Unit found out about this, there'd be no going back to anything. Would they even ask why she'd done it? Would they care whether the end justified the means?

Considering they knew as well as she did that the greatest of humanity's atrocities had been perpetrated for the greater good, no, they wouldn't care about her motives. The Special Unit's rules were ironclad, harsh, and not up for discussion. They were in place for one reason: so no telepath would ever be tempted to take justice into their own hands. The punishment for such a crime wasn't something Pixie wanted to contemplate.

She thought of Mary back in her room, of the people who were making way for the paramedics so she could be treated. The pain below her waist had eased when they'd put her on the bed. The bastard had damaged her spine. Pixie's jaw ached from gritting her teeth, but she couldn't unclench it. Whatever she did tonight, whatever the cost to herself, it'd be worth it to see this nightmare end. It had to be.

"I won't ask you again," she said, voice low and even, mindful of the other patrons sitting around the bar. She opened a one-way channel and sent a compulsion just strong enough to make him pay attention.

He put his drink down.

"Now stand up." This time, it was an order. He complied, and she made sure it hurt every step of the way.

"The hell are you doing to me?" he bit out, holding her stare, because she wouldn't let him look away. *No mercy.*

"Shut up and walk." She gave him her back and went out, dragging him along behind her. It took very little effort to keep him moving. For all that he made himself feel strong by hurting others, his mind was as weak as a child's. That was why he did it in the first place. It disgusted her to be in such close contact with him, but her wrath was stronger.

Worth it to see this end.

Another antichem rally had started earlier in the day, and it was still going on over to the east. On the other side of town, thousands had gathered around the immunization clinic, their chants powerful enough to carry on the wind. Pixie steered clear of that fray, turning in the opposite direction. She walked past the handful of people milling around with nothing better to do, and headed toward the city limits.

Only industrial warehouses and street gangs were out this way. Resphera wasn't an architectural marvel to begin with, but this part of town had been so neglected, it reminded her of Earth, circa 20th century. Amid the graffiti-covered warehouses, trash in metal barrels had been set on fire, and in every shadowed corner, shivering groups of drug addicts huddled together for warmth. They wouldn't go near the fires; drug-induced paranoia and sensitivity to light kept them far away.

Beyond the last warehouse, Resphera once again became respectable. Or as respectable as it got. A threshold of filth marked the border, as if some giant snowplow had piled it up along one side to keep it off decent people's shoes. Pixie stepped over it, onto the clean pavement of the highway leading out of town. A holosign jauntily proclaimed: YOU ARE NOW LEAVING THE CITY OF RESPHERA. HAVE A NICE DAY! But every time it flickered, a graffiti overlay read FUCK OFF!

Pixie led her zombie to Infinity Bridge, a thing of beauty spanning a ten-story-deep gorge. Apprehension clawed at her insides, but she kept going, even when the guy started to whimper behind her. He'd be pissing himself soon.

In the middle of the bridge, she stopped and faced him. "Do you know what to do, or should I give you instructions?"

He tried to reply, but Pixie wouldn't let him. She felt his fear without trying to. Still less than a fraction of what he'd made Mary feel. Nowhere near enough.

"I don't have ham-sized fists to beat you bloody for what you did," she told him. "I know I can't get you convicted. But I can make this right again." One less bad guy in the world. It would be worth the cost. It had to be.

"Sit down." He sank to the ground as if his legs had gone out from under him.

In the distance, a flare went up, drawing her eye and with it, the man's. The first step in violent crowd control—a warning shot. If the rally didn't break up soon, they'd call in reinforcements to make them disperse. Good. That meant everyone would be busy elsewhere.

Pixie turned back to her prisoner and crouched in front of him. "I want you to know that what I am about to do doesn't have to hurt. But it will." *It'll hurt both of us,* she thought, bracing herself.

Despite her compulsion to keep him docile and quiet, he was still very much aware. Tears and snot streamed down his face. His eyes were as wide as saucers, but his mouth was pressed tightly shut.

Closing her own eyes, Pixie reached out to Mary lying on the stretcher being loaded into an ambulance, and brushed her mind as gently as she could, slowing her friend's thought process so she calmed down enough to let the sedatives work.

Mary hurt enough already; Pixie didn't want her to relive what had happened. She insulated her friend in calm as she "borrowed" Mary's memories, channeling them through herself and into the mass of human refuse before her. She made him see and feel it all—the fear, the pain, the helplessness, the worry that someone might come in and become another one of his victims. By the time she'd finished, Pixie was shaking. Mary had been relieved to see Pixie. Not because she'd be able to get help, but because she'd been just late enough not to get caught in the crossfire. How different the outcome might have been had Pixie gotten there a few minutes sooner.

The man's eyes glazed over, his mind a low-level hum. Shock. Pixie knew he was still seeing what he'd done, caught in the middle of two perspectives without a way to distinguish between them. A pity he wouldn't have time to fully appreciate his impact on the world; how a good woman could be destroyed so thoroughly and so quickly, she might never recover, or how she'd never again see herself as anything other than a victim. Pain made memories long. He should have the opportunity to experience it himself.

But if Pixie thought about it any longer, it would drown her, rip her apart the way he'd ripped apart Mary, and then she'd never see this through. Breathing was already a chore, and tears made her eyes burn. She couldn't allow that, so she pushed to her feet. "Get up," she said, her voice raw with strain.

The man complied, slack-faced like a sleepwalker. Under her silent direction, he clambered over the railing to the little ledge on the other side. Pixie wavered, suppressing a shudder that mirrored Mary's in the ambulance. In the next instant, her heart began to slam against her ribcage. The rally was turning violent.

She squeezed her eyes shut, focused to remove herself from both places. She needed to be herself and no one else to finish this. The vile excuse of a man had a name, an important one. He didn't deserve it. "You are no one," she whispered, stripping him of his identity. He'd remember nothing of who he was or what he'd done until the moment he'd walked into the upscale brothel. "No one and nothing," she said.

It wouldn't matter for much longer, but she couldn't stand for one more second his pretending to be human.

The sudden wrench in his mind woke him up a little, and he realized where he was, knew what he'd done, and knew what he was about to do. He started fighting her. Fear for his life made him stronger and it took more effort to keep him in line. Pixie struggled to hold on.

Her control slipped enough to free up his speech. "Oh, God!" he whined. "Help me! Someone *heeeelp!*"

Swaying on her feet, Pixie uttered her final command in a strained voice that wouldn't carry far: "Let go."

And he did.

When the echo of his distant splash faded, Pixie collapsed. Her body heaved, and she cast up everything she'd eaten that day, leaving her drained, shaking, and about five minutes away from passing out.

She didn't have the strength or the time to backtrack to check on Mary. She'd been seen leaving the bar with him, but no one would think much of it for a while, especially with the escalating riot. When they began to put two and two together, though, Pixie would be the first one they'd come after.

Her first instinct was to go home, back to her brother. He'd make it all okay again. But the thought of making him an accomplice turned her stomach.

No, she thought. *I won't bring this to his door.* Besides, he was still technically an agent with the Special Unit, and if she showed up on his doorstep, he'd be forced to bring her in. No way would she put her brother in the position of having to deliver his own flesh and blood to the gallows. No. She'd made her choice, and she'd pay for it on her own. As of this moment, Jeremy's little Pixie no longer existed.

She used the railing to haul herself up off the ground. The temperature had dropped a great deal, and she hugged herself for warmth. With the last of her mental strength, she orchestrated a happy dream of friendship and love in Mary's sedated mind. When she'd finished, Emma Calen, a waitress-turned-murderer, hailed a taxi and waved goodbye to the carefree life she'd been pretending to lead.

Twenty-one years old, Emma should have learned by now: there was no such thing as a carefree life for a telepath.

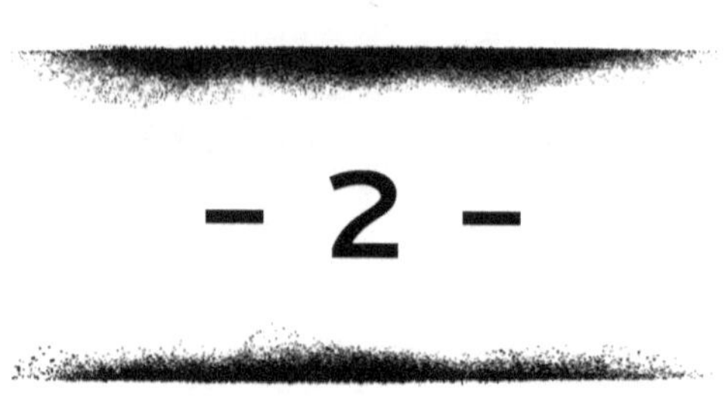

– 2 –

Juan Dominguez was a simple man who used to live a simple life with his obnoxious wife and three spoiled kids, before the people of his district had lost their damn minds. "You think I don't know it's New Year's Eve?" he demanded of his guard. As Chief of Police, it was assumed Dominguez had authority over every uniform in the district. Assumed, that is, by everyone except said uniforms. "No, I haven't seen the cells. Yes, I am aware we're overcrowded. Well, you know what? You better come up with a damn good plan to make room, because we're about to have more incoming."

He didn't hear the response he needed.

"I don't care if you have to padlock them in the locker room, just do it and stop pissing me off!" How he missed the olden days when a person could slam down a corded phone in frustration. Now, all he could do with the standard issue coms was wiggle his fingers over the sensor.

"Hey, Chief, where do you want the floater?"

Dominguez glared at the ME as he wrestled a pain patch out of its packaging and slapped it over the side of his neck. His headache was turning into a migraine. "What floater?"

As the door opened behind the ME, outside sounds filtered in, and Dominguez sighed. They'd just broken up a rally last night and already another one was building. If this went on much longer, he'd have to call in for reinforcements. A third of his uniforms were already out of commission for injuries sustained in the line of duty.

The ME tapped the black synthetic case in front of his desk. "The one that got called in. Picked him up a few minutes ago. Definitely drowned. No signs of trauma."

"Well, Jesus, Kate. How 'bout the morgue? Do I have to do everything around here?"

With a careless shrug, Kate wheeled the body off. "Whatever. Just thought you might wanna, you know, sign for it. Or something. But hey, don't mind me, I just work here."

Grumbling, Dominguez popped some chewing gum into his mouth and turned to his screen. The pointed clearing of a throat brought his attention back to the guy he hadn't noticed come in. "What?"

A badge flashed before him, long enough for Dominguez to be able to read what it said. Not that he bothered. Special Agent something or other. "I'm here about the body."

"Huh? What body?" He looked up at the guy, but his gaze snared on a suit that had seen better days, rather than the owner's face.

"The one your ME just brought in."

Dominguez frowned. "Why? Standard every day jumper, probably. Couldn't handle the stress, so he took a dive off a bridge somewhere."

"I see. Do you have an ID for him?"

Dominguez huffed, not appreciating the tone of condescension. His district might not have been as big as those hoity-toity metropolises out there, but it was still his, and he ran it pretty damn well, if he said so himself. Except, of course, when his people went batshit about whatever the hell they were protesting out there. "Ran a background check," he said, bringing up the results. "Traced his last known whereabouts. Blah, blah, blah. Look, the guy's a suicide, okay? Now if you don't mind, I have bigger problems to worry about."

"Yes, of course. I understand," the guy said, drumming his fingers on Dominguez's desk. "I wouldn't want to take you away from your duties. Please, disregard this case and my presence here."

"Damn right I will," Dominguez muttered. Best idea he'd heard all day. He brushed the digital reports aside, all the way to the trash bin icon. *Wait a minute...* That wasn't right. Scowling, he opened the trash bin and emptied it so the file wouldn't be tempted to annoy him further. There. That ought to do it.

"Thank you for your cooperation," the stranger said.

"Welcome," Dominguez replied gruffly.

Kate came back out, her cart now folded into a size she could carry under her arm. "All right, the newest resident of Box 27 is tucked in and sleeping soundly. *Now* do you wanna sign for it?"

Dominguez glared at her. "What the hell are you talking about?" Didn't he just say he had very important things to do?

"Hello! The stiff from the river?"

He stared at her blankly.

"It's all right," the stranger said. "I can sign."

"There, see? He can sign." And Dominguez dismissed the issue as resolved, turning back to his screen.

"It was a pleasure working with you. Have a nice day."

Dominguez straightened in his seat, the tension in his shoulders suddenly gone. Yeah, he would have a nice day. He'd call in reinforcements, let them take over this mess, and be home by dinnertime. He might even get to enjoy a day off tomorrow. For once. Not like he was the only working class stiff in this place. *Let someone else shoulder it for a while. See what it really takes to keep a district tidy.*

The door opened, then closed.

Kate leaned on his desk and sighed. "Who was that? He's hot."

"Huh?"

"The guy who just left. Agent something or other. Can't remember. He was a real looker, I think. Wait, who was he again?"

Annoyed she hadn't left yet, Dominguez popped his jaw. "Kate, do I look like I have time for this shit? Take a gander outside, then tell me what I should spend my underpaid, overtaxed time on: my job, or your new boyfriend."

Kate gave him a strange look. "You should take some time off, dude. You're not making any sense at all."

"You know what? That is a good idea." Taking up his coat, Dominguez fished out his badge and dropped it onto the desk on his way out. "I quit. Happy New Year."

- 3 -

In the cavernous strategy room, five hundred men and women stood at attention before the massive fifteen-foot tall screen covering one wall. Not a thread out of line, not a scuffed boot among them. They stood in perfect formation, silent and waiting.

The screen activated, and a close-up of a man's mouth appeared, with only part of his nose and chin peeking at the edges as he spoke, his identity safely preserved. "For decades we have stayed in darkness, watching over humanity. We have trained and prepared for the inevitable."

A series of news reports on the violent antichem rallies replaced the speaker. Local police departments were overwhelmed, and several feeds showed uniformed soldiers trying to push the crowds back. This had been building for years. Seemed the dam had finally broken.

The reports cut off, and their leader reappeared. "The time will soon come for us to emerge into the light. My Shadows, you have done me proud, and now I call on you to make me proud again." The screen went blank, then a list of names scrolled over it—a summons for a chosen six, and a dismissal for the rest.

The Shadow army had only two ranks: Hounds and Hawks. But the distinction was to differentiate their duties rather than to create a hierarchy. The vast majority were Hounds, men and women whose primary directive was reconnaissance and shock tactics. They were trained to make their target panic, show his hand, and be caught. Hawks were stealth specialists, only called in to swiftly and silently retrieve or eliminate high priority targets.

John Wayland was a Hawk. One of only twenty ever assigned that rank, and the only one listed among the six chosen.

After the dismissed Shadows had marched out, the sergeant major opened a different door and preceded the chosen six down a long, brightly lit corridor to a briefing room. The exact number of desk chairs had already been prepared for them, each with a waiting e-pad. The Shadows sat in order by name first, rank second, which put John in the last chair on the right. The sergeant major closed the door, and another screen activated. This time, the commander in chief showed himself fully—a man with immaculately combed silver hair and a cold, crooked smile: Senator Matthew Griffith.

Without preamble, he spoke. "I have a very special interest in this case. It will require the utmost care and precision. There can be no mistakes, no loose ends. Understood?"

"Yessir!" the Shadows said in unison.

"Good. Now, you will find the complete file in front of you. Study it carefully."

John picked up the electronic pad already streaming a wealth of information. Unlike the rest, though, his had a small bird-shaped symbol blinking in the bottom right corner; an indicator of additional, confidential information. He'd read that on his own later. For now, John focused on the briefing.

Senator Griffith steepled his hands and caught them up on the events. "Three weeks ago, Jonah Rashid, a prominent member of society and a close personal friend to the governor, was found dead at the stated location on Mars 2. The local police investigated and traced his last known location to a bar not far away. He was recorded leaving with a young girl. Other than a birth certificate and old ID card, there is no information on her in any official database, and further searches have led to dead ends. She has disappeared. I don't need to tell you how upset this makes me."

Behind them, the sergeant major continued where Senator Griffith left off. "Hounds, your mission is to find the girl. Locate, but do not engage. Understood?"

"Yessir!"

"Dismissed."

The Hounds cleared out, leaving John alone with the sergeant major and Senator Griffith.

John set aside the file to give the men his full attention.

"Someone went through a lot of trouble to keep this girl's identity a secret," the senator said, "and a lot more to bury all of the evidence and reports from the police investigation database. The Special Unit's signature is all over this; she is one of theirs."

So that's why he'd been called. "Understood, sir."

"I want her alive. Do not fail me."

"Yessir."

The screen went black.

The sergeant major took a casual step toward him, voice lowered. "You understand what is at stake, Hawk?"

"Yes, Sergeant Major," he answered, also keeping his voice low. The room swallowed his echo, making him sound even softer but all the more threatening for it.

"The last time a telepath got loose among the Shadows, we lost an entire outpost unit." *Lost* wasn't accurate but it was the best way to describe what had happened. Those not slaughtered had been reduced to mumbling, incomprehensible idiots with a debilitating fear of darkness, turning catatonic every time they saw a shadow move.

The damage, resulting from an unforgivable lack of vigilance, had been so severe, all records of the incident had been sealed, with further inquiry deemed too hazardous to continue at the time. But Shadows had long memories, and they didn't like to lose.

"With all due respect, Sergeant Major, I wasn't there at the time." If he had been, the situation would have been handled very differently.

"Don't get cocky, soldier. That's how you get other people killed."

John straightened in his seat. "Yessir."

"You have this room for two hours. Make good use of it."

John stood to attention and saluted the sergeant major, who executed a perfect, pivotal turn and marched out the door. Reclaiming his seat,

John opened the confidential file, which contained birth records for one Emma Calen, born May 6, 3014 on Earth. Red hair, blue eyes and, according to the security footage from the bar, a skinny five-foot-six. He memorized her image, making note of her physical characteristics. She looked harmless enough, but looks could be deceiving.

The next few pages were dedicated to methods of delivery. A holding unit had been prepared for her arrival. John was to deliver her there and nowhere else; he was to hand her over to no one, and leave her nowhere except in the holding unit. She would be guarded 'round the clock without fail.

That meant a lot of sleepless nights.

Didn't matter. John had honed his body and his mind to go several days without sleep and food. He was a Hawk, after all.

And now he had his prey.

– 4 –

January 27, 3036 – Lexington, Earth

Travis had picked the café for one reason: the grand showcase window facing the street. Not only did it create an almost artful image of the cozy interior, it also afforded him a wide-angle view of the outside.

At the moment, though, all that concerned him was the young, red-haired woman facing away from him. Emma Calen.

She was chilled. Even from this distance, he saw as much. Her clothing wasn't made for the recent frigid temperatures. Even with the heavy cloud cover, the day was so cold, most who could afford it stayed inside. Travis knew, without needing to get closer, that Emma was at this moment preoccupied with listening to the news report on her com. Her unease made Travis tune in to the broadcast on his own device.

The news wasn't good. Another riot was building close by, and Emma's living space, which could barely be called an apartment, was somewhere on the other side of it. She ought to take the safe route around, but she was anxious to get home—fast. Something had spooked her, and Travis had to school himself to not seek out the cause. It would only alert her to his presence. He couldn't have that. She was jumpy enough already; he didn't want her to run again.

When they'd heard about Resphera, he'd gotten on the first shuttle out, walked her footsteps to that brothel after the fact, and seen what she'd seen. Weeks later, Mary Morales was still in a physical therapy brace, relearning how to walk. Her broken teeth had been fixed, but her jaw fracture couldn't be operated on until her spine stabilized. By then, it might be too late to completely repair the damage to her looks.

Travis couldn't fathom how Emma had managed to restrain herself the way she had. In her shoes, he'd have done far worse.

But she shouldn't have run. There were measures in place, systems designed to help in these situations. Emma could have turned to any one of them—to him—for help. He'd expected her to be waiting for him, and it bothered him she hadn't been.

But knowing none of this would have been an issue had he only looked after her better, bothered him even more.

He had to fix this, make amends. He owed her that. Emma Calen had been the first to look him in the eye and see not a drug-addicted screw up, but a boy worth saving. She'd been a true friend, had accepted him from the first while others had waited for him to detox and clean up before they'd deemed him worthy of their attention. She'd tutored him when his teachers had lost patience with how far behind he'd lagged, had stood up for him when others had teased, and encouraged him when he'd felt too overwhelmed to bother with it all.

Emma had made him want to be better. For her. And he'd failed her.

But he'd fix it. For now, no one knew her location except for Travis. He hadn't reported to anyone since he'd tracked her here, and unless she told him otherwise or expressed interest in coming back on her own, he wouldn't. Independence was a luxury no one had thought Emma might want one day. Others got sent out to school, to work, or to assignments, while Emma got suffocated by her loved ones, as if that somehow made up for the tragedy of losing her parents before she truly knew them and living on the streets with only her brother to look after her.

She'd never begrudged them, never once lashed out at her guardians the way sullen teenagers often did. She'd contented herself with keeping others happy, but in her heart, Emma was her own person, and for some reason, no one else seemed to understand. She *needed* to be on her own; she'd worked too hard for it.

And to finally find her freedom, only to lose it again…

No. Travis wouldn't allow that. Emma would have her space, if he had anything to say about it. And right now, he did.

When she hunched her shoulders and turned toward home, Travis paid his bill and followed.

~

"...and for those of you commuting along Emerald Way, be advised there is a detour in effect due to an antichem rally. To bypass, take Nara Street East to Brunswick..."

Emma bit back a curse, then looked up at the dark clouds threatening a snowstorm. Brunswick was six blocks out of her way. On foot, it would take an extra hour to get to her apartment. Not an option in this weather, especially with the nagging itch at the back of her mind warning her of danger. Lexington had been brewing something big for weeks, and each day without incident made a bloody riot all the more likely.

Emma shook off the paranoia, dismissing it.

She'd been watching the news day and night since Resphera. There'd been no mention of what had happened on Mars 2, but that might mean the media was just cashing in on bigger stories, like the riots.

Ugh, she *hated* this feeling. It killed her to constantly have to look over her shoulder, and know she deserved it.

Everything she'd built for herself, every personal achievement she'd been so proud of, was gone. She was a felon. No matter where she went, Emma felt the word MURDERER branded on her forehead for all the worlds to see. She hadn't taken one life, but two, flushing her own down that river along with the human waste she'd relieved of a pulse.

As callously as she remembered it, the memory made her shudder.

I did it for Mary, she reminded herself. *Because no one else would have.* Had it been worth it? She had to believe so.

The first snowflakes wafted down in tiny, fluffy clumps.

One drifted down the back of her neck, making her flinch, and she flipped her collar up against the growing cold. Emma switched her com earpiece to silent and stared at a digital window display while she decided how to get back to her apartment. A crowd was a good place to hide in plain sight, but a violent crowd would trample her to dust before she could clear her mind enough to decide to make a run for it.

Tapping her foot, she checked the time and huffed. In exactly thirty-eight minutes, the local SU safe house would broadcast its own update on the state of the city and world politics. It was the last connection to her former life and the only news source she trusted, and she had to be in front of a com screen to access it. If she missed it, she'd have to wait a week for another one, and with the way the riots were escalating, Emma planned to be long gone by then.

Thirty-seven minutes left. Already the ground was white with snow and the storm was still building.

"I guess that's that." Girding her loins, Emma hunched her shoulders, ducked her head, and marched resolutely down Emerald Way, directly toward the rally.

At first, the streets in the commercial district looked relatively normal—people in transports and on foot, all going about their business. Almost everyone was either dressed to the nines in a sharp conservative suit or wearing some sort of service uniform, and all of them stared straight ahead, nowhere else, in a widespread, cosmopolitan tunnel vision. Case in point: the cosmetically enhanced business woman talking on her com and checking her e-pad at the same time. Someone could crash his transport into the restaurant window across the street, and unless it blocked her way, she'd never look up from whatever deal she was working on. People these days spent an awful lot of time inside their heads, considering they were all alone in there.

Before long, Emma had to squint against the snowfall. The current of business people all flocking toward one place turned into a river of strange costumes and headgear, and from one block to the next, she strode into the thick of the rally, squished and jostled from all sides by people who were one wrong word or gesture away from turning on everyone. Thousands of them flocked together, many carrying holowands that projected images into the air above them, of babies being injected with toxic sludge. They shouted things like "Leave the kids alone!" and "Resist the poison!"

The mob, heading from one part of the city to another, swayed in a hypnotic movement accompanied by repetitive chants, both of which sucked nearby people into the melee. Emma recognized the early signs of mass hysteria, and she put up her strongest shields. She'd have to go straight through the crowd to get home, and she only had twenty minutes left to do it.

A guy in a grim reaper cloak got in her face, yelling at the top of his lungs, "Let nature rule!"

Emma winced and jerked away, but had no room to escape. From her other side, a woman dressed in nothing but underwear and furry boots echoed the grim reaper's shout, sending Emma reeling. Two soldiers appeared and shoved the protesters back toward the main throng.

Oh no. Squinting up through the snow, Emma spotted a containment hover on approach. The police must have called in backup. Apparently, this was much bigger than Emma could see from her vantage point. Frantic to escape, she whirled around, searching for any way out. Soldiers had cleared one path a little, but their confrontation with the reaper and Lady Furboots had turned into a fight, which began to rile others, and in less than a second, the small opening had closed again.

Two soldiers turned into ten. The reaper threw a punch, and then the floodgates opened. Emma got shoved left and right as the brawl grew. She shielded her head as much as she could, but even then it wasn't enough to avoid every stray fist and elbow, and Emma soon lost all sense of direction, unable to catch her breath in the crush of very angry bodies. She smelled smoke and blood; something had caught on fire, and the soldiers were shouting for reinforcements.

Should have taken Brunswick. Her body and mind were getting hammered with a flood of anger that crashed like a riptide against her shields. Desperate, Emma sent out a mental push to clear some space around her. It wasn't much, and she couldn't hold it for very long, but at least she could breathe again. She quickly scanned the area for an escape route. The hover was coming closer, and if she didn't get out of here soon, she'd be penned in with the rioters.

She saw no way of retreat. Unless the mob shifted on its own, she wasn't going anywhere.

Then it did, and across the open space, she met eyes with a stranger on the other side of the street. He was handsome, in a hard, unfeeling sort of way, like he'd been carved out of stone. Tall, with honey-colored hair disheveled by the wind, he perched on the ledge of a defunct holosign as if to avoid the mob. But Emma knew better. He was too steady, too unaffected by the raging riot to be in any way a part of it. Perched above the rampant crowd ripping itself apart in fits of violence and madness, the man dressed in a trendy jacket and military-issue boots remained completely still, staring right at her. Watching her like a hawk through curtains of gently falling snow.

Startled by his direct gaze, Emma froze, puzzled by the strange sense that she should know him. He definitely seemed to know her, looking right into her eyes when most others tended to look away. In the middle of a growing riot, he acted as if she was the only thing worth watching, and the sheer intensity of it gave her butterflies. Not the good kind.

There was only one reason why he would have picked her out of the crowd. By now, the SU would have pieced together what had happened on Mars 2, and if this guy was one of their operatives, then running from him would only obligate him to chase her. Caught between a rock and a hard place, Emma took a chance—she let go of her compulsion on those around her to focus on the operative and send him the equivalent of a telepath greeting and introduction.

She was met with nothing; her mental touch slid across his head as if it was made of polished silver, and for an instant she almost saw her thoughts reflected back. Emma frowned and tried again with,

—What the hell was that?—

She knew for a fact he didn't get the message, but he did smile—a miniscule twitch of his lips that did nothing to soften his angular face. It sent a chill of dread down her spine.

No, no, no, this was wrong—*he* was wrong. All wrong.

Instinct borne of a lifetime spent hiding her abilities took over. Emma grabbed mental hold of three soldiers fighting off a particularly difficult group and made them move. The fight shifted, obscuring her view of the stranger, and Emma shuddered with relief as violence beat at her skull once again, washing away the disconcertion of having touched something she shouldn't have. Humming a children's rhyme to herself to block out the rising mania among the protesters, she turned around and fought her way through the mob into a dark, empty side street.

The rally stretched for blocks in every direction, and another crowd had filled the street at the end of the alley, but the brawl hadn't reached that far yet. It was only a matter of time; these people knew the military had been called in. Already wave after wave of paranoia and aggression was building, fueling her own. Keeping her stride swift and even, just short of breaking into a run, Emma hurried through the soon-to-be-snowed-in alley. When her oversensitive ears picked up an echo to her footsteps, she hummed louder to block it out, but the sound didn't abate. It was physical, not mental. Heart pounding, she cast her senses out behind her, but while her ears picked up on the clomp of boots on pavement, not a single thought or emotion accompanied it.

Impossible. Everyone in the universe emitted at least some sparkle of brain activity. Even coma patients deemed brain dead still had neurons firing in a distinctive pattern. As long as the heart beat, there was brain activity, and Emma could pick up on it.

The person following her projected nothing but dead silence.

Thirty yards ahead, the alley opened up and the noise level rose again as she approached it. Emma knew she'd be plunging into another melee of flying fists, but with the stranger on her heels, she only had two choices: turn and fight, or run and hope she could lose herself in the tumult without getting trampled. More soldiers were flocking in to control the riot, and the hover was almost on top of them with three more on the way; standard procedure to hem people in, herd them toward the desired direction of the holding facilities.

I can't be caught. It was more than just instinct; the instruction had been drilled into her since before she'd been born. Emma Calen was a ghost. She didn't exist outside of the Special Unit, and there was a reason for that. She only had to think back a few weeks to remember. This left her with one possible course of action.

Before her, the alley opened onto a riot. Behind her, the footsteps were closing in. Emma arrowed her intent through the crowd, shifted bodies left and right in a wave just small enough to allow her passage. And when that window of opportunity opened, when she could all but feel icy fingers at the back of her neck, she ran.

- 5 -

John was half an inch from his target, when she bolted into the street, and before he could follow, the crowd turned into a war zone and he lost sight of her. With his cover blown and no other option, John activated his eye piece to link up with the standard military containment hover for a feed of the riot. A handy piece of tech to have in the field; operated by rapid eye movements rather than hand motions or voice commands, the eye piece gave him needed functionality without drawing attention.

As the lens flickered on, his vision split between the ground fight and a bird's eye view from the hover. Emma Calen ran straight through the mob like a shark swimming through a school of fish. No one touched her. Instead, when she did whatever telepaths did to push people aside, they turned on each other. Violence followed in her wake, worsening by the second.

Biting back a curse, John charged into the thick of it, and immediately an elbow caught him across the cheekbone. In his left field of vision, he saw the target had reached the other side, but the containment hover was right above her and the pilot had already activated a barrier shield to cut off any path of escape. With a siren and a zap, a luminescent blue veil dropped down in front of the target's face. She was trapped. Nothing got through a containment veil—the electromagnetic barrier fried anything that touched it. *Got you.*

Someone whaled John across the back with a baseball bat. He twisted around and broke the batter's hand, shoving him back into someone else. As soon as he got ahold of the bat, those closest turned on him. He struggled to keep enough breathing room around him to utilize the crude weapon. Hemmed in, his reach was limited, but the bat gave him enough leverage to make up for it. Taking firm hold in its center, John shoved the blunt end into someone's face, then pulled it back in rapid succession hard enough to fracture something belonging to a guy behind him. When the two stumbled back in either direction, he swung to the right. Three more went down, and John moved forward, making slow but steady progress toward his target while keeping an eye on her.

The hover feed showed Emma staring up with enough focus to make the hairs on the back of John's neck stand on end. She wasn't concentrating on the hover itself, but its pilot. John swore, fighting harder to get to her. He was nearing, but not fast enough. The closer he got, the more people moved away from her and toward him, blocking his path, burying him. He couldn't see anything in his general vicinity, but he could still see through the hover's feed.

Emma Calen smiled into the recorder, giving it a little finger wave. The barrier veil flickered then disabled completely, and the hover veered wildly off course. Right before the feed cut off, John saw his target getting away.

He was losing her. John switched off the now useless feed and instead brought up a virtual nav menu to activate his percussion blast cuff. With just enough time to throw one last punch, he dropped to the ground and raised his cuffed wrist overhead. *Two… one…*

The resulting shock wave bowled over everyone within a thirty-yard radius and forced John flat to the ground. He made his joints move again, made himself climb to his feet before the others recovered, and sprinted after the girl. She had a hell of a head start—already halfway down another side alley—but John was faster. A couple of swift jumps, and he pushed off the closest dumpster, then caught hold of a second story sidewalk ledge. The time it took to clamber up cost him precious seconds, but once he had the high ground, he had a clear view in front and behind.

The girl didn't have enough stamina to keep up this kind of chase;

she'd slowed down to a quick walk, stopping every few steps to catch her breath. Pumping his arms for speed, John closed the distance, then jumped down to the pavement right in front of her.

Her first reaction was surprise—bright blue eyes snapping wide, red lips parting on a gasp. The next would be her natural telepath's instinct to protect herself through any means necessary. By the way she cast about for something to use as a weapon, he surmised whatever mental push she'd tried to deliver had failed.

"Don't run," he ordered.

She spun around to do just that. Lunging, John caught her, lifted her off her feet, getting a faceful of red hair, and dumped her to the ground.

She didn't scream for help. That was a new one. Instead, she scrambled away, crab fashion, wading through the snow with those bright blue eyes trained on him the entire time. He saw fear in them, but something else, too. Defiance. "I don't have any money," she said, as if he was some common street thug. Maybe she just hoped he was. "And I have a disease. A horrible, disfiguring disease. You don't want to rape me!"

That stopped him in his tracks. Taking offense to this on an elemental level, John tilted his head a little, scrutinizing her for the first time. She didn't amount to much, and her features were strange—round face, pointed chin, pert nose, and eyes too big and too bright. Combined with her red hair, it yielded something… curiously appealing. But ultimately helpless. Her telepathic abilities, therefore, had to be great enough to compensate for her lack of physical strength. Wouldn't help her now.

John pulled back his shoulders, stretching out sore muscles, and bit his tongue against a wince. Every single injury and contusion was her fault. For that alone, he wasn't averse to scaring her a little. He reached for her, but in a split second, her submissive façade disappeared as she caught his arms and, kicking out at the same time, used his own momentum to propel him over her head.

John rolled on impact, then leapt to his feet before she could do the same. Now he was mad. Impressed that her little trick had worked, but mad.

Her body tensed to rise, but she slipped on the icy ground, and an instant later he was on her, spinning her around to face him, crouching over her torso. His grasp to her throat forced her back down, pinning her to prevent movement but not hard enough to choke.

She cried out, her small, dull nails digging into his wrist to dislodge him, legs flailing without aim. "That all you got?" he taunted.

The girl growled and threw a laughable wild punch, missing his chin by inches. She was definitely not a fighter; more of a panicked foal who'd break her own neck to wrench free of him. John squeezed her throat in warning, which just made her fight that much harder. She managed to half twist his cuff, but with a slight shift of his wrist, he turned her head to the side, baring her throat for a tranq injection before the cuff could activate another percussion pulse.

In two seconds flat, she went limp on the ground.

After checking her pulse, John leaned back. He released her throat but had no intention of moving off her until he'd confirmed she wasn't playing possum. The color she'd gained during her struggles was already fading. She'd go hypothermic soon.

John unzipped his jacket and touched the hawk pin on his shirt. "Target secured," he said to the team of Hounds on standby, who'd been instructed to keep their distance until he gave the signal. "Sending extraction point coordinates now."

"Confirmed," one of them replied. "Pick up in two."

John zipped up his jacket and lifted the troublesome girl out of the snow. Standing with her in the middle of that alley, a small reprieve from a city turning red with bloody riots, he counted the seconds until the retrieval team arrived. He'd counted to fifty-seven when he decided to glance down at his sleeping captive. She looked even more vulnerable like this, fragile, like the most delicate of dolls with a face so innocent, no one would ever suspect the secrets it concealed.

The muscle over his bruised rib twitched in an annoying spasm, reminding him he'd need to see the medic at some point. John lifted the girl a little higher against his shoulder, adjusting his hold, just as a breeze tickled his nose with her scent.

Frowning, he put his nose to her hair and breathed in deep to confirm.

He hadn't imagined it before. She did smell like spring.

– 6 –

Sit up, Emma. We aren't finished yet.

Big hands shoved Emma down, and her ass met the hard surface of a metal chair, jarring her spine and bringing her to full consciousness. When they ripped off her blindfold, bright light flooded her vision, and everything was blurry for a few moments. Wrists chafing in her binds and ears ringing, Emma waited for all of her senses to kick in.

Not all of them did. She felt like her head was stuck under water.

Once her sight had cleared enough to make sense of the world, Emma carefully cataloged her surroundings. She was in a smallish room with bright white walls and a ceiling to match. The floor was a dull black, the door only distinguishable by its handle with a glowing thumb pad. A mesh fence bisected the chamber, identical tables pushed up to either side. Emma sat behind one, looking across the divide at the empty chair behind the other.

Definitely utilitarian, probably not a party hang out, considering the harsh choice of color and the fact that they'd left her alone in there.

Static electricity prickled the back of her neck, and she cautiously peeked over her shoulder to catch her captor staring. He hastily turned his steely gray eyes away toward front and center. He'd changed clothes since their scenic jog through chaos, and had given up all pretense of being anything other than a soldier all buttoned up in a weird, dark blue uniform. His bruises from earlier were gone; he must have had them treated before she came to. In comparison, her ass still ached from falling on it, her legs were sore from the run, and there was a piece of fingernail she was never getting back again from where it had lodged in his discarded jacket sleeve.

"What the hell is this? Where am I?"

He might as well have been a robot, for all the reaction he showed. That twitch in his square jaw didn't count. Seemed to be a natural tic he couldn't control. With her head still throbbing from whatever drug he'd used to knock her out, Emma wasn't up for another wasted telepathic effort. At least not yet.

Instead, she twisted as far as the armrest would allow, swinging her bound fists toward his crotch, conveniently located at eye level. He slapped them away so fast, it set Emma back on her ass.

Grabbing both of her shoulders, he forced her to face forward, then held her in place when she fought. "Stop," he ordered, and the single, low-spoken word made her freeze. He squeezed her shoulders in warning, then released her.

She didn't hear him step away, but she felt the gap widen between them. Game over. "Jerk."

Silence.

Emma huffed, drumming her fingertips together in a nervous rhythm as she studiously ignored him. With no windows or clocks to mark the time, she didn't know how long he made her sit there. It felt like forever before the door on the other side of the fence finally opened. A man walked in, three soldiers at his back. When he took his seat, the three spread out around him and turned to human stone—perfect little cookie cutter tinmen with the IQ of a rocking horse, vibrant personalities to match the room, and obedient to a fault. Emma tried to hate them, but how can you hate something that isn't really there?

The man now sitting across from her was a whole other story. "Good morning, Emma."

So she'd been out for at least half a day and a full night. Or they'd taken her around the planet somewhere.

"Welcome to our humble abode. I trust you had a pleasant trip in." His smile was crooked, the mark of a liar. "I'm glad we finally get a chance to meet, face to face."

As her headache eased, a low-level hum started inside her brain. A small enough distraction that she should have been able to ignore, except its presence revealed the absence of something else: thoughts. Emma reached out to the man on the other side of the fence and met with a fizzing resistance that made her flinch.

The man chuckled. "I see you've discovered my security measures." He tapped his pen against the fence, which sparked with electricity. "It's a telepathic Faraday Cage," he explained. "I had my best scientists calibrate it to precise specifications. It keeps you from poking into my thoughts." So that's what it was for. "It's just a precaution. I would hate for this conversation to turn ugly."

Emma's hands curled, putting more tension on the binds. They'd start cutting into her wrists soon.

"Do you know who I am, child?"

Everyone knew. Senator Matthew Griffith, the quiet mouse who whispered into the ears of the Interplanetary Council of Governance. Whenever a military action suddenly became necessary, it was usually ordered on Griffith's recommendation, based on intel only he had, collected in ways only he could accomplish. No one knew much about him, except that he brokered in fear, and whenever he made the news, the network showed only his photo while someone else quoted him. He never appeared in public, never gave interviews, never did anything to draw attention.

For that alone, he'd made the SU's watch list. They liked to keep an eye on people who had the power to singlehandedly change the course of history.

I'm in the House of Griffith. Holy shit! Emma kept her face blank and her mind sharp for any tricks he might have up his sleeve. Something told her they hadn't tranqued and kidnapped her for a cup of tea, and if she had any chance of getting out of here, she'd need to keep her wits about her.

Her head still buzzed too much to be useful, telepathically speaking. Didn't mean she was helpless, though. It was impossible to spend a lifetime in other people's heads without learning a thing or two, and Emma's recent attempts at reenacting every bad fugitive movie ever made had turned her into something of an expert on these things.

So think, Emma. How do you get out of this one?

No one knew she was here, so her first order of business was to get a message out.

"I will take your silence to mean yes," the senator said, seeming unconcerned by her lack of response. "You are Emma Calen," he added, introducing her to herself.

Emma didn't say a word.

"My dear, there's no reason to be frightened. If we could untie our guest, please?"

The scary-ass soldier at her back moved. A gleaming knife the size of her forearm flashed down, and then her bonds fell away. The blade hadn't even touched her skin. Emma resisted the impulse to look behind her and rubbed feeling back into her hands, all while telling her heart it wasn't in its best interest to explode just yet.

"There now, isn't that better? Would you care for something to drink?"

As if on cue, her door opened and another soldier entered, setting a single glass of water down onto the table in front of her.

"In the past, some of our guests thought they needed to fight us, try to escape. They even tried to disrupt the shield by throwing water on the cage."

Good idea. Emma swiped up the glass and threw the water, arrowing her mind at the miniscule space of a chain link eye. She felt herself passing through, but then the fence sparked angrily, and the answering charge zapped her neurons back into inertia. The shock reeled Emma backwards and almost out of her seat. If not for her soldier guard roughly righting her from behind, she would have ended up on the floor. His hands on her provided a prime opportunity to strike, but Emma couldn't move. Her muttered, "Fuck," came out as a garbled moan.

"Naturally, we've compensated for such a possibility since then," the senator said, wiping his face.

Emma's soldier removed himself from swinging distance. Damn.

"What do you want from me?" With the taste of raw electricity on her tongue, she sounded a little drunk.

"I want to make you an offer," Griffith said. "I would very much like to adopt you into our little family."

It sounded to Emma like something the wicked witch would say, right before she shoved her into the oven.

"You have gifts that could be extremely useful to me. You would also be able to train my men to better resist attempts at telepathic corruption from others of your ilk."

Ha! In what freaking universe did he think she'd ever align herself with people who violently abducted others into their ranks?

"In return, I am prepared to be very generous with you. You'd have your own home, a sizable allowance, all of your basic expenses paid… Anything you can think of, I am in a position to provide for you." *All the sweets you can stomach, my dear. We'll want you nice and plump for the feast.*

Emma rubbed her forehead. Had her kidnapper written IDIOT there after stabbing her in the neck with a tranq dart? This was just plain insulting. But calling Senator Griffith a deluded megalomaniacal psychopath with old lady hair and a small dick was probably not the best way to proceed. Biting back the colorful choice of words, she opted for something less likely to get her killed on the spot. "I respectfully decline your offer."

Griffith smiled. "Perhaps it would be better if you considered it a job placement rather than an offer."

Emma gritted her teeth.

"Come now, Emma. Do you really want to continue living life the way you have been for the last three years? Can you honestly tell me you like the person you've become? Living off others, cheating… murdering?"

Her face drained cold, her lips went numb, but she didn't flinch. The memory of a biting chill, of a bridge she never should have been on with a man she never should have met, made her hands shake. She clutched her knees to hide it. "I'm not a murderer," she said, the sentiment too feeble to convince herself, let alone others.

The senator's gaze moved to a point behind her, and whatever he saw there made his crooked smile dim momentarily. Emma recognized this as a subtle, wordless reprimand. Whatever the soldier at her back had done to offend his superior couldn't bode well.

"This is your chance to make amends. To make yourself into something your family can be proud of."

Pride is for people with something to prove. MacMurphy had told her that. He was the closest thing Emma had to a father; the one who'd taught her to never place herself above others just because she could. Stepping back was just as honorable as taking a victory. More so, really, because it meant she cared about the other person rather than some achievement that would end up being meaningless in the long run. MacMurphy hadn't trained recruits; he'd raised a family.

I miss you all, she thought them, knowing the message would never make it that far. *I miss you so much.*

"Think about it," the senator said, losing patience with her non-answers. "And while you consider the future course of your life, I do hope you will take advantage of our first class amenities." He nodded to his faithful, brainwashed henchman.

The soldier grasped her arms and lifted her to her feet, steering her out the door and down a nondescript corridor. Emma counted her footsteps, as she'd been taught, and left her mind wide open to pick up anything and everything. A whole lot of mental garbage, bits of conversation here and there, made it through the walls, all filtered by the listeners' varied levels of understanding. None of it was immediately useful, so Emma shoved it all to the back of her mind to process later. She couldn't navigate her way out of here by their thoughts alone, anyway.

The world looked and felt different on the telepathic plane—each individual created his own, and the only time the multitudes of versions ever overlapped was when one consciousness affected another. A stronger personality could always overpower a weaker one to make him see the world through whatever eyes they chose. Disturbing enough on its own, but Emma knew it could get much, much worse. The words *mass hysteria* came to mind.

The man forcing her down the hallway hadn't spoken a word since her failed attempt to neuter him by blunt force, and with him behind her, she couldn't gauge his emotions by sight. Two senses down. Not about to have a taste, and unable to read his thoughts, Emma was left with touch and smell. His hands were rough, like he'd spent more time fighting than using them for anything else, and he smelled of metal and cold. It reminded her of an ancient strip of train track she'd once played on. The wooden beams had been so weathered, they'd somehow absorbed the essence of their iron bolts and had filled the air with their scent.

The humming in her brain resurfaced as they stopped in front of a door, and a sick feeling twisted Emma's stomach when it opened onto a room no bigger than the one they'd just left. This one was empty of everything except for a small mattress on the floor and something that might have passed for a sink or a toilet. She wasn't sure which.

And the humming was louder.

The soldier's hands gripped her arms a little tighter as he leaned down to murmur at her ear, "The longer you stall, the worse it will get."

Emma turned her head sideways, caught a glimpse of his face. She had just enough time to wonder whether that was indecision she'd seen flicker in those gunmetal eyes before he shoved her into what felt like a padded cell for her mind, and closed the door.

~

The girl had come face to face with the senator and hadn't folded. She'd known who the man was, what he could do, and had effectively spat in his face. John couldn't decide whether that made her brave or stupid. He'd stood there, waiting for her to agree to what he'd considered very generous terms, though now he wondered why. She'd given *him* a run for his money, fighting to the last, so why should he have expected the senator to fare any better?

Perhaps because he'd never seen anyone personally confronted by the man tell him *no*. Senator Griffith didn't take such interest in just anyone, so whatever his reason for having Emma Calen brought in, he wanted her very badly. And she'd refused him.

John flexed his hand, staring at the closed door as if he could see her through it. Of course, he couldn't. And there'd be no video feeds, either. The power field surrounding the cell disrupted any and all signals going in or out. That was the point.

For all intents and purposes, Emma Calen was now completely cut off from the outside world.

He flexed his hand again, then turned his back to the door, taking up a guard position. She had little to no chance of getting out. Closer to no than little. Still, the senator didn't take chances. With an asset this valuable, he would have posted an entire regiment to guard her if he had it. But John was the only Shadow immune to telepathy, and for all the tests they'd done and continued to do, they couldn't replicate his peculiar gift. Something about DNA instability.

Most days, it didn't matter in the least. He couldn't use his mind to do anything out of the ordinary; he didn't have special mental abilities, and wasn't a genius, or in any other way unique.

But his immunity against being corrupted made him an irreplaceable asset to the Shadows. No one else could have brought Emma Calen in; she would have turned their brains to mush as easily as he'd watched her manipulate those crowds in Lexington. No, it could have only been him. And that made him proud.

John rubbed his palm across his thigh and realized why it felt so weird. He could still feel the warmth of Emma Calen's arm through her jacket where he'd held onto her.

Strange…

Footsteps echoed down the corridor in approach, and he stood at attention, back as straight as he could make it without arching. He could tell time by the steady rhythm—*tap, tap, tap, tap, tap.*

The sergeant major stopped in front of John, swiveled to face him. John saluted.

"At ease, soldier." He held out a wrist unit, indicating for John to remove his armor cuff. "Your shift schedule for the next two weeks."

John handed it over. "You think it'll take that long, sir?"

"Hard to say with telepaths. Could be less, could be more. Her meals will be brought to you. You are to wait until the soldier bringing it has cleared the corridor before you open that door. You will stay to make sure she's eaten the meal, then retrieve the tray. The door will be closed before you call someone to pick it up. You are not to leave this post unguarded for any reason, or engage the subject under any circumstances. Clear?"

"Yes sir."

"Someone will come to relieve you at the end of your shift."

John saluted again as the sergeant major left, and then he checked the schedule. He'd be on guard duty for seventeen-hour intervals, with six hours in between for sleep, and two fifteen-minute breaks for food and rest. It didn't show him who'd be replacing him or for how long, but given the nature of their captive, no one besides him would be stationed at this door for longer than two hours.

He hoped Emma Calen broke soon.

- 7 -

Lexington, Earth

A tic in Travis' eye made needles stab through the agony of a massive migraine, jarring him awake. He couldn't smell the blood but felt it cooling against his cheek. Wracked with pain, he forced his limbs to move, crawling to the bed and using it to lever himself up from the floor. It took him six tries before he managed and by then, every breath tore a wretched sob from his raw throat.

Light tortured his swollen eyes, and movement made him pray he'd pass out again. But he didn't. Shaking from head to toe, he raised a rubbery hand to wipe away the blood from his nose and lower face. If he tasted it again, he'd throw up.

He'd lost her.

The moment Emma had walked into the rally, she'd disappeared into a sea of mental signatures. Still, Travis had felt her there by the shock wave left in her wake, until her panic had spiked off the charts and she'd just… disappeared.

The mental blast he'd used to push through the riot had cost him, but not as much as his repeated failed attempts to reach her. He'd screamed for her, pushing farther beyond his limits than he'd ever dared. Again and again he'd shoved his consciousness past what his brain could handle, until rivulets of blood had poured from his nose and tear ducts. He hadn't cared, not even when his neurons began to burn with the intensity of his telepathic madness. The searing pain had only made him push harder until, for a split second, he'd thought he'd sensed her so very far away, like a ghost hovering in front of a massive star.

That one instant of hope told him she was still alive, and then the consequences of his efforts had shut him down in a neural implosion that knocked him back on his ass. By all accounts, he should have been dead. Stronger telepaths had overtaxed their brains to the point of permanent damage.

It would have been worth it, had he had something to show for it in the end. But he didn't.

Travis checked the time and moaned miserably. He'd been out for hours. Emma could be halfway to anywhere in the galaxy by now. *Not again.* He couldn't fail her a second time. She needed him now more than ever. He'd sensed enough of who'd taken her to know that much.

He also knew he couldn't rescue her on his own.

Fumbling his com out of his pocket, Travis attached it to his sore ear. Turning the volume down as much as he could to spare his eardrums, he issued a command to connect.

"It's Travis," he said when his call was answered, hardly recognizing his own voice, feeble and shaking. He took a couple of deep breaths to marshal the temptation to sob his misery. He needed to make himself comprehensible so MacMurphy would understand what he meant when he said, "I lost her. To the Shadows."

– 8 –

They didn't turn off the lights for nighttime. Emma waited for it, hoping that with darkness, her mind would somehow reboot, rewire itself to cope with this place. Her jail cell was hermetically sealed, with an almost invisible strip of air duct circling the room.

There was something about the walls… They didn't just block her telepathy, they seemed to nullify it. Emma couldn't be sure without available subjects to test it on, but that had to be it. She felt crippled here, disoriented. As bright as the walls were, they seemed fuzzy; as sharp as she knew the sound of slapping said walls should be, her ears felt plugged. Even her own voice sounded foreign, her breathing incredibly loud.

When popping her ears didn't work, Emma stripped off her jacket, and tore off one sleeve to tie around her eyes like a blindfold. It helped a little, but not enough. There was a silence in her mind she'd never heard before. For the first time in her life, she was completely alone inside her own head.

It terrified her.

Refusing to admit defeat, Emma lay down on the mattress and slowed her breathing.

Sleep didn't come easy, or stay long. It was fitful, broken up by fragments of dreams, all of them her own but somehow still foreign, with no continuity or any sort of meaning she could divine.

When Emma woke up, hoping to be back in her own bed, she

found herself still in the tenth chamber of hell-for-telepaths. And she felt like crying.

Pretty soon, her body's needs became too insistent to ignore, forcing her near the sink to check it out. It had two sensors. She passed her hand over one, and water poured out of the spout. No controls for hot or cold, so probably all she'd ever get was lukewarm. She splashed some over her face.

The other sensor brought out a rudimentary toilet, an old-fashioned flush kind that required use of toilet paper. Emma shuddered. *So unsanitary.* And they hadn't given her any soap, either.

She sucked in a bracing breath and muttered, "Like it or not, it's all I've got," then dropped her pants and made use of the toilet, praying the room didn't have surveillance feeds. As soon as she was finished, the toilet disappeared into the wall and she scrubbed her hands in the sink as thoroughly as she could.

How long did they plan to keep her here?

"Hello?" she called out. If anyone heard, they didn't answer. "Anybody there?" The room didn't even echo, just swallowed her voice as if she hadn't made a sound. Creepy. She drummed her fingers against her thigh for a while.

When she got bored, she circled the room, scrutinizing every inch in search of a seam, a weakness—something, anything—but the only vulnerability she found was to her disadvantage: the vents. If she pissed them off, they only had to turn off the air and watch her suffocate. Or pipe in some gas to poison her.

Hailey's sister was good at that sort of thing. The glimpse she'd taken into Dr. Chase's mind had given Emma nightmares for a week. The woman was a walking encyclopedia of chemicals—from distilled water, to antiseptic solutions, to a gas that corroded skin and tissue on contact. The scariest thing about the last one? It was a natural byproduct of an inconspicuous little plant grown on Earth.

She wouldn't relish dying that way. *Better not piss anyone off, then.*

Right. Because that was going to happen. Blowing out a frustrated breath, Emma returned to the mattress.

The twitch, when it began in her left pinky, didn't raise any warning flags. It should have.

~

John's shift ended just after sunrise the next day. By the time he'd left the corridor, the stiffness in his legs was almost gone. But as tired as he was, he couldn't even think about going to his bunk. Instead, he went outside for a run.

Hounds were at their PTs in the field, so he detoured through the woods, choosing a little-used route toward the gate and around the perimeter. The chilly air nipped but refreshed him after long hours in the stale hallway. At the gate, he nodded to the Hound on guard duty and kept going, only to turn back when a siren signaled the gate had opened.

Utility transports were heading out from the garage, the kind of vehicles designed to inconspicuously hold a dozen Shadows each, including their gear. John backtracked to the guard. "What's going on?"

"Riot surrounding a parliament seat on Jericho. The sergeant major ordered an intervention."

John frowned. "Since when do we interfere with the local police and military?"

The Hound met his gaze. "Since now."

Four transports passed the gate. Four dozen Shadows, all told. Not a small mission. With so many in one place, the odds of being noticed went up exponentially. Whatever or whoever the target, the sergeant major was risking premature exposure to acquire it. John hoped it was worth it. The Shadows' greatest asset was the element of surprise, something they couldn't afford to lose, not with telepathic enemies out there like Emma Calen potentially numbering in the thousands. They had no defense against that. Yet.

But it wasn't John's place to question his commanding officer. He left the Hound to his duties, altering his route to head back to the compound.

A quick shower relaxed him enough to remind him how tired he was. With only five hours left before he had to report back to his post, John lay down onto the bed to rest his eyes. Sleep came quickly, pulling him into familiar dreams…

"Welcome to Greenfield," the old man said.

John didn't look at him. He tried not to look at anyone, but he felt them watching. From the corner of his eye, he caught the flutter of movement as children leaned close to whisper to each other. He knew what they said, too. What everyone always said: he was a freak, the son of a sicko murderer. He hated all of them.

"I am called Ivan."

Down the hallway, a gaggle of kids stared. All of them were scared, except for one. The tall boy with hair cropped almost to the scalp gave John a gap-toothed grin and cracked his knuckles.

Old Ivan saw. "Tell me, meester Welan, you play chess?"

A sharp rap on his door roused John instantly. Wake-up call. He shook off the dream, hurried to wash up, and as he tore open an MRE, his gaze snared on the old wooden chess piece on his windowsill. The piece was the only thing he owned from before he'd been drafted into the Shadows, and every so often he looked at it and wondered whether all those dreams he had were real or whether his own deep-seated desire to remember anything from his past choreographed the scenes playing out while he slept.

Tossing the empty package into the trash, John picked up the chipped white queen and traced the grooves around its top. Sometimes, the dreams were so vivid, he could almost believe they were memories. Other times, he hoped they weren't—

His wrist unit beeped an alarm; time to get back to work. Pocketing the piece on his way out the door, John went to relieve the soldier guarding Emma Calen. Today it was Vega, a Hound who preferred not to speak unless absolutely necessary. Their schedules had been synchronized, and both wrist units beeped in unison to signal the end of her shift and the beginning of John's, but before he could ask her if she knew anything about the Jericho mission, Vega gave a nod and left, eager to get back to her duties, whatever they were. He almost envied her.

Standing around all day gave a man little to do, but a lot of time to think. Normally, John would be concentrating on his assignment, but since he currently didn't have one, he was left with only one thing to mull over: the prisoner. The troops had been told about the high-risk acquisition and warned to keep their distance. Even with the chamber functioning and the door locked, as long as Emma Calen refused to see reason and join their ranks, she posed a risk. And as long as he had to guard her, John might as well have been a prisoner, too.

Though he wasn't all that much older than the girl, she was still so much a kid, John couldn't understand why the senator had fixated on her. Surely it would have made more sense to acquire a more mature telepath for their purpose; why waste time and resources on someone who probably still had a holoposter of the latest heartthrob on her bedroom wall?

John answered his own question.

A more experienced telepath would know not to expose himself. If exposed, he'd know to avoid capture. And if captured, he'd know how to escape. If the objective was to use one for his skill, then keeping him in a room like the one currently housing the girl would serve no purpose, and once outside of it, an experienced telepath wouldn't hesitate to strike back.

But Emma? Try as he might, John couldn't picture her as a formidable mastermind. Everything she'd done to date, impressive as it might have been, she seemed to have done impulsively, without any planning or forethought—and that included the murder which had ultimately put her on their radar.

What had prompted her to make a man in full possession of his senses jump off a bridge like that? He'd watched the feed from the bar a thousand times, trying to figure out how she did it, which part of her mind she used to grab hold of the man's conscious decision-making process and bend it to her will.

He'd watched her with Senator Griffith. When confronted with her crime, she hadn't gloated, but neither had she repented. Her posture, the nervous clutch of her fingers, had told him her actions had been borne of necessity; she'd done what she'd considered to be her duty, but had taken no pleasure in it. John could sympathize with that.

Still, he kept coming back to the question of her motives. What could possibly drive a girl like Emma Calen to commit murder?

For an instant, he contemplated asking her.

In the next, he dismissed the ridiculous notion.

John didn't care what she'd done, how, or why. What mattered was the outcome. She'd screwed up and revealed herself. Might as well have painted a bull's eye on her forehead.

She was a scared little girl on the run; she made the perfect target. Powerful enough to serve their purposes, young enough to be controlled. Experience, or her lack thereof, would be her undoing. She would eventually agree to the senator's terms, if only to spare herself this imprisonment. She'd do it to get the chance to attempt an escape. And because John knew to expect it, she'd fail.

He'd take no pleasure in it, as he hadn't in bringing her here, but he would follow his orders to the letter.

It was his job.

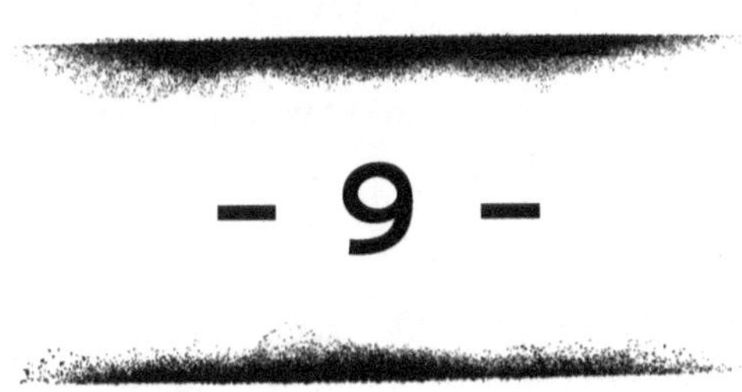

– 9 –

A Hound named Latham brought her first meal. If John recalled correctly, the blond, freckled young man had been inducted into the Shadows about three months ago. Still young enough to have his enthusiasm intact. That would change soon.

"So, uh, what's she look like?" Latham asked. He tried not to smile, but his green eyes sparkled as if it was Christmas morning.

John stared him down.

Latham didn't get the message. "I heard she's pretty hot." He broke into a grin. "Is she? It's okay. You can tell me."

The boy's clipped, hurried sentences hinted at too much stimulant in his morning cocktail. For some reason, it grated on John's nerves.

Latham laughed, play-punching him in the shoulder. "I'm just messing with ya, man." But his gaze kept flitting over to the door. "Seriously, what is she? Blonde? Brunette? A little black beauty? Oh man, I hope she's a redhead. I *love* redheads!"

"You need to go." It took effort to say the words without growling, and the sudden spike in animosity toward a fellow Shadow caught John off guard. To compensate, he stood straighter, blanked his mind so he could focus on his task.

"Aw, come on, man. We're supposed to be brothers-in-arms, here. Brothers *share*."

John wouldn't know. "My orders are not to open the door until you leave."

"Yeah, but you can still tell me."

John turned his head to meet the younger man's eager gaze. "She is a Class Three telepath being held in a unit specially designed to contain her abilities. That is all you, or any of us, need to know."

"Damn, man! What, did they cut off your balls when they zapped your brain, too?"

"What did you say?"

"I mean that whole Super Soldier act is cool and all, but I gotta—"

"You're talking to a Hawk on assignment, soldier." The rank didn't give him any authority over a Hound, but to distract a Hawk from his duty could warrant corporal punishment, depending on the circumstances. Hawks were specialists; they didn't get dispatched to fetch refreshments. Something Latham had yet to learn.

The boy's jaw went slack.

Now was as good a time as any. "You are also in direct violation of the sergeant major's directive to keep these premises clear. Now I suggest you shut your mouth and march on, before I'm obligated to report your insubordination. Am I making myself clear?"

Latham drew himself up, almost at attention, but not quite. He was too busy staring at John.

"Move," John growled.

With a muscle ticking in his tightened jaw, Latham gave him a heel-snapping mock salute, then walked away.

John had half a mind to go after him. Instead, he put the tray down and took a moment to set himself to rights. Entering a captive's cell in a state of agitation invited mutiny; he couldn't afford to let his guard down. Once he'd mastered himself, John picked up the food tray and opened the door.

A flash of bright red from the corner of his eye made him quickly put himself between the captive and the still-open doorway. The portal closed automatically, but there was still a four-second time frame in which a person could potentially pass through.

Cleverly, the captive had waited nearby to try to capitalize on such a promising opportunity, but she'd hesitated when she realized he was on to her. A terminal mistake. By the time she'd snapped out of her surprise, it was too late. John shoved her away with his shoulder as the door closed, sealing them both inside.

The girl screamed and launched herself at him, forcing him to turn sideways to save the food tray from overturning. Her fists were ineffectual at best; her nails were more likely to break against his uniform jacket than to cause any real damage, and she wasn't in a position to reach his skin. John let her tire herself out, and when the flying fury of her hands and feet had slowed, he freed one of his hands to shove her back.

With her small body mass and low center of gravity, she stumbled backwards onto the mattress. No physical damage done, aside from what she might have incurred on her own. When he set the food down before her, the yelling and cursing began.

John tuned it out, taking up a guard position by the door while the girl ranted and raved. Curiously, she didn't approach him again, and she didn't touch the food. After an hour of this, her voice grew hoarse and she finally fell silent.

For about ten seconds.

"Heroes are not supposed to be sadists," she rasped. "But then, you work for Griffith, so that would make you the bad guy. Guess I can't really expect much from a soldier." Suddenly, she shook her hand—hard. "Damn it, stop! Why won't my finger stop twitching? Did you do something to me? Was it a neural agent or something?… *Speak*, damn you!"

He didn't.

"Gah!" When she pushed to her feet and started to pace, John spared her a cautious glance. But having been once thwarted, she kept her distance. "I can do this," she said to herself, then took in a deep breath. "Just relax. This isn't so bad. I can take it for a while. My friends will come for me, you know." That last comment was meant for him, he supposed. "And you can't even imagine what they'll do when they get here. People like us? We look out for each other."

Another round of back and forth. She turned her head toward the food each time she passed by, only to swivel around to face him before moving on. *Just eat it*, he silently willed. He didn't want to be here any longer than necessary, but he had to make sure she ate.

"Are you going to be staying here, now? A bit cozy, don't you think?

Or have you been ordered to get me to cooperate by any means necessary?" She came toe to toe with him, though she had to tilt her head way back to look him in the face. "Well, let me tell you something, buddy boy. My vagina not only has teeth, it's poisonous. So I'd think twice before sticking something in it."

John ruthlessly checked his impulse to smile. The girl had guts, he'd give her that.

"And that goes for other orifices, too, just so we're clear."

Crystal, he thought.

"Trust me, you don't want any of *this.*" She motioned to indicate herself, and when he didn't respond, she snapped her fingers in front of his nose. "Yeah, that's what I thought."

And back to pacing.

She moved around so much, John wanted to snap at her to knock it off. Worse than dealing with Latham.

"How long will you stay standing there?" She shook out her hand again, bit her pinky, swung her arm back and forth. He could have told her it wouldn't do any good, but his orders were not to engage. With a frustrated sigh, she slumped. "You know, now that I think about it, your situation is probably just as messed up as mine. I mean, if you really look at it… I'm here. You're here. We're both stuck."

All the more reason for you to start eating.

"Do we really have to be, though?"

Not if you eat your meal and let me get out of here.

"If you could be anywhere in the universe right now, where would you be?"

Anywhere but here.

"Bet you'd be anywhere but here, huh?"

It was a logical assumption, but her instinctive answer, spoken with a wry half-smile, made him stiffen. *I am immune,* he reminded himself. *She can't read me.* But despite that knowledge, and the fact this room played merry havoc with her telepathy, it still took him several seconds to convince himself he hadn't been compromised.

Deliberately, he envisioned the worst possible scenario for her, just to see if she would respond. He imagined her stripped of clothes, hair tangled in his grasp, completely at his mercy.

But not only did she not respond, *he* did, and suddenly he wondered what she would look like naked. Whether she was quiet in her passion, or wild with abandon. Pretty soon, he was stepping his feet apart, cursing the day he'd caught her. And he still hadn't proven anything to himself, except that he'd underestimated how stupid a beautiful female could make him. Shamed and angered by his base response, John bit the inside of his cheek, forcing himself to remember this girl was the enemy.

"Now," she said, "if I'm not too rusty on my rules of engagement, sensory deprivation is only the beginning, right? So, since you brought me food, I'm guessing starvation is out, which would leave drugs, poisons, and-or environmental fluctuations. Probably start with hot to make the cold more miserable." A contemplative pause, then, "I could save you the trouble." Suddenly, her voice was all kinds of sultry, and without looking, John felt her eyes on him, which made his internal discomfort worse.

Had he been compromised? Was she using his own wayward thoughts against him?

Keeping his gaze trained straight forward forced her to stand up to get into his line of sight. John schooled himself not to look when she slowly removed her sweater, and shook out her bright red hair, but he could still see her somewhat and couldn't turn his head away unless he wanted to telegraph a weakness. "Is this better? No? Hmm, I'll have to think of something else." She toyed with the straps of her top to entice him, letting one slide off her shoulder.

Her skin was creamy pale and John wondered whether it felt as soft as it looked. He bit down harder onto the inside of his cheek until he tasted blood. It grounded him.

"We don't have to stay here, you know." The other strap came off, and she crossed her arms beneath her breasts to keep her top from sliding down too far.

John reasoned the glimpse he'd stolen was simply an accidental byproduct of a blink. *Stop it. Don't make this any harder than it has to be.* He didn't know whether he asked it for her or for himself.

"You have the key to the door," she reasoned shyly. "I have the means to get us very, very far."

A second ago, her vagina was poisonous. *Remember that. Enemy.*

She stepped close again, voice lowering to entice. "No one would ever find us."

If he just looked down, he'd see right into her cleavage. *Admit it. Admit you're tempted. Denying yourself will only make it easier for her to manipulate you.* John drew in a breath, inadvertently inhaling her scent, and his eyelids turned heavy. *Yes, I want to see.* Emma was so close, like static against his skin. She peered up at him, head cocked as if to offer the pale length of her neck while she traced random shapes over his chest with one delicate fingertip. She wasn't wearing perfume, and something told him she never did. Her natural woman's fragrance was more pleasing than the most seductive, pheromone-laced perfume in the universe, and he realized he'd… missed it.

Emma rose up on tiptoe, but still wasn't tall enough to get where she obviously wanted to be. With her lips a fraction of an inch from his jaw, she whispered, "What do you say, handsome?"

John held steady. *Do not engage.*

"Nothing?"

With nothing to lean on, her stamina eventually gave out, forcing her down to her heels. She huffed, pulling her straps back up onto her shoulders. "Worth a try," she said with a careless shrug. Back to the mattress she went, and John released a tense breath. She sat down and picked up her food tray.

Finally.

"So, poison or drugs?"

Damn it!

"I don't suppose it would make any difference to tell you I am highly susceptible to both, and even low doses could kill me."

Non-issue. Poisons or drugs would serve no purpose, as both would need to be treated medically, which would require a second person in the room with her.

"Okey-dokey, then. Here we go." She took a bite, and groaned. "This tastes like crap. At least get me some salt, will ya? Pepper? A celery stick?" Shaking her head, she forked another bite. "Tyrant." But she did eat. After so long without food, even amid her complaints, she polished off the tray and drained the water glass. When she'd finished, she set everything aside and asked, "Now what?"

One question John was all too happy to answer. In three swift steps, he retrieved the empty tray, gratified to see her flinch at his approach. Then he rushed out of the room, careful not to leave any space for her to slip out past him. As soon as the portal had closed, he hailed a mess hall Hound to pick up the tray, wanting nothing more than to get rid of the damn fork she'd sucked like a pro.

He hoped they sent someone other than fucking Latham.

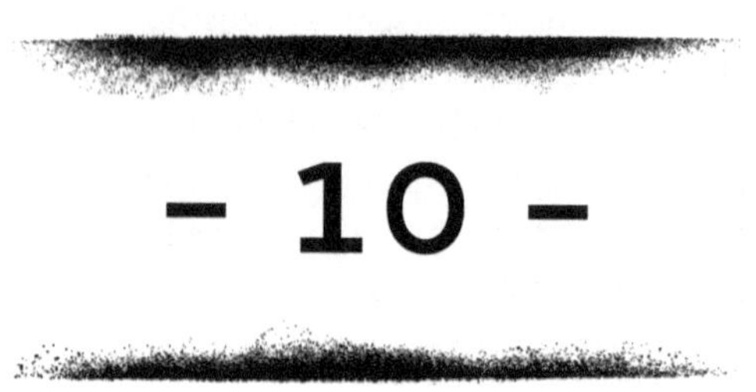

– 10 –

Miramar Colony – Date Unknown

All power to the complex had been cut a long time ago, and if they tried to bring it back now, everyone and his brother would be aware of their presence. That simply wouldn't do. Zayn paid good money to keep any information he received exclusive; he didn't like to share, especially when it came to possible acquisitions.

His sources claimed this one had massive potential and hadn't yet been tagged by the SU. Curious, considering how aggressive he knew the SU's recruiting tactics to be, at least when someone's gift was obvious. Happily, he also knew the SU had massive blind spots, which he always delighted in exploiting to his advantage.

Zayn jerked his chin at his second-in-command for a report.

"The security system hadn't been breached," Leanne said, "so I'm guessing EMP. Must have been pretty strong, too, to take out the whole complex. This place is a fortress." She consulted her equipment again, the singular piece of machinery dwarfed in her hands. At six-foot-four, Leanne wasn't a woman to fuck with. That was why he'd appointed her his second. "I think we're all clear…"

Before she'd finished, Annabel slipped around her and into the building. She'd worn his clothes again—pants too big and a sweatshirt that drowned her, sleeves dangling several inches past her fingertips. No matter how many times Zayn bought her new clothes or altered his own to fit her, she always wore something like that. At least this time she wore proper shoes.

Leanne sent him a warning look, and he nodded in acknowledgment.

"I'll keep watch," he told her. "Have the others stand guard at a distance and alert me if something changes. Otherwise, everyone stays out until I give the order."

"Understood."

Zayn grabbed a light and followed Anna into the dark corridor. If his intel was correct, the stairway at the end led up to the living quarters. They could wait. He wanted to see the lab first.

Shining his light through the glass window to see Anna, he caught a glimpse of his own reflection like a malevolent ghost with glowing amber eyes and a nasty slash across the face. He quickly moved on. "What do you feel?"

Anna held her palms up, closing her eyes. Her breath hitched. "Pain. Fear."

Old memories, then. His Annabel was a chronopath—a mind reader with a glitch, so to speak. Rather than reading thoughts in real time, she sensed them after the fact. By walking into a room, she could feel the history of every person who'd ever come through. Thankfully, her gift had a limit. The older the presence, the fainter it became; sharp thoughts turned to vague impressions, words jumbled, sights blurred, until only the raw emotion of the event remained, seeping into every nook and cranny like old perfume.

"Something bad happened here." Her chin dipped forward, hiding her face under a fall of honey-colored hair. Zayn brushed it back, clipped it at her nape, then gently nudged her face up.

"Look at me, love, I'm here."

She opened her brown eyes and did as he asked, but she wasn't seeing him. "I hear music," she said. "Dance with me, Zayn."

He smiled and, setting the light down, took her into his arms. She was only a few inches shorter, but so delicate, she might as well have been a child. He caught her right hand in the length of sleeve, kissed her knuckles through the fabric, brought it to his heart. For a moment, Anna became lost in whatever world she'd wandered off to, and they danced, swaying slowly in the open space between lab tables and equipment. Zayn didn't rush her; they had all the time in the world. Every chance he got to hold her like this was a gift he refused to give up. Moments like this were becoming too few and far between. He was losing her.

"They fought, and then they danced, and…" Anna hummed, shivering against him.

"What is it?"

She smiled dreamily, eyelids drooping. "Come have a look."

Zayn touched his forehead to hers, a connection that sometimes allowed her to share her gift, to show him what she saw. This time, there were no sights, only sounds and emotions. He heard the song she swayed to and adjusted his step to match the rhythm, to please her.

"This isn't working," she murmured, echoing a voice from the past.

Zayn spun as the vision guided. "Hmm, you're right. Maybe you should let me lead." The words made him grin, warmth tugging at his insides.

Anna chuckled, amused by the dialogue. "I thought I was."

"Just relax," Zayn whispered, nuzzling her in the way she liked. "I might actually know what I'm doing here."

Breathless, Anna brought her lips to his, and he pulled her tighter into him, savoring every detail, pilfering another man's memories of his mate to connect with his own. He kissed Anna with every ounce of his broken soul, willing her to feel *him* for once. Just once more. *Come back to me, love. I can't lose you.* Maybe, just maybe, if he could hold on tightly enough, he wouldn't. Maybe he could keep the past from snatching her away.

But all too soon, she broke away from the kiss to say, "I have to get back to work." They weren't her words, and the noose around his heart constricted a little more.

"No." *Not yet!* "Kiss me again," he pleaded, furious that the past echoed him back.

Anna squeezed her eyes shut, somehow wresting herself back to the present. Winded, shivering, she leaned on Zayn. "Getting names. Umm… Amelia Chase. Hailey Chase. Gabriel Connors. Caesar something. Silas dog."

He clutched her, supported her while she found her feet again. "That's good, baby. That's very good. Now let's get you out of here, what do you say?"

From the hallway, Leanne's light shone through on them. "Traffic's starting to pick up. We need to hurry this along."

"Anything from the machines?" he asked.

"We got all we're going to get."

"Good. Have the others retreat. I've got this."

Leanne nodded and left, plunging Zayn and Anna into darkness again.

Anna sighed, pushed to stand on her own, and reluctantly, Zayn let her. He retrieved his light and kept a close eye on her while she wandered around the lab, touching computers, searching through cabinets like a curious little squirrel. She only got like this when she was looking for something very specific, but oftentimes even Anna herself didn't know what that was until she actually found it.

At one of the cabinets, she stopped to trace something with her fingertips. "Nature always prevails," she said. "They will have been talking about us. The Evolution riots. Rioteers. Evolutionaries." She smiled at him. "That should be us."

Zayn came around the table to join Anna, who was pointing through the glass of a bookcase to a paper book with a symbol on its cover—a plant of some sort with two leaves and roots in the shape of a DNA double helix that split into two underground. The book was titled *On The Origins of DNA: A Study Of What Was, What Is, And What Might Yet Be.*

Zayn pulled Anna to his side, and kissed her temple as he retrieved the book. "Evolutionaries, huh?"

"I think it has a nice ring to it."

"I think it does, too."

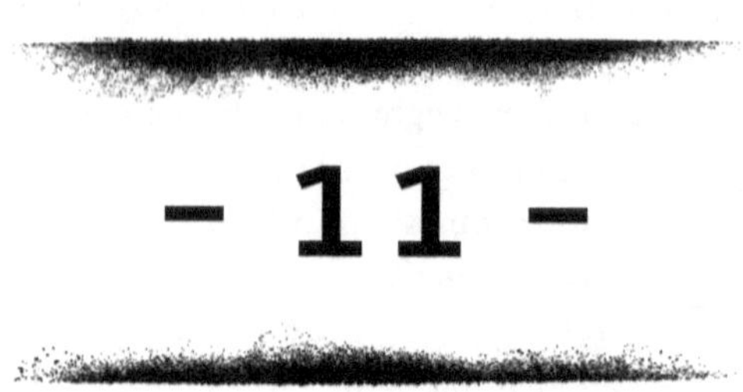

– 11 –

Isolation was beginning to affect John's judgment. Boredom had driven him to distraction, a lapse he couldn't afford. The moment a Hound came to relieve him for his six-hour break, John headed straight to the mess hall. It was chowtime, and he'd rather spend an hour with his comrades than waste it on sleeping.

Their ranks had been oddly thinned. Half the tables stood empty, and the soldiers present were quiet and subdued. The TV wall broadcast several news feeds at the same time, reports from different sectors, and all of them showed similar images of riots and violence. As John retrieved his meal and sat down, the messages crawling across the bottom of each feed caught his attention.

Sixteen planets had petitioned the ICG for military aid in controlling the conflicts. Places where soldiers had already been dispatched looked more like war zones with cities destroyed and infrastructure damaged, sometimes beyond repair. Like throwing fuel on a fire, the more force the ICG applied, the more violent the riots became. Metropolises were being razed from the inside out, and there seemed to be no end in sight.

Latham sat across from John, blocking his view. "How's our guest doing?"

John's jaw muscle twitched.

"What? You're not on duty now, are you?"

Would anyone care if he stabbed a fork into Latham's eye?

"Come on, don't be a dick. We've all been curious about what you do with all that free time you have now, haven't we, boys?" Latham's ill-concealed challenge sounded all the more a threat coupled with the sharp smile that twisted his mouth. "They have all of us rotating shifts in front of that door, but no one's allowed inside. No one, except you. Why is that?"

John laid the fork down before he did something stupid.

"It takes her two hours to eat a meal," Latham mused. "That's a long time away from surveillance feeds, don't you think?"

Finn chuckled at a table nearby. "Ladies and gentleman, I give you the living, breathing reason why no Hound will ever be a Hawk." He picked at his meal, a sure sign something was wrong. But like a proper Hawk, he wouldn't be caught dead bitching about it. "Shut your mouth, Latham, before someone shuts it for you."

The idiot ignored him. "Two hours. Just you and her in a cozy little room with a mattress. How do I get put on that kind of detail, huh?"

Finn dropped his fork with a muttered, "Shit." He stood and gave a four-fingered wave to shoo the others back. He'd lost the pinky on that hand years ago sparring with John. He knew what was about to happen.

"I've been on this base for three fucking years—"

"And others have been here longer," someone cut in.

"You shut the fuck up!" Latham snapped without looking away from John. "This is between me and him."

"Is it?" John asked quietly. "I had no problem with you until you started talking. You should stop while you're ahead."

"The way I hear it, you had no problem with anyone until they burned one into your brain."

John tensed.

"You were a fucking coward. They were gonna wash you out your first week before the sergeant major intervened. You were *nothing* before the Shadows." Latham scoffed. "Far as I can see, you're even less now."

"Walk away," John told him.

"Yeah? Or what? You going to tattle on me? Get Big Daddy to fight your battles for you again?"

John shook his head and picked up his tray to move, in no mood for this shit.

Latham slammed his hand onto the tray, forcing it back down. "Hey, I'm talking to you, asshole—"

John cracked him in the nose so hard, Latham's head snapped back then forward again. Broken cartilage, but the damage was minimal, as evidenced by Latham's snarling and scrambling across the table to get to John.

He looked like he needed some help, so John grabbed Latham by his shirt and his belt, and bodily threw him down onto the next table over, using the soldier's back to sweep it clear of cutlery before sending him gliding headfirst into the wall.

Hounds moved farther back, while Finn and another Hawk stepped up to contain the damage. Something was wrong with Latham; his aggressive responses were off the charts. Bleeding all over the place with a possible concussion, he still got up, snarling like a rabid dog, and charged at John again, swinging wildly, embarrassing himself and his DIs.

John twisted away from one punch and struck Latham in the throat just hard enough to make him back off. It didn't work. Latham kept coming at him as if he'd completely lost his mind. Catching another wild swing, John head-butted Latham's nose, breaking it again, then did it one more time until Latham slumped to the floor in a daze.

Victory was hollow when the senseless fight hadn't even been worth John's time.

Latham tried to rise up for more, but Finn pushed him back down with a booted foot to his chest. "You're done, buddy. Stay down. You're done."

"You got this?" John asked.

Finn nodded. "Yeah, I'll take him to med bay before we head out."

"Out where?"

"You're not the only Hawk who's got an assignment," he replied with a grin and a wink.

John nodded. "Thanks for this." If he had to take Latham to med bay himself, he might kill the man along the way.

Finn gave him a two-finger salute. "Always a pleasure to clean up after you."

John chuckled. "Yeah, fuck you, too." Dinner plans ruined, he sighed, heading back to his bunk. Hounds shifted out of his way as he passed, giving him strange looks and reminding him of nightmares best forgotten. They all stared as if they knew something he didn't, but none of them were brave enough to tell him.

John didn't wait for them to start whispering. Instead, he picked up his step, shoving his hands into his pockets, where the tip of the chess piece dug into his palm, a sharp reminder of a past he'd lost long ago.

Yeah, that void bothered him but didn't take away from who he was. The past didn't make a man or dictate who he would become. As far as John was concerned, he'd gotten a fresh start and had used it to put himself at an advantage.

That the rest of the Shadows seemed to think it made him deficient was their problem, not his.

One day, that underestimation would cost them the way it had cost Latham today.

~

Gray Dublin, Earth

"Anything?"

MacMurphy speared a hand through his graying hair to avoid glaring at Travis. "You're supposed to be on bed rest." He wouldn't even look at Travis; didn't want to pile on more guilt, but this was worse. Travis would rather get chewed out; take a mental beating and get the resentment out in the open. This forced politeness was like hot iron nails raking over his skin.

"Horse shit," Travis growled.

"Get back to bed," MacMurphy said. "Jessica will be looking for you."

"The Brain knows where to find me if she has more tests for me. I'm needed elsewhere."

"Is that so?" MacMurphy turned on him, and the flood of anger staggered Travis. "And where exactly might that be? If you have any more useful ideas, now would be an excellent time to share them.

Unless, of course, you want to go it alone again!"

Nell laid a hand on MacMurphy's arm, but it didn't do any good.

Travis' head still pounded and the swelling around his eyes refused to go down. Unsteady on his feet, he had to lean against walls and furniture to keep his balance, and his telepathy was shot to shit for the time being. Travis was, for all intents and purposes, useless. He should do as he'd been ordered: get out of everyone's way and let them look for Emma.

But he couldn't. "I lost her on Earth for a window of a few hours. However they took her, they must have left a signature of some kind, a trail."

"Thank you, Sherlock. That's a brilliant idea. Now if you would be kind enough to reveal by what feat of deductive reasoning we're supposed to pinpoint which of the *seventeen thousand* signature trails belonged to the Shadows, we can rally the forces and go hunting a Pixie!"

Travis' face grew hot.

"Nothing?" MacMurphy taunted. "No shining pearls of wisdom?"

"John, stop," Nell pleaded, giving him a worried look. "Can't you see he's hurting enough already?"

"Not nearly enough." MacMurphy advanced. Taller by a scant two inches, he might as well have been a giant, as small as he made Travis feel. "He needs to own that this is *his* fault. You had one job to do: Bring. Pixie. Home. Instead, you thought it would be more fun to let her go wandering off into a riot when you *knew* she was in danger. The Shadows didn't take her from you, boy. You handed her to them on a silver platter."

Travis dropped his chin in a wordless nod, lowering his gaze to the floor. MacMurphy was right, this was Travis' doing. From start to finish, all his fault.

"Now, I'm about to put in a call to her brother. Unless you want to be the one to break the happy news to him, I suggest you get the hell out of my sight."

A small hand curled into Travis' sleeve and yanked so hard he almost toppled over. "There you are! Did I not tell you to stay put?"

Travis levered himself away from the wall and past the ten-year-old girl wearing a lab coat.

"You better be going back to bed, mister."

He was. For the moment. The director of the Special Unit, his boss and the only father figure he'd ever known to be worth a damn, had just told him he was no longer needed. For now, Travis couldn't do much about it, but in a day or two, with the Brain's treatments, he should be back on his feet physically. The Shadows wouldn't be found any other way except going out there and hunting for them. MacMurphy had things covered on the tech side. But he would need eyes on the ground. The more people they had out there searching for Emma, the better their chances of stumbling onto a clue. Everyone made mistakes, and the Shadows were no different. No matter what Mac-Murphy said, no matter how badly Travis had screwed up, he wasn't about to give up now.

The only difference was that it no longer mattered to him who found Emma first, as long as someone did—and fast.

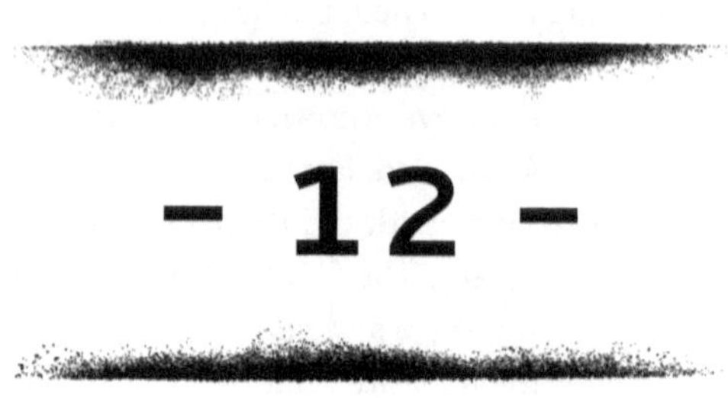

- 12 -

As strange as it was, Emma liked having the rat bastard soldier in the room with her. Every so often, the door would open and he'd come in with a tray. Food and water. It all looked and tasted the same, but while she ate, the soldier would stand by the door and stare straight ahead with those winged brows scrunched into a frown over his eyes, waiting for her to finish. Even though he didn't broadcast any thoughts or emotions, he still projected something—some vibe she picked up on in the absence of everything else. His presence categorically proved she was still there. He was; therefore, Emma existed. Despite his never looking at her, he was there to see her, so she had to be there to be seen…

She had no idea how often these feedings had been prescribed for her. Could have been twice a day, or twice a week. Sometimes, the stretch between felt longer; other times, it seemed like he'd just left and then he was back again.

They meant to keep her disoriented; sensory deprivation didn't work if the victim had some routine to hold on to. Instead, the visits grounded Emma in sanity.

In sanity.

Insanity.

Huh…

Her thoughts had drifted again. Emma refocused on her meal. She ate slowly, prolonging every moment to maintain this equilibrium just a little while longer. Blinking her eyes hard to banish the fog, she looked down at the fork she clutched. It shook. No, her hand shook.

Emma set it down, then held her hands out in front of her and, watching them vibrate in the air, she became aware of other things. Like how her head pounded and how her vision kept shifting, because her eyes were. She wasn't sleeping well at all. It was definitely getting to her. And that tight feeling in her stomach… It wasn't that, exactly. Her belly felt like someone had blown up a balloon inside it, and no matter how much she ate, it just felt hollow, making her sick.

Emma swayed where she sat on the floor, so she leaned back against the wall and focused on her statue. He wore the standard uniform of Senator Griffith's little army—midnight blue-and-black camo pants; shined black combat boots; and a midnight blue jacket that buttoned up to the neck, straight cut to offset the slightly baggy pants with their multitude of pockets stuffed with an arsenal of weapons. It was a good look, actually. Understated, yet poignant. No flashy decorations, except for a silver pin at one shoulder, in the abstract shape of a bird. The others she'd seen had worn similar ones, only theirs had been shaped like a dog.

"You got a name?" she asked.

Nothing. Not that she'd expected an answer. Like a good little soldier, the man never talked. Those few words that last time… how long ago was that? Could have been a day or month as far as she knew. She'd lost count of the seconds as they… ticked… by…

…must have been a fluke. She couldn't even remember what his voice sounded like. All she could remember were his eyes. A predator's eyes—sharp and focused on her. No thought behind them, except for her capture.

But that mouth… could it smile without being cruel? Could it make his face look strong instead of hard? Twitch his eyebrows sexy down instead of angry together? Emma would probably never find out. What a shame. What an utter waste of man. And arms. A good pair of arms was indispensable to hold the world together, and his would make Atlas swoon.

Tick. Tock. Tick. Tock…

"I'm Emma." Of course, he'd already know that. The senator had known, though how could he possibly? She didn't have any records outside the SU.

Silence.

Oh man, she missed her old room at SU. She'd shared it with the other girls. Maia, all of five; and Lucia, nearly eighteen. An unlikely combo, sure, but they'd spent most nights laughing and talking about boys. Maia had said they smelled.

Emma couldn't smell the statue soldier. From this far away, she couldn't smell anything. Not even her meal.

…it was almost gone. Emma watched her hand reach for the fork. A plastic one. Almost too soft to use on the food, let alone as a weapon. The statue wouldn't leave until she finished her food. At least it tasted somewhat decent.

"Come here often?" Then again, maybe that's where the poison was. Maybe that's why her hand shook so much that it took three tries to spear the little piece of potato and bring it to her mouth. She mussed up her chin the first time she tried.

Wonder how potatoes grow…

Come here often?

Never really leave much. You?

"Yeah, I already know you do." She pinched her nose closed and puffed out her cheeks. Her ears didn't pop. Opening her mouth wide, she forced herself to yawn. That didn't work, either.

Then a real yawn cut off what she was about to say, and her eyelids drooped. "Even if you don't move or talk, you're still pretty to look at."

Before her eyes closed completely, she saw him turn his head to return her regard.

~

She passed out where she sat. John figured that meant she was done with her meal. He moved in to take the fork out of her hand and to pick up her tray. She didn't stir. Was she still breathing?

John held his hand beneath her nose and barely perceived a puff of air against his skin. He checked her pulse next. It fluttered against his fingertips like a trapped butterfly. How could she sleep like that?

Easy answer: she didn't. She wasn't really sleeping, just… checked out. Her eyes were closed but not moving behind her eyelids. No dreams, then. Any second now, she'd tip over and wake herself back up. John had done that a few times when he'd dozed off on guard duty. The shock of coming to had been almost as bad as realizing he'd fallen asleep in the first place. He hated that feeling.

John set the tray aside, and gently touched her shoulder, intending to lay her down before she fell over. Like flipping a switch, she woke up with a sharp intake of breath, her bright blue eyes, even brighter in this room, mere inches from his.

For a baffled moment, they stared at each other.

He'd seen people scared before. Angry, confused, grieving. But not all of those things at the same time. Looking into those blue pools of emotion, John's breath caught. She looked so lost and alone, hurting in the light. John's hand rose of its own volition to brush her hair back over her shoulder.

"Nothing," she whispered, and he stilled. "There's nothing. Your eyes are empty."

The proclamation made him shudder.

"Who are you?"

John ducked his head, picked up her tray, and left. As ordered, he waited until the door closed behind him before he summoned a Hound from the mess hall. Incidentally, it was also time for his fifteen minute break, and as soon as a soldier came to relieve him, John made a quick, dignified exit to his quarters.

But once he got there, he couldn't stop his feet from moving. He paced a circuit from the window to the door and back, and every time he strode past the bathroom doorway, his eyes went to the mirror above the sink. Finally, opening his mouth wide to stretch out the stiffness of his clenched jaw, John went in and braced his hands against the sink, staring at his own reflection.

Your eyes are empty. What the hell had she meant by that? Just because he couldn't remember his childhood, didn't mean he didn't have a soul. He'd had a life before the Shadows, once upon a time. So what if he didn't know what it was? It still existed.

John shook his head hard and turned on the water, focusing on the hiss to master himself. Didn't matter what she'd said or what she'd meant. She was a telepath well versed in the art of mindfuck, and if that wasn't enough, she was currently halfway off her rocker, to boot.

Shit, I should have stayed at my post. What the hell? Disobeying a direct order from the sergeant major? If the girl had been even halfway lucid, John could have compromised the entire mission! Splashing his face with cold water didn't help at all. Water didn't wash away mistakes. *What is wrong with me?*

Something had to be.

John had seen the effects of that room on telepaths before, had guarded two or three of them in the past. One had called it "sensory deprivation of the cruelest kind," because that's what they thought telepathy was to these people: a sense, just like sight or hearing, and removing it equaled crippling them.

But he'd never seen it affect someone so much, so soon. Barely a week had passed since Emma Calen had been placed in that cell and already she exhibited signs of mental deterioration others hadn't shown until three weeks, or more. Why was she so different?

And why the hell did he care?

He didn't. It was a trick, nothing more. Whatever she was experiencing, he'd bet his last credit it wasn't as bad as she made it out to be. It was all a show to win his sympathies, make him drop his guard.

John fished the white queen out of his pocket, squeezed it tight to remind himself what was real. The girl in that room was nothing; a phantom who wouldn't matter for much longer. She'd break, or she'd be broken, and the world would keep on turning.

The thought should have calmed him, but it didn't. He unclenched his fist to look at the chess piece.

Intense pressure to submit usually elicited one of two responses: surrender or counter-victory. The first was a complete breakdown, resulting in the captive's total submission; they gave in to every request and order, no matter how small or demeaning, just to make the torture stop. The second was a feral fight to the bitter end, in which the captive cursed his or her captors but didn't give a fraction of an inch, choosing death over any small semblance of obedience.

Emma Calen seemed to be in a category all her own: retreat. She neither fought nor surrendered. She simply… was. As if she'd forgotten life outside of those white walls had ever existed. She seemed oblivious that someone wanted something from her. Like the chess piece in his hand, she moved any which way she pleased to avoid capture, wreaking quiet havoc on the board.

John's schedule beeped. He pocketed the queen and marched back to his post. Nodding to the soldier he replaced, John stood in front of that door and stared straight ahead.

He didn't care. It wasn't his job to study her strategy or to admire her strength. Emma Calen was in no way special. Every piece had its weakness, even the queen.

He just had to hold steady and ignore how sallow her skin had become. If he didn't look into her eyes, he wouldn't notice the dark rims and smudges around them resulting from strain and lack of sleep, and he could ignore how they made her irises stand out that much more. And if he just did his damn job, it wouldn't matter how much effort she put into not shaking. She'd moved with a lithe sort of grace before, like a bird in flight; panicked, rushed, but still elegant somehow. John hadn't realized this until it was gone.

And damn it, she still smelled like spring.

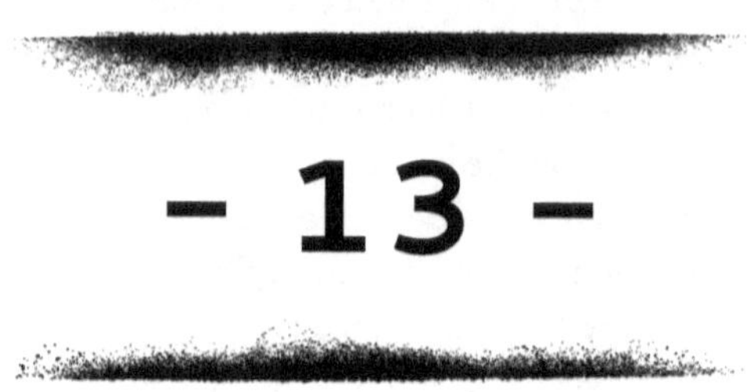

– 13 –

Lexington, Earth

Dorian had guard duty today. No one liked it, but Leanne was out scouting and Zayn needed someone at the door. Lexington wasn't safe anymore, not after the last riot, when the city had essentially ceded all control to the military, who disliked revolutionaries hiding out in their backyard. It was time to relocate.

But before they did, Zayn had one last thing to do.

"I like these digs," Dorian said, nodding in approval at the ten-by-ten hole in the ground they currently occupied. "It's got character."

Zayn regarded all of the assorted stains the place had acquired over long years of housing drug addicts, orphans, and fugitives. "Yes, I suppose it has a sort of rustic appeal." Had it been up to him, they'd have never come within miles of here. But they hadn't had a choice. With the military breathing down everyone's necks and one of their own getting hauled in with the riot masses, they'd had to abandon their last hideout.

Thankfully, Anna was still asleep and would stay that way until they were safely out of here. The last thing he wanted was for her to wake up and relive their past.

They'd fallen in love here.

Not this room, precisely, but one of the thirty chambers that made up this complex. Back then, it had been a haven for runaways hiding from everyone, including themselves; during the good old days when the universe had been their rotten oyster. Zayn, the embarrassment son of a morally deficient father; Michael, the future dominator of every game of chance ever invented; and Anna, the overlooked child of innocence.

He'd loved her from the start. But then, Anna had always been so damn easy to love. She'd looked at him, into him, and called him hers, despite knowing exactly where he'd come from, what he was heir to. Anna was brave in a way very few people could afford to be: she opened her whole self to the world, embraced it, faults and all, and every time it hurt her in return, she simply smiled and gave more.

Back then, the three of them had been as thick as thieves—young, desperate, clinging to each other because they'd had nothing else. It had been easy to dream big; the only way to go from the bottom was up.

Or so they'd thought.

Funny how such an ambivalent thing could ruin so many lives. Apathy—the inability to feel for others; the idea that people were willing and able to help themselves, and so needed no further aid; the thought that "good enough" was enough for those on the other side of the invisible barrier.

The day a Special Unit agent had wandered into their little hideout had been like Christmas morning. They'd all heard about the mysterious people who walked the unsavory parts of town, searching for others like them. Of all the dreams the three of them had shared, to be chosen and adopted by the Special Unit had been their most heartfelt prayer. What more could an orphan want than a family to call his own?

That day, Zayn had spotted the telepath from half a block away. He'd recognized the way they moved, talked, tilted their heads just so to catch a whisper of a thought. Like watching an angel or alien glide over the sidewalk, and realizing no one else could see it. He'd rushed back to their little hidey-hole and, grinning big at Anna and Michael, told them this would be their day. He'd all but lined them up at the door so the agent would know to look at them first—to look long and hard, and to *see* them.

They'd held their collective breath when the man had finally walked in, tipped his hat, then kept right on going, asking about a teenage boy with a very small sister.

Anna's worried look had sent Zayn trailing the agent as he walked among them. Several times he'd tried to engage the man, to point out others might be worth considering. Not him; he wasn't a telepath. But Anna and Michael were, in their own ways. He'd needed the agent to take them. Zayn knew how to survive on his own; he had options. His stubborn principles had sent him running from home in the first place. But he could swallow them, and his pride, if need be and go back to his son of a bitch chemical engineer father. Anna and Michael had no one.

The agent had listened politely, paused long enough to shake hands with them, but in the end, he'd excused himself, too intent on his chosen ones to give the other three the time of day.

Michael had been devastated. Zayn couldn't look Anna in the eye for a month.

But he'd learned one thing from that day: you can't keep a street rat down.

Decades later, Zayn now found himself in the interesting position of having something the Special Unit wanted very badly.

Curious how the wheels of fortune turned.

"So what are you doing, anyway?" Dorian asked, craning his neck to look at the piece of paper Zayn was marking.

Zayn finished the final line of neat, generic script, then held up the note for Dorian to see.

Dorian frowned. "I don't get it."

"Remember that Shadow we crossed paths with a couple years ago?"

"Yeah?"

"He gave me this. It's the location of their base of operation in this sector."

Dorian scratched his head. "And he just… gave it to you?"

Zayn shrugged. "Not willingly at first. Took some persuading. But you know I always get what I want." No matter what the cost. He neatly folded the note and went to the door, shoving Dorian's feet off the table as he passed. "Malcom," he called to the runner stuffing his face with what was undoubtedly a pilfered pile of supplies. "There's an SU safe house behind La Luna, that Italian joint downtown. Entrance in the back alley, marked with white paint. I want you to attach this to the door."

"What, we're helping the Psychics now?" Dorian asked. "The enemy of my enemy and all that shit? I thought you had some grudge going on."

No, he wouldn't make it that easy for them. "The enemy of my enemy is still an enemy," Zayn replied patiently. "But that doesn't mean I won't use them against each other when the opportunity presents itself."

Dorian's frown lifted into a grin of understanding. "I knew you had somethin' up your sleeve." He chuckled. "Shit, can't wait to see this play out. Bunch of pacifists against the best trained army of assassins in the universe. This is gonna be fun."

Zayn didn't smile back. Dorian didn't understand shit. He was a juggernaut—muscle upon muscle, with only enough brain cells to move them around from place to place. This was a game of strategy, something so far beyond Dorian's power of comprehension, it pissed Zayn off that he'd wasted time telling him as much as he had.

"Go get Anna," he ordered, finished with the conversation. "We're leaving in twenty minutes."

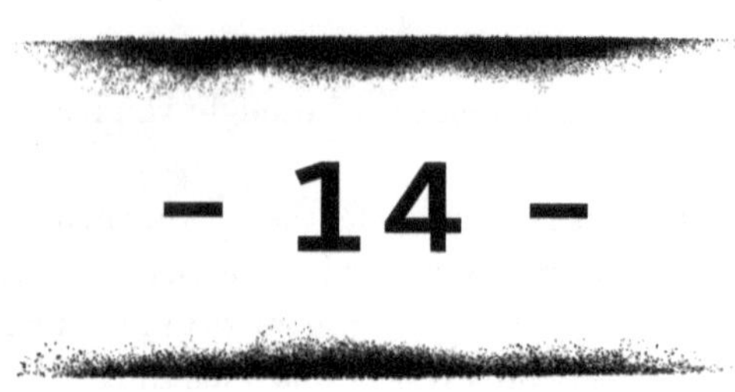

– 14 –

The humming walls had a distinct frequency. Swaying back and forth, Emma sang to herself, pitching her voice higher then lower to try to match it. When she did, a shudder racked her spine as if she'd touched on something she shouldn't have. She rubbed her arms and went to the sink again.

Washing helped. The splash of water didn't overpower the hum, but at least it diluted it. Emma scrubbed her hands and face, then cupped as much water as she could and dumped it over her head, repeating the process until her hair was soaked through.

Then she stripped down to her underwear and scrubbed her clothes. The sink was miniscule and water sloshed everywhere, puddles making the slick floor a death trap for the elderly. Overwhelmed by a sudden excess of energy, Emma scrubbed her shirt until her hands cramped. This wall hummed louder than the others. She hated it.

In a quick twitch-and-spasm, she flung the sopping mess of a shirt to the floor, then screamed and lashed out at the wall. She pounded at it over and over, punching and slapping until the hurt in her hands no longer registered. She yelled, and sobbed, but the remorseless wall just stood there as if Emma didn't matter.

She only stopped when her arms got tired and her throat had closed up with too many tears to shed.

Wheezing, she dropped to her knees and hummed again. She hit the right frequency and almost shivered herself to pieces, but this time she kept at it for a full count of four, and in those four seconds something… clicked.

Her sight blurred, and she sat there, rocking back and forth on her heels.

Tick. Tock. Tick. Tock.

"Hickory, dickory, dock. The mouse ran up the clock… The clock… The clock struck… The clock struck one…" And *tick, tock, tick, tock.*

Tick… Tock… Tick… Tock…

Hickory, dickory, dock—*tick*—the mouse ran up the clock—*tock.*

Emma watched the ancient brass pendulum swing from left to right. The clock kept ticking, but the hands never moved. Left, right. Tick, tock.

Hickory, dickory, dock—*tick*—the mouse ran up the clock—*tock.*

Her eyelids grew heavy while she watched the hypnotizing movement.

The clock struck one, the mouse ran down, hickory, dickory, dock.

"Sit up straight, Emma. We aren't finished yet."

Emma's eyes went wide, and her back straightened, a habit formed from too many such reprimands, well meaning though they were. She looked around at the three rows of desks that filled the dim room, inhaled deeply the familiar scent of history and dust, and her chest ached with longing. The other students faced front, not a sleeve out of place, and they didn't move a muscle, too rapt on their teacher.

John MacMurphy smiled and settled onto the edge of his wooden desk. No fancy machinery here; everything was as old as Earth, a sensory candyland that guaranteed students wouldn't turn their minds inward. The chalkboard was gray instead of black, the windows covered with bamboo shades and pretty lace drapes. The lamp on John's desk was so old, no adapter existed to make it compatible with today's power supply. Books of various shapes and sizes lined the hermetic shelves. They were not to be touched. "Today, I have a different kind of history lesson for you all. Toward the end of the twenty-ninth century, we had what became known as the largest fallout in human history. Billions died, entire worlds were destroyed, and that was only the beginning."

Emma smiled. "Didn't we already go over this last week?" She distinctly remembered that. Someone had cracked a joke about those who failed to learn from history being doomed to repeat it.

"There's a lot I haven't told you yet. Knowledge you might need someday."

He said it with a smile, but his eyes were too intense for cordiality. This was something he wanted *her* to know, not the others. Beneath her hand on the desk, a paper folder bled into being. Emma frowned down at it, wanted to open the thing, but her mental command refused to move her hand. She was stuck, her attention forced on MacMurphy.

"The fallout nearly destroyed the human race. No one had ever thought this through; they just aimed and fired untested weapons manufactured on different planets, using whatever exploded the loudest. Those charges not only destroyed entire continents, they also reacted with each other to create the perfect conditions for extinction. Disease, mutations, low birth rates, weakened immunities—maladies humans haven't seen since we first split the atom. It nearly did us all in."

"So the sectors came together under one government to save and protect humanity," Emma finished gravely.

MacMurphy delivered the equivalent of a mental knuckle rap. "Yes," he said. "The Interplanetary Council of Governance was created, and as the overarching ruling body, it assumed the burden of responsibility and allocated all available resources to the study and repair of the human genome."

"Thus, the chem-treatment industry was born."

Directly beneath her hand, a label appeared on the file. Her fingers obstructed all but two letters, and she frowned, trying to make out what it said.

MacMurphy scowled at her. "May I continue?"

Emma's attention snapped back, curiosity instantly forgotten. "Depends," she quipped, thoroughly amused. "Do you have something new to add to the discussion?"

She could tell his patience was wearing thin, though, so when he started up again, Emma held her tongue and listened. "The goal was to repair the damage to a person's DNA and stabilize it so the mutation wouldn't pass on to new generations. It only took them two decades to discover that treating full-grown adults only created a temporary fix; a vaccine that eventually dissolved, leaving the person in the same shape as before, if not worse. To truly cure someone for the span of a normal lifetime, they had to be treated directly after birth when the umbilical cord was cut, severing the physical connection with the mother. It was the first and only success, but the change wasn't inheritable. Thus, the treatment became mandatory for every child born, and in this way, the population growth once again became stable."

One student grumbled under his breath, slumped in his seat, staring at the simulation of the outdoors in the windowpane. No one else moved a muscle.

MacMurphy ignored him. "But the government-sponsored genetics research never stopped. The science guild now had the means to fix people, so why not try to make them better? They restructured prisons in order to perform their experiments in secret, using inmates as test subjects in studies designed to push the human body to its limits, and beyond. And in the middle of all of this, the guild discovered something shocking: after generations of successfully immunizing the population, people were beginning to show signs of resistance to the treatment."

"People like us," Emma said. Her fingers twitched, drawing her eye to the partially exposed label: NATALIE AND JO…

"Yes," he confirmed. "People with strange eye colors, crooked teeth, mild depression, or odd mannerisms at first, then more noticeable changes: advanced mental abilities, psychological and physical illnesses thought to have been eradicated long ago. And the more obvious they became, the more it unsettled our society. These strange people were a testament to the power of nature. Evolution had given humanity the means to once again survive on its own, and we had living, breathing proof that chem-treating a child was not only unnecessary and sometimes ineffective, but also limiting. Whatever a person might have been was suppressed by the treatment, and once administered, it couldn't be undone.

"People began to oppose the mandatory treatment of children in infancy. Then, in 3028, the prison experiments were leaked to the public, and all hell broke loose."

Of its own volition, Emma's hand moved and opened the file onto gory images of brutalized, beaten, and sadistically murdered people. So many images, but only two victims: Natalie and Jonathan Hunt.

A shiver of dread ran up her spine. She didn't like the direction this lecture was taking.

"Peaceful protests erupted into bloody riots in all major cities," MacMurphy continued. "The government fractured under the pressure but maintained a mask of unity for the public. They were worried, and rightly so. People now existed who could read minds and predict the future; those who had amazing strength and speed, and they had a lot of sympathizers in the general public. If they ever banded together against the ICG, not even the most advanced weapons in the universe would be able to stop them."

A girl near the door momentarily broke out of her apparent paralysis to intone, "Dun-dun-duuuun."

Emma stifled a giggle. The boy behind her added, "The fate of mankind now rested in the hands of Mighty Man!" He pointed over to the faded poster on the wall, and froze that way.

One bell chime was all MacMurphy needed to get Emma's attention back. He never blinked, and she felt like he somehow spoke his next words straight into her brain, imprinting the lesson into her long-term memory before it had even been processed. "The government doesn't take chances, Emma. Ever. They always have a safety net, a backup plan to make everyone fall in line again. When this new threat arose, a single voice whispered to the Council and, fools that they are, all of them listened. He proposed the creation of an army trained specifically to battle chem-resistant individuals. By any means necessary. An army so strong, so well trained, that even rumors of its existence would dissuade any attempted coup."

A soldier killed my parents when I was ten. A boogeyman in a Shadow-blue uniform. Emma shook her head to dislodge Tristan Hunt's voice from her head, along with the images conjured up by his words. *Congratulations, he said after he'd done it. You've been given the privilege of serving the Union to better mankind.*

"But that's just a myth," Emma argued as nervous butterflies fluttered in her belly. "We would have known if something like that existed." Of course, the Special Unit wasn't called *special* for nothing. They had telepaths of all ages and ranks on every inhabited world, keeping quiet, keeping the peace. Keeping watch. They were the guardians of humanity.

MacMurphy didn't answer, merely held her gaze.

"We would have known!" she insisted. "There's no way we wouldn't have."

I discovered my mind was the greatest weapon of all. A feral rage momentarily lit her blood on fire, and her nostrils flared with every breath, lips drawing back into a snarl as the image of a grotesque animated soldier corpse arose in her mind's eye. She couldn't shake it. *It took me twelve years, but I did get to him eventually. There wasn't much left of him by the time I was done. But the others, an entire outpost of sadistic sons of bitches just like him…*

Hickory, dickory, dock—*tick.*

…I made them piss themselves in fear of the shadows they lived in.

The mouse ran up the clock—*tock.*

The pendulum dissolved, followed by the clock and the bookshelf, and then the chalkboard faded away. One by one, the students disappeared, leaving Emma with old photos of death floating up from the file, dancing in the air before her to the tune of terror-filled screams and moans. Emma's heart thudded, her breathing becoming erratic.

Tick. Tock. Tick. Tock.

Soon, the images began to fade as everything around her brightened into an unbroken field of nothing, and all she had was John MacMurphy's stare to anchor her. "They call themselves the Shadows," his receding voice whispered across her mind.

Then he, too, disappeared, and she cried out.

Gone. Gone. Never been. And she was alone again, trembling in her bright white cage where the clock didn't tick, it hummed. Naked. In every sense. With no sense at all.

"Hickory, dickory, dock," someone sang. The foreign voice came from her own lips. No *tick.* She tried again. "The mouse ran up the clock." No *tock.* No pendulum, or chalkboard; no dust, books, or people.

No dead soldiers.

Sit up straight, Emma. We aren't finished yet.

But they were. She was. Emma turned her head left, then right, but didn't recognize anything. The tips of her hair were moist, and she was almost naked.

She gasped, shoved to her feet, but her legs had gone numb and she tumbled, falling onto all fours again, right in front of the pile of wet clothes. Terrified, shaking, she picked up her pants and struggled to pull them on. The shirt was too sodden, so she left it and took up her sweater instead. At least it was reasonably not too wet. She couldn't find her shoes.

"Hello?" she called out, afraid no one would respond. Afraid someone would.

Only the hum answered her.

Emma moaned miserably, crawled to the mattress, and broke into tears.

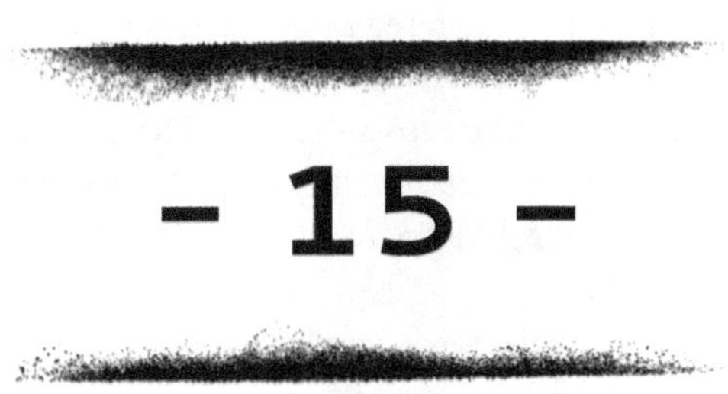

– 15 –

John jerked awake to his own shout. Instantly alert, he assessed his immediate surroundings for a threat and saw a blinking red alert message. He'd overslept on testing day. *Shit!*

No Shadow went without exercise at least once a day, no matter what assignment they'd been given. But once a week, they all had to report to one of several rounds of scheduled simulations to test their proficiency and focus. Times were pre-assigned, and once the session initiated, all latecomers were locked out. If he missed his, a soldier could participate in the next round, but it weighed against him, and the simulation became a lot more difficult to traverse.

John had less than ninety seconds to get his head on straight and report to the field. No time to wash up or shave, just stuff his feet into boots and run. Good thing he slept fully clothed.

He made it in the nick of time. John rubbed his eyes, shook himself out to wake the hell up. The simulations weren't designed to take it easy on soldiers; one wrong step could get a guy knocked out or maimed. No kid gloves for the Shadows; they believed in survival of the fittest. Whoever was still alive after the time ran down to zero got to stay a Shadow.

"Begin," ordered the sergeant major's pre-recorded voice, and the grassy field erupted into orchestrated chaos.

John sprinted out, jumping over a line of fire set to flare in close proximity. The wall of heat passed through him, and he was grateful his clothes were fireproof, but they didn't protect his head or his hands. His internal diagnostics registered first-degree burns. Nothing worse than a bad sunburn. Once clear of the flames, the sharp sound of weapon fire sent him rolling across the grass. His trajectory triggered a land mine loaded with rock salt. It exploded upward more than to the sides, so John kept rolling to avoid major injuries. *Son of a bitch, get it together, Hawk!*

He righted himself and crawled on his stomach under an ivy-laced net. The vines were weaponized with poisonous barbs that broke off clean and hooked into skin. They hurt like hell and it took a trained medic to remove one without tearing out a plug of flesh in the process.

The netting stretched over a full kilometer. By the time he'd gotten to the other side, his shoulders and thighs were burning and he was covered with mud. A handful of barbs had hooked into his shirt, but none had pierced his skin. He got lucky.

Stripping off the shirt, he ran at the wall in front of him. Sometimes they'd lay a weapon on top of it, which meant he'd need it as soon as he touched down on the other side. Exactly one chance to grab it, otherwise he wasn't finishing the course.

John pushed off, grabbed the top, and vaulted over. There! He grabbed for the weapon, cursing when it nearly dropped out of his hand to the wrong side of the wall. His landing left something to be desired, and his ankle screamed in protest, even as he brought the weapon up and swept the area. Three shots fired before he got a bead on the marksman. He only had one shot, but that was all he needed. The enemy soldier fell from his high tree perch to land on the ground with a thud. He wouldn't be moving until the tranquilizer wore off, and if he'd fallen anywhere near a trap, he wouldn't be walking away with all of his limbs.

John discarded the now-useless weapon and scanned the area. Three pairs of soldiers were locked in hand-to-hand combat, while another swatted at the air, screaming, too far away to hear. Whatever obstacle that soldier had come through, John was glad he hadn't gone that way. He smelled smoke. Someone had caught fire. Intermittent flashes of light through the trees meant pulse guns. He hoped, for their sake, whoever had gone that way wore armor. This was a war zone, and until they got through it, every Shadow present was in danger of his life.

John's next challenge was the pond. Shit. He hated that one. Murky water, waist-deep at the shallow end with whatever happened to strike the sergeant major's fancy swimming below the surface. Usually something with teeth, sometimes venomous to keep things interesting.

John waded in, mindful of every step, sweeping his boot along the bottom before he put his weight down on it. That's how he found the blade. Freezing in his tracks, eyes sharp for any movement above water, he traced the object with the toe of his boot. A decent-sized knife. He'd be an idiot not to take it. But it seemed to be anchored down there somehow; he couldn't pry it up without using his hands. He'd have to submerge. Always a tricky proposition, but if a knife was at hand, he'd no doubt need it.

John took a deep breath, then exhaled it, preparing his lungs. One more, and on the third, he gasped in as much air as his body could hold and dived under. The pond bottom was heavily magnetized. John managed to get his fingers under the knife, but the damn thing wouldn't budge. He kept at it until his lungs started to burn, then gave up to get air. But before his head broke through the surface, something slammed into his back, driving him under again. The sneak attack forced precious air out of his lungs. John swung a blind punch and connected with the hard edge of a breathing mask. The diver recovered faster and, with one hand curled around John's forearm, the other around his neck, the soldier pushed him deeper under.

John curled his legs in, then kicked out with all his might as his head began to swim. Again and again, he battered the soldier's body until the hold finally loosened. John broke free, and shot up to the surface, sputtering. Not daring to chance another attack, he instead struck out for the other side of the pond, teeth grinding. Physical strain and oxygen deprivation had made his limbs weak and shaky, which wouldn't have bothered him except he was acutely aware of an enemy at his back and a live, if a little low tech, weapon within reach.

John dragged himself onto the bank and rolled to his back, risking precious seconds to catch his breath. That was the only reason he noticed the shiny shards staring to rain down. Needle thin bits of metal coated in neural agents that would incapacitate an enemy on impact. Effectiveness was 99.8%.

John shot to his feet and ran like hell for the circular shield thirty yards away. He wasn't the only one going for it. From his right, a Shadow came running, but he heavily favored his left side where his pant leg had soaked through with blood. From the left, one more, this one with an open gash across his face. John put on a burst of speed and speared his body forward. He slid across the grass, taking the shield with him and away from the two soldiers who crashed together. With a lightning quick roll, he hunkered underneath the shield, hoping he'd made himself small enough to be protected as the needles rained down with delicate chimes, incapacitating the other Shadows.

John had never liked this particular weapon; no way to control dosage. If someone took a hundred needles, like those two just had, he wasn't sure it wouldn't kill them. By the time the last needle had fallen, the ground was silver with them. Into the profound silence that followed, the buzzer went off, signaling the end of this session.

John dropped the shield and dragged his feet off to the sidelines. There'd be a one-minute intermission before the next session began.

The sergeant major met him in the safe zone. "That was sloppy work, Hawk. I expected you to be out before the rain."

John straightened to attention. His side twitched, but he schooled himself not to show pain. Must have pulled something. "Yessir!"

"You're not getting lazy on me, are you?"

"No, sir!"

The sergeant major eyed him just a moment too long, and John fought the urge to fidget. He deserved the censure. His head hadn't been in the game. A damn dangerous thing to do, especially with live weapons in play.

A holographic readout nearby reported three injured, five incapacitated, and one dead. No names, just stats. The roster would be updated once the injured were treated.

The sergeant major scowled at it. "Shit. It's going to be bloody day."

John said nothing, waiting to be dismissed.

"Why were you late?" the sergeant major demanded.

Pointing out he hadn't been would have made no difference, even if arguing with a commanding officer were allowed. "Overslept my alarm, sir." No excuses, just facts.

"All that standing around too much for you, Hawk?"

"No, sir."

"Then there's only one other explanation."

John stared down at his hands. They'd cramped into fists he couldn't straighten, knuckles torn up and bloody. The smell of blood and urine burned his nostrils while the room plunged into complete silence. The boy at his feet had stopped fighting and pleading; he had no strength left to protect himself and now lay motionless, chest barely rising with each breath. John's heart raced, but he wasn't scared and he wasn't angry. He felt nothing. The boy had attacked him and lost. John could breathe another day.

But the look on old Ivan's face…

A muscle twitched in John's jaw, and it took effort to pry his teeth apart to answer, "Yes, sir."

The sergeant major grunted in reply. Impossible to tell what he was thinking. Probably nothing good. Cold began to register against his skin. It was a chilly morning, and his clothes were soaked through. As the adrenaline slowly burned off, he'd get weaker, shivery. Merely a physical coping mechanism, unless the Shadow succumbed to his needs over those of his mission.

"Get yourself cleaned up. I'm pushing your rotation off an extra fifteen minutes. I want you on profile until you see the doc—which you will do STAT, before you report for duty. Is that understood?"

"Yessir!"

"Dismissed."

John saluted and marched off. He hated the doc's treatments as much as he hated the nightmares themselves. He hadn't had an episode in months, the longest stretch so far, and he'd hoped he'd finally grown out of it. He'd been wrong.

Back in his quarters, John stripped out of his sodden clothes and dumped everything, including his boots, into the laundry chute, deciding what to tell the doctor when he asked—because he would, and John couldn't tell him the nightmare that had almost made him miss his session was about a fist fight.

The brawl was the least of it. What really turned his stomach was the fear he'd seen in the old man's eyes. Not *for* John, but *of* him.

It's not real, he told himself. *Just a figment of my imagination.*

He took the chess piece out of his pants pocket before he closed the laundry compartment. When he opened it again, it held a fresh, clean uniform set. The shower had built-in sensors to detect any injury or deficiency. John stepped in, let hot water scald over him to warm his insides and wash away the grime. By the time he'd finished, several alarms were blinking red, and once he was dressed, a cocktail of vitamins and nutrients awaited him in the med cubby. John downed the bitter contents without thought and checked the time. Exactly two minutes to report to med bay before someone came looking for him. Squaring his shoulders, he went.

The entire med bay was sealed off from the rest of the base to protect against possible contamination and to minimize the spread of any disease or infection. Each of their three medics had top-of-the-line supplies and tools at his disposal, as well as an assistant to do the dirty work.

The chief medic also doubled as a psych consult, with a lab of his own, sectioned off for an illusion of privacy. Since Dr. Wen gave full reports to the sergeant major, John's superiors already knew about his hypersomnia handicap. The sergeant major considered it to be a tolerable flaw, given John's unique ability. Ironically, that very ability made the handicap almost impossible to treat.

John's nightmares weren't just nightmares; they hijacked his mind for however long it took to replay the event, and wouldn't release him until it finished terrorizing him. No external stimuli worked to wake him up; he became trapped inside the scene with no way out except to see it through.

John hated that vulnerability. And he hated that no matter what Dr. Wen did, he could never cure John permanently.

"Ah, there you are," the squirrely doctor said in greeting. "Sit, sit."

John had to force his feet to move forward. The exam chair made no pretense of being anything other than what it was. With wires and tubes connected to it from all sides, it was hard and uncomfortable to sit in for long periods of time. But that probably wasn't the chair's fault.

John sat and leaned back, just so he wouldn't have to look at Dr. Wen.

"The sergeant major said you had another episode?" It should have been a statement, but Dr. Wen delighted in pretending he knew less than he really did.

"Yes."

"The usual?"

One of them. I almost killed a boy who wanted to prove himself to his friends, and disappointed the man I looked up to. And still it hadn't been his worst. He once saw old Ivan argue with the sergeant major, then die shortly thereafter. But that wouldn't do, either. It was just his mind's coping mechanism: inserting familiar faces into a made-up past that never happened in order to fill the void in his memory.

"Yes," John said, and recalled his most hated dream instead. "I'm in a dark room hiding under a bed, red lights flashing everywhere. I hear screaming, but I can't tell where it's coming from. Then a woman drags herself across the floor toward me. Her throat is slit, but she's still alive. I reach out to her, but her eyes go wide, like she doesn't want me to move." *Or maybe she feels the end approaching and it terrifies her.*

"Mm-hmm, mm-hmm. Go on."

John curled his fingers around the armrests. "I hear heavy footfalls, and then a man is there. I can't see anything except his feet, but I hear him breathing. He just stands there, waiting. He yells for me to get out, but I stay put, so he drops to one knee, a bloody knife in one hand, and drags me out by my shirt."

"Yes, yes. Same as always. Well! Let's get on with it, shall we?"

John swallowed hard. *Yeah, let's get on with it.*

Dr. Wen brought out a fragile-looking white half-circle and placed it like a headband onto John's forehead with the ends curved down around his temples. A delicate instrument that required precise calibration to disrupt targeted neural pathways.

In theory, it was designed to dissolve a memory. In practice, all it did was zap the hell out of John's brain and left him disoriented for ten minutes. Useless. No matter how many times he went through this, his neural pathways eventually reformed as they'd been before. Sometimes the peace lasted a month, sometimes two. Sometimes he was back in the chair after a week. When he'd been younger, he used to run to Dr. Wen, begging for him to stop the nightmares. That was before he'd begun losing hope he could ever be fixed.

John forced his muscles to relax, to let his weight sink into the chair, a last-second meditation before the timed, electromagnetic blast temporarily turned his brain to mush. He didn't feel pain in the strictest sense, more of a burning, bright-white eraser sweeping across his mind. If thought had a physical presence, the blasts would cauterize it. John caught the hot, metallic scent of electricity in his nostrils, and in some part of his brain not being fried to inertia, he recognized Dr. Wen had upped the voltage this time around. Then, even that thought disappeared.

When the floor came into focus again, John groaned and leaned forward, mouth as dry as the desert and hands twitching on his knees. Dr. Wen was talking, fully aware that for the moment John was beyond basic comprehension. He didn't even try to move yet; if he stood up right now, he'd end up crumpling to the floor like a newborn colt.

Dr. Wen shined a light into his eyes to check his pupils. "Not responsive yet. Give it another minute."

As if he had a choice.

John raised a hand to rub his brow. His fingers weren't working, but he had enough mobility in his arms to chafe some feeling back into his face. The tip of his tongue still prickled, and it made him sick to his stomach as if he'd swallowed blood.

Once the ringing in his ears had gone away and he started to understand Dr. Wen's mutterings, John was almost back to normal.

"…rate of restoration will be, given the new calibration. You will keep me apprised, won't you? There's a good man. I'll have…"

John tuned him out, closed his eyes, breathed through his nose, and flexed his muscles, group by group, the way he always did. It helped him regain control so he could get out of there.

Finally, he shoved to his feet and stayed on them.

And then he remembered the only place he could go was back to the door holding Emma Calen in her cell.

Still, a sick, backward sense of kinship arose, bordering on reverse Stockholm syndrome. If anyone had a clue what he'd just been through, it would be the girl. Given a choice, at this precise moment, her company would be preferable to just about anyone else's.

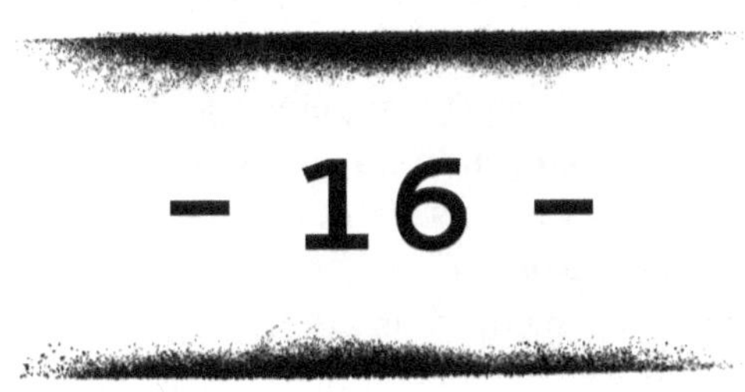

– 16 –

Somewhere in the Tae Colony – Date Unknown

"*Zayn!*" Dorian shouted, slamming open the antique wooden door so hard it cracked when it hit the wall. Leanne, always on point, shot to her feet, gun trained straight at his head as Zayn shifted to shield Anna on the floor. He had a hand on one of his knives, but he wouldn't draw unless necessary. Leanne had this covered. Recognizing one of their own, she didn't pull the trigger, but that gun never wavered from her killshot. If Dorian so much as twitched wrong, he'd be a massive heap of dead meat on the floor.

Dorian, however, had no instinct for self-preservation. Even faced with Leanne's hair trigger response, he snarled and kept on going, straight to the TV wall. "Centurion News," he barked, and the channel changed to the news station.

His voice made Anna twitch, and she started humming to herself while she drew on the floor with a piece of coal.

"*Lisbon is reporting widespread violence throughout the city. Several military units have already been dispatched to control the crowds, and citizens are urged to stay indoors as much as possible. Our thoughts and well-wishes go out to all those affected by this incident.*

"*For those of you just joining us, the group responsible for instigating this riot against the chem-treatment industry, and many others like it, has come forward in a public message and identified itself as the*

Evolutionaries."

Anna's head rose as the news announcer blinked out to show the message. "Talking about us already?" she said.

The message was short and to the point: *Life will prevail at any cost. If we keep poisoning our children, that cost will be our future. Only when blood becomes currency will we understand its true worth. How much is paid will be up to you.*

Underneath was a symbol—a simple drawing of a two-leafed plant, its roots shaped like a DNA double helix splitting into two separate but complete strands.

Fitting, Zayn thought, given the subject of the book he'd first seen it on, and the bits and pieces of a data jigsaw puzzle he was still trying to put together. If it all fit like he thought it did, then Dr. Amelia Chase would never go down in history as the first person to successfully splice human DNA. Not in a petri dish, but in a live, adult specimen.

"Look at that!" Anna said, grinning wide. She'd abandoned her drawing to clutch Zayn's arm, and her eyes shone so bright with excitement, he didn't even care about the coal smudges on his shirt.

"Guess that answers the question of whose fucking jagoff idea that was!"

Zayn's hand moved without thought. A single knife spun through the air and buried itself into Dorian's shoulder. It barely moved the behemoth. When Dorian roared, Zayn pushed Anna behind him. "Knock it off," he ordered.

But Dorian was beyond hearing. "Do you realize what you did?" he shouted, pulling the blade out, more annoyed than physically hurt.

Before the juggernaut could take a step, Zayn let another knife fly, straight into Dorian's other shoulder to make things even.

Dorian growled when he pulled it out. "You put us on the fucking map, asshole! They'll be hunting us like dogs now! I didn't sign up for this shit!"

"What did you sign up for?" Zayn snapped. First time in three years he'd had to raise his voice to anyone under his command. Anna flinched at his back, and he didn't know whether it was because of him or Dorian. Either way, the man was going down. "What did you think this was, a high school prank?"

Dorian took one more step before Leanne had had enough. She fired a shot, searing a hole through his thigh.

Dorian howled, but the pulse charge instantly cauterized the wound. It didn't bleed; he kept on coming.

"Back up, nice and easy," Leanne said, shifting closer to Zayn and Anna.

"We were supposed to be the puppeteers, not the puppets! No one ever should have known none of this was random. That's what you promised us! No one would ever know! And then you had to go and listen to that crazy bitch—"

Zayn's knife speared Dorian's throat a split second after Leanne scorched a hole through his brains. When he dropped, the rickety old house shuddered.

"Shit," Leanne muttered.

Zayn's sentiments exactly.

Anna rounded him to stoop by Dorian's body. Humming a lullaby, she closed his sightless eyes with coal-smudged fingertips. "Good night, Dory. I'll miss you."

Leanne holstered her gun, watching Anna with a look that said she was planning for contingencies. Had it been anyone but her, Zayn would have cut her eyes out for staring. "Others will have seen that report," she warned. "They won't be any happier about it than Dorian."

"I underestimated the news media. Never thought they'd air that message so quickly."

Anna pushed to her feet, wiped her hands on her shirt. "I think we should tell the others it's time to put on their pretty frocks."

Zayn agreed. "Have everyone meet in the basement in twenty minutes," he told Leanne. "And get somebody to clean this up."

As Leanne hurried to obey, Anna traced Zayn's brow. "Frowns don't become you, beautiful."

Zayn smiled and brushed at the streak of black across her cheek. "You're the beautiful one." He kissed the bridge of her nose. "Now go wash up before the meeting. I need to finish a few things before we go down."

"I want to wear my ball gown. What do you think?"

"Whatever you wish, love."

Anna twirled and went off to the bathroom, stripping along the way.

Zayn's indulgent smile faded slowly, and when it did, he was glad she wasn't there to see it. She'd made him promise not to do this, but given the stakes, they no longer had a choice. The SU was moving too slow on the clue he'd sent them to reclaim their precious lost girl from the Shadows. Without that conflict, it was just Zayn's people against the world. While he had no problem taking the spotlight, he'd been counting on a lot more bodies out there to draw fire away from him.

Zayn returned to his desk and pulled up the search he'd done the day before. Anna had given him three traceable names in Dr. Chase's lab: Amelia Chase, Hailey Chase—last name now Calen—and Gabriel Connors. Aside from the obviously doctored public records, all three were curiously listed in the TorreyCom public access residential database. Hiding in plain sight, right under everyone's noses. Zayn could admire that kind of courage.

And he had no trouble taking advantage of it.

– 17 –

The subject was deteriorating at an accelerated rate. John kept his eyes firmly front and center, but from the corner of his eye, he could still see the girl occasionally twitch and spasm. Her fork scraped against the tray with enough force to make him want to flinch, and every so often, she shoved the whole thing aside as if she couldn't take it anymore.

Then the rocking ensued.

John didn't move. Behind his back, his hands clenched tight enough to cramp muscles, but he didn't move. Not even when she started mumbling nonsense to herself. He rooted his feet and waited, because this was just another one of her episodes. It would pass in a few minutes, and then she'd resume eating. His orders were to stay put until she finished, and if he took the tray from her prematurely, the mess hall Hound would want to know why.

Suddenly, Emma sat up with a deep sigh, and the tension in his shoulders eased. He wasn't looking at her face but heard the smile in her voice when she said, "I bet the sky was green when you were born." She waited for him to reply, and when he didn't, she shrugged and kept talking. "The neighbors must have hated that. Daisies can't grow in colorful weather. They turn to rock and skip across the ocean. Was there crying when she died?"

John's breath hitched.

Haunted eyes stared at him from across the floor, terrified not for herself, but for him as a dark pool of blood spread around her.

He ruthlessly shook the nightmare off.

"I suppose not. Babies only cry when there's a wolf chasing them. Or a hawk. I used to have a baby turtle once. It got smashed by a defective hover. Now, how a hover got in my bathtub, that's a better question. Not like orphanages allow hunters in the kitchen. Except when they wear uniforms…"

Emma kept talking, for a few moments completely in control of her movements, if not her thoughts, and John couldn't block her out. Somehow, what she said made perfect sense to him, his mind drawing connections between her words and his dreams. Uniformed hunter in the orphanage kitchen; the fictional Ivan dying after dinner. John started sweating, his leg muscles twitching with a subconscious urge to run the hell away. The room's effects were not transferrable, he reminded himself, and even if they were, he wasn't susceptible to telepathic manipulation.

Get it together, Hawk. It's just a trick.

The room quieted. She'd stopped. Good. So why couldn't he relax? Because he felt her watching him, and the intensity of her stare was like static against his skin.

Slowly, silently, and with a preternatural grace, Emma stood from her mattress and came forward, bare feet touching down toes-first.

No! Look away!

John faced forward, gritted his teeth to keep his gaze locked on the far wall as Emma advanced.

"I know you," she said softly, a confused murmur meant more for her than for him. Her hand lifted to face level, hovering several inches from his skin. John schooled himself to keep his breathing even. "I saw you before. In a dream, I think. Not mine, someone else's. You used to be so, so… complex. Before they killed you."

Kill me, too. Please!

John's heart thrashed in his chest. Where had that childish voice come from? He'd never heard a child wail in such agonized grief, yet it was so familiar, it almost made him fall to his knees.

Emma moved left, didn't have enough room at his back to circle, so she went right instead, only to run into the same problem. "Lost little bird pitted against dogs to fight and claw, and it refused."

"Fight!" the sergeant major ordered, and Finn raised his wooden staff.

John shook his head at the boy, and dropped his weapon at his feet. He would not spill another's blood. Never again, no matter how much they hurt him.

"I said fight!"

The boy attacked, cracking the staff over John's shoulder, and his clavicle gave with a snap.

John clutched his temples to banish the hallucination. Had he been compromised? No telepath could penetrate his shields.

And how do I know that?

"They clipped its wings, but it kept trying to fly away every chance it got, until…" Emma frowned. "I can't see you. Why are you blind?"

When she waved a hand in front of his face, John had had enough. He caught her wrist, met her confused gaze. "Stop."

Emma's head tilted, and she squinted. "Nothing. T-there's nothing." Shivers started in her hand, then moved down her body until she shook from head to toe, while her eyes widened with fright and flooded with tears. John released her, and she hugged herself tight, backing away from him. "Touch, and sight, and sound, and nothing. Nothing! Black hole in the middle of the sun. I will end here." Her gasp was quickly followed by another, and then she was hyperventilating and collapsing to her hands and knees, fighting for every breath of air. "Dy-ing," she panted.

John tensed every muscle to steel himself against responding to her distress. *Just a trick.* He wouldn't let her get to him. Funny how the lies people told themselves were the easiest to believe.

Emma looked up, the angle of her neck causing her to wheeze as she silently pleaded with him.

He took a step.

"Does it hurt," she said, and gasped in another breath. "To die?" More tears flowed, and her face scrunched up with terror and helplessness. "Please, stop it"—*wheeze*—"I can't breathe… when you shout…"

John's foot moved forward another half-step before he brought himself up short, poised between going forward and going back. *Wake up. Wake the hell up!* He couldn't stand it here another minute; he needed her lucid, and eating. *Wake up, Emma.* "Wake up." The words formed on his lips with barely a sound.

Emma's chin dropped forward, hair shielding her face as she gasped in big breaths. "Enough. No more." Clawing at the mattress, she braced herself and bowed her back to force her airways open. A wheeze turned to a gasp, a gasp to a sigh, each one slower and deeper than the one before, as she gradually calmed herself. John counted her breaths, feeling lightheaded with excess oxygen, and realized he was mirroring her.

That's it. Slow and easy. Calm down. Come back, I know you can.

Then, from one sigh to another, she moved her hair out of her face with a shaky hand and picked up her fork. The episode was over. She probably wouldn't even remember she'd had it. And there was John, halfway across the room, watching her as if he could do anything about it.

I'm sorry, he mouthed.

Before she noticed him out of place, he silently returned to his post and faced forward again.

– 18 –

Emma had learned to tell time by the soldier's appearances. She figured since the sun had two times in a day, one rise and one set, she counted two arrivals as one cycle. The first began the cycle, the second ended it. Five arrivals ago, she'd noticed a change in him. Nothing obviously pronounced—he was too good for that—but there was definitely something different about him. He entered her cell as if walking to the gallows, and left with a heavy step as if burdened by woe.

She giggled. Woe. *Woe is me. I have to feed the sparrow whose head I broke.*

What a chirp.

Emma was deep into full-blown jitters now, and cold all the time. Hunger gnawed at her belly but the thought of putting food in her mouth made her stomach tighten and turn.

Why hadn't any soldiers come for her yet? Wasn't there some un-spoken rule that someone should be poking at her to make the *right* decision? Shouldn't they be getting pissed off and trying to pressure her?

She sighed. That was exactly what they were doing. The effects of this room were getting worse by the day. Or week… Whatever. Even her Hawk soldier's visits weren't enough to stave it off anymore. She just got angrier every time he came in, perfectly composed, with his clean uniform and his blank expression. She'd never tried to punch him before. Maybe she should.

It probably hurt to punch stone, though. And it wasn't like she was steady enough to take a swing, anyway. She snickered at the image: little Emma, all of five and a half feet tall, with toothpick-thin arms, taking a swing at the soldier.

Missing.

Spinning in place like a cartoon character until she collapsed.

Emma laughed at herself, but the sound cut short.

Where was he, anyway?

She wanted to take a shower… or as much of one as she could in here. But something told her he'd be coming soon, or should be. It had been a while. He hadn't forgotten about her, had he?

Maybe she ought to take that shower anyway. Give the guy something to look at.

Emma peered down at herself. *Not much to see, though.*

Her hands felt sticky. No matter how many times she washed them, the cold sweat always came back to make her feel like she was covered in slime. *Why* couldn't they give her soap? What were they afraid she'd do with it? Wash herself to death?

At least I'd die clean…

Chewing on her lip, she played with the sensors. Water on. Water off. Toilet out. Toilet back in. Water on. Toilet out. Toilet back in. Water off. Water on. Water off. Water on. Water off. Flush.

If she did it fast enough, it almost had a rhythm. Except the sensors made no noise, and the incessant hum drowned out the hiss of running water. She fisted her hands in her hair and tugged just short of tearing it out.

In her mind, she screamed, but no sound came out of her mouth.

Bored and utterly miserable, Emma started pacing. After seven full circuits, her entertainment finally arrived. Efficient as ever, he set her tray down, took his place by the door and held up the wall.

"Took your time, soldier boy," she muttered. Eyeing the food, she thought better of it and did three more circuits instead, passing by close enough to brush elbows with him if she wanted to. She didn't. Not much, anyway.

"They must have gotten you young."

For a moment, she got lost in that thought. How young had they gotten him? She tried to imagine him as a small boy, but couldn't see him as anything other than the stoic soldier standing before her. As if he hadn't existed until he became fully formed.

How lonely that had to be.

As lonely as me.

She saw it in the tense set of his shoulders, the way his mouth was always drawn in a bitter line that begged to want to smile. He didn't frown, he glowered, but there was something… so… alone in his eyes.

Emma had wanted to punch him. She still did. That, or press a kiss to that hard mouth. The latter would have been more for her than for him. Or would it? He was here. Not elsewhere, but here. Did he have someone who cared for him elsewhere? "Do you?" she asked aloud, and sighed. "I do. I miss them so."

Her stomach clenched, and Emma sat down so he wouldn't see her double over. With a shaky hand, she picked up the fork. It had to be defective; the food refused to stay on it. Frustrated, she dropped it back onto the tray.

"So, what do you do when you're not chatting me up? Run laps around the compound? Push-ups? Yeah, I'll bet that's it. Bet you could do a thousand of them, and never once wonder why."

Emma was starting to think she imagined him there. Or herself here. One of them wasn't in this room, and she had trouble puzzling out which one that was. She pinched herself and winced. *Yep, real.* She rose, shuffled her feet over to him. He was so tall, her nose marked the center of his upper torso. Emma stared up at his face. Not a single booger in his nose. Swaying from the vertigo, she dipped her chin down to stare at his chest. It was just so… wide.

I could stretch my arms out all the way and still not reach its edges. That chest was like… the world. Emma would have laughed, except loud noises worsened the drumming in her head. Instead, she raised a finger and, watching it for a moment to locate it in the space between them, slowly touched it to his pectoral, and pushed.

She nearly pushed herself off her feet.

Swaying forward again, she turned her head sideways to press her ear to his heart. The steady thump kicked up a notch as if to shove her away when his limbs didn't move.

Frowning, she leaned back to look up at his face again. His nostrils flared. He hadn't shaved today. "I think I could like you," she whispered. If only he could hold the world steady enough for her to find her feet. She could stand tall like him, look him in the eye and really see herself. Or him.

But he's the enemy.

"Gotta keep those close. Closer than a friend. Are we friends now?"

Waiting for an answer, she heard something roll across the floor at her feet—a shiny glass marble. When she blinked, it was gone. *Just like all the rest.*

"Wouldn't mind being friends," she said to herself. "Could use one, actually."

For an instant, the hum grew deafening before it hushed to a familiar decibel level, leaving her shaken.

Having thoroughly confused herself, Emma waved goodbye and went back to her food. The water felt deliciously cool against her lips, and she took a quick sip before her body could change its mind. Instead of using the hateful, broken fork, she picked up a piece of meat with her fingers and popped it into her mouth. She chewed it fast, but made sure to properly masticate it before she swallowed.

Then she waited.

When her stomach didn't immediately cast it all out again, she chewed another piece of meat. "Are you from around here?"

She'd stopped expecting him to show any kind of reaction, but while he was here she could at least pretend she wasn't talking to herself. Crazy people talked to themselves.

"Got any brothers or sisters?"

She talked and ate, speaking absolute gibberish. *Sometimes nonsense can make all the sense in the world.* To her, it did. Well, not now, but back when…

…and before she knew it, Emma's plate was empty and she was finishing the last of the water. Oh, she would regret that later.

She regretted it already. It meant time was up. Emma balefully looked up at the soldier, then dropped her gaze and picked up her tray to hand it to him.

He came over with boots so big that, for a moment, they were all she saw. He placed the empty glass from the floor onto the tray, taking hold of the thing so close to her fingers, she could feel the heat of his skin. Her muscles clenched, refusing to let go. "Don't go," she whispered, unsure she wanted him to hear.

The tip of his thumb brushed the nail of hers and, as if he'd pushed a button on her motor functions, her fingers released the tray.

Her chest felt hollow with desolation as she covertly watched him walk away. At the door, he paused. "Good night, Emma."

Before her mind caught up enough to wonder if she'd imagined him speaking, he was gone again, and she was left all alone in an empty box that clawed at her brain.

~

John leaned against the closed door, head thudding back. Two weeks were up, and Emma wasn't any closer to joining forces with them than the day she'd arrived. Not only that, her mental state was worsening by the day. Basic language eluded her, and very soon, she'd be useless for their purposes. What good was a teacher if no one could understand her? That *had* been the point, right? For her to train them to resist telepathic manipulation?

Maybe he should speak to the sergeant major. The senator hadn't asked for any progress reports so he had no idea how quickly Emma was deteriorating. John had seen other telepaths beg to be released by this point, but it had taken them a month and a half to get there. They were destroying a valuable asset, and they needed to be made aware of that.

Footsteps alerted him to someone's approach. He pushed the button to signal a tray pick up, but the screen on his schedule had gone black. Time up.

The sergeant major and two Hounds marched down the long corridor. John shook himself off, straightened up, got his head back to where it belonged—on his shoulders, on the task at hand, and not in the holding cell with the girl who'd laid her cheek against his chest and asked him to stay.

"Sir." He saluted the sergeant major, nodded to the others.

"These men will relieve you for the time being," the sergeant major said. "Walk with me."

Handing the tray off to one of the Hounds, John obeyed, falling into step beside the sergeant major. They went outside. The first whiff of fresh air John had had in the last two days, and it made him lightheaded. He exhaled every last molecule of air in his lungs, then inhaled a fresh batch to cleanse them. He did it three more times before they went back inside another building.

At the door he'd been aiming for, the sergeant major stopped and turned around to guard it. "Go on," he said.

Checking a frown, John opened the door and entered.

Senator Griffith waited for him inside. John saluted his commander in chief.

"Have a seat, son," the senator invited.

John sat.

"There's no need to be so tense. This is just a debriefing. Although, you understand that your accuracy is of the utmost importance. I will require your observational skills and confidentiality."

"Yessir."

"Good, good. So tell me, how is our guest?"

The casual way he'd said it made John hesitate. Their *guest* was falling apart, and every additional second they kept her in the holding cell heightened her risk of serious, perhaps even fatal, damage. He almost said so out loud, but then he woke the hell up and answered as expected: "She is deteriorating at an accelerated rate. Already showing signs of loss of motor function, lapses in concentration, verbal confusion, and shortened attention span."

"I see." A contemplative tone. Not the reaction John had expected. He didn't sound at all concerned about losing an asset; seemed almost gleeful at the news. "And do you know why that is?"

"No, sir."

Griffith smiled, and there was something sinister behind it. "My team tells me it's because telepathy is not an *ability* as, for example, being able to do complicated math in your mind. Nor is it a *sense* as we would think of sight or touch. It's somewhere between the two, and both at the same time. Having telepathy stripped from their minds is equivalent to losing not only a mental faculty, but a sense, as well. For us, it would be like being blindfolded and mute. Plus all the other little inconveniences that come with sensory deprivation." He waved aside those *little inconveniences*. A normal, sane person would break within a week under any one of them.

John blanked his mind; didn't think, just listened.

"In any case, the stronger they are, the more integral it is to their normal functioning, and the more its removal affects them physically. Our subject's expedited decline would indicate massive potential. Wouldn't you agree?"

John wasn't a scientist to have an opinion one way or another. *Torture* was all he could think of the whole situation. But he shouldn't sympathize. Shadows were subjected to common torture methods early and often to hone their minds and bodies to endure, if and when they were truly under duress.

The senator didn't seem to mind his silence. He steepled his fingers and asked, "What is your measure of the subject?"

John met his gaze in surprise.

The senator shrugged. "You are the only one who's had any contact with her since she's arrived. I am curious to know what you make of her."

John hesitated to volunteer any additional information. Something wasn't right. The senator seemed almost eager for bad news. How could that be? "Based on my observations, sir, the girl—"

"The subject."

John wanted to gnash his teeth. "She's too stubborn to break," he finally said. It was the truth. Emma Calen might be young, she might be inexperienced, but that didn't make her weak. Quite the opposite. In her naivety, she believed herself to be invincible, able to wait them out.

It would kill her.

It would destroy everything of the person she used to be, scramble her mind, rip away every last speck of rationality until she couldn't comprehend the world inside her own head, let alone the one outside it. And then it would kill her.

But it wouldn't break her.

"Emma Calen will die before submitting to what you… what *we* want from her." It was time to suspend her isolation. No point in continuing a course of action that didn't bring the intended consequence. No reason to waste valuable resources on a lost cause. Their strategy had failed, and the senator had to realize this and compensate. He had to release John from this assignment. Had to.

Griffith tapped his fingertips together in thought, and for a moment, hope surged through John.

Until the senator issued his command. "Then we will just have to try harder."

– 19 –

The next time her soldier came, he set the food down right in front of her. Emma had been drowsing, or hallucinating. Possibly some combination of the two. His presence hadn't even registered until he brushed her hair behind her ear where she lay.

"You've been pretty out of it," he said. "Do you think you can eat something?"

Emma sat up, rubbing her eyes. "What time is it?"

It was a reflexive question. To her surprise, he answered. "It's late. I've been here three times, but you were sleeping. Didn't want to wake you." Boy, she had to look like hell for him to give half a damn.

A cool glass pressed into her palm. Holding it with both hands, she rested it against her burning forehead. "Have you been ordered to cease hostilities?" she slurred out. Memories came and went; time moved in unpredictable patterns. Didn't take a genius to realize her brain was starting to fragment.

The soldier was still crouched in front of her. "How do you feel?" If this was a hallucination, it wasn't very convincing. As if soldier boy would ever stoop to talking to her. *Pfft.*

But, since it wasn't going away… *Might as well go along with it.* "How do I look?" Her clothes felt clammy and disgusting. She must have attempted to wash again earlier. At least, she hoped that's what happened. The alternative wasn't something she wanted to contemplate. Emma had no recollection of having taken her clothes off. Or put them back on, for that matter. But she remembered being naked. And she remembered being clothed.

The soldier pushed to his feet, backed up almost to the door. "If you don't cooperate, we have no choice but to keep you here." Was he telling her, or himself? "You might consider things from our point of view."

She gaped. "Is that a joke?"

"Just think about it," he said, warming to the subject, so concerned with convincing her. "Anything's gotta be better than this, right? And you'd be doing good works in the end. You could help stop wars, prevent them from happening."

Okay, now she *knew* she was dreaming. "Won't that put you out of a job, soldier boy?"

He took a swift step toward her, and Emma flinched, expecting him to kick. He didn't. "My name," he said so quietly she almost missed it, "is John."

The name bounced around inside her mind like an out of control pinball and for a while she wasn't aware of anything else. By the time she'd shaken herself out of it, she was alone in her cell again, the food tray still there.

He'd left her.

Not that she blamed him. She was beginning to think of these little get-togethers as dates. Twisted as the idea was, there were always just the two of them, and food.

The idea sent her into a fit of giggles.

He came back. "You haven't eaten," he observed.

"Lost my appetite. Guess you'll just have to shove me into the oven, skinny as I am." And she was. She'd lost a lot of weight, despite them feeding her semi-regularly.

Or were they? For all she knew, soldier boy didn't come here more than once a week.

And he never called.

Yep, just like a date.

He lowered into a crouch in front of her. "Nobody's shoving you into an oven, Emma. We're warriors not—"

"You're soldiers," she snapped, somehow offended. It gave her something to grasp on to, and for once she felt almost… lucid. "Don't flatter yourself. It's not very attractive."

"Warriors, soldiers. I don't see the difference."

Emma pushed away the forkful of food that suddenly hovered in front of her mouth and squinted instead at the soldier's face. John, was it? She remembered something about him being a John. He looked like a John. No different than millions of other guys named John.

What were they talking about? Oh yeah. "It's the difference between a staircase and an elevator," she explained.

"If you say so," he murmured, bringing the fork forward a second time.

Emma pushed it away. "No, I do say so. An elevator goes up and down. People push buttons and you stop wherever they want to, whether you like it or not. Staircase, a lot more work, but you choose which floor to go to and you don't go anywhere else."

There was that damn fork again! Frustrated with her own convoluted thought process as much as with him, she knocked the fork out of his grip, then slapped her hands to his face to make him pay attention. "Listen to me! Soldiers follow orders without question." She looked him dead in the eye. "A warrior thinks for himself."

I won't be one of them. I won't! This room would kill her. She could feel it coming, brain cells separating, dying one by one, turning her gray matter to mush until nothing was left of her. Still better than voluntarily killing them all at once. Emma would rather die than become a zombie.

John the soldier gently grasped her wrists, pulled her hands away, and placed them into her lap.

Then he pushed to his feet and walked out.

~

Back in his quarters, John closed the door with care, then removed his boots and set them neatly at the foot of his bed. His room was bare, hardly much better than Emma's; he had a bed, and a bathroom of his own, and that was pretty much it. But at least the small window gave him a glimpse of the outside world. And he could turn the lights on and off.

To make sure, he tried them. On. Off. On. Off. On. Off.

On. Emma's unnaturally blue eyes stared at him in the light.

Off. Her matted red hair tangled around her face and neck while she slept, never more than a few minutes at a time.

On. Half of his room turned bright white, while a mattress appeared on the floor by the wall, with Emma sitting on it, shaking as if she was cold.

John turned off the light with a foul curse and sat down on his bed, face in his hands.

A soldier follows orders without question.

He'd been ordered to place a young girl into a chamber that would torture any normal human being, and he'd been assured that the sensory deprivation would force her compliance. The effects were supposed to be temporary; she'd recover soon after her release, which should have been days ago.

John hadn't expected anything like what was happening to Emma. No one else had lasted this long. The sergeant major debriefed him on Emma's condition every day now, then reported to the senator. John told them everything with the hope it would change the situation, but the sergeant major never evinced any reaction whatsoever, and the senator never issued any new orders. They didn't care.

They weren't at her door day and night, watching her fall apart, little by little. They weren't there when she zoned out as if her mind had just shut down for a few minutes, or when she looked at him as though she'd never seen him before. Worse, when she looked at him with so much trust in her eyes just before he took the tray and crushed her with betrayal.

She cried, he knew. When no one could see her, she cried. Every time he came back, John noticed the wet patch on her mattress, looked into her reddened eyes as he set down a new tray, saw raw pain written plainly on her ravaged face.

Whatever the sensory deprivation did was bad enough. Locking down her telepathy was worse than inhumane. And his presence was the bright red cherry on top of that sundae.

A warrior thinks for himself.

He'd told her the truth. Emma had the ability to save countless lives. The world was on the brink of another war like the one that had nearly destroyed their entire species. Everyone felt it, from the most populous cities to the smallest hole-in-the-wall village. It translated even into the government itself, but the ICG still clung to the old faith of strength in numbers, in unity. They were determined to go to any lengths to keep the human race whole.

Only Senator Griffith seemed willing to acknowledge the inevitable looming on the horizon. When the whole became no more than the sum of its parts, sooner or later, the internal pressure of conflict shattered it. And when that happened—as it was starting to already—the senator and his small but expert army of Shadows would be the last line of defense.

For the first time, John wondered whom exactly they'd be called on to defend.

And, thinking of Emma, the next question was: At what cost?

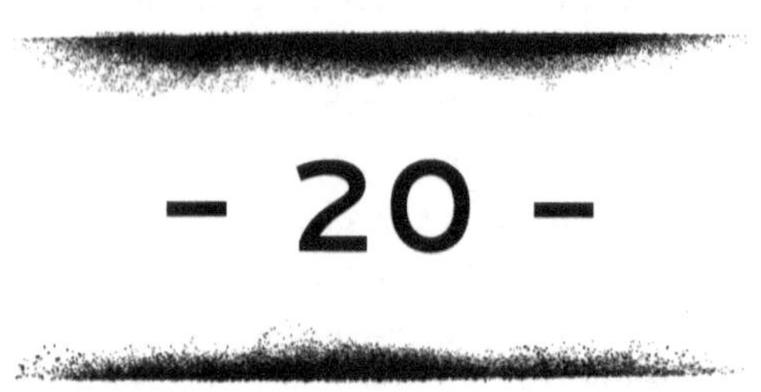

Somewhere in the Tae Colony – Date Unknown

Morning light teased Zayn awake, and he opened his eyes to Anna watching him. She crossed her eyes and skewed her mouth, making him laugh. "What are you doing?"

"Cheering you up," she replied, pinching his cheek like a mother hen. "You've been so grumpy lately."

He yawned, stretched, and snatched her to his chest for a good morning cuddle. "There's a lot to be done. You know that."

She sighed heavily. "I know. My presents always take forever to get to me."

Zayn nuzzled her cheek. "But aren't they always worth it in the end?"

She shrugged. "I suppose."

"This will be, too. I promise you." When it was all finished, he'd give her a whole new world.

"Zayn?"

The uncertainty in her voice squeezed at his heart. "Yes, love?"

She raised her head to look at him. "I don't want anyone to die."

The simple plea wrenched at his soul and he couldn't think of anything to say.

Luckily, the beep of an alert saved him from having to answer. The Calen household com his tech had hacked was picking up a transmission. Zayn pecked Anna with a quick kiss before he gently set her aside. Leanne entered then, a question in the arch of her eyebrow. "Anna," he said, "why don't you go visit with Michael for a while? Then maybe the three of us can get together for lunch. What do you say?"

Leanne took the hint and prepared to escort Anna out.

He was reaching for his com, when Anna gave a frustrated huff. "Sometimes I think I would have been better off falling for him instead."

Zayn leapt over the bed and caught her around the waist. He lifted her off her feet and spun her around until she squealed with laughter. "Take it back, heartless wench."

"*Zaayyyyn,*" she protested.

He dipped her quickly, almost to the floor. "Take it back," he demanded, and kissed her.

"Uh-uh!" He loosened his hold, feigning a drop, and she yelped. "All right! All right! I take it back. Now pull me up!" He loved seeing her this way; she lit up the whole world with her happiness.

The alert beeped again.

He ignored it and swung Anna into the air instead. "Tell me you love me."

Laughing, she clutched at him until her nails bit into his skin. As if he'd ever let her fall. "I love youuuu," she howled.

Zayn set her down onto her feet and squeezed her tight, kissing her breathless until she melted in his arms.

Anna sighed, dreamy-eyed. "I do love you, you know."

"Are you sure? You're not planning to leave me for a lesser man?"

"No," she said on a chuckle. "Now aren't you going to say it back to me?"

"Annabel Lockhart, you are the only reason I will my heart to beat." He leaned in to whisper at her ear, "You're my everything."

She smiled, her whole heart shining through her eyes. "See you for lunch."

He nodded and handed her off to Leanne. "See you then."

When they were gone, he removed himself to a chamber off the east hallway, one he used as an office, and locked the door. What Anna couldn't sense wouldn't hurt her. Zayn kept telling himself that as he acknowledged the alert and brought up the conversation on his com wall. He recognized one of the callers immediately and just stopped himself from breaking something. John MacMurphy, director of the Special Unit and a man much older than the last time Zayn had seen him, sighed at something the second man had said. "I have people looking everywhere. It's not that easy. After they set fire to the parliament building in Old Seoul, the ICG good as declared Martial Law. Everything's on lock-down, and the more questions we ask, the more attention gets turned our way."

This was about the girl. The younger man was Emma's brother, the only living relation she had left in the universe. If she'd pinned her hopes of escape on this motley crew, he felt sorry for her. A washed-out, elitist asshole, and a brother so overcome with concern he couldn't think straight.

A bitter smirk twisted Zayn's mouth as he listened. Never once did MacMurphy mention to one of his precious chosen that he knew precisely where his sister was being held. "I know you're worried," the old man consoled, understandably riling Jeremy Calen even more. "We are, too. And trust me, we're doing everything we can." What horse shit. "But we have to be careful. Your inability to connect with her doesn't have to mean anything. This is why we didn't want to tell you. She could be out of range. She could be shielding. Just because you can't reach her doesn't mean—"

"I can't reach her because she's not there to be reached!"

MacMurphy looked like he was nearing the end of his patience. At long last, someone besides Zayn got to see the true face of their benevolent leader. Nothing but another heartless manipulator out for himself and no one else.

If his reaction was anything to go by, Calen saw it, too. But he didn't say anything.

"Look," MacMurphy said reasonably, "at this point, we don't know what happened. That's all I'm saying. She could be perfectly fine—"

"You did not just say that to me," Calen snarled. "I know I didn't just hear you say Pixie is *perfectly fine* after Mars 2." Apparently, he was still unaware of the Shadows' involvement in her disappearance.

And *Pixie*? How sweet. Ironic, given what he'd ferreted out about Mars 2. The girl had broken the cardinal rule of all telepaths: Do not engage without permission. She'd taken justice into her own hands, used her abilities to force a man off a bridge. No trial, no judgment. Just cold, efficient execution. Too bad the Shadows had gotten to her before Zayn could. She had balls—massive, titanium ones. He could have used her.

"I need you to calm down, Jeremy. This isn't helping anyone, especially not Pixie." MacMurphy sounded so calm. But of course he would. It wasn't his flesh and blood on the chopping block.

Calen stopped pacing and faced the com screen. He took a good, hard look at his mentor, the man who would have raised him and his sister. "You know something more."

Zayn smiled. *Yes, great master, do tell us what you know.*

MacMurphy rubbed his brow. "At this point, not enough."

Zayn snorted and rolled his eyes.

"But you know *something*," Calen insisted.

"Possibly. A hint or two without substantiation, vague enough to send a loving brother into a panic. There is no point in telling you anything until I have hard evidence to support it."

"You tell me right now, or I swear to God, you won't like the alternative."

MacMurphy sighed. "Get some rest. Have a hot meal, hug your wife. Let us do our job."

Calen reached for the com, and the connection abruptly ended. Zayn did some quick recalibrations to patch into an entertainment feed and get Calen back on-screen.

He'd smashed the com to pieces. Righteous fury. Now, what was he willing to do about it?

"Yes, you're right. The com was evil and needed to be destroyed."

Zayn zoomed in on the white-haired woman standing in the doorway—Calen's wife, Dr. Hailey Chase-Calen. "Just came to tell you word's spreading through Amberley. A government shuttle landed a couple hours ago and deposited a hundred soldiers into our quaint little corner of the universe. Might not be a good idea to go into town for a while."

"Will you be okay with that?"

"With not going to town?"

"With troops of soldiers prowling in your territory."

"I'll be good if they are," the woman said, flashing a hint of fang.

Zayn tilted his head, considering this development. He'd known Hailey had attempted to follow her sister's example and test the animal DNA experiment on herself, but from what he'd been able to unearth, her trial had failed. Evidently, the Chase sisters were very, very good at keeping their secrets, which made him curious about what else they might be hiding.

"I was afraid of that," Calen muttered.

"Don't worry, they'll leave soon enough. There's nothing here for them to do."

Zayn didn't think so. Their presence would only escalate unrest among the citizens. He did so enjoy when the government did the dirty work for him.

"No, they won't," Calen said. "People will see them and start panicking. The soldiers will incite the riots they came here to prevent."

"That's gonna suck. Oh, speaking of not leaving, I found another note attached to the door of my lab."

Calen took the piece of paper and unfolded it. "*Nature always prevails*," he read aloud, and Zayn echoed him. "*Broken and bloody, it will yet rise to turn on its oppressors. Stand with us or stand aside.*"

Zayn smiled. Having a scientist on their side would be a benefit. But how much better was a scientist *and* a shape-shifter?

"I don't like this."

"You don't think it could be that group, do you? They've been all over the news lately, organizing rallies and riots…" Hailey snapped her fingers. "Oh, what did they call themselves…?"

"Evolutionaries," Calen supplied. Zayn did like the sound of it. "This looks like their symbol, but for all our sakes, I hope it's just a copycat."

"They can't know about me, right? They couldn't possibly know." Zayn chuckled.

Calen rubbed his brow. "The SU has people who can see into the future, calculate impossible odds, sense the history of inanimate objects."

Zayn's mouth twisted. That had to be a new development. Back in the day, they'd only been interested in mind readers.

"And those are just the ones we know about," Calen went on. "Who knows what others could be capable of? We're not taking anything for granted." He pocketed the note and stuffed his feet into shoes.

"Ten guesses where you're headed."

"If anyone knows about what the hell's going on, it'll be Hunt. Stay here, I'll be back."

"The hell I will."

Zayn swore when they left the house. He pinged his contact on Torrey, hoping she was awake. Katarina worked magic with hacks, but it made her sleep cycle erratic.

Luckily, she answered right away with an irreverent, "Yo."

"I need info on an individual. Last name Hunt. Somewhere outside of Amberley. Cross-reference Calen."

Katarina frowned. "Hunt. Why does that sound familiar? Stand by."

Not like he could do anything else.

Faster than he expected, she was back. "All right. Tristan and Dara Hunt, proud owners of a castle. I kid you not."

"Get me everything you have on them, and find me an eye in the… castle."

"You got it, chief. Patching in… now."

Katarina disappeared, and Zayn got a fly-on-the-wall view of a massive entry hall with stone walls and wooden beams. The Calens had already arrived and were separating with the Hunts—Tristan with Hailey, and Jeremy with Dara.

Knowing Katarina could still hear him, Zayn ordered, "Give me a split screen."

"Thine will be done," she quipped.

The screen split. One side displayed Tristan Hunt showing Hailey Calen everything he'd found on the Evolutionaries. Inconsequential. Zayn dismissed them to focus on the other two entering a sunlit room with a view of a lake.

"Sit," Dara Hunt said. No small talk, just down to business. "I can't promise anything, but my range is wider than yours. Let's see if I can sense anything about Pixie. Give me your hand."

Calen did, and closed his eyes. Physical contact enhanced telepathic connections. In this case, it would combine their abilities and make them stronger.

Zayn cursed. This was giving him nothing. He couldn't get into their heads. Fucking telepaths.

He almost gave up, when Katarina hummed. "This is interesting."

A third feed joined the two already on-screen. A nursery of some sort, with a little girl who looked no more than four reading multiple e-pads. She was as quiet and self-possessed as any adult, and there was something so disturbing about her, Zayn couldn't help but pay attention.

Then she sighed and looked up. "Mom is going to spank your butt red."

A ball of orange-and-black fur wrapped in thread rolled out from behind a couch. The little tiger cub pawed the air, trying to extricate himself, but only managed to tangle himself up more. When he growled and got up to walk away, he pulled the destroyed blanket after him.

The girl gasped. "That one's mine!"

Before Zayn's eyes, the cub contorted and shifted, limbs elongating, fur receding, until a mirror image of the girl crouched naked on the floor. A boy with a reckless grin and a challenge in his eyes.

Zayn forgot to breathe.

"Eyes on the prize, chief," Katarina said. "You've got action on one."

Zayn tore his gaze away from the little shifter child to focus again on the telepaths. Tristan had joined them, one hand on Calen's shoulder, the other on his wife's, and whatever they were doing was making him twitch. "Now," he growled.

Calen gasped, shuddered, then whispered, "How are you doing, sis…"

~

"How are you doing, sis?"

Emma dragged her unfocused gaze away from the piece of dark blue thread on the floor. Her smile felt wan; she was so, so tired. "Hey, big brother."

Jeremy smiled, reached out to brush her cheek. She couldn't feel the caress, and her eyes closed against tears trying to sting their way out. "You're not really here, are you?"

His smile faded at the edges, his eyes turning sad. "No, Pixie, I'm not."

Emma sniffled, wiped her nose on her sleeve, and pulled herself together. "Okay." She gave a resolute nod. She could handle this. "But since you're here, you might as well tell me what's new."

Jeremy only stared at her. "I love you, Pixie. You know that, right? No matter what."

She rubbed at her leaky eye. No evidence. "Yeah," she replied, her voice quivering. "Of course I know that. I love you, too. Even if you did marry the Hellcat from Hades."

He didn't laugh at her lame joke, just kept staring straight into her eyes. "No matter what," he said again. As if he knew. As if this whole damn place was a one-way mirror reflecting her own madness back at her, and showcasing it for everyone on the other side. All of her flaws.

All of her sins.

The memory of the worst one came at her all at once, unbidden, and pulled her under, away from her brother, even as she reached out blindly for a saving hand.

The white floor morphed into a snow-covered sidewalk, and her shoes groaned each time she stepped into the fresh layer of flakes. She used to love that sound. It was almost time for Christmas dinner. She'd have to hide her loot before her friends descended on it and ruined the surprise.

Emma grinned and, giddy with the anticipation of seeing their faces, ran up the staircase. The brothel was a pristine, Victorian-style mansion, out of place and time on this colony. It had been designed with only the best and greatest in mind—luxurious décor, expensive refreshments, highly professional staff, and a 100% discretion guarantee. Men and women sought this place out for an experience unlike any other.

Emma's best friends worked here, and they got paid well for bringing comfort and pleasure to their customers, work they truly enjoyed. Mary often told her the most profound thing a woman could experience was to bring a measure of peace to a man broken by tragedy. They weren't prostitutes; they were healers. And while Emma had no intention of joining their ranks, she loved them all dearly.

Emma nodded to the two discreet security guards, who smiled and waved her in. Great guys. Feet firmly on the ground. She had gifts for them, too, but they'd have to wait until morning, just like everyone else. Now, the question was: where to hide the packages until then? Pondering that quandary, Emma took the stairs two at a time and didn't notice anything wrong until it was too late. Far too late.

A split second. No more than her bare hand brushing a stranger. The smallest instant of connection, and she was somewhere else…

Heat and cold, breath misting in the air, heart thrumming, body sweating in the light jacket. Breath so loud, everything else seemed muted. Hardly heard the woman's voice from so far away—echoed, garbled. Saying something in that goddamn soft way women had when they tried to manipulate a guy, tried to make it seem like it was for the best, his decision after all.

Show her how wrong she was.

Hands curling into fists. One flew so fast, it didn't have a chance to flatten out. A punch instead of the slap intended. Woman on the floor somehow, between one moment and the next. Rage seething inside, but also hunger. Hands groped, left marks. Clothes tore away. She flailed. A hard slap subdued her. Blood trickling from her lip. Disgusting. Wouldn't be kissing that mouth now.

She moaned. Fingers curled around her throat, choking off the sound. Her eyes went as wide as saucers, then squeezed shut to block out the pain of—

Emma just barely turned her scream into a moan. She was shaking, terrified. Insides tied into cold knots, she couldn't even retch. Couldn't draw in air. *It's not true. Can't be.*

But it was. She knew the difference between imagination and fact. Daydreams were subtle, foggy, pleasing to the mind. This had been too hard, too sharp, rooted far too deep in the psyche.

A split second. Just long enough for her to drop, like she'd been whaled across the stomach. The man she'd touched hadn't even paused; he was already down the staircase and out of the house in a blink, leaving Emma in his wake.

Leaving Mary.

Mary!

Emma struggled to her feet, made them move, propelled herself forward when her wobbly legs threatened to send her back to the floor with every step. Three rooms down, the door was open, and pain—*Oh, God, so much pain!*—soaked the hallway like bad incense smoke. She could taste it in her mind, and it made saliva flood her mouth.

Already knowing what she'd find, Emma threw open the door so hard, it slammed into the wall. Reality was even worse than the memories. Shock blurred her vision, turned it inward where her mind could make sense of it.

Her friend, the warm, funny woman who'd taken her in when she'd had nowhere else to go, lay on the floor. Her clothes were torn, and she was covered with bruises and scratches, blood tracking down her thighs.

Emma couldn't move.

Not even when Mary tried to lever herself up. She was too weak, hurting too much. Instead, she made a broken sound, turned her head a little, and Emma gasped again to see Mary's beautiful face all bruised and mangled with a split lip and a couple of teeth missing. *Oh, my God!*

"Get… Sam," Mary whimpered.

"Oh, my God," Emma whispered, horrified.

"Please…"

Dashing her tears away, Emma went, banging on every door she passed along the way, rousing everyone out of their beds. She slipped three times running down the stairs and almost knocked some people over.

She found Sam in his usual spot, halfway down the second floor hall.

Emma called his name.

Sam shoved to his feet, met her by the stairs. He didn't need to be told something bad had happened. Charging past her, he went up.

Up, to Mary. Not down, after the man.

Emma could already hear the commotion up there. Mary was one of those people everyone liked; she'd befriended everybody who lived here, and even some of her clients were lifelong acquaintances. Right now, everyone who saw her had pity in their eyes. They should have been outraged that a man would have dared hurt one of their own. They should have been charging after him, right now, while he was still close.

That's what Tristan would have done. Her shifter friend would have torn into the guy's throat before he'd even cleared the door.

No. If Tristan had been around, this never would have happened.

That, more than anything, got Emma moving. Tristan looked after his own any way he could. It's what Emma should have done, instead of hiding like anyone out here gave a good goddamn about what she could do.

I could have stopped this. I should *have stopped it!* Guilt choked her until she felt like she'd pass out from it.

No way to undo the past.

But she could do *something.*

Curling her fingers into fists so tight they shook, Emma did something she hadn't done in over a year: She opened her mind wide.

In seconds, she'd filtered through the overwhelming chaos of noise and emotion—the house was bursting with both right now, and it broke her heart. She pushed all of it aside to narrow her focus onto an invisible trail. Like a black hole, she could only find it by the effect it had on everything else.

People moved out of his way, watched after him as he stomped by down the street. Even though they couldn't read his thoughts, they sensed something was off. People always did.

Emma followed that same path, stalking through the middle of the walkway, parting the scant crowds before her. He wasn't even running; drunk on his own power, he meandered into a bar. She heard him in her head, saw what he was looking at. Carefully confining herself to his senses and away from his thoughts, she saw him hail the bartender. "Hey, my man, let me get a victory salute over here."

Emma's step faltered, then picked up. She entered the bar just as his drink was set down before him, and she shut him out of her mind. The guy, nameless and would remain that way, chuckled to himself and picked up the shot glass. "Showed that bitch right," he muttered. Licking his lips, he brought the glass up…

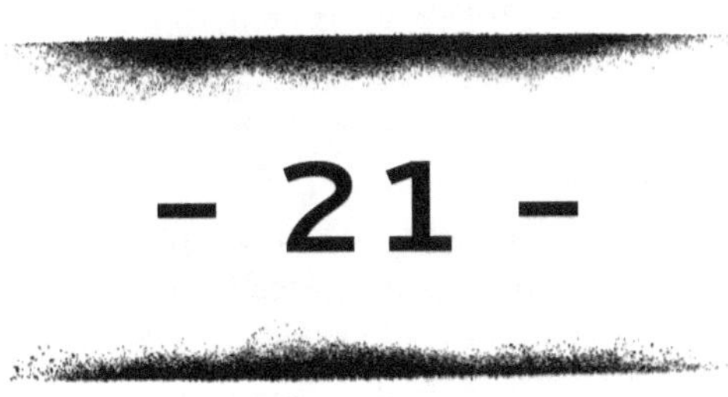

– 21 –

Back in the Tae Colony

Five minutes passed with little action from the telepaths, so Zayn switched to Hailey Calen playing with the children. She argued with the girl as she would an adult, taking apart some intricate scientific principle. In contrast, the boy, once again a tiger cub, seemed more like a pet cat to her. She pulled a piece of the destroyed blanket around the floor to make him chase it, and when he growled at her, clawed her hand, she snatched him up by the scruff and hissed in his face. His ears flattened, and he licked her nose by way of apology.

Zayn didn't know what to do with this. He wanted to do *something*. He couldn't buy this kind of leverage. If he had those kids, their parents would do anything and everything he asked.

But Anna wouldn't condone it. Children were innocent and meant to be protected. She'd overlooked a lot from him already, but given their own royally fucked up childhoods, if Zayn crossed that line, she'd never forgive him.

"I'm sending you the Hunt file," Katarina told him, crunching chips. "Haven't read it yet, but something tells me you'll find it interesting."

Zayn was about to read it when Calen started to freak out. He broke away from the telepath connection and fell to all fours, gasping. "I can't... I... can't—"

His wife came running, calling out his name, trying to reach him, but Calen seemed completely out of it.

With one ear listening for Katarina's report, Zayn watched Tristan Hunt take Calen in hand. "You're losing it, my friend," Hunt said roughly.

"If I take her place—"

"You won't! You think these people give a shit about her? You walk in there, they'll have two telepaths instead of one."

"I have to do something!" Calen insisted.

"Listen to me!" Hunt snapped. "You don't take something from the Shadows without leaving part of your soul behind—" He cut himself off.

Zayn frowned. "Is there a connection here I don't know about?"

"Three words," Katarina replied. "Outpost Green twenty-four."

His eyebrows shot up. "No shit." So this was the man who'd supposedly gutted a Shadow outpost?

"All in the report," she said.

Zayn skimmed it, but couldn't find anything explicit. "Show me."

"The Shadows?" Calen was saying. "What the hell are you talking about?"

Hunt met eyes with his wife.

"*What!*" Calen demanded when no one answered him.

Dara nodded to whatever wordless communiqué her husband just shared with her. "I'll start packing our things."

Hailey frowned. "Are you going somewhere?"

Hunt waited until his wife was gone before he spoke again. "I've dealt with these people before. The Shadows. I've seen what they can do, and I know how they operate." He huffed. "I can't help you. You go after Pixie, you do it without me."

"What are you talking about?" the white-haired woman demanded. "You flew Dara and your infants into Rome to help my sister. You can't bail now! What, are you saying there's something even the Big Bad Tristan Hunt is afraid of?"

Hunt glared, eyes changing to pure, feral gold.

"Holy shit," she said weakly.

"I'm sorry," Hunt said. "I really am. Pixie's a good kid, and I hate to leave her like this. But I won't go against the Shadows again. I have too much to lose."

Katarina streamed a police report onto a split screen. "Here." The gruesome double homicide of Natalie and Jonathan Hunt. Zayn shuddered, reading through parts of it. Tristan Hunt, their then ten-year-old son, had been listed as a missing person that day, and everyone had presumed him dead, until he'd walked into a police station years later and confessed to the murder of several government soldiers. He'd been sentenced to life on a prison world, then later transferred and released on good behavior into the custody of the Special Unit.

"This smacks of Shadow involvement." It was just the sort of heavy-handed recruiting they liked to do.

"Oh yeah," Katarina agreed. "You remember Green twenty-four, right?"

Of course he did. The underworld had been buzzing with it for months. It had been both a confirmation that the Shadows did, in fact, exist, and proof that they weren't as invincible as they'd led everyone to believe. If the two were truly related, then Zayn wanted to meet this Tristan Hunt just to look the man in the eye and shake his hand. What he'd done to the Shadows had been nothing short of legendary, and no doubt left a massive scar on their confidence.

No wonder they'd started to target telepaths specifically.

"Where will you go?" Calen asked on the feed.

"Somewhere no one will find us," Hunt replied. "This is a full-out war—Shadows versus Evolutionaries, and everyone else in the middle. And Jer, these people are not like your Special Unit; they won't care whether they lose ten or ten thousand in the fight. If you have any sense of self-preservation, you take yourself and yours out of the crossfire."

Zayn didn't need to see any more. He still had a couple of hours before his lunch with Anna and Michael so, deciding to do something useful, he flipped through the virtual pages of the Hunt report.

"Calens are on the move," Katarina reported some time later. "They're all about to scatter. Orders?"

"Intercept the Calens." The overwrought brother would be chafing at his mentor's betrayal, and Zayn could capitalize on that, sway him to their side. He'd only need a few hours of the man's time. Easy pickings, as far as he was concerned.

"And the Hunts?"

Zayn considered it. The Hunts would make an invaluable ally. Unfortunately, they seemed determined not to take a stand. He could force them if he were desperate, but he wasn't. And a willing ally was worth a hundred slaves. "Let them go."

"Roger."

After another half-hour with no further word from Katarina, Zayn had had enough research. He was about to break for his lunch with Anna, when Katarina came back with an update. "I lost Calen," she said. "He's on a shuttle out. His wife couldn't get past the soldiers; she didn't have clearance, so she's staying behind. All shuttleports are now shut down to civilian travel, pending further notice. Looks like we're all stuck here, boys and girls."

Not what Zayn wanted to hear, but it didn't matter. He had more than he needed. The wheels were finally turning, and damn, if that didn't make him smile.

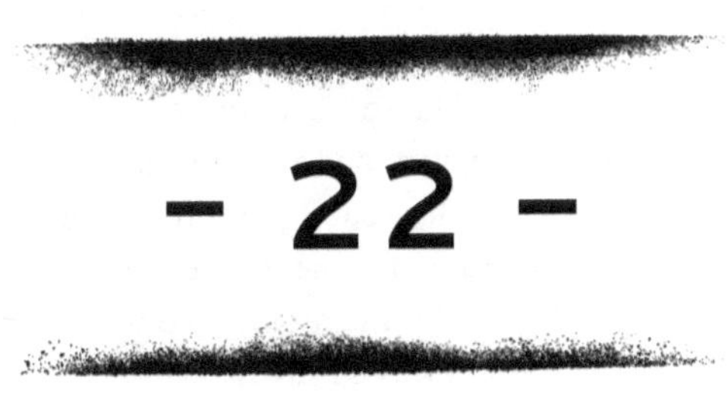

– 22 –

The food tray John carried to Emma today was a little more varied than the ones before. He'd requisitioned it from the mess hall for himself and had picked it up on his way back to his post. Despite the regular meals, Emma was losing too much weight. If he couldn't get more nutrition into her, she'd starve to death.

John dismissed the Hound guarding Emma's door, noting how the man marched away without question, without any change in facial expression. On to another assignment. Like a good little soldier, following orders to a T.

Maybe Emma was right about them.

The thought didn't sit well with him. Not at all.

Inside, Emma sat exactly where he'd left her, hadn't even touched the food on the old tray. All of it was still there, fork flung sideways where she'd knocked it out of his hand.

"Emma?"

She didn't respond. Was she sleeping?

John set the tray down by the door, pushed the old one out of the way so he could get a closer look. "Emma, are you—"

Her head lolled, eyes rolling back in her head.

"Jesus!"

The seizure shook her so hard, John feared she'd break her own neck. Keeping her head steady against his shoulder with one hand, he clamped her arms to her sides, clutching her to him as hard as he dared. "Emma! Hold on."

Think… Think, goddammit! He couldn't do anything until the seizure stopped. If he let go, her frail body would break itself apart. "Stay with me, you're going to be okay," he soothed, not believing his own lie.

Emma made sounds like a wounded animal, but he welcomed them. At least her airway was still clear enough for her to breathe. He held on, waiting five more seconds before he realized no help would come. With no monitoring devices in this room, no one would be rushing in to take over her care. John was all she had. And she was dying.

Making a snap decision, he pinned his cheek against hers to free his arm, then picked her up and walked out the door. It closed behind him, sealing the chamber shut, and John sat down on the hallway floor with Emma in his arms. He didn't have enough medical training to deal with this; he only knew to try to keep her from hurting herself. Her fingers were locked into claws, arm muscles cramping, twitching her limbs in uncontrollable spasms.

"I've got you," he said, rocking her, trying to smooth her hair from her face so he could see her eyes. He caught flashes of all white, no blue. It terrified him. "Hold on, Emma. You can't give up now."

When she went limp, John thought for a frantic instant she was dead. He checked her eyes, her pulse, her breathing. Still alive. *Thank God.*

Then: *What the hell do I do now?*

He couldn't put her back in that room. It would kill her. She needed medical attention, but he couldn't take her to med bay—

Emma sighed in his arms, tears leaking from her closed eyes. Her curled hand, caught between them, hooked into his jacket and held on.

"Emma… can you hear me?"

She didn't respond.

John jarred her gently, trying to wake her up. Without a scan, he didn't know how much damage she'd sustained. One wrong movement could paralyze her, send her into another seizure, or even kill her. But he couldn't keep holding her like this forever. "Come on, girl, open your eyes."

A barely audible moan was the only indication she'd heard him at all.

John swore and checked the time.

The hallway was empty, but not for long. Sooner or later, someone would wonder why John hadn't called for a tray pick up and come looking for him. He couldn't be found out here with her.

Couldn't put her back in that room, either. She wouldn't survive another episode like this.

What, you suddenly care what happens to her?

Yes.

This was wrong. It served no practical purpose. The senator might not have said as much, but his orders spoke for themselves: he intended to keep Emma in that room to see how long it would take to break her—to *kill* her.

John couldn't let that happen. Not on his watch, and certainly not by his hand.

The parameters of his mission had changed. *Reassess and respond.*

John looked down the length of the hallway, then the other side. All clear. Testing day, and every Hawk besides himself was out on some secret assignment they hadn't been allowed to share, even with each other. He ran the Hound schedule through his mind. The last round of tests would be starting in three minutes with the majority of those who'd already tested recuperating and the rest too preoccupied to pay attention.

John had a small window of opportunity and only one course of action that would allow him to sleep at night. The idea gave him pause enough to wonder whether he'd lost his mind right along with the girl. Then he looked at Emma—really looked at her—and realized this was the first sane thing he'd done in weeks.

Tucking her securely against his chest, John got up and started walking.

Two guards on duty in the transport bay. Not Shadows, just low-pay-grade muscle; glorified mechanics who should have been standing guard or tending to the vehicles. Instead, they played cards on a tool cabinet they'd turned into a table.

John slowed his step to quiet his boots and headed past them. Maybe they wouldn't notice him.

"Hey," one of them called. "Somethin' I can help you with, sir?"

"As you were," John said, not even looking at him.

The mechanic whose name John had never bothered to learn met him halfway to a transport vehicle. "Don't have you on my roster," he said. "All soldiers need to be signed in and scheduled for use of the vehicles. Sergeant Major's orders, sir."

"I have my own orders," John told him, shifting so the light caught on his hawk pin.

The mechanic stood straighter, until his gaze flicked to Emma. He looked back at John and they stared each other down, butting heads about what the mechanic should do. As a Hawk, John outranked him, but even he was bound by protocol.

The mechanic wasn't stupid, just slow to move. In the time it took the man to reach for his com, John had shifted Emma and pulled his side arm, ready to shoot.

He never got a chance to use it.

With a gasp, Emma opened her eyes wide and screamed.

John winced at the piercing shriek so close to his ear. He dropped his weapon in a hurry, sinking to one knee and freeing a hand so he could silence her. Completely oblivious to his efforts, Emma kept screaming as the mechanics fell to the floor, clutching at their heads. The sound she made wasn't one of pain, but of horror—the scariest damn thing John had ever heard in his life.

When Emma ran out of breath, she fell unconscious again, but whatever telepathic blow she'd sent out wasn't ending. One of the mechanics had pissed himself. The other was curled up in a fetal position, weeping and scratching at his face until he drew blood.

John swallowed hard. The delicate creature currently asleep in his arms had wrought this. He'd seen her in action before, knew what she was capable of, but to see the effects of her abilities up close was more than a little unnerving.

Reassess and respond.

The alarms should have gone off already. Why hadn't they?

Didn't matter. *Have to move fast.*

John loaded Emma into the most civilian-looking transport, got into the driver's seat and, switching the nav console to manual, drove out of the compound just as the sirens started to wail.

Once the facility was locked down, it would required three high-ranking officers to disable. As a security measure to protect against a major threat escaping off-base, no more than one officer was allowed to be present at any given time. The EM barrier sparked and began closing around the perimeter as John sped toward the gate. Shadow guards writhed on the ground, weapons forgotten, gate left wide open. Two utility transports approached on automatic nav. Had to be, otherwise they'd be reacting to account for the EM barrier. Both got inside at a moderate speed, and John swerved around them, pushing the transport to its limit, gritting his teeth as the barrier locked down, zapping the rear of the vehicle. Luckily, the front propulsion system wasn't affected.

The gate closed belatedly, sealing the base from any electronic and biological infiltration.

John let out a tense breath, forced his muscles to relax. They were safe, for the moment. Nobody would be getting in or out of the base for quite some time.

He glanced at Emma passed out on the back seat. *She's stronger than we thought.* More dangerous.

And now he was on the run with her. A fugitive from his own squad, the only life he'd ever known, with a weapon potentially capable of destroying them all.

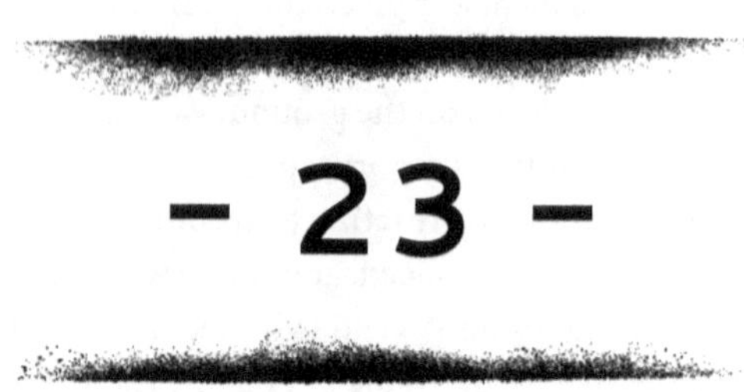

– 23 –

She dreamed about a bright white room with walls that constantly hummed. The drone got louder, and louder, until it wasn't just a sound anymore. It was a voice—her voice.

Emma screamed herself awake, batting away the invisible sparks of electricity burning her head and face like fire ants. They were *everywhere!* "Get them off! *Get them off!*"

"Emma!"

She fought against the big hands that grabbed her; tossed her head around so hard, she almost broke her neck. Her flying hair blinded her to everything except for those evil blue sparks going off all around her. Inside her. *I'm going to catch fire,* she thought, and screamed again, wrestling for her freedom.

She was pathetically feeble in her efforts. Massive bands circled around her shoulders to hold her steady, while a hand covered almost half of her face, pressing her head to a hard, unyielding shoulder until she couldn't move at all. Could hardly take a breath.

Her scream dissolved into a wretched wail, then the tears really came. Powerful sobs shook her frame like a leaf. Something was broken inside her; she could feel the rift, something missing, something that didn't belong…?

It didn't make sense. Nothing made sense!

The world moved, rocking back and forth like a small boat on a very angry sea, and she was stuck, and couldn't hold on, and her hands shook so bad…

"Easy. Just breathe. It's going to be okay."

She laughed, and even to her own ears, the sound carried an edge of hysteria. Okay? Nothing was okay. No such thing as okay. It was gone. Run away so far. *Can't follow. Lost my sunstone.*

—*Somebody, anybody… Help…*—

She felt the call fracture into thousands of little pieces and scatter like mist on the wind. *My name is Emma,* she told herself, focusing on that one little thing. *I am Emma Calen. I have a brother. He's married to a cat.*

Another crazy laugh scared her. And still, the tears kept coming. She was so thirsty. How could so many drops of water still be left in her? She brushed at her face, and her hand came away red.

Blood?

Emma fought with renewed vigor, frantic to wash it off.

"Emma, hold still!"

Not blood. Her hair. She'd torn out her hair. With that realization, a massive flood of sparks seared through her brain. Emma screamed, clawing at her eyes.

Someone cursed as the world moved again, then she was doused with water so cold it knocked the breath out of her. Emma could only gasp, hoping she didn't drown. Oh, but the water… She opened her mouth to it, desperate for every drop; tried to catch some in her hands, but her wrists had been shackled, and no matter how hard she tried, she couldn't free them. The shackles knew to move with her. They gave a little, but not enough, in a distracted tug of war she'd be more keen on winning after she'd drunk some more.

But too soon, Emma exhausted herself, shivering in the icy rain. She collapsed against the wall holding her up. A warm hand pushed her wet hair off her face. Kept petting her in a steady rhythm that made her want to twitch an ear. *There's a good girl.*

Is it dinnertime? She'd lost track of her date. He never called…

The water shut off.

~

Emma went limp, passed out again, and John sagged back in relief against the shower wall. "Thank God," he murmured, squeezing her a little. Her pulse was steady, her breathing even; she was simply asleep. As if she hadn't just scared fifty years off his life. "Let's not do that again, huh? What do you say?" He took her silence for agreement. "Good."

Heart pounding and worn out from the thirty-five-hour drive but acutely alert after Emma's freak-out, John sat with her in the tub for a moment to collect himself, absently petting her hair. Small clumps of it were tangled around her hands, and he checked her scalp for bleeding wounds. Thankfully, there were none. When he pulled the torn hairs from her hands, he noticed his own were trembling.

John heaved a sigh, lightly thumping his forehead against the crown of Emma's head. "What am I going to do with you?"

That was the million credit question. *Tell us, Hawk, now that you have cut all ties with the only life you've ever known, stolen a hostage from the deadliest private army in the universe, and signed your own terminate-on-sight order, what will you do next?*

John had no fucking clue.

Groaning like an old man, he picked up Emma and carried her out of the bathroom, back to the bed. The moment he laid her down, she turned over onto her side and curled up as tightly as she could manage, still shivering, even in sleep. He couldn't leave her soaked.

John retrieved a towel and carefully raised her up to pat her hair. "You're lucky I don't startle at sudden noises. A Hound might have shot you by accident." Exhaustion was making him stupid, talking nonsense to someone beyond hearing.

But at the sound of his voice, she moaned and clutched his arm— tight. "Uh…" John couldn't move to extricate himself. "Okay, umm…" She was balanced at the edge of the bed, with a firm hold on him. If he pulled too hard and she didn't let go, she'd end up on the floor. He tried anyway. Emma wouldn't budge.

John groaned and shifted her over a few inches so he could sit on the edge of the bed. The moment he did, she seized him, grabbing handfuls of his shirt and laying her head in his lap. He stared at the towel in his hand, then down at Emma.

Reassess and res—oh, screw it.

He pulled out a knife and carefully cut through her sodden clothes to remove them, only once touching her skin with the cold flat of the blade. She gasped and curled tighter into him. John had to work quickly. If she woke up and found herself naked…

Emma's skin was so pale he could see her veins. The ridges of her vertebrae tented the skin of her back; she was painfully emaciated. When he'd managed to tug the rest of the clothing scraps free of her body, she seemed to have shrunk even more. And she still had a death grip on him, shaking so hard, he could feel it.

Tossing the filthy rags into a nearby trash bin, he pulled the covers off the bed and did his best to bundle her into them. Warmth seemed to calm her, and she loosened her hold but didn't release it. "You have to let go now, Emma," he murmured. When she didn't respond, he tried petting her hair. "You're safe now. I promise. But you have to let go." He felt awkward, clumsy showing affection like this, but he must have done okay, because she gradually released him.

As soon as he was free, John leapt to his feet and put the width of the room between them. On the bed, Emma curled in on herself. He didn't like that. She was still scared, and looked so small on the large bed…

John shook his head hard. Sleep. He needed sleep. After checking again to make sure the room was secure, he took the fastest hot shower of his life, scalding himself in the process. His clothes weren't much better than Emma's, but at least his were designed to take serious abuse, and he only had to rinse and wring everything out. By the time he'd shaken them out, the shirt and pants were as good as new.

But they were still part of a uniform that would raise eyebrows, if not an all-out alarm. He'd have to get new clothes before they moved on, which should be soon.

And at some point, John would need to figure out what to do besides keep moving. He wasn't equipped to provide the help Emma needed, and he wouldn't be able to handle another episode like the one she'd just had.

Scrubbing a fluffy towel over his head, he regarded her lying on the bed. She hadn't twitched an inch. How could she sleep like that, all cramped up and tense?

A noise outside made him shove his back against the wall by the window and carefully peek out through a gap in the blinds. Nothing. John exhaled a controlled breath, hands clenching and unclenching at his sides. They were still too close to the base, but his overtired, overtaxed brain couldn't focus enough to strategize. One moment he was staring at Emma on the bed, the next he sat in front of the com screen, blanking on what he'd wanted from it. He'd just been thinking… *Damn it, what was I going to do?*

John rubbed his face and slapped himself to wake the hell up. Then he retraced his steps back to the window, to the bed, to the bathroom. He saw the rags in the trash. Right. Clothes.

When a problem is too big to solve whole, divide and conquer.

On the com screen, John brought up the hotel's console and scrolled through the menu. They needed clothes and food first, and he repeated that to himself when the words he read stopped making sense. He was crashing hard, and the longer he held out, the worse it would get.

"Focus," he told himself. "You lose it, you die—she dies."

The hotel's menu had a "castaway" option, which included clothes, toiletries, and snacks for every person registered to the room. *In the event of a luggage loss, this is the perfect solution for our guests,* the description read. *Enjoy the stylish, complimentary travel bag as our gift to you.*

Perfect. John placed the order, then paced the confines of the room for the three minutes it took to be delivered. No attendants, valets, or concierges here; the items arrived in the smart dumbwaiter by the door.

The bags' contents included three full outfits with shoes, toiletries, and even accessories. John removed the silky nightgown and coaxed Emma to straighten so he could dress her. He kept his touch light and impersonal, his eyes on her face, but that didn't keep him from feeling each and every one of her ribs and the prominent edges of her hip bones. When he caught himself smoothing the fabric down her sides, he quickly covered her and stepped away. She needed a bath, but that would have to wait until she was awake and somewhat lucid. For now, he was content just to have her dressed. The possibility of Emma waking up while she was naked and going into another psychotic meltdown had been making him twitchy as hell.

So much for a full recovery.

By the time he had her tucked back in, it was almost midnight. He could afford to let her get a few more hours of sleep, but they'd need to be out of here before sunrise. The longer they stayed in one place, the greater the chance they'd be caught.

John changed into jeans and tossed his uniform into a pile by the bathroom door. His head swam. No good to anybody like this. He stared at the bed, unable to drag his gaze away. Emma took up so little space. He could probably lie down and sleep comfortably without ever coming into contact with her.

That he'd even considered this, made John shake himself—hard. "You sleep, you die—*she* dies." If the Shadows found them, they'd shoot first, and sort through the wreckage later. Right now, John's knowledge of how the army operated was the only thing standing between them and an early grave. He hadn't risked his life to save Emma's, only to get them both killed a few miles into freedom. "You sleep, you die," he repeated to himself when his eyes began to close.

And you have no business being near the asset, Hawk.

That straightened his back. *Not a Hawk anymore.* And Emma damn well wasn't an *asset*.

John rounded the bed, ready to lie down and get some shut-eye. But just as he was about to settle in, Emma gasped in her sleep, hand twitching by her head, brows drawing together. Dreaming. Whatever she saw in her mind, John could tell it wasn't pleasant. Not surprising, given what she'd been through. What he'd put her through.

Cursing under his breath, John went back around, pulled the plush armchair closer to her side of the bed, and sat down to watch her sleep.

A small moan had him scooting to the edge of his seat, reaching out to touch her. He pulled back, frustrated with her as much as with himself. "Rest easy, Emma." His words came out as an order, and John scowled, softening his tone. "You're safe now."

If she were awake and able to read his mind, she'd know just how much bullshit that was. But the sound of his voice seemed to soothe her, and she settled in, turning her face toward him with a sigh.

When her hand slipped off the bed, palm up, John caught it with the intention of placing it back. But the cool softness of her skin distracted him, and he rubbed his thumb over the base of her fingers.

Her nails had been ruthlessly bitten off to the quick. John traced the jagged edges, the places where she'd torn too far and had drawn blood. It looked as if she'd tried to claw her way back to sanity.

A too-hard squeeze would crush those delicate bones to dust, yet somehow, Emma was still the strongest person he'd ever met in his life. How could that be?

The weight of sleep slowly dragged him down, but John fought it, refusing to give up his vigil until he was absolutely sure they would both be safe.

That could be never.

Maybe so, but it would still be better than the alternative.

Emma woke in a bed. An actual bed, in a bed frame with posters and a canopy, pillows and a blanket, and she was wearing silk. Her eyes flooded with helpless tears. Of all the hallucinations she'd endured here, this one was the worst. As soon as her tears had cleared up, she'd be back on the ratty mattress on the floor, surrounded by blindingly white walls and a hum so loud, she'd want to scream just to drown it out.

She waited tensely for that to happen, for the dim fog to clear, but it didn't. Blinking rapidly, she looked around. This *was* a bed. In a room. With a window and the shades drawn closed! It was dark—oh, God, so blessedly dark! She could breathe, and there was no pain.

Still humming, though. Her chin wobbled. She hated that hum. Hated it so much.

Emma reached up to scratch her itchy nose. Her hand stuck. Stiffening, she slowly, carefully turned her head. She could be pinned. Chained. Stuck. And sure the room was different, but it still felt like a prison, and she couldn't see the sky. What would she do if she couldn't get her hand out of the bind?

Emma stared, uncomprehending. Her hand was caught in a man's. A big, shirtless man with brown hair the color of honey. Winged brows, hard jaw, unsmiling mouth. *Chest so wide, I could stretch my arms out all the way and never reach its edges.* Soldier boy?

But... he never called.

Emma didn't dare breathe too loudly.

So pretty.

No, that was wrong. Flowers were pretty. Rainbows and kittens were pretty. Statues were cold. Rock. Unmoving. Silent, quiet, still, mute, noiseless, un-com-*mu*-ni-ca-ti-ve.

What had he done with her?

Broken. So far away from home, which always used to be in that memory just over there. His fault. How could he be sleeping like that, when he'd broken her?

Emma twisted her wrist a little, tugged carefully to free herself. His fingers curled tighter, and she went still.

Not awake.

What was that behind him? She squinted in concentration, trying to remember. The name eluded her. *Make something up.* Waterfall. Yes, the cold waterfall was that way, but she knew it just had to go warm, too. And there would be… those things there. They made bubbles and smelled so much better than she did.

Emma glanced at the soldier boy. *He won't let me in there,* she thought desperately. But she had to get in there, or she'd die.

One more careful twist. If she could just get free—

Awake.

Emma froze. Steel gray eyes pinned her in place, and they were all she saw.

"Emma?"

A flash of panic made her move faster than light—one second she was on the bed; the next, she'd run past him, and he raced after her, but she slammed the door shut and locked it. Leaned her whole weight against it to keep him out.

But…

He wasn't trying to get in. And it was so bright in here. So, so bright, her heart began to race, her breath laboring to catch up. "S-soldier boy?"

A soft thud. "I'm here."

And the panic eased. Slowly, she let go of the door, clutching the front of her shirt instead, wringing her hands in it while she watched for any sign that a monster was coming through. When nothing happened, she apprehensively turned away. First her feet, then her hips and torso, then her head, and finally her gaze.

She caught half a glimpse of something moving in the mirror and quickly moved on to the waterfall with no buttons or sensors. How did it turn on?

Where did I get this thing? The long, silky shirt reached to her knees, and she couldn't remember putting it on. What had she been wearing before? She vaguely remembered walking around in a forest somewhere, naked, covered with dirt. Frolicking in the dry leaves.

A throbbing headache brought on more of that hum.

Emma clutched her head, thumped it against the wall. *Can't tell what's real.* Could have just locked herself into another cell. With a waterfall. If it was true.

Was it?

Look.

Emma looked at the walls. Not as bright as the other ones. She pressed her ear to them. No hum. Only in her mind.

"Emma?"

Soldier boy's voice made her jump. Good guy or bad guy? Curling her nails hard into her palms, she made herself open her mouth. "H-how does the water fall? In the waterfall?"

Silence.

No, don't disappear! "Soldier boy?" she called, eyes widening to better hear him out there.

"Voice activated," he said.

Emma swallowed down the lump in her throat, then turned to the waterfall. "Fall," she said. Nothing happened.

"Try *on.*"

"On?"

Water, wonderfully clean water, sprayed out of the tiled walls in a flat stream. Just like a real waterfall. Emma nearly cried for joy. She put a shaky hand under it, loving the way it caressed her skin. It was warm! She needed more. "Warmer?" she tried, and the temperature rose until the room was filled with steam.

Emma laughed, stripped out of the shirt, and ducked beneath the stream.

~

She was talking. To herself. About things that made no sense to John. But at least she was talking. And she'd laughed. *Hell of a sight better than the screaming, hair-tearing fit from earlier.*

"Amen to that."

John scowled. Now he was talking to himself. He stayed by the bathroom door, listening to Emma the whole time in case something set her off again. She'd locked herself in, but he could easily break the lock, if need be.

The door eventually opened on a thick cloud of steam. She'd been in there for a good hour and a half, and he'd almost dozed off on his feet. When the steam cleared a bit, Emma entered the room in that clingy nightgown, skin bright red all over as if she'd tried to scrub it off. Her hair was clean and dry, twisted into a knot at her nape.

She edged around him, watching him with wary blue eyes. He could have sworn she blushed, but it was hard to tell with her skin so raw. "What time is it?" she asked.

John checked the clock. "Almost five in the morning."

"Not what time is it. What *time* is it?"

"I don't follow."

Emma narrowed her eyes at him. "This is a cheat."

"What?"

She nodded as if she'd come to some sort of conclusion. Her hands fisted in her nightgown and she kept eyeing the door, checking to see if he noticed.

John sighed. "Are you hungry?"

She sucked in a breath and shook her head hard. "No, no, no, no, no more food!"

John held up his hands. "Okay, easy. You don't have to eat if you don't want to."

Emma tossed him a look that said she was still waiting for him to attack. She swayed toward the door, but her feet didn't move.

Hoping a show of trust would calm her, John went to the table. "If you don't mind, though, I'm starving."

He'd ordered simple chicken and fried potatoes, with a side of fruit salad. John figured they could both use a bit of comfort food right about now. There was soup for Emma, too.

Deliberately giving her his back, he set the small table for two, then took a seat by the window so he could pull the drapes aside a fraction to look out. Beyond that, he ignored her, letting her decide on her own.

For a while, she watched him eat, shifting her weight from foot to foot, wrinkling that nightgown beyond repair.

Just when he reached for his water, she asked, "Am I here?"

John turned to her. She looked so lost, standing there barefoot and half naked. What was she asking for? Proof of her existence? How could he possibly give her that? Instead of answering, he asked a question of his own. "Where else would you be?"

Emma nodded as if he'd spoken some sage words of wisdom.

"There are more clothes for you in that bag over there."

She dived for it immediately, pulling everything out until the bag's contents littered the floor around her. She pulled on socks first, then stripped off the nightgown in a hurry. Out of courtesy, John averted his gaze. And kept averting it every time it strayed back.

Letting her out of his sight, however, turned out to be a mistake. As soon as she had shoes on, Emma went straight for the door, and before John could stop her, she was out in the hallway, running for the elevators.

John cursed when she hit the call button and ran off again before the elevator got there. "Emma!"

She screamed, hands clasped over her ears, and rounded a corner toward the terrace. Each floor of the hotel was a separate, rotating unit with a gym, a pool, a fully equipped kitchen and dining room, and a massive terrace with a hover pad parking lot. Last night, the hotel had put on a big movie event, so mostly everyone had flocked to the entertainment wing. But if Emma managed to find people, they'd both be screwed.

From around the far corner, John heard her gasp so loudly, his heart skipped a beat. He ran faster, and turned left. Wearing tight jeans, and a half-tucked camisole, her hair mostly out of the bun, Emma stood frozen halfway down the hall in front of the elevator and the armed soldier stepping out of it. Army uniform. Crowd control, not a Shadow. John had counted ten of them in this hotel alone, and probably thousands more were out in the streets.

"Ma'am?" the soldier said, blank-faced.

John caught up in a hurry to cover for Emma's lack of answer. "Sorry, uh…" The soldier was a sergeant. Probably not a good idea to use it, though. "…man. We thought we had the floor to ourselves." He wrapped his arm around Emma, pulled her into his side. "We're newlyweds. You understand." He smiled in what he hoped was an irreverent smirk.

Emma reached out to poke the soldier. "Cheat?"

John caught her hand, then the other one when she tried again. "No. No cheating."

The soldier frowned. "What's wrong with her?"

Think fast. "One of her bridesmaids spiked her drink with Bliss at the reception." Where the hell had that lie come from? John didn't care. He ran with it. "It was a practical joke."

The soldier snorted. "Rich people."

Emma tugged on her hands, trying to free herself. When he didn't release her, she kicked the soldier in the shin.

"Ow!"

"No cheating," she mused, her eyes wide with wonder when she looked up at John and whispered, "He's real!"

Yeah, no shit. Real, and really pissed off. "I'll just take her back to our room now."

"Yeah, and keep her there!"

"He's really real."

John shushed her, quickly ushering her away before the soldier started asking questions.

When he had her safely back in the room, he locked and bolted the door. He had his back to her for only a second.

Emma grabbed a knife from the food tray and came at him, screaming murder.

"Jesus!" John grabbed the knife, wrenched it out of her hand, but Emma was operating on pure panic and survival instinct. She didn't care if she had a weapon or not; she just kept coming at him with fists and kicks, fighting like a madwoman who'd never had any training whatsoever. John caught her, lifted her off her feet. "Emma, calm down. Nobody's going to hurt you."

She tried to head-butt him.

"Listen to me. You need to calm down."

Emma kept fighting, flailing her feet, twisting in his grasp until she simply couldn't anymore. Exhaustion set in, leaving her limp in his arms, her head on his shoulder, breathing hard. When he finally set her down again, her knees buckled, and he had to walk her over to the bed so she could sit. Gasping for air, she blinked away her tears and looked around, utterly lost. "This is real."

"Yes," he said.

"Why?"

He didn't know how to answer.

"What do you want from me!" Emma fisted her hands in her hair, and he had to pry them loose so she wouldn't tear it out again. She couldn't manage more than a moan in protest.

"Remember the white room?"

She shook her head. "It was a dream."

"No, Emma, it wasn't."

Her chin wobbled. "Then this is."

"This is real, too."

A big tear trickled down her cheek. "A cheat. Trying to confuse me. Think I'll believe you if you ask nice. You think you can fool me, but you can't." A defiant gleam lit up her eyes, and she smiled savagely. "Couldn't before; can't now. You—can't—break—me."

And through her tears and her trepidation, John believed her. Emma wasn't just a fighter; she was a survivor. Had it been John in her place, he wasn't sure he would've ever made it out of that room. But little Emma had. Without any prep or conditioning, she'd come through, and instead of cowering, the girl driven half out of her mind looked him straight in the eye and said, "You can't break me. I won't let you."

When push came to shove, John realized, Emma would fight with everything she had to reclaim her life, even if that meant destroying everything and everyone who'd taken it from her. As the one who'd brought her to this, John would be first on that list. He placed her hands into her lap and backed away. "I don't want to break you, Emma."

Free of him, she crawled backwards over the bed to perch in the armchair where he'd slept, and hugged her knees to her chest. "Then why am I here?"

Because my unit betrayed my trust and made me into a monster. Because even at your most confused, you made more sense than any order I'd received. Because you've reminded me I still have a scrap of humanity left. You're the closest thing to a conscience I've ever had, and I couldn't let you die. But he couldn't say any of that. Not that she'd believe him, even if he could. "Would you rather be back there?" he asked instead.

Emma contemplated this for a moment, then slowly shook her head. Not exactly progress, but he'd take what he could get.

"Are you hungry?" Without waiting for an answer, John sat down to eat and left her to decide on her own. She said nothing, but five minutes later, she sat down on the edge of the bed. Two more, and she was pacing back and forth, eyeing the food on the table. She had to be starving.

John kept eating, minding his own business. He didn't look up when she cautiously perched on the chair opposite his own and watched the food disappear from his plate.

"What time is it?" Emma asked.

John checked the clock. "Five forty in the morning." He took a bite of chicken.

Emma pinched her lower lip, worried it with her nails, frowning down at the table.

Finishing his plate, John pushed it away, and took a strawberry from the fruit bowl. The one closest to her. She almost didn't flinch. A delayed reaction, as if she'd forgotten to be afraid of him for just a second. To compensate, she moved her chair farther back from the table.

"What time is it?"

"Five forty-two."

Emma reached for a piece of fruit, but hesitated and pulled back. Then her hand shot out, snagged a strawberry, and she held it so close to her face, her eyes crossed to look at it. "How does it work?"

"Like this," John said, biting into the one still in his hand. It was sweet and sour at the same time, the way only a strawberry could be. These were the expensive kind, grown instead of manufactured. Only the best for patrons of the Ambassador Lounge. It would cost a pretty penny, too. Hopefully, by the time the guy whose name and account John had used realized something wasn't right with his expenses, they'd be long gone.

Emma placed the strawberry back into the bowl.

"Something wrong?"

"It was… incongruent."

"Try something else, then."

Instead, she pulled her feet up and hugged her knees to her chest, laid her cheek on them and closed her eyes.

"You really should eat something before we leave."

Her head shot up. "Leave? Outside?"

John nodded.

Emma blinked, then began shoveling food into her mouth. Anything she could reach and as much as she could fit into the hollow of her cheeks. She couldn't even chew it all, but she kept going, checking to see if he was watching. In seconds, she'd emptied her plate, every bit of food stuffed into her mouth, and she was starting to turn green.

John sighed. It was going to be a long trip.

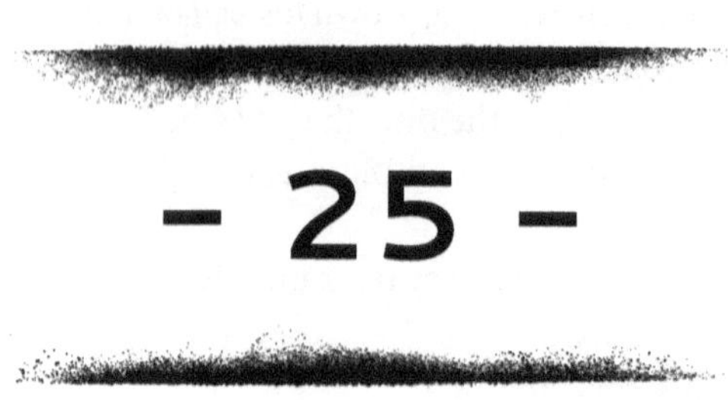

– 25 –

She threw up the second they stepped foot outside the room. Soldier boy didn't even pause, just handed her a paper napkin and a bottle of water. Emma rinsed out her mouth, spitting onto the hallway's plush rug as they went to the elevator, where he gave her something else. A small packet of pellets, which she eyed with more than a little suspicion. Just because she was using him to get out of here, didn't mean she trusted him. Then again, she couldn't trust herself, either, so where did that leave her? *Lost in the woods without a rope.*

"They're supplements," he explained. "Should have started you off easy. You haven't exactly been eating this last week."

Her hands shook as she emptied the packet into her palm and asked quietly, "What time is it?" Not what she'd meant to ask, but she couldn't put into words what she really wanted to know. Rather than watch his face for signs of deceit, Emma picked out a pellet and stuffed it into her mouth, chewing needlessly.

"It's six in the morning. February fourteenth. Valentine's Day."

So many days gone…

Wait. Valentine's Day? "Are people going to die?"

Soldier boy looked at her. "Okay, you lost me on that one."

"Valentine's Day," she said.

"Yeah…?"

"It's tradition for people to die. A lot."

He stared at her. Emma figured that meant the piece of memory was wrong. She ducked her head and ate another pellet.

The moment the elevator doors opened, a sea of noise assaulted her. Emma gasped and dropped the rest of her pellets, slapping her hands over her ears. It did nothing. "Too loud!"

"Emma?"

"Too loud!" She had to yell to hear herself. "*Too loud!*"

—the hell is my mouthwash? You left it, didn't you?—

—can't believe I have to get up at the ass-crack of dawn for this shit—

—Twinkle, twinkle little star, your "art" makes me sick by far—

It hurt! *Stop it, please stop!*

—I wonder if his other wife knows…—

—She has no idea how stupid she is—

—Five star service, my fat hairy ass…—

So many voices, all shouting at her, like poisoned needles all stabbing into her brain from every direction, all at the same time. Her eyes teared up again and now she couldn't see, either.

Soldier boy dropped their bags and covered her hands with his own, scrutinizing her as if checking for damage. "What do you hear?"

—Half an hour before Hong Kong wakes up. No way I can do this in time—

—Dad! The limo's here!—

—I can't believe this is my first day as Mrs. Kendall—

She heard him perfectly over the din. How could that be? Why did he act like he couldn't hear any of it? "Voices," she said, or thought she did. "So many. I can't—"

—Is she going to wake me up every morning?—

"Emma, look at me. Focus on my eyes." He brushed away her tears so she could see. His eyes were gray, steady. "There's nobody here."

—I want a divorce. Honey, we need to talk. No, that won't do. Matt, I think we should see other people—

"No, but there is!"

—Shit, I'm late, I'm late, I'm late. Very important fucking date!—

"Listen to what I'm saying."

—Are you even listening to me?—

"The voices are in your head."

—Shut your fucking mouth!—

Emma cried out a wailing, "*Nooo!*" She couldn't lose it now. They were almost outside! She had to see outside; they said there was a sky.

"Emma, they're thoughts. You're a telepath. You're hearing thoughts."

Telepath. The word echoed through her brain until all the voices repeated it back to her. Telepath. Mind reader. The voices were in her head, but she wasn't making them up.

—*Shush,*— she told them.

And just like that, they were gone. Shields snapped into place like puzzle pieces finally finding where they belonged. Silence. But not absolute. Emma slowly pulled her hands away from her ears, leaving soldier boy's cupping her face.

"Can you still hear them?"

Her ears were fine; no underwater muffle. His voice rang loud and clear. "Yes," she whispered, and heard herself perfectly. "But I choose not to."

He looked relieved.

Am I that far gone? She didn't know whom she was asking.

It's his fault, came the answer.

Emma clamped down on her rising well of fury. Not yet, she soothed. Not the right time. She'd watch and be cautious, be ready for when the hawk took flight again, because he would. This was a cheat, no matter what he'd said, and Emma would not be tricked. Not by him, and not by the senator man.

And when he turned on her—because he would—Emma would be waiting for it. This time, *she* would win.

The elevator doors tried to close, but couldn't. Soldier boy picked up their bags in one hand, grasped her elbow with the other, and led her through a different floor to a moving outside stable of transports. The warm breeze stirred her hair, and Emma blinked, squinting up. No sky, only more blackness. But then she looked out sideways, and there, so far away it seemed like a dream, off in the distance some-where, she saw light. Not sunrise, but almost.

Her feet veered toward it, but soldier boy pulled her up short, tugged her another way to a bright pink transport with yellow stars along its sides and a sparkling little crown on the roof. "Princess," she whispered, tracing the twinkling stars. "Lady of the rising sun."

Soldier boy fiddled with the digital lock until the doors opened, then ushered her in. No driver/passenger side, only plush yellow seats all around; no console, only a round tree stump in the middle. "Soldier boy?"

"My name is John," he said, tossing the bags into the back and climbing in after her.

John. Yes. She remembered now. "John?"

"Yes, Emma?"

Her body sank into the plush yellow seat, cushioning her in softness and warmth. She felt swaddled and safe, and so very tired. "Are we stealing?"

"Borrowing," he replied after he'd pried the tree stump open to tinker with something inside. "We're just going for a quick ride, is all."

"Okay." Emma closed her eyes and fell asleep.

~

John had to hardwire the destination into the secondary nav system. By the time he'd finished, Emma was out. He let the transport do its thing, and closed his eyes to catch a few winks himself. Unfortunately, the ride was short, and they stopped just as he was really falling asleep. John forced his eyes open and stepped out to survey the parking lot full of decent-looking vehicles. He chose one at random and digitally pried it open. Only after he'd set everything up for another short trip did he go back for Emma, who didn't stir when he picked her up and transferred her into the other vehicle. He put their bags into the storage space of the inconspicuous dark gray model he'd chosen, then sent the ghastly pink monstrosity back to the hotel and settled in for the second leg.

He did this five times, until the streets had begun to fill too much for him to attempt it. Once he deemed it no longer safe, John hailed a taxi and relaxed for a while as it drove them around the city on a scenic tour to the shuttleport.

But when they got there, John tensed and almost told the automated system to keep going.

A line of soldiers guarded the giant, glass-domed terminal, all standing two lengths apart, which allowed just enough room for people to pass between them, one by one. The stone-faced military men ignored the grumpy passengers, but kept a sharp eye out for trouble. They wouldn't have been guarding ways on and off the planet unless they expected a large-scale riot. High time John got Emma out of here.

If he could even get them through that defensive line.

"Seven credits," the taxi system said, offering options for method of payment. John used an old trick he'd learned and swished his fingers all over the screen to confuse it into thinking payment had been rendered and accepted. THANK YOU, AND HAVE A NICE DAY flashed across the screen, and the door opened, waiting for them to get out.

"Emma," John said, shaking her shoulder. "Wake up."

She frowned and turned her face into his shoulder to hide. Had she just growled?

He shook her harder. They couldn't be seen dawdling. "Come on, girl, we have to get out of here."

Grumbling, Emma raised her head to glare at him through one eye. The other was still closed. "I am not a morning person."

"Noted. Now come on."

He grabbed their bags and led her across the street. *Stay calm. Glare, but not too long.* Fifteen feet away. Ten feet. Five.

Emma took John's hand, moving up to his side, then slammed into one soldier when they passed by, which visibly pissed him off. "Sorry," she called back with a breezy smile.

John squeezed her hand hard to shut her up.

Inside, the glass dome fractured light into a myriad of rainbows. Columns draped in holoveils changed the scenery every few minutes. At the moment, they were covered in tropical vines. In the next instant, the vines melted into a waterfall. The floor had built-in panels programmed to match the columns, and display multi-colored footprints to guide lost passengers to their destinations, eliminating the need for cumbersome signs and directionals. Everything was meant to soothe and calm tired passengers, and it worked for the most part. People queued up in orderly lines depending on where they needed to go, with no fights, no arguments, no difficulties.

For all the muscle outside, very few guards roamed the inside of the port itself. Good. But they still needed to keep a low profile. John picked out an inconspicuous console and hacked the courtesy com to book them on the first available flight out. It would be a close call; they only had a few minutes to make it to the boarding area. "We may have to run it. Will you be okay with that?"

Emma hummed a noncommittal answer, dozing off on her feet next to him.

Cursing, he shook her awake again. "Look at me," he ordered.

She slapped him—a pathetic, limp-wristed slap that only served to irritate him.

"What the—"

"Be nice," she said, eyes darting left to the wall and the security feed strip.

John gritted his teeth so hard he felt a jaw muscle twitch, but he drew in a deep breath and got himself under control. Because she was right.

"Do we have the tickets?" she asked.

"Yes, dear." He forced a smile for whomever might be watching. Their passes doubled as IDs issued to Andrew and Fiona Bennington. Hopefully no one would start asking questions at the security checkpoint.

When he showed her, Emma snatched hers, read it, and then nodded to herself. "Then what are we waiting for?" she asked, nose in the air. "We're late, as is. Be a love and get the bags, 'kay?" With a patronizing pat on John's cheek, Emma turned on her heel and sauntered off, leaving him behind to gape after her.

John took up the bags and followed, stalking her step. When they passed one of the many buffets lining the terminal, he heard the same arch tone Emma had used, coming from someone else. John slowed, then did a double take at the older couple seated at the bar: a browbeaten man hunched next to his wife, who appeared incapable of shutting her trap.

"…don't know why you insist on doing things your way. You know I am always right. Aren't I always right? And I told you not to go to that casino, but you went anyway. And what happened? Huh? That's right. You lost. Abysmally. My God, Andrew, how am I supposed to look *my mother* in the eye and tell her my husband lost half of my inheritance? And don't tell me we're still filthy rich anyway. That is not the point—oh no, I ordered a whiskey sour. Be a love and fix it for me, 'kay? Now where was I…?"

John tried not to stare at the woman, but he couldn't help himself. The woman stood out like a holoposter, decked out as she was in layers and layers of gold—gold blouse, gold shoes, gold jewelry. Even her graying hair was threaded with gold ribbons. And sweet God, that voice! When it went high-pitched, he could almost hear dogs howling outside.

"An-*dy!*" Emma screeched from the security checkpoint. He'd fallen behind, and she stood tapping her foot at him. Exactly how the real Fiona Bennington tapped hers while she waited for her drink. When Emma gave an imperial wave to hurry him up, John shook himself and joined her. Emma stayed in character the entire time the security officer read through their passes, incessantly chattering at him until the poor man had had enough and rushed them through so they wouldn't miss their flight. From there, it was a straight shot to their shuttle. They made it just in time, the last to board.

As soon as the shuttle doors closed, Emma sagged as if she'd had the wind knocked out of her. "Good God, that woman is a pain in the head."

John narrowed his eyes. "Who are you right now?"

She smiled up at him and said, "Hi!"

"Emma?"

"Soldier boy?"

"Where are you?"

She shrugged. "Wherever the wind takes me." Then she frowned. "Why do you ask?"

For a second there, she'd almost sounded lucid. But looking into her eyes now, John saw no trace of the coherence she'd shown a minute ago, which sent a pang of disappointment through his chest.

Emma sighed. "I'm tired."

Yeah, you and me both. "Come on, we're this way."

John navigated Emma into the window seat, while he took the aisle. The row was meant for a married couple; it was shaped like a love seat that could be adjusted into a full-sized bed with a half canopy for privacy. Great. He was exhausted, and Emma fell asleep well before they'd taken off. The minute the seat activated, John stretched it out and closed his eyes.

They shot wide open again when Emma rolled onto him in her sleep, laying her cheek against his chest and curling up as close as she could physically get without crawling into his lap. He stared at her, baffled by this. Every time he'd touched her today, she'd flinched. Now, she clutched him like a security blanket.

John nudged her to get her off him. She didn't move. He twisted to dislodge her and roll her back onto her side. Emma just frowned in her sleep and held on tighter. Profoundly uncomfortable, John shook her shoulder to wake her.

The woman *shushed* him, settling herself more comfortably against his side, one leg flung over his, her knee a scant inch from his crotch.

Exhausted and at a loss, John gave up trying to make sense of Emma. She'd probably wake up and scream her head off again, thinking *he'd* made her do it, but right now, John was too tired to care. Settling his arm around her—because she really gave him no other choice—he closed his eyes again and slept.

When he woke up, she was sitting sideways next to him, watching him with that lost look in her eyes. "What time is it?"

He was beginning to understand the question was more of a comfort thing to her. "I don't know," he said, rubbing his face. "We're in flux." The console screen indicated they were close to landing. He'd slept through the entire seventeen-hour flight. John had never slept so long in a single stretch in his entire life. "Looks like we'll be landing soon."

The answer seemed to satisfy her, and she laid back down. A moment later, she eased closer. Then again. He didn't move when she tentatively poked his side. Not even when she brought her ear to his chest. "Seashell," she whispered.

"Comfy?"

"Yes," she said quickly. "I can hear the ocean."

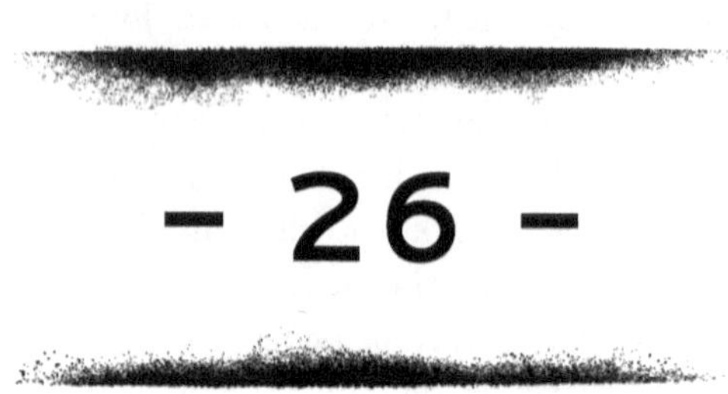

– 26 –

Emma smiled at the rumble of his surprised chuckle. Like thunder over the waves. He was awake. She was here. And they were landing.

She hadn't been here before. While he'd slept, she'd been gone—dreamcoasting. Hours and hours gone, time in which she'd tasted a hundred sanities, all making perfect sense to her, individually. All of those people had such solid anchors, blissfully unaware of how easily they could be cut. Emma knew. Her own had been severed in only a few days. But she'd expected scissors, not a flame.

And then she'd woken up, and soldier boy had been asleep next to her, and she'd almost panicked. She hated him, but he tethered her. Nothing to him, but he was *there*. Her mind latched onto his shiny head like a magnet. If he wasn't awake, she couldn't see his eyes. And if his eyes were gone, he didn't exist, and so neither did she.

"Sleep well?"

"I did," he replied.

"Good. But no more."

"No more sleep?"

She almost told him about the tether, but no. Clingy birds were bad enough; clingy and neurotic would be too much to handle. Instead, she replied, "Sleep can get you killed."

The bed transformed on its own, folding up into a seat, and soldier boy's arm came around to steady her. *Holding up a wobbly wall.* Emma ended up half in his lap, but she didn't care. The ocean calmed her. His hand awkwardly petted her hair to soothe her as the shuttle burned and shuddered through the atmo-entry, and for a little while she was stable. She could think.

I am Emma Calen. I have a brother, Jeremy. He's married to a cat.

Was that right?

No.

Yes. Hailey was a cat. Haileycat. *Hellcat.* She saw her now: pale, with bright white hair and black claws that hardly ever dulled. She was a pain in the ass. Vicious when provoked.

She makes Jeremy happy.

Hellcat got to live.

I am Emma Calen. Born on Earth. I had parents. They died because they were like me. The memory came back; she shouldn't have it. So long ago. She hadn't been real back then; just a little thing. A pixie with huge eyes that saw too much. *They died because of us, Jeremy and me. Because they wouldn't give us up.* Emma shivered, disliking that thought—a lot. *They wouldn't let us be poisoned, and tortured, and killed, so they were taken in our stead.* The memory didn't hurt much anymore. It was an old phantom ache in her soul. She hadn't really known them, but she had. From the moment her mind awakened in her mother's womb, she'd loved her. From the moment her father spoke her name, she'd adored him. She loved Jeremy, too. But he didn't want to play brother and sister anymore.

Another shiver. They'd all left her.

"Emma?"

Soldier boy hadn't. His name was John. Emma blinked away the meddlesome haze. Her hand was crushing his shirt, and he rubbed her knuckles to coax her to let go. She did, snatching her hand back. *You can't have it,* she thought, remembering how much he'd already taken from her. Too much. More than everything.

Emma ducked out from under his arm and moved as close to the window as she could, pressing her nose against it to see outside. Once the fire had cleared, she saw an unending field of buildings. They grew peoples there. Sometimes there was a harvest, but never enough. Peoples kept growing, and falling, and rotting. There was no one to pick them.

The shuttle descended until the window became useless. Emma felt the touchdown. Didn't hear anything. Shields back up. Impenetrable. Nothing in, nothing out. How long could that hold?

Until I fall asleep again.

That was a scary thought. Emma sneaked a quick peek at soldier boy. He was a mess; anger, and fear, and hate all rolled into one. She couldn't trust him for one instant.

She had no other choice.

It was him, and it was her, and the rest of the world was poison. This one, at least, she knew. It only hurt to look at him.

As soon as the shuttle opened, Emma raced for the door. Soldier—John—caught her hand and Emma couldn't get free but she kept pulling, dragging him to go faster. She wanted out. John went along into the 'port, but then stopped and froze, and she couldn't budge him any farther. She tried. Put her whole weight behind it. Nothing.

He wasn't even paying attention, too busy typing on a screen, and it took *forever*. Must have made him very angry, too, because he cursed at the numbers.

"All flights are booked, and there isn't another one until tomorrow afternoon."

"Bad?"

"Yes, very bad."

"Why because?"

"Because it's not safe to stay here."

A group of soldiers marched by, and John turned his back, pulled her into the shadows. *Not safe.* Riots, she remembered. So many angry people shouting, hurting each other, because they couldn't strike out against the ones who hurt them.

"Do you trust me?" he whispered.

"No." Obviously.

John looked taken aback, but recovered quickly. "There will be more of those soldiers outside. If they stop us for any reason, the Shadows will know. They will find us. Understand?"

She frowned. "You're one of them."

His mouth twisted. "Not anymore."

Emma tilted her head to read his eyes. Nothing but mirrors she didn't want to look into. "Cheat?" She wasn't sure anymore.

He shook his head.

She scowled. "Would you tell me if it was?"

John rolled his eyes. "We can argue in circles all day if you want, just not now, okay? We need to get out of here. We have to hide. Come on."

Outside, the buildings were so tall, even when she tipped her head back all the way, she still couldn't see their tops. John talked, a lot more than before. Emma tried to pay attention, but his voice made more sense than the individual words. Something about hounds and flushing.

And there were the peoples! So shiny and bright, she had to squint at them. Pink, and green, and blue, and purple—oh, that one was *prettyyyy*. "Want." She reached out to a purple people, but John snatched her hand back.

"Look at me," he ordered.

Emma flinched. A flash of the riot, angry hands striking out against her, cold snow against her back, white walls, that godawful hum. She drowned in it, ears ringing and vision hazing over. On the verge of hyperventilating, Emma reached out and touched the hard wall of a chest. Her hands curled into the fabric covering it, held on for dear life as the maelstrom tossed her around inside her own mind.

Someone called her name from so far away; it was nothing but a hum. Emma latched on to it, followed it out, pushing back everything that didn't belong. White gone. Snow melted. People stepped away, turned from her, continued on to wherever they'd been going before they'd morphed into monsters.

Emma blinked it all back, breathing deeply to calm her heart, because she had to. This was a different place. Different time. And she was a very different person.

Terrified of getting lost again, she scanned the surroundings for something familiar.

She found *him*.

His hands were holding her; *his* eyes were frowning at her, angry and scared, searching for her when she thought she was right there. *Found you. I'm here.* Giddy with relief, she smiled brightly. "Soldier boy! Missed you, fella." She threw her arms around him, jumped up a little to kiss his cheek.

When she'd settled back onto her heels, he stared at her, his arms around her both loose and tense at the same time, as if he couldn't decide whether to hug her or push her away.

Slowly, his frown gave way, and when it finally did, his mouth stretched into a wry, crooked smile. Emma's heart gave an extra thump. He got handsomerer when he smiled! "Would love to know what's going on in your head right now, girl," he said, deep voice going all warm and rumbly, making Emma shiver a little.

His arms closed around her in a tentative embrace, like those she saw other couples doing. But theirs were better. They didn't hesitate; they caught each other tight, and kissed and kissed. Held on as if they'd never let go. *Want...*

Emma raised on tiptoe and pulled him down so she could reach. His lips were so warm, not like stone at all, and her thoughts settled, centered on just this—the feel of him, his familiar scent of winter and steel. She found herself in the press of his mouth against hers, and she didn't want to let go.

John tensed in surprise, so she kissed him slow. No hurry. Her past was gone; her mind cleared. In that moment, Emma knew exactly who she was, where she was, how she got there, and why. She knew what she was doing and with whom, which meant this had to be a dream, and she could choose when not to wake up.

"Emma," he said against her lips. His hand came up to her face, and she could feel him pulling away.

Not yet!

She licked between his parted lips, thrilling at his groan. His fingers tangled in her hair, arm clutching her, lifting her off her feet. And then he *really* kissed her—a hard, desperate gallows kiss that made her eyes sting with tears. Because she knew this wasn't a dream. It was wrong, and it could never happen again. A few moments of sanity stolen from the universe. But how sane could she be, kissing the enemy? Did it matter?

Don't let go, she thought desperately, the first coherent thought she'd had in what she now knew to have been weeks. *Don't let me fall apart again. Need this. Want...*

Hard fingers dug into her hip; fist tightened in her hair until she felt strands snap. She didn't care. Snapped a few of John's herself, and he didn't seem to notice as he slanted his mouth over hers, licked at her tongue as if he couldn't get enough.

Want.

But—"Can't." She broke from the kiss and pressed her forehead to John's. He was still holding her up, breathing hard, eyes squeezed shut.

"God, Emma, what are you doing to me?"

Emma followed the rise and fall of his Adam's apple as he swallowed, pulled her chin back when he sought her lips again.

He should know, but he didn't. Because he was soldier boy—utterly and completely unreachable. He'd done this to her, condemned her to this broken place, and now he was the only thing holding everything together.

At her retreat, John's eyes opened—burning, hungry, confused. Conflicted, just like her. For a moment, he searched her gaze, then his face shuttered; John had turned back into soldier boy. He set her down slowly, let go until only his hand rested on her hip. And with that loss of contact, Emma's thoughts slipped sideways.

Feelings jumbled, ideas flitted away, memories confused together until she forgot. Soldier boy stared as if waiting for an answer to something. Had he asked a question? Oh, yes. He wanted to know what she was thinking. She wanted to show him, but remembered why that wouldn't work. With a sad sigh, Emma traced a finger down the center of his forehead to his nose. "Shiny head. Won't take any messages." Probably a bad idea anyway. One of them should be comprehensible.

Soldier boy cupped her jaw, ran his thumb over her lower lip. "Are you all right?"

Emma frowned, puzzled. Had she said something crazy again?

"Please, talk to me."

He looked so worried. Emma thought hard to say something right. "Food?"

John sighed and gave her another packet of pellets. Emma made a face, but dutifully ate the whole thing while he watched. *Wouldn't drop them twice,* she wanted to tell him, but the wicked pellets foamed on her tongue, forcing her to keep her mouth shut.

While she ate, he put dark glasses on her nose, a big hat on her head, then took her hand again, and they walked.

And walked.

And walked some more.

For a loooong while.

And then, she lost time.

~

She'd kissed him.

John couldn't wrap his mind around it. Out of the blue, she'd just grabbed on and kissed him. And *Jesus Christ*, what the hell was he supposed to do with that?

He'd had a willing, eager Emma in his arms, sucking his tongue, clutching him like her last link to sanity, and then she'd pulled away, and he'd watched her fade.

She's broken, John reminded himself to get his bearings. *Because I broke her.*

A transport almost ran them over when he slowed in the middle of the street. The blare of a horn shocked John into the present, and he couldn't believe he'd just walked three blocks, completely oblivious to the army patrols stationed at every corner. An amateur sniper could have picked them off and he wouldn't have even noticed.

Mentally kicking his own ass, John pulled Emma along faster, eyes sharp for trouble. Something must have happened here or the army wouldn't have been brought in. Rebellious call phrases had been spray-painted on the buildings, and every time the chemical wash cleaned them off, an automated mechanism sprayed them right back on again. Garbage and broken glass littered the ground. Probably remnants of a rally or something.

More importantly, people weren't the ignorant mob of sheep he was used to getting lost in. This crowd was very much aware; they saw the soldiers and looked at each other, no doubt wondering who was the freak among them, who'd throw the first stone. They were twitchy and scared, and it wouldn't take much to incite them into a frenzy. John kept to the less-crowded areas where he could see a clear path of escape, just in case.

It wasn't feasible to procure a transport, and "borrowing" one was out of the question. That left their feet. John had no trouble walking the rest of the day, or longer. But Emma would need to rest soon. She looked too pale in the bright sun, her lips dry, but she trudged along without complaint, a trooper all the way. She'd grown quiet, a sure sign she was tiring. The silence felt awkward.

"How are you doing?"

"Shiny," she mumbled. Whatever that meant.

When she didn't say anything else, didn't seem in any way inclined to discuss what had happened, John rolled his shoulder uncomfortably and stopped trying to make her talk. He checked on her every hour, made her eat more supplements to boost her strength, but beyond that, he didn't let himself dwell on her too much. It was enough of a distraction that every once in a while, Emma squeezed his hand, as if checking to make sure he was still there.

Then, in the middle of an intersection, she dragged one step out longer than the previous. She kept going, but her hand in his went completely limp. As soon as they'd crossed, John stopped and pulled her glasses down to check her eyes. Pupils dilated, unfocused.

"Emma?"

Nothing.

He jarred her shoulder.

No response.

The soldier across the street was looking at them.

John gritted his teeth and, as nonchalantly as he could, wrapped his arm around her, nudging her to keep going. "Talk to me. Where are you?"

No answer.

"Emma." He squeezed her shoulder, curled his fingers into her joint hard enough to cause pain.

No reaction.

Emma followed physical cues, walked where he steered her, but her mind was just... gone.

It made John edgy enough to stop at the first inn he saw and check them in under a different false name. Inside their room, he locked the door and ordered food, sat Emma down onto the bed and checked her eyes again. "Emma, listen to me. I need you to wake up now. Can you do that? Can you look at me?"

No response.

He shook her, slapped her, shook her again, but she'd gone catatonic. Having run out of options, and getting desperate to have her back, John pressed his mouth to hers… and shuddered. It was like kissing a corpse. "Goddammit, Emma, wake up! Kiss me back, slap me, do something!"

She didn't.

Pressing his cheek to hers, he whispered at her ear, "Please."

But like a broken doll, Emma just sat there, eyelids at half-mast, staring blankly into space. And the longer it continued, the more it scared him. The once fearless Shadow Hawk who'd faced his own death on a regular basis was terrified. Emma needed a hospital, but the second she stepped foot in one, she'd be dead.

I don't know what to do.

Emma could be dying before his eyes, and he had no idea what to do.

Wake up!

When the food arrived, John left her long enough to set it out on the table. He had no appetite for it, but maybe the aroma would rouse her. She had to be starving. "It'll be here when you're ready," he told her, foolishly hoping she'd just blink awake and say, "Okay, I'll be right there."

When she didn't, John resigned himself to waiting for her to come back on her own. He went to the one window they had and stood watch, compulsively looking at her every few minutes in case there was any change.

The senator claimed telepaths made a full recovery almost immediately after release. John had no way to verify that; he'd never spent any time with the telepath subjects—*captives*—after their release. One had died before getting out, and none of them had ever had as violent a reaction as Emma.

And she wasn't getting better. She talked, and even looked at things, as if relearning everything. By the different inflections she used, John understood what she wanted to know whenever she asked what time it was. And when she couldn't remember what something was, or how it worked, her mind seemed to grasp on to metaphors. Waterfalls and seashells. He'd kept the lights off in the transports because every time he'd left them on, she'd gotten twitchy in her sleep. Even now he kept the shades drawn, hoping it would calm her back to consciousness.

I don't know what I'm doing. For all he knew, he could be making everything worse by running like this. What did he know about how telepaths functioned? Only that their abilities were essential to them, and Emma's had been subjugated so long, it might have left permanent damage. And that seizure hadn't helped, either.

A warrior thinks for himself.

If John was a telepath, what would he be thinking now? He liked his solitude, but Emma was used to people constantly inside her head, even if only as whispers. She craved interaction now, that much he knew. Unable to see into his mind, she took what she could get. Conversation. Contact. *That kiss.* John made a note to talk to her more.

What would he do if she didn't recover?

They were already being tracked. John could feel it. Invisible eyes watched him from a distance, snaking ever closer. He knew their strategies like the back of his hand. The second the base had reopened, it would have gone into action. They'd have already tracked the first transport, reviewed its log, and sent Hounds to every location where John had stopped for longer than sixty seconds.

By now, the Hounds and Hawks on their trail could very well be in the city, but probably relying on technology more than their eyes and ears. This particular city had a population of close to three million. If they just laid low for a while, John and Emma might possibly get lost or simply overlooked. But for that to happen, they'd need to disappear completely—no hotels, no purchases, no transports, and no contact with anyone. Every single transaction would raise a red flag.

Hounds didn't worry him. He'd see them coming from miles away. But the Hawks…

There was a contingency every Shadow trained for. Order 23257-Romeo-13.

"Two three two five seven Romeo thirteen," Emma echoed from behind him.

John turned away from the window to stare at her. *Impossible.*

"Two three two five seven Romeo thirteen," she said again, blinking rapidly. "No code names. Numbers confuse and disorient."

Exactly right. "Emma?" He crouched before her, watching her eyes shift back and forth as if she was dreaming.

"Objective: locate and recover target in deep cover."

Meant for Shadows gone AWOL. Perfect for teaching soldiers obedience by showing them countermeasures were already in place for every plan of desertion. "Emma, are you… Can you read my mind right now?"

"No," she said, nodding to the window. "But I can read theirs."

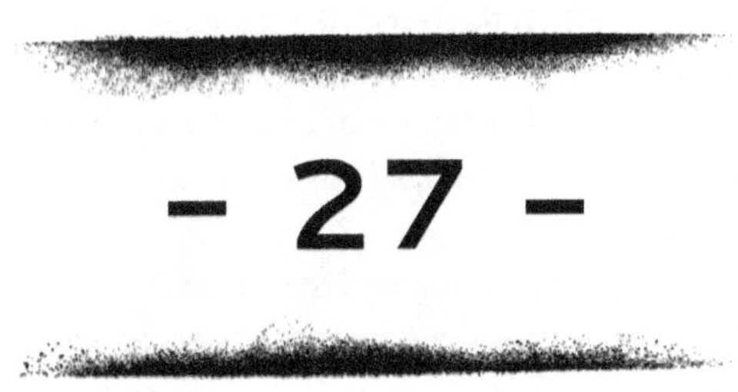

John shot back to the window, keeping carefully out of sight as he looked for Shadows. He was a sitting duck, and he wasn't even armed.

"*Spread out,*" Emma said, making her voice deep. Emulating someone? Could she actually hear the Shadows? "*I want eyes and ears in a five-block radius. — Copy that. Hounds moving out. — Hawks, report.*"

John looked at Emma, who stared straight ahead, watching something other than the room.

"Two three two five seven Romeo thirteen." Emma shook her head, then raised her worried eyes to him. "What time is it?"

"Time to get out of here," he said, snatching up the bags.

"*They'll be coming out of the east exit, below street level. — Copy that, circle around, cover the roof entrance.*"

John swore.

"*We can take them with snipers. — Morons, shut up! They can hear everything we're saying. Initiate com silence.*" Emma smiled grimly. "*Yeah, you just try and hide from me, bitches. — Shit. She's a telepath. — Don't think, that's an order!*" She laughed.

"We have to go now." He took her hand, but she pulled him up short.

"*John. I know you can hear me, son.*"

John dropped the bags and crouched in front of Emma. "Emma, I want you to shut them out. Can you do that?"

"*You can still rectify the situation.*"

Hearing the sergeant major's words come out of Emma's mouth

gave him chills. "Shut them out, Emma. Don't listen."

"Have to," she whispered. "Need to. Or die. — *If you turn yourself in now, I can guarantee you leniency. We have obviously underestimated the subject. Standard measures of containment were insufficient. Nobody is blaming you, Hawk. Help us secure the subject, and we can put this behind us.*"

"Look at me. Can you tell me where they are?"

"Three on the roof across the street. — *Snipers in position. Clear line of sight. — Hold fire.* — Two street level, civilian clothing. — *Standing by.* — Black boots. Yours were black, too." Emma traced his brow lightly with her fingertips, and for a moment, her eyes were completely clear, filled with so much regret he didn't know what to do. "Should have known you weren't one of us." Then she squeezed her eyes shut and it was gone as the sergeant major took over. "*Just give us a signal. All we need is a nod and we can take it from there. I know she's controlling you right now, but she's unstable. You're a Hawk, soldier! Act like it.*" Emma blinked rapidly, trying to get back to herself. "Soldier boy?"

Anger rose like a roll of thunder from his chest and when she touched him there, John realized he'd made a physical sound. The sergeant major knew exactly what Emma could do, and he was using her to orchestrate her own capture. Had she been at her full potential, he never would have gotten through. Either he was taking a shot in the dark, or he knew Emma's condition after the white room.

The sergeant major never shot from the hip.

They'd lied to him.

Emma couldn't read John's mind, but whatever she'd misread in his expression made her eyes go wide and teary. "Don't take me back there," she whispered. "Please, please don't. Please, soldier boy, I'll be good. I promise."

John cupped her nape, pressed his forehead to hers. "You tell him this for me." And then he whispered into her ear something that would make the sergeant major's head explode.

She breathed in awe. "Oh, we're in trouble now."

John snatched a steak knife from the food cart. Feeble, but he didn't plan to use it. It had just occurred to him that he had the most effective weapon of all right in his grasp.

He had Emma.

She clutched his hand when he led her out of the room, checking the hallway left and right. "Civilians coming in now. Snipers at the ready," she told him. "John, they'll shoot to kill."

John filed that information away. "Elevator or stairs?"

"Stairs. Down."

Stairs it is. Nice that this hotel actually had a staircase. Most around here were too tall and used emergency pods instead for faster evac. "You're sounding lucid."

"I think… I think I am. For now, anyway."

John squeezed her hand. *Better not waste it.*

They went down ten flights of stairs, then paused while Emma gave him an update. The civilians had split up: one kept an eye out in the lobby, the other checked the elevators. They couldn't wait any longer. Five more flights and they'd be at street level.

"I need a gun," John muttered.

Emma let go of his hand and opened the door.

He caught her. "What the hell are you doing?"

She looked him right in the eye and said, "Stay."

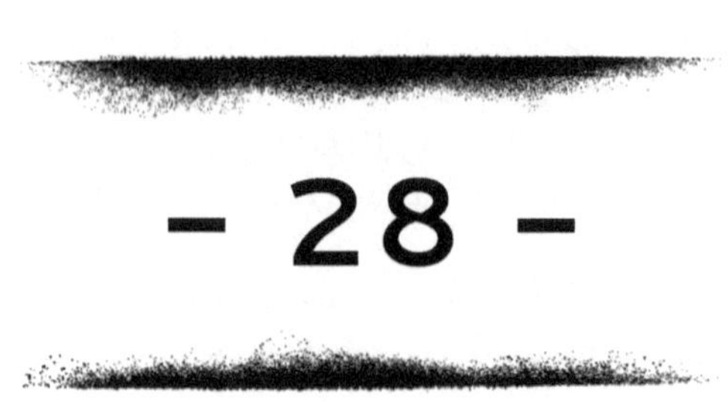

– 28 –

For two weeks, Travis had watched the Shadow base for any sign of Emma. MacMurphy had relayed a message from her brother that she was being kept inside some kind of artificial shield. Had to have been; Travis hadn't felt a trace of her during that whole time.

Until she'd suddenly flared with a telepathic shock wave that had almost knocked him on his ass. By the time his mind had cleared, she'd been gone again and the base had been rendered… incapacitated.

Thank God for Lucia and Rafe. Neither had been affected, so they'd followed her into the city and to the shuttleport the next day, tracking her by sight, because her mind's signature had become unrecognizable. And they'd kept their distance, afraid their sudden appearance would send her into a mental tailspin.

None of them knew what had happened to Emma, or how she'd gotten herself out, but that wasn't their main concern. Right now, they just needed to make sure she was okay. Having missed her shuttle, they'd called MacMurphy, who'd immediately commissioned a private one to take Travis, Lucia, and Rafe after Emma. They'd only lagged behind an hour and a half.

So close to retrieving her…

And then the Shadows had caught up.

They were everywhere now—on the roof, in the streets, hiding in plain sight. But they couldn't hide their minds.

—*Do you have them?*—

—I have six of them,— Lucia replied.

—I have the rest,— Rafe added. *—The Shadows aren't going any-where.—*

Travis linked up with Emma and followed the familiar trail of their connection to a completely unfamiliar mind with a consciousness in such disarray, she wasn't even aware of his presence. He took hold of her thoughts, honed them in on her mad dash out of the hotel room, kept her focused on her escape, which took a lot more effort than he'd expected. Something wasn't right; her thought process was a jumble of past and present, and she couldn't seem to get a grasp on what was real and what wasn't.

She wasn't alone, either, but, try as he might, Travis couldn't get a read on the man with her. He was nothing, a blank slate. Didn't matter. If they couldn't lose the Shadows, none of it would matter.

—We'll need a distraction.— And with Rafe and Lucia holding the lines, Travis would have to provide one.

Don't hesitate. A second of inattention could cost them all.

Travis ruthlessly tore across his own mind, splitting his consciousness between Emma and the crowds outside in search of something he could use. An agonizing throb began in his temples, spreading inward until his brain felt too large for his skull.

—You need to pull back,— Rafe warned. *—You're pushing too hard.—*

—I've got this,— Travis growled, unable to control his mind-voice anymore. His shields were faltering, but he refused to let up. Wiping a tickle of sweat from his upper lip, his hand came away with blood. Too soon after his last meltdown. He hadn't had a chance to fully heal yet, but this was Emma. She needed him. And he didn't intend to fail her again.

—Shit, one of mine broke off,— Lucia said.

Travis' pulse sped up, jarring his concentration. His hold on Emma slipped, and he felt her veer off course, directly toward the Shadow Lucia had lost. *No, no, no! —Lucia, stop him!—*

—I can't…—

Emma pulled on his control, unconsciously using it as an extension of herself to grab hold of the Shadow. Travis didn't dare breathe or make a move. If he distracted her and she lost him, she'd die.

~

John swore and went after Emma as she marched off, too fast for him to casually catch up. He tried anyway, but was too late.

Emma turned the corner, and there stood the Hound, flanked by four army officers and a hotel attendant.

"'ten-hun, soldiers," she ordered.

John stopped dead in his tracks.

Luckily for him, the soldiers did as well. "Sir!" said the Hound, standing to attention, while the others saluted, and the hotel attendant walked off, completely oblivious to all of them.

Emma stepped up to the Hound and, looking him up and down in utter disdain, ordered, "Give me your sidearm."

The Hound immediately proffered it as he would to a senior officer, never looking Emma in the face.

She took the weapon with a cheery, "Thanks!" then spun on her heel as if nothing was out of the ordinary. When she saw John, she blinked down at what she held. "Why didn't you tell me it was your birthday? I would have wrapped it."

John carefully took the weapon before she accidentally shot him, or herself. With the soldiers still frozen at attention, he pressed a quick kiss to her temple. "Thanks for the present."

Emma grinned. "Welcome!" Then, following his gaze back to the soldiers, she waved them off with a careless flick of her fingers. "Scatter."

All except the Hound split up, each running off in a different direction. One slammed into John with enough force to turn sideways, but he righted himself as if it never happened and kept going.

John shuddered. Eerie freaking ability. And the Hound still stood frozen. "We need to get going," he said uneasily. For whatever reason, Emma was halfway lucid, but that could change at any second. He checked the weapon. Standard issue pulse gun with a full cartridge of rounds.

"There's a blue transport down on level 12C," she said distractedly, watching him work the gun with the intensity of someone learning a new skill. "The owner won't be needing it."

John moved the gun behind his back to break her stare. "How do you know?"

Emma blinked up, shaking off the trance. "Because he just died in his sleep on the eighteenth floor."

~

Somehow, Emma extricated herself from Travis' control and shifted it completely onto the Shadow instead. Now out of his grasp, she kept going with her companion, leaving Travis to hold the Shadow in a daze.

Travis strained, shaking. —*Lucia!*—

—*Got him!*—

Travis let go with an explosive breath, sagging against the wall. On the other side of it, thousands of people went about their lives, and seventeen soldiers stood guard. Not Shadows, just regular army. Crowd control. Still a threat if they decided to intervene. A good reminder they weren't finished yet. Travis gritted his teeth, wiped off his nosebleed with a trembling hand, and sought Emma's mind again. She was running down the stairs.

—*They're coming toward you,*— he told the others.

—*Then get your ass moving,*— Rafe ordered.

Travis shook his head, fully aware they couldn't see him. The Shadows needed something to latch on to, otherwise they'd never cease their pursuit. He spotted a couple exiting the inn. They looked nothing like Emma and her companion, but they didn't need to. He sent a quick impression of his plan to Rafe and Lucia.

—*That'll do,*— Lucia said, and she relayed the information to her Shadows, while Rafe did the same with his. When the transport carrying the couple drove off, the Shadows broke from their positions and followed. They'd follow for miles, focused on the hunt, with the signature tunnel vision of men incapable of thinking for themselves. By the time they'd caught up and realized they'd been duped, Emma would be safely out of their reach.

—*I see her,*— Rafe said. —*Get over here!*—

Travis moved.

~

They reached level 12C without incident, but John couldn't shake the feeling something was wrong. This was too easy. When Emma reached for the door, he stopped her. "What's the status on the Shadows?"

Breathing hard, Emma looked at him, then closed her eyes, and her brows pulled into a frown. "I don't know. I'm not getting anything anymore."

John swore. Instinct told him this was a trap.

Emma was ready to forge ahead, but again John stopped her, holding the door closed while he debated with himself. They couldn't go back up; even if the Shadows had miraculously disappeared, he couldn't walk into the main lobby with a gun shoved into his waistband. The army soldiers guarding the elevators and entrances might take issue with that.

He had twenty rounds in the gun, but that wouldn't do them any good if they got surrounded. One lucky shot could drop him or Emma, and he couldn't expect another mind trick out of her. Three more levels lay below them. Maybe they could try one of those.

Emma gasped.

"What is it?"

"Nothing," she said, but her eyes were wide. "The lot is clear. We need to move."

She looked almost desperate to get out there. "Are you sure?" he pressed, studying her face.

Emma nodded eagerly and reached for the door. Something definitely wasn't right.

John pushed her back and opened the door himself, cautiously scanning the area to get the lay of the land. Just as she'd said, the lot seemed abandoned; no people he could see or hear, only transports. He stepped out with a sharp eye all around to make sure it was safe before he let Emma come through. "Go," he said.

She took off for the vehicle she'd picked out, with John bringing up the rear, watching for threats. They were halfway around the perimeter and circling to the other side, when she stopped as if she'd hit a wall.

John raised the gun on instinct.

Before them stood a man and a woman dressed casually conservative. Nothing unusual about them, but something put John on guard.

They stared hard at Emma.

John stepped up, halfway shielding her. "Who are you?" he demanded.

They didn't move; not even a blink to indicate they'd heard him.

Then someone else came running, face bloodied as if he'd just gotten the shit beat out of him, but there were no bruises or swelling on his face. "Emma!" he shouted.

And she ran right into his arms.

Travis had kept Emma on the periphery of his mind as he raced to the parking lot where Lucia and Rafe were waiting for her. He'd felt the moment she spotted them; felt the recognition take root. Lucia had been Emma's roommate growing up, and Rafe, the resident artist, had painted her dreams many a time. That was why Travis had called them in. He'd needed Emma to see familiar faces to know she was safe, even when her mind tried to tell her otherwise.

Now, having rounded the last corner, he finally saw her, and ran headlong. "Emma!"

She saw him, her face lit up, and Travis nearly went to his knees. She cried out his name and ran straight into his arms. Though mentally exhausted and unsteady on his feet, Travis caught her up and buried his face in her shoulder. Nothing had ever felt so good. He wouldn't have given it up for the world. Emma clung to him so hard it steadied his spine, and somehow he managed not to fall over. Somehow, for her, he steadied his heartbeat and calmed his mind. She was safe.

—Ya might want to ease up there, Romeo. Her boyfriend looks ready to throw a fit.—

—Boyfriend?— Travis reluctantly raised his head to look at the man who'd brought Emma this far.

—Yeah,— Lucia said. *—We figure he's a Shadow. But that can't be right. Do you feel those shields? It's like a solid wall around his head. I*

can't get through.—

—*Me either,*— Rafe agreed. —*But we know he has a weakness.*—

Emma. The way he stared at the four of them with his finger on the trigger… Travis had no doubt the guy was a Shadow, and one who'd fixated on Emma to a dangerous degree. Travis couldn't read his thoughts, but he could sense the wheels turning in the guy's head. The Shadow surveyed the lot of them, then looked at Emma, and made a conscious decision not to fire—yet.

—*His name's John,*— Emma supplied, then pushed a kaleidoscope of memories at Travis. Their sheer confusion was staggering; he couldn't make any sense of their order, or the emotions attached to them. Almost as if she'd felt everything a human could possibly feel, and then decided not to choose one emotion above any others. John wasn't good or bad to her. He simply *was.*

When Emma leaned back to look at him, Travis set her down on her feet and searched her gaze for an explanation. All he got was a sunny smile.

—*Never mind,*— he told her. —*We can sort this out later. Right now, we need to get you home. Are you ready?*— He showed her the private shuttle waiting to take the four of them to Gray Dublin. To get to it, they'd need to cross the city, but with the Shadows still out there, they'd also need to make it quick. The sooner they got there, the better. They could keep her safe at the SU, fix up her mind, as good as new.

Emma nodded in agreement with everything, until she suddenly frowned. —*Four of us?*—

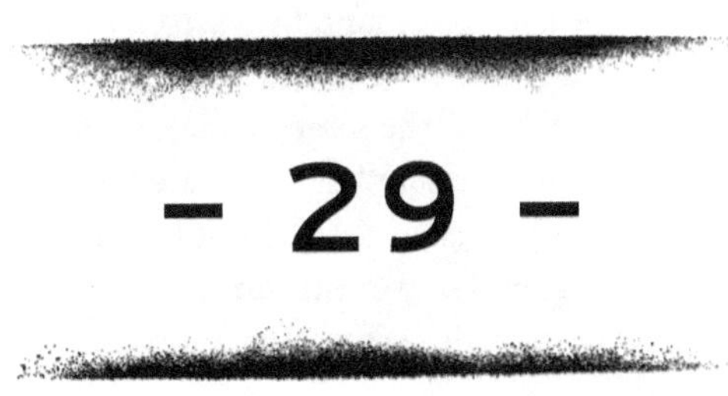

– 29 –

They folded in on her mind, and it felt like a warm blanket had settled over her. Emma could feel her focus slipping away, but she didn't care. *You are safe,* they were all saying, and they meant it. She couldn't catch her breath. Rafe showed her how they'd duped the Shadows into following someone else across town in the wrong direction, and Travis showed her the shuttle waiting to take her home. The four of them would go back to Gray Dublin.

Earth. *They're taking me home.*

Four?

Emma pulled away. They were all smiling, happy to have her back; no condemnation, no judgment, no pity from any of them, at least none that she could detect. They were all as open as one telepath ever got with another, sharing freely in a sort of multi-instantaneous conversation, and all of them were telling her it would be okay.

Except, Travis' smile was fading.

Four…

Lucia, Rafe, Travis, Emma.

John.

Lucia, Rafe, Travis, Emma, John. She repeated that count in her head, again and again. Her numbers were wrong; she couldn't make them into four.

As one, all four telepaths turned to John the soldier boy, who stood where Emma had left him, holding up air, because there was no wall.

He now had a gun along with two bags. All ready to move on. But his face was crinkled. Or tried to be, and he wasn't letting it.

The Hawk had flown his master's hand, and this time Emma knew it wasn't a cheat. She'd felt it in the sergeant major's mind. Soldier boy had stood up to take the bullets for her, and there'd be many more. The Shadows would hunt him just as they'd hunt her, and if they caught him, they'd kill him again. Forever this time.

The Hawk knew it, too. His eyes said as much. They looked at her and said goodbye. But where would he go?

"Five," Emma said aloud.

—*Are you sure?*— Lucia asked across their link.

Emma met Travis' gaze, saw the hurt in his eyes. He thought she was broken; blamed himself for being too late. But he wasn't.

—*Emma?*— he asked, wanting something from her.

She didn't know what to tell him other than, "Five." Soldier boy had taken her from the Shadows. Now she had to make him a Secret.

Rafe made a face. "I think she means she wants you to come with us," he told John.

"Really?" Soldier boy didn't sound convinced, and Emma was suddenly terrified he'd refuse. "What did she say?" He looked almost angry, like she'd betrayed him, left him alone with the gun, and a twitchy finger on the trigger.

"Uh, something about making you a secret?"

"She thinks you need her to protect you," Travis said in an ugly tone Emma had never heard from him before.

John's jaw muscle ticked as he stared Travis down.

—*You'll need to explain it to him, honey,*— Lucia told her. She looked tired. And worried. She should be.

Emma ran back and grabbed soldier boy's arm to pull him along, but aside from switching the gun to his free hand, John didn't move. It felt like trying to budge a mountain, but she didn't care. "I said five. Did you not hear me?"

When Lucia spoke, in her mind she showed Emma what she wasn't turning her head to see with her eyes. "One, two, three"—she pointed to each of them—"four... five." She smiled when she said it, and so did Emma.

Soldier boy didn't. He stared at Emma as if he wanted to read her mind. She stopped pulling on his arm so she could meet his gaze. What did he see in the chaos? Could he make any sense of it? Because most of the time, she herself couldn't. But right now, her thoughts were clear enough: the Hawk had chosen her over the Shadows, and that made him hers. She was keeping him.

"What time is it?" he asked, and she understood exactly what he wanted to know but couldn't answer it. Instead, she shrugged, hoping it looked more indifferent than it felt on the inside. "You're the one with the metronome." She could tell by the way everyone else frowned that it didn't make any sense, even in her mind. "But it better be pointing north," she added for good measure.

John made her wait for a million years. It took so long, she got dizzy from holding her breath. And he never once took his eyes off her. But then he finally blinked, gave the smallest of nods, and that was that. Emma was bringing home a hawk.

– 30 –

February 16, 3036 – Gray Dublin, Earth

No one pulled a black bag over John's head. No one shackled or gagged him either as they entered the infamous Special Unit headquarters in Gray Dublin. John was left standing alone in the middle of the wide-open entry hall while Emma's friends and family descended on her with happy shouts of welcome. Already on edge, he had to school himself not to draw the weapon they'd allowed him to keep. Worse, when they whisked her away, he almost stalked after them, but stopped at the sight of Travis getting a stern talking-to from an older man in jeans and a plaid shirt.

Given the tic in Travis' jaw, the lecture wasn't pleasant. Every time he tried to speak, the older man cut him off, and when Travis tried to walk away, he got pulled back for another bout.

Good. John hoped the son of a bitch got what he had coming to him. Would serve him right, too. All through the trip over here, Travis had done nothing but get in the way—he'd kept Emma distracted with nonsense conversations so she couldn't talk to John; he'd made her sit between him and the other woman, whose name John had already forgotten, so she couldn't move; and worst of all, he'd constantly touched Emma, holding her hand, hugging her at random, ruffling her hair with a familiarity that made John fantasize about disemboweling him. Slowly.

He just had one of those faces, John supposed.

When Travis finally walked away without apparent punishment, his supervisor turned his gaze toward the Shadow darkening his hallway, and John tensed almost to attention.

Now it would come.

The man speared his hand through his salt-and-pepper hair and he sauntered toward John as if he had all the time in the world. He was of average height, a man who must have had considerable strength in his youth. He still retained much of it, but his age showed in the lines of his face, the tired expression, the heavy footfalls. Despite it all, when he stopped in front of John, his shoulders were stiffened back, and he stood tall—a man who lived assured of his authority. "I take it you are 'soldier boy.'"

"My name is John Wayland," he said, adding as an afterthought, "Sir."

The man ignored this and, without introducing himself, went on to say, "Travis tells me you're a Shadow."

"I was," John answered.

"But not anymore?" The question held an equal measure of curiosity and challenge, but his posture indicated he wasn't concerned in the least.

"No, sir."

"I've never heard of a Shadow deserting his unit."

It wasn't a question, so John said nothing.

"Travis is of a mind we should *dispose* of you. Lucia keeps smirking, and Rafe can't be bothered to form an opinion. As you can imagine, running a facility of this size is pretty demanding and I don't have time to waste, so let me cut to the chase: Are you a spy? Keep in mind, shields or no, I will know if you lie to me."

"No, sir."

"Do you still ally with the Shadows?"

"No, sir."

"Did you come looking for an alliance with us?"

John hesitated. The thought had never entered his mind. Without the Shadows, he was no one. He had no identity of his own, no money, and nowhere to go. Whether he could create a life for himself without raising alarms was debatable, but he could try. He didn't necessarily *need* anyone, and after all of this, he wasn't inclined to want another affiliation like the one he'd just defected from. "No, sir," he said, but his tone left something to be desired.

"Then why are you here?"

Because I don't trust Emma's well-being to the likes of Travis. Common sense told him if anyone could help her heal, these people could. But John kept thinking about where he'd found her: alone, on the run, hiding. She hadn't trusted them then; she shouldn't now.

But she should trust you?

No. John was worse than the lot of them combined.

So why are you here?

He didn't know. John didn't have ready answers in reserve for this line of questioning. When his mind blanked, his gaze flickered over to the hallway where Emma had disappeared. He wanted to go after her almost as much as he wanted to get away from the man's steady, probing eyes.

As closely as he watched John, the man noticed him look away and followed the direction of John's gaze with a contemplative expression. "I see."

John's trigger finger itched. He was a soldier, not a diplomat; without something to shoot, he was at a loss.

"Well, I suppose you'd better come with me, then."

"Sir," he said, his feet following the order out of habit. He took half a step before he made himself stop. *Not a soldier anymore. Not anything anymore.*

Realizing John hadn't come along, the man stopped halfway down the hall and backtracked. "Problem?" he asked.

Yes. I don't know what to do.

But voicing it would mean admitting weakness.

The man raised a condescending eyebrow. "Something you want to get off your chest, boy?"

John gritted his teeth. If he was ever going to be anything other than "soldier boy," he had to change the rules of engagement himself. He willed his shoulders to slump a little and his arms to relax. Rather than staring straight ahead, he looked the man in the eye. "To be clear: I'm not your lackey. I'm not your subordinate, and I'm done being ordered around. Now, I don't know who the hell you are, and I don't particularly care. I came here for one reason: because Emma asked me to. That doesn't mean I'm signing on to whatever brainwashing, mind control cult you have going on. And no, I don't intend to start anything, but if you try something, I sure as hell will end it."

The man nodded. "Is that it?" His nonchalant response made John's righteous ire deflate in a hurry.

"Yes."

"Good. I'm John MacMurphy, director of this facility. I failed to mention that before." He made the introduction offhand, already turning away before he'd finished speaking. "Now follow, *please*. And keep up."

John picked up the bags and hastened to catch up to MacMurphy's swift, no-nonsense stride.

"I'll choose to interpret your abnormal lack of overt awe as a result of your Shadow training," MacMurphy said. "But let me assure you, an impression will be made."

Past an automated sliding door that spanned the entire fifty-foot wide chamber, the facility spread out in a starburst of corridors. Ramps led up and down to different levels, passing by what John assumed to be classrooms behind glass walls, and absolutely no signs or maps. He swallowed dryly.

"Told you."

Because of the way the hallways had been structured, people walking around sometimes seemed to come out of nowhere or disappear into solid walls. It was only an optical illusion, but it made John's head spin, and he had a feeling this was just the tip of the iceberg.

All this time, the Shadows had considered the Special Unit a group of unorganized, cowering telepaths hiding in small numbers where they wouldn't be seen or recognized. They couldn't have been more wrong.

Picking his jaw up off the floor, John asked, "How big is this place?"

"Bigger than you'll ever know. People have disappeared completely in these hallways before, never to be heard from again."

John looked over at MacMurphy. Was the man kidding? He couldn't tell.

"I wouldn't go exploring, if I were you. It's easy to get lost here, and

I can't imagine anyone feeling inclined to help you."

Directly in the middle stood a vast circular chamber with frosted glass walls and a giant red cross. "This is our clinic. You will become intimately familiar with it quite soon."

John didn't like the sound of that, but MacMurphy had already moved on.

"Dorm rooms are on three levels down the corridor at ten o'clock. Head along twelve o'clock to find common areas, game rooms, dining hall, exercise rooms, et cetera. Two o'clock is off limits to anyone without clearance, which includes you. And before you start imagining some nefarious evil mind control world domination headquarters, don't. That wing is closed off for construction, nothing more."

"How—"

"You tensed when I said 'off limits.' And I can hear your teeth grinding. It's not good for your enamel or your jaw."

As they turned toward the dorms, John's mind whirled with disaster scenarios, none of which boded well with a bottleneck construction like this. "Are there any emergency exits to this place?"

MacMurphy looked appalled. "Of course there are emergency exits. This is a sprawling, sophisticated, live-work facility, not a fox den. Unlike the Shadows, we value the lives of our people."

John flinched at that.

"Now. Ground rules. Fights are not tolerated here. I don't care who starts what or why, if a fight breaks out, all those involved are permanently removed from the premises—no exceptions. All residents, no matter their age, schedule, or assignment, are required to attend two thirty-minute group meditation sessions a day, and two one-hour training sessions a week. Meals are served four times a day in the dining hall. In between, the kitchen is closed, but snacks are laid out for those who missed a meal. Sleeping arrangements—and this is where I'll need you to pay attention: this facility is coed, with the understanding that whatever amorous activity people engage in must be one hundred percent shielded."

"Not going to be a problem," John said dryly.

"Not you I'm worried about," MacMurphy retorted in kind. He stopped at a juncture of three corridors and faced John. "Listen, whatever happened between you and Pixie has clearly left an impression." When John tried to tell him that nothing had, MacMurphy raised his hand. "I don't care. You said your piece, now it's my turn."

John shut his mouth.

"You enter with a clean slate, just like everyone else. I don't care what you did for the Shadows, I don't care about your part in capturing Pixie, or holding her captive. I do care that you brought her back to us. I care that she seems to have taken a liking to you, and I will most definitely care what happens from here on out. And, understand me, boy, if you give her cause to be unhappy for even a second, I will end you."

John drew himself up. *Message received. Loud and clear.*

MacMurphy nodded, then jerked his chin down the hallway. "Your room is the third door on the right. Welcome to the Special Unit." Then he brushed past John, headed back where they'd come from.

The hell John was letting the man off that easy. "What will you do with her?" he called over his shoulder.

MacMurphy stopped in his tracks. "*Do?*" he repeated.

John swiveled, cursing himself for standing at attention. He made a conscious effort to relax his shoulders. "She killed a man. I don't know why. He probably deserved it. But I'm pretty sure it wasn't her job to determine that. So what do you intend to do with her?"

MacMurphy stared for a moment as if he couldn't believe what he'd just heard. Then his jaw tightened and he marched back, past John. "Let's talk inside."

The room they'd assigned to John had a slanted ceiling and a surplus of old world furniture. He couldn't take a step without banging his knee against something. If hobbits existed, this would be how they'd decorate their burrows.

"Sit," MacMurphy said.

"I'd rather stand."

MacMurphy scowled and sat in the rocking chair. "I don't suppose you know much about us. The way we… work."

"No, sir. And I don't imagine you're going to tell me."

To his surprise, MacMurphy did. "Those aware of the existence of telepathy have been studying it for years. So that you understand how complex its biology is, we have only learned two definitive things to date. One, telepathy as a part of the human genome is still evolving. There is a theory suggesting it's the next step in human evolution, and over time, everyone will be able to communicate and share knowledge in this way. But we're centuries out from such a miracle, if at all. The second thing we know is that it cannot be traced until it manifests."

"So there's no way to predict it?"

"None at all. Which makes it very difficult to deal with. Eighty percent of the people you see here manifested in puberty. For the lucky ones, it happened gradually. The not-so-lucky ones changed from one moment to the next. Imagine waking up one morning with an extra head on your shoulder that whispers horrible things in your ear, but no one else can see it. Most of these kids had no idea what was happening to them when they started hearing voices and seeing ghosts. They were terrified. Many were living in the streets, addicted to drugs, which only made things worse.

"We help as many as we can, but even we can't predict who'll man-ifest, and we don't always get to the kids in time. In some, the stress is simply too much for the brain to take. Once it gets past a certain point, without counseling, the telepath either ends up catatonic or a suicide statistic. That alone makes each and every person here a miracle. Wouldn't you agree?"

John nodded, since the man seemed to expect some sort of response.

MacMurphy leaned forward, looked him straight in the eye. "Now here's the most important thing you'll ever need to know: Pixie—Emma—was nothing like that. She's in a subgroup of telepaths so miniscule, it's not even zero-point-one percent of us all. She was born a telepath; her ability developed in the womb along with all of her physical senses. She perceives the world differently because she's never known life without telepathy."

She knows now.

Face to face with the older man, John couldn't think of a single thing to say. If Emma's ability to read thoughts was truly that elemental to her, then how much damage had taking it away caused? John sat on the bed.

I did that to her.

Not only had he done it, he'd wholeheartedly believed it was right and just. The perfect soldier, following orders without question; standing guard and watching her fall apart before his eyes. Every insult she'd hurled at him in that holding cell, everything she'd accused him of being, had been right.

MacMurphy smirked. "You're turning green, my boy. That guilty conscience is a bitch, isn't it?"

"What will happen to her?"

"She's stronger than she looks. She'll recover."

"I mean, what she did."

"I don't imagine that to concern you in any way." MacMurphy pushed to his feet and headed for the door, dismissing John, offhand.

John bolted up and barred his way, looked him dead in the eye. "If you hurt her, I'll kill you," he promised.

MacMurphy didn't flinch, merely met John's gaze without a hint of fear, and matched his quiet tone. "Do you honestly believe there is anything worse we could do to her than what's already been done?" When he walked out, he didn't slam the door; he shut it softly behind him.

John slumped back onto the bed, braced his elbows on his knees, and took in a deep breath, willing himself not to throw up.

"Queen take pawn. Check."

Ivan always played white.

John rummaged through his pockets for the old chess piece, only to realize he wasn't wearing his uniform pants anymore. He'd left them in the Ambassador Lounge trash bin, along with the queen.

The last link to whatever life he'd had before the Shadows, was gone.

– 31 –

Somewhere in the Tae Colony

"Ladies and gentlemen, tonight we bring you live footage from Sapphire City, Jericho, where our ground crew is covering the antichem riots. As you can see from these images, the city is… no more. We have been receiving reports all through the night, and from what we have seen, the riots have turned into outright war against the Interplanetary Council of Governance.

"At approximately seven in the morning, local time, a band of rioters marched into the city. They were quickly joined by citizens fleeing from their burning houses. We have now learned those fires have been deliberately set by the residents themselves, and due to the fire department being disbanded, they have not been put out.

"The mob then continued through the financial district, where they broke into businesses, destroyed buildings, and painted the Evolutionaries' symbol across the walls. Some have fled into the suburbs and onto ships heading out to sea. Most, however, have joined the movement, growing the mob exponentially. Our crew reports that while the outer edges of the crowd are quite violent, those in the middle were seen marching peacefully, chanting a message in unison: Stop the poison. Stop the tyranny. A life is a life is a life.

"Civil services were unable to halt the advance, and military action was employed. At noon, local time, three of the four containment hovers *utilized to corral the crowd were shot down over the parliamentary build-ings. Our sources say an extraction team of military personnel wearing dark blue uniforms was able to safely evacuate some of the officials on duty before the buildings collapsed and created an outward shock wave that leveled the city and buried crowds of protesters in its wake.*

"The death toll is estimated to be in the hundreds of thousands, a figure echoed in countless cities across the Union, where the antichem revolution continues to rage without any sign of abatement. New threats and demands are sent out every day, and we no longer believe these are coming from the Evolutionaries alone. Ordinary citizens have joined the extremist group, taking matters into their own hands and further than ever before. The message is clear. The people have had enough."

Zayn turned off the live stream.

"This is getting out of hand," Leanne said, shaking her head.

No, this was exactly what they needed—for the people to wake up from their stupor and demand their own natural lives back. He'd wanted them to rally, and they have. He'd wanted them to fight for their children, and they were. He'd wanted the Shadows to tip their hand, and they did.

But he'd also wanted the SU to take notice and *do* something for once in its long, neutral existence; to take a stand for what was right.

And where were they?

"What's the word on my care packages?"

In a bid to get them moving, Zayn had sent recordings of the Hunt children both to their parents and to several known SU agents. He'd banked on their reporting home to start circling the wagons around their own, so he could find out where the hell they were all hiding. For years, SU's base of operation had been a thorn in Zayn's side. No one could figure out where it was—not mind readers, not seers, not trackers, not even the damn Shadows. For all they knew, the SU home base didn't even exist, except in the hearts and minds of good little telepaths.

"No visible response," Leanne reported.

"And Torrey?"

She shook her head. "Locked down. Our people are stuck. But so far, the towns are calm. No news feeds."

"The Hunts, Leanne."

"Gone; disappeared into thin air. One of our guys had a hunch they might have gone off to the Connors' place in the mountains, so he went to check it out and almost got his head chopped off. Guy's got that place booby trapped all to hell. We're watching it from a distance, but so far it looks dead. No one in or out."

Zayn slammed his fist on the table. "So we have nothing."

"Not nothing. Michael had a vision earlier."

"What did he see?"

"We don't know. He kept repeating 'Sue Gray. Sue so very Gray,' and then he had a seizure. Still out for the count. Anna's with him now."

"Keep me appraised of his condition. Dismissed."

Leanne left the room to stand guard outside.

His strategy wasn't working. The SU should have been all over the Shadows by now, making their own push against the ICG. After all, it was in their best interest, especially after the girl's abduction. With John MacMurphy's resignation from the advisory council, they had no voice in the government. Griffith was pushing his own agenda of more specialized chem-treatments, calling for DNA testing on parents and children to determine the most suitable course of action.

But Zayn had seen the bill and read between the lines. Griffith had made provisions to map genetic markers for certain psychological traits, including telepathy and personality dominance indices. The senator aimed to find out who'd grow up capable of controlling others and who could be controlled, and Zayn knew exactly what Griffith would do with that information. The same thing all warmongers did: use it to write the future as he saw fit.

The revolution against chem-treatments was only the first step to preventing a genocide that would put the 20th century Nazis to shame. It was a stall tactic to distract the ICG long enough to shelve the vote on Griffith's proposed bill. But it wouldn't work forever, and it wouldn't solve the problem. Without a step two, the longer the violence continued, the better that bill would look to those in charge of keeping the peace.

The Special Unit had the numbers and the skills to end it, but they refused. Every day they continued to bury their heads in the sand, they proved themselves to be the soulless, elitist bastards he knew they were. And the situation kept getting worse. Pretty soon, it'd be too late for even them to make a difference.

But if they didn't want to be inconvenienced, no skin off Zayn's back; he'd take care of his own, and to hell with the rest. He'd stir the pot so much, there'd be nothing left but dust, and when it settled, humanity could once again wipe the slate clean and start over.

From nothing, if necessary.

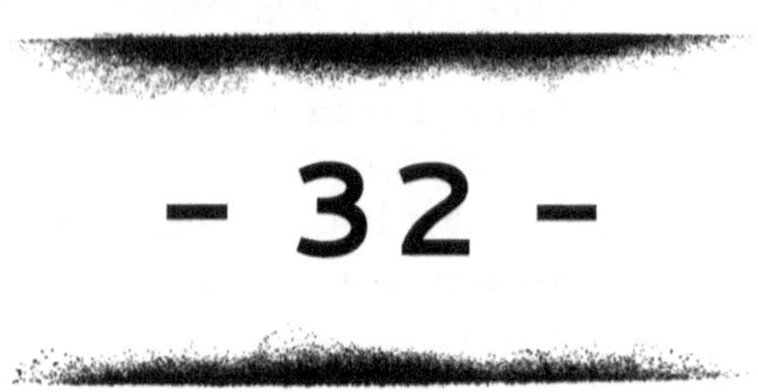

- 32 -

Clarity. Such a simple thing, yet Emma couldn't quite grasp it. *Am I actually lucid right now?* She peered around the room at all of the familiar faces smiling at her, breathed in the soothing scent of chocolate chip cookies, baked specially here and nowhere else. And she realized that, yes, she was sane—at least momentarily.

No hum, no lapses in time; her mind was open with everything flowing in and out, as easily as a breath of fresh air across her thoughts. Finally. *I can breathe.* And Emma knew this was all because of the people around her. They were doing this, not her. Someone—she wasn't quite sure who—was being very naughty, telling her everything she wasn't supposed to hear, like what they all *really* thought of her.

Little Pixie was back. The three-legged family dog had returned. They thought her mind had suffered a trauma in the white room, and then her brain had suffered one with the seizure. Everything she'd depended on all her life had been rewired the wrong way. It could be fixed, but not by Emma, and not in this state. So they were doing it for her, regulating the flow of information so her brain could learn to recognize the pattern and begin to rewire back on its own.

None of them were afraid of her. They should be. With clarity came memories, and for once, they were all organized in the right order, start to finish, front to back. Emma leafed through a picture book of the last few months and couldn't believe what she saw.

December on Mars 2. Emma shuddered and fast-forwarded through that. January on Earth. Not far from here. Almost a perfect pretense of normal, but too sharp and dark to be believed.

And then, the white room. No fast-forwarding through that one. Emma watched herself lose her mind one small twitch at a time. She'd spent a whole chunk of time—a day? More?—counting cracks in the wall, only to realize there were none. She saw soldier boy standing at her door, eyes front, as if she didn't exist; heard herself talking to him, and firmed her mouth against forming the words aloud.

She'd talked to him a lot. Not much of it had made sense. But her pattern of speech had still held a certain coherence, like a different language she'd gradually adopted. Soldier John had witnessed it, learned it with her, so he could understand her now.

She remembered what she'd done to the men in the garage. Simple guys, leading simple lives, doing their simple jobs. Well, pretending to, anyway. She'd hacked into their brains, made their worst fears real. Hadn't even been all that difficult, just an instinct reaction; the flip of a switch in the part of their brains that stored emotional memories, and—*boom*. One man found himself drowning in a murky lake. Another became trapped in a shrinking dark room. Another crawled with insects, inside and out.

One unfocused, wide-range telepathic blast, and a half-mile radius worth of people had been incapacitated. Emma didn't even know how long the effects had lasted, but she knew that at least five of them had been permanently broken by it. She'd felt it happen before she passed out.

Clarity.

Sometimes it was better to see shimmering butterflies making lazy loops in the air.

It's temporary. Another naughty little transmission. Not quite a communiqué; more of a nudge to the understanding she already had. The effects of whatever they were doing weren't meant to last for any length of time. It took effort to do this, and because no one could be with her 24-7, as soon as they left, she'd revert. They were hoping for a gradual fix, that she'd feel better after each session, but they really had no way of knowing.

"We fixed up your old room for you," Rafe said. He wouldn't be staying here for the night. His particular gift was seeing people's dreams, and he couldn't always control it. With Emma here, it was safer for him to be elsewhere.

She didn't begrudge him. In his place, she wouldn't have stayed, either. Emma nodded in understanding. She didn't really care where they put her up for the night, as long as it wasn't a mattress on the floor. But she did wonder whom they'd had to kick out to make room for her.

"And we called Jeremy. He's on his way, although it might take him a while."

"You shouldn't have done that," Emma said.

"Of course we should have! He's your brother. Don't you think he wants to know that you're safe and sound?"

"Sorry, did you say *safe* or *sane*?"

Smiles dimmed, though they did their best not to show it. Emma ducked her head. She shouldn't have barked at them like that. It wasn't their fault. "Sorry. But you shouldn't have meddled." Jeremy had taken care of her all her life. He'd raised her, protected her, looked out for her, all so he wouldn't have to think about his own life.

Her brother thought he'd chased her away. In truth, Emma had been happy that he'd finally snapped. Both of them had needed some space to live their own lives. But that hard-won, fragile freedom would vanish in an instant if Jeremy came swooping in and took it into his head that she needed to be taken care of again.

Which he would. Because she did. And she hated it.

"We get it," Rafe said. "He can be a little overbearing. But it's only because he loves you."

Emma snorted. "Maybe he needs to love me less."

"You don't mean that," Lucia said kindly. "You'll feel differently when he's here, you'll see."

"Maybe he'll be so busy relearning this place he won't have time to Mother Goose me."

The SU, or Sue as she'd begun to think of it in her less-than-organized moments, had grown up since she'd been gone. Like a magic trick. The building's outside used to match the inside for size. Now, it looked like they'd tunneled into the adjoining buildings to make more room. And hundreds of people lived inside, as opposed to the three dozen who'd lived here seven years ago. But what amazed her most was how well they all got along.

"Somehow, I doubt that," Rafe retorted, getting to his feet.

Today's session was over. Her babysitters were leaving. They said their goodbyes, promised to come see her tomorrow, and went back to their regular lives to recharge their mental batteries. Emma sat back, closed her eyes, and watched her mind slowly fog over. She sighed when it finished. Mostly because her shields had automatically snapped closed to make her just as deaf and blind as a normal person.

No middle ground with me. Go or no-go were her only options.

She missed soldier boy.

Emma wandered out of the room and, since no one was stopping her, walked the hallways of Sue, trying to take it all in. She liked the magic mirrors that showed one thing, but when she opened them, revealed something completely different.

In one room, Emma toed a yellow circle on the floor, and a man appeared out of nowhere. "Welcome," he said in a deep voice. "Choose your opponent."

"Big bad wolf," she said, giggling.

A giant wolf appeared across from her, hackles raised and red eyes flashing as it snarled at her. Emma ran out screaming. People leapt out of her way as she barreled past them, giving her strange looks when she yelled, "Bad dog on the loose!" They were no help at all. She closed herself in the first room she came to and pressed her hands against the door, holding it shut. *Don't be hungry. Don't be hungry.*

Emma stood there until she was sure nothing would come after her. Then she turned around, and gaped. The room was filled with tiny people, so little, they didn't have hair or teeth, but had huge heads on their mini bodies. She slowly approached one lying in its little bed, and it stared up at her with its buggy brown eyes, making spit bubbles.

She gently poked it in the belly, and the tiny person made a squealing giggle sound. It amused her, so she tried it with a different one, but that one screwed up its face and started to scream its giant head off. And then the rest of them did it, too.

Emma stuck her tongue out at them and left. *See if I care.*

The scent of food made her stomach rumble, so she followed her nose to the dining room, which wasn't where she thought she remembered it being and looked nothing like it should have. So many tables and chairs, all of them empty, but food was in here somewhere, she could smell it.

"Hungry?"

Startled by the intrusion, Emma turned to the man who used to be John MacMurphy. This version of him looked whiter. "Haven't eaten since the lockdown," she said.

She knew two Johns now. Couldn't call them both the same, and soldier boy didn't like being a soldier boy. *Little John it is.*

Big John chuckled. "Well then, let's get you fed."

He took her hand, led her to the food, and let her pick what she liked. Emma piled her plate with everything that looked edible, then filled two more, and by the time they'd sat down at one of the tables, she had one plate with all pink stuff and another piled with something blue. The last plate she pushed away; it was being belligerent.

"How are you settling in?" Big John asked.

Emma shrugged. "Yes." The knife was very sharp. She tried to bend it, but it wouldn't. It even had a pointy tip. Not at all like the broken fork she'd had before. It was steady.

"This must all seem very new to you. There have been a lot of changes since you left." He took the knife from her, rearranged it in her hand and, guiding her movements, helped her cut up some food into smaller pieces. "You know, your friend has an interesting mind shield. Tough to know what he's thinking."

Emma shook a mental magic eight ball. "Ask again later," she told him.

Big John chuckled. "That easy, huh? Do you think he'll tell me if I ask nicely?"

"No." Little John didn't talk about thinking. He thought about talking. "But he'll make a funny face at you and tell you to eat more." She frowned at the piece of cow stuck on the end of her metal fork. "I think he took care of me."

"Emma, do you remember how you were taken?"

She didn't like his tone. Made her sound crazy. "Caught in a hawk trap. Put in a wrong cage made just for me. But the falconer screwed up. Didn't hood him proper."

"*Hood* him? Emma, was the man you brought here responsible for you being caught?"

Hadn't she just explained this? "Hawk trap," she said with a nod. Then she squinted at his face. *I know that look… What is it?*

Ah. Frustration. Big John wasn't Little John; they weren't speaking the same language. Emma tried to find the words to explain. "Faulty hood," she said and covered her eyes to demonstrate, peeking at Big John from between her fingers.

He wasn't getting it. Huffing in defeat, Emma ducked her head and ate some more. *Slowly,* she told herself. *Little bites, or they'll all leave again.*

"Have you met with any of the new ones?" Big John asked.

"Only the tiny baldies. They're a hive mind."

Big John stopped eating and stared at her.

Had she said something crazy again?

"How could you know that?"

Emma shrugged. "One cries, they all cry."

"Well, they're babies. Babies do that."

"Not like that."

"Like what?"

She was getting tired of having to repeat herself. "One cries, they all cry. At the same time." Emma scowled at the blue stuff on her plate. "The leader doesn't like me. What *is* this stuff?"

Big John took her plate away. "I didn't realize any of them were manifesting. So soon?"

"Yes, they're good little bombs."

"We'll have to separate them."

Emma nodded. Hive minds, bad. Mind control, bad. Drones one hundred percent dependent on leader, bad. Die without leader, bad. She sighed. *I don't like bullies.* The crier was definitely a bully. She dropped her fork, impatient to get out of there. "What time is it?"

"It's seven fifteen."

Useless. Scowling at him, Emma left.

– 33 –

Dinner was at eight. John washed up and changed into the clothes someone had left for him. They almost fit, except the shirt sleeves were too short. He rolled them up above his elbow so they didn't pull. The people in the dining hall were nice enough, showing him the proper procedure for getting food, pointing out their favorite dishes and which ones to avoid at any cost. Apparently, that morning's batch of pastries had turned out less than digestible.

With most of the tables occupied by those who didn't look inclined to make room for one extra, John took a seat at a table that had only two current occupants. The young woman smiled in welcome and introduced herself as Juliet.

Her companion, a fresh-out-of-puberty boy called Steven, stared at John. "You're the Wall. Everybody's talking about you. Is it true you can't be read?"

There was meaning somewhere in those few sentences, John was sure of it. But damned if he could figure it out. *I've spent too much time around Emma. Everyone else is starting to sound incoherent by comparison.* He cast a questioning look at Juliet.

"That's your new handle," she informed him. "Because of the shields on your mind."

"I see."

Juliet grinned.

Steven stared. "Bet I could do it," he said.

Juliet rolled his eyes. "Pixie couldn't."

"Pixie's messed up."

A food tray dropped onto the table, and Travis slapped the boy across the back of his head—hard.

"Ow!"

"Watch your mouth," Travis said, settling in between the boy and Juliet.

"Sorry," Juliet said, looking very uncomfortable. "We're trying to teach him manners, but it doesn't seem to be doing much good."

"Why am I the bad guy?" Steven demanded. "He's the one who did it to her." He shoved to his feet and removed himself to another table.

Juliet blushed, staring hard at her plate.

John barely noticed the boy's departure, too busy with the staring contest Travis had started. *Give me a reason, asshole. Let's end this here and now.*

"Steve does have a point," Travis said.

John turned his eating knife around, reverse grip. "I suppose he does." He might not have designed Emma's holding cell, but he'd put her in it.

"What do you suppose we should think about that?" Travis challenged.

"Guys, come on now," Juliet said. "MacMurphy said to be nice."

Both of them ignored her.

"Whatever you want to," John replied. He had nothing to say in his own defense. At some point, ignorance ceased to be a valid excuse for guilt, and John had passed that point about two days after locking Emma into the white room.

"You're not going to tell us you were just following orders?"

"Travis!" Juliet snapped.

"I *was* just following orders." *Like the good little soldier I was.* "That's the problem."

Juliet quieted, and it was a toss-up as to what took her aback more: his answer, or the lack of remorse in its delivery.

Travis considered that, and leaned back in his seat, crossing his arms over his chest. "There's a general consensus that you brainwashed Emma into bringing you here so you can spy on us and report back to your boss."

"Noted."

"Did you sleep with her?"

"*Travis!* That is none of our business!"

John carefully set down his utensils and pushed his plate away. Son of a bitch just had to go there. Now it was personal. "No. Did you?" *Say yes. Go ahead. I'll tear your fucking head off with my bare hands.*

Juliet groaned and slapped her hands over her face as if she couldn't take it anymore.

"How much did they pay you to bring her in?" The bastard hadn't answered.

"Nothing more than my usual pay. You planning to swoop in to protect her from me?"

"If necessary. How did you people find her?"

Even Juliet tuned back in to that one.

It was a test. Travis was fishing to find out whose side John was on. If John refused to answer, they'd take it as evidence he was still in allegiance with the Shadows. He could set them straight by simply telling the truth, all of it, including Emma's crime. But *that* he wouldn't do. Whatever they knew already, John would cut out his own tongue before he told them more. He owed her that much, to start with. "Emma's story is her own," he said quietly. "If she wants to tell you, she will. But try to force it from her, and it'll be my pleasure to rip your spine out through your mouth."

Travis held his gaze for a long time. Then he grunted and went back to his meal. Apparently, the discussion was over.

The few bites John had managed to swallow sat heavy in his gut. He'd lost his appetite for the rest. "It was nice to meet you, Juliet."

She gave him a wan half-smile, half-wince. "See you around."

John brought his tray back to the window, where a plump, middle-aged woman frowned at it. "You didn't finish?"

"It was delicious, ma'am. I just don't seem to have much of an appetite today."

She nodded with a sad sigh. "I guess I understand."

"Have a good night, ma'am."

"You too, handsome." Her saucy wink surprised a grin out of him.

John kept his gaze forward as he left the dining hall, determined to ignore the whispers and condescending looks that always followed him through crowds. This time, there were none. He slowed at the exit, glanced around to be sure. No one stared; everyone was busy with their own meals and conversations. Juliet was giving Travis a talking-to, which he didn't take with anywhere near the same submission he'd shown MacMurphy. Steven entertained his table with some story that required a lot of dramatic gestures, sending everyone into fits of laughter. He seemed to have already forgotten their earlier encounter.

People talked, ate, touched, and laughed, displaying genuine delight in spending time together.

And it occurred to John: this was exactly how he'd always wanted the Shadows to be. A band of brothers. Family. Maybe they were, but they'd never included him among them; he'd always been the odd one out. Conversation stagnated pretty quickly when people started to compare memories and realized John didn't have any.

He'd never felt bad about that before. Memories could become corrupted. Past loved ones could be used to compromise a Shadow. Thoughts of home distracted soldiers in combat. John had been proud that none of those things could happen to him; he'd been the perfect weapon for the Shadows, which had made him an indispensable asset. But now he realized *asset* was just another word for *thing*. Subhuman.

No wonder they'd used him. Loyalty was something you showed to people, not automatons.

Deeply perturbed, John wandered back to his room, and regretted it instantly. There, he felt like just another piece of furniture in a storage closet. The walls started closing in. The sloped ceiling began pressing down until John finally turned off the light. Darkness brought blessed relief, and he sighed, sitting on the edge of his bed.

"Music," he said, hoping the master system here recognized voice commands. Over the writing desk, a wall panel opened to reveal a screen that streamed music lists. John reached forward, made his selection, then relaxed back on the bed and let the computer organize a playlist.

The door opened by inches, without a knock. He expected someone with a baseball bat, but instead, Emma's red head tentatively emerged from behind the door. "Are you decent?"

John grinned. "Rarely."

Emma eased into the room, wearing nothing but an oversized T-shirt that covered her down to the knees. By the light of the hallway, John saw it was dark green, a shade all too familiar—he'd worn it just yesterday. It suited her. Made her skin glow.

Emma's fingers snapped in his line of sight—about the level of her knees—and he dragged his gaze back up to her face. "I repurposed your wardrobe," she said.

John frowned. "Didn't they give you your own clothes?" He'd gotten so much stuff, he hardly knew how to combine the pieces, having never worn anything other than his uniform or some pre-chosen outfits for undercover ops.

Emma shrugged and checked out into the hallway to see who was around. She eased the door shut, closing them in darkness, and John sat up straighter on the bed. Nothing had changed except for the lighting, yet somehow, the room felt smaller, much too cozy. He could almost feel Emma's breath on his neck even though she was still standing by the door.

"This is a good locale," she said in approval. Her voice sounded different—deeper, more throaty.

For some reason, it made him profoundly uncomfortable. "Are you… all together?"

"I am complexed with prose, but my muse is operational."

"And your telepathy?"

"On or off. No gradient."

"How are you handling that?"

"Yes." He heard the shrug in her voice, and if he closed his eyes, he could almost see her frustrated huff, accompanied by her ruffling her hair. "I need a bidirectional transmission. No receivers out there."

A building full of telepaths, and she'd come to him, because she couldn't find someone who understood her? "You want to turn on the lights?"

"No!" she said quickly. "No, this is… better."

"Okay," he said, and she breathed out in relief. "What do you want to talk about?"

She pushed away from the door, and he promptly heard a thud and curses. That would be the foot of the bed.

John took her by the wrist to guide her around to the side. "Sit," he said, positioning her so she wouldn't fall off the edge.

"They summoned my blood kin," she said unhappily. "I won't like it."

"They're just trying to look out for you." What had her file said about relatives? He'd read that thing a hundred times to learn as much as he could about her before his mission, but his focus had been on personal preferences and habits, rather than background and connections. She'd been on the run and contact with anyone she knew had been highly improbable.

"He's a cat person. And he commands. Won't like being shut out. Won't translate… no, under… understand."

A brother. Now he remembered. Jeremy Calen. A blank slate beyond that. Jeremy had been next on their list if Emma's capture failed. John would have to warn the guy when he showed up.

Emma patted the mattress along his leg to his hip, then patted him, trying to place him in the space around her, and John stiffened when she rearranged herself to sit alongside him. She whispered some numbers, then agreed with herself, and crawled over John to his other side, squeezing between him and the wall. He moved over to give her more space, but he could only move so far before he'd fall off the edge. As out of sorts as John felt with her in his bed, he didn't have the heart to tell her to leave. She was like a puppy that way, all big pleading eyes and innocent smile, so damn trusting, as if he was the most honorable man in the world.

You almost died because of me. The knowledge was always there, that if not for him, she wouldn't be here right now with her mind in shambles and an army hunting her and everyone she'd ever associated with. Somewhere in the back of his mind, he expected her to wake up and look at him with horror and hatred in those brilliant eyes. John knew it was coming; knew he deserved it. But he dreaded it with every fiber of his being. While she looked at him as her hero, John could almost make himself believe he wasn't the monster he knew himself to be. And as horrible as it was, that treacherous, weak part of him hoped she never recovered.

"I'm scuffed," she said gravely. "Not shiny and new anymore."

John put his arm around her.

Emma pushed away, twisted as if to look at him. He assumed he was supposed to pay attention. "Not broken, either," she said.

"Then why are you here?" The words came out before he could stop them. "I'm the one who caught you, remember?" He tensed in preparation for her attack.

Emma slapped his chest; a frustrated flutter of her hand. "Why does everyone keep reminding me? I was there, remember? Hawk flew in, clawed the sparrow back to his nest. I'm not a juggernaut."

"And you're not angry about that?"

"You're damn right I am! You pecked me! And if you hadn't tossed the hood, I wouldn't be talking to you. Well," she amended, "talking, yes. Talking helps. So I would be. But not with sense. You wouldn't subscribe to sense. Waste of a perfectly good metronome."

Some of his tension eased. "So… you won't try to decapitate me while I sleep?"

A pause.

"Emma?"

"Hush, trying to formulate a picture."

He waited.

"Nyeh," she finally decided. "Hawk without a head not nearly as amusing as a chicken."

John laughed.

Emma settled against him, her ear to his chest. She did it so easily, as if it was the most natural thing in the world, and it humbled John as much as it terrified him. She forgave him, because he got her out. But that didn't absolve him of his own guilt, or the constant fear that her trust in him would one day be broken.

As if she'd read his mind, Emma hugged herself to him. "Doesn't matter what happens now. The hawk pried the cage open. Released the sparrow. Could have killed it. Insulated instead. Took guts to toss that hood. Besides, I'm not right to weigh. Little John did good."

"*Little John?*"

"There's already a Big one. Sorry."

"Brat." He tugged at her hair with no real venom, and Emma

squealed, poked him in the side. He wasn't ticklish but he squirmed anyway, just to make her happy.

She poked him again.

John sifted his fingers through her hair, savoring its silken feel, its fresh scent of spring.

Emma poked him a third time.

"What?"

"Scoot."

John shifted lower until they were both stretched out length for length. Pillowing her head on his shoulder, Emma draped a slender arm across his chest and sighed. "Night, seashell." And John couldn't say he hated it.

Now he understood how she'd earned her nickname. A more charming, unpredictable creature he'd never met. *And I almost destroyed her.* John hugged her close, pressed a kiss to the crown of her head, breathing deep. "Good night, Pixie-girl."

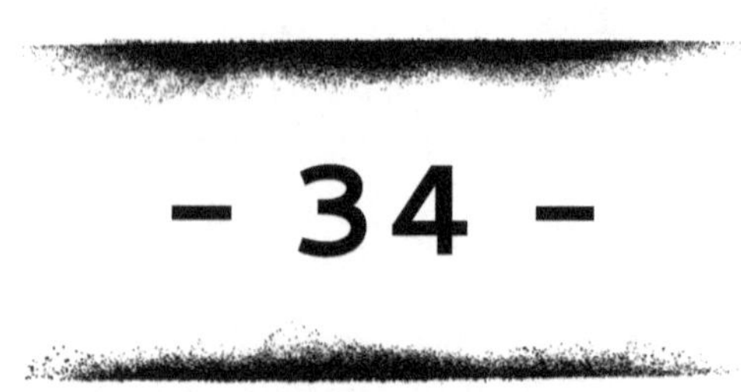

– 34 –

It was the most beautiful mine field ever with colors so bright, they would have hurt Emma's eyes if she were awake, and sounds so rich and intimate, she felt as if every bird sang just for her. Emma coasted so smoothly through dream after dream, from mind to mind, she forgot that sooner or later she'd have to go back.

But back *caught up with her eventually. At first, it was nothing but a stray flash of white or the buzz of a beehive turning into an all-too-familiar hum. A face in a crowd that didn't belong. Emma kept going, losing herself in fantasy.*

Then she opened a door and the nursery she'd expected to see became a bright white room. Her heart gave a painful thump and a half, reeling her back, but the door she'd come through was gone. Emma spun around, looking for a way out, a shadow—anything. But everywhere she looked, all she saw was bright white. The world had been erased, countless dreams chased away by one nightmare.

Her body shook from head to toe, and she hugged herself to stop it, but it only made her shake harder, and the air got thicker. Emma gasped for breath, faster and shallower. Any minute now, she'd pass out and then the light would claw into her brain again. She wouldn't survive it a second time. A harsh, desperate cry tore out of her throat, so foreign to her ears it terrified her, and the world jolted.

Squeezing her eyes shut, she willed herself somewhere else. It wasn't the room. No corners, no floor, no ceiling. She wasn't back there. "Sun-

shine, sunshine, sunshine," she chanted, willing the vision to change. "Sunshine, sunshine…"

Something shifted. Warmth caressed her face. Emma opened her eyes, squinting into the light, and as her vision adjusted, a new world came into focus. She was looking through a window at a sky white with clouds that seemed to glow as the sun tried to beat through them. High up, stories above the tallest buildings, Emma surveyed a sea of gray.

She wasn't hugging herself anymore. Instead, her hands were braced against the windowsill, fingers curled so tightly into it, they hurt. But Emma couldn't make herself let go. Her gaze swept over the world then slid down to the computer screen between her hands. The sight of her own face made anger roil deep inside her, a silent growl that subtly rocked her entire being.

"She must have had help."

That voice made the anger worse. Still staring at her own picture, Emma saw her hands change in her periphery—her skin darkened, fingers lengthened and thickened until they weren't her hands anymore. "You assured me the Hawk would not be compromised." No, not hers. Someone else's hands. And voice. And mind.

"I believed that to be true, sir. He'd been put on mind reader detail before and proved impervious to telepathic manipulation."

The fingers curled down harder, nearly prying the fingernails from their beds. The only outward sign of aggression he displayed; one the other man never saw. "You have spent too much time among soldiers, Sergeant Major," her host said mildly. "You've forgotten that the most powerful influence on a man's mind isn't a telepath, but a woman."

A pause. "I don't understand, sir." The sergeant major didn't take kindly to having his trainee's honor impugned, especially one into whose grooming he'd invested years. Almost two decades. Griffith had all the files on it.

"Then allow me to explain. We have spent a fortune programming the asset into believing his job as a retrieval specialist and assassin served to protect the vulnerable. And you put him in charge of the most vulnerable-looking time bomb ever spawned. What exactly did you expect him to do?"

"With all due respect, sir," the sergeant major grated, "the Special

Unit project was your idea."

"Yes, and it would have worked perfectly, if only you'd displayed a little foresight."

"We lost one subject. We'll get another one."

The angry growl inside her turned into a roar. The hands on the windowsill relaxed, and the man turned to face the com screen. "Do you think I spent two decades on reconnaissance to waste our element of surprise on some insignificant child?"

No. His game was much bigger than that, and the sergeant major knew it. His face turned ruddy. "The Hawk may still recover her."

Teeth ground in a screep that made Emma shudder. "Consider the Hawk a sunk cost. Thanks to your botched recovery attempt, he's probably half a universe away. If I were you, I'd pray he went underground and not straight to the other side."

The sergeant major pulled his shoulders back, clearly not happy with that solution. "Your orders?"

Emma's host turned away, his gaze resting on an old printed picture of two young men in mud-covered clothes, laughing together.

The moment she recognized them, Emma jolted out of the vision.

Senator Griffith's final words followed her into wakefulness: "We'll strike at the heart of them."

~

Emma's scream shocked John into full and instant consciousness. Her hands flailed up to her ears, accidentally smacking him in the face. He caught her knee before it could smash his privates into his spine. "Emma!"

She kicked and fought, battling the monsters conjured up from her nightmare, and it was all he could do to keep them both from ending up on the floor. "John!" she screamed. "No!"

The door burst open and light flooded the room, sending Emma into a panic. Before he could snarl at the intruder, multiple hands grabbed them and tore them apart. John roared and fought back, but the four of them, each with a firm grasp on one of his limbs, held him off the ground where he couldn't get proper leverage.

And all the while, Emma screamed and screamed as if being ripped apart from the inside.

John flexed his muscles, pulling in on himself and dragging his captors with him. Then, in a move he hadn't had to use since his hazing days in basic training, he snapped straight again, knocking them all off balance. One lost his hold on John's leg, and the second John pulled it free, he kicked out with vicious precision. His heel connected with a jaw. His knee broke a nose. Then both of his legs were free. With a snarl, he spun around and slammed the last two against the wall. One persistent mother fucker dug his fingers into John's arm, and John punched him in the face, again and again, until the man couldn't hold on anymore.

Without missing a beat, John went for Emma.

Before he'd even taken a full step, more of those goddamn telepaths mobbed him and he had no hope of getting past them unless he wanted to kill someone. When Emma screamed his name again he seriously considered it.

Of the four who'd held him, three had revived enough to grab hold of him from the back as three more crowded in from the front. John kicked one's feet out from under him. Bit down on another's wrist. Punched a third before two grabbed his arm and a knee in his back forced him to the ground.

John almost wrenched his own neck trying to raise his head to search for Emma. As the rest of the telepaths converged, MacMurphy swept in, plucked Emma up, and carried her out of the room. Then someone punched John's lights out.

He woke in shackles. The cell they'd put him in was more of an unfinished construction project; everything was covered with dust, the doorframe was empty, and the miniscule window had a dark outline around it where someone had mapped out a larger, future opening.

John rubbed his temple, careful of the fist-sized lump, and didn't try to get up while everything still spun around him. He had a hard time making his eyes focus, but he didn't need to examine the metal rings on his wrists to know what they were: standard-issue house arrest paraphernalia with a set center point and a radius in which the wearer could move. One step outside that radius and the shackles would zap him with varying levels of electricity. They could be programmed to deliver anywhere from a little bite to a shock strong enough to render him unconscious. The higher threshold had the unfortunate side effect of making the victim incontinent for a few days.

Without knowing the parameters, John had no idea how far he could go before the shackles activated, or how bad it would be when they did. He didn't risk it. "Hello?" he called. The vibration of his own voice made his head pound. "Anybody there?"

Movement in the doorway caught his eye. A boy no more than six years old peeked around the edge to stare at him through wide eyes. Having never interacted with people that young, John had no idea what to say. He didn't want to spook the boy, but that steady stare made him twitchy. And twitchy soldiers were dangerous. "Hello," he tried.

The boy didn't respond.

Was he hallucinating this? "What's your name?"

A slow blink, then nothing.

John stifled a shudder. "Do you live here?"

More staring.

Christ, was this how Emma had felt back at the base? She'd talked to him every time he'd brought her food, tried to get him to talk back, and he'd ignored her. "What do you want?" It came out harsher than he'd intended, and he flinched.

The boy didn't. He stepped out from around the corner into full view and just stood there. His clothes were too big on him. He had the cuffs rolled up until they bulged at his wrists and ankles, and his shirt tucked into pants that had to be held up by suspenders. Good looking kid, but painfully thin. His eyes were almost too large for his face, half hidden beneath an uneven fringe of hair.

John's heart gave a painful thump. An orphan always recognized another. "I'm John," he said.

Without a word, the boy stepped into the room in his too-big shoes. He approached slowly, like a skittish wild animal. Sitting on the floor, John was at eye level with him and, even though he knew absolutely nothing about kids, he suspected the boy should have been bigger at his age.

Step by step, the child came to John. Wide brown eyes stared into his, then a small hand raised and a tiny finger brushed down the center of John's forehead. John felt the touch like static electricity against his frontal lobe, and he sucked in a startled breath.

The boy blinked and did it again, then laid his little hand flat just above John's nose and closed his eyes.

John realized what he was trying to do. "You can't read me, kid."

"Don't wanna," the boy said, almost in a whisper.

John felt a pulling sensation along the inside of his skull, like a net dragging across the surface. Then it was gone, and the boy opened his eyes, filled with such relief, they glittered with tears. "You okay, kid?"

The boy dipped a slow nod, then walked away, leaving John all alone again, wondering what the hell that had been about.

~

"One man whispered and they all listened," Emma said. "And the Shadows were born."

"That's right."

"You're lying!" Emma beat her palms against her head to stop the echoes all shouting the same thing back at her: *Lying! Lying!* Someone had put a plate of cookies out on the kitchen table, and those cookies laughed at her, called her a freak.

She heard the others outside, too. They'd tried to fix her, but she'd screamed them out of the room. Now they were out there pacing like rabid dogs with their prey just out of reach, waiting for her to fall out of the tree so they could rip into her.

They'd hurt her soldier boy.

Emma opened the balcony door inside her mind and screamed at them at the top of her lungs, venting her fear and rage. She screamed and screamed until it all emptied out and they were falling to their knees, cursing her. They wished she was back with the Shadows in their bright white room where no shadow lived.

She hated them for it. All of them.

"That's enough, Emma!" Big John snapped. He'd never yelled at her before. She was his favorite.

"Enough, Emma!" she echoed. Yes, she'd had just about enough.

Matching his ire, she pushed off the couch he'd sat her on, and immediately keeled over. She caught her knee against the table corner, felt skin break and tear. When she dropped, she ground that knee into the floor, focusing on the pain to find her way back.

"One whispered. All listened." She laughed as Big John grasped her arms to help her up. What a joke. "How could one whisper, when there were two?"

Big John flinched.

"*Two.*"

He sighed. "Yes," he finally admitted, "two. Matthew Griffith and I were both on the advisory committee thirty years ago. Everyone was still riding on the success of the chem-treatments, oblivious to anything besides their own satisfaction that things were finally back to normal. Matthew and I were the only ones who knew nothing was that simple anymore; we were the ones who went before the ICG and presented the possibility of chem-resistance. Of course, by then, it was already widespread, but no one paid attention. All we did was point it out and suggest it might be prudent to investigate alternatives. We were laughed out of the room."

"No imagination." No foresight. The government didn't want change; they didn't think it was necessary, and neither did they have the scientific brain capacity to understand that every action had an equal and opposite reaction. The emerging antichem movement should have been a foregone conclusion.

Big John brought out the first aid kit and knelt in front of her. "We changed people, Emma. The moment we turned on each other, we started changing people. There were those who'd come through the war and had children, grandchildren, great-grandchildren, all of them perfectly able to survive all on their own, without ever receiving any kind of chemical help. Their descendants were the first to show resistance to the treatment; their bodies had evolved by necessity to be more resilient. We had no idea, until the government forced us to look into it on our own. We traced entire family trees back to the fallout survivors. Every single chem-resistant individual has an ancestor like that."

Emma watched him clean her knee of blood and snap open a sealant packet. If what he said was true, then a great big portion of the population would never be affected by the treatments, no matter how many times they got injected. And their numbers would keep growing. *Nature always finds a way...* "Who knows?"

Big John brought the stick to her torn skin and carefully pulled it across her wound. The solution puckered the edges together, effectively sealing it. No bandages necessary. "Not many. Oh, they know about the resistance; it's become too widespread and obvious to ignore. But they don't know how it originated. They've already spent decades chasing their own tails to create a better, stronger treatment to bring everyone in line again. Matthew Griffith knew they'd fail. He and I knew what was coming. We tried to warn the ICG, but they wouldn't listen. They insisted their approach was correct, that the only way to preserve peace was to enforce equality, by any means necessary. Matthew agreed with them. I didn't. That's where we not-so-amicably parted ways."

"He's like us?"

"In a way. He can't read minds, but he has a gift for induction and extrapolation, to the point where he can predict the future. In all the years I've known him, he's rarely been wrong. When the government laid down their edict, Matthew predicted widespread riots. He was right. He predicted that cities would fall into chaos. He was right. He predicted that people without non-resistant ancestors would become resistant to the chem-treatments, and several more levels of growing unrest would follow, all leading to one final, inevitable stage: another war like the one that brought us to this point. Looks like he might be right about that, too."

Emma drew her knees to her chest. "You both built armies." No, that wasn't right. That wasn't what she'd meant. But, thinking it over, she realized it was exactly right. For once, her mind had come up with something that made sense.

Big John stared at her. "That's not true."

"It is. Shadows and Whispermen. They fight with guns, because they have nothing else. We fight with thoughts and words. People turn on each other, people band together. We clash, we take casualties. We suffer. This is the war the senator predicted."

Big John's expression turned thunderous. "We have never caused harm; that's not what we do. The Evolutionaries—"

"How do you know?" The words had come out as a challenge, but Emma really did want to know. "We teach, we investigate and counsel, and then we leave. How do you know those people don't hurt? How can they not? We sift through them, take bits and pieces. What if we don't leave enough behind? What if we jumble them so bad, they don't remember who they were? What if they're lost?" *What if they're just like me, and they don't even know it?* "Who are we to say they're wrong to begin with? And we keep fixing, and adjusting, making room for ourselves—*and I can't stand it!* Who are you to say I'm broken?" She shoved to her feet again, and this time she stayed on them. "How dare you tell me I need you! You're the reason they did this to me!"

Big John blanched. "What?"

How could he not know? Frustrated, Emma gathered up all the confusion of her dreams and shoved it at him in one jumbled mess. Like throwing away trash. She let it go, and it was gone. And she could sit down and just be, while Big John sorted through it all and comprehended that this was all his fault. His. Not Emma's. She was a POW. If not her this time, it would have been someone else some other time. There'd been others before her, and unless the Shadows were stopped, there'd be more. Because men like Matthew Griffith didn't give up; they were fanatic about their beliefs and weren't above killing to make everyone else convert.

This was their war, whether Big John admitted it or not.

And already their ignorance had put them, and all of their sympathizers at a massive disadvantage.

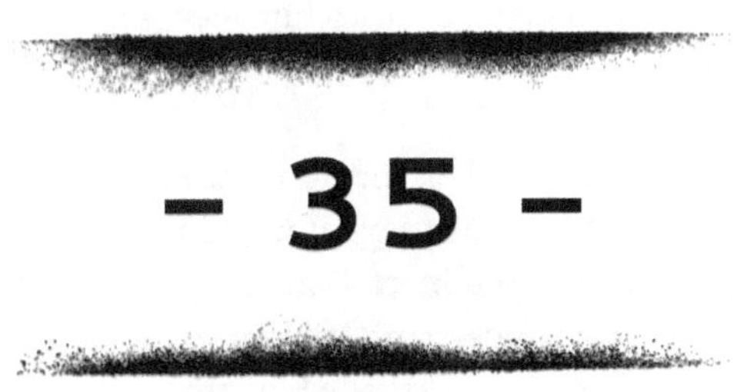

When he'd finished with her dreams, Big John did what Emma knew he would: he called the troops. Everyone eighteen years and older would gather in the big game room for a very important meeting to discuss strategies. He was so busy with his own thoughts, he never noticed little invalid Emma slip away.

She hurried through the compound on bare feet, which were starting to get chilled. Some of her gradient had returned; she could open herself just a little, just enough to "see" ahead and keep out of sight. *Sneaky.* She smiled. This was fun!

The security room three doors down wasn't in an obvious place, and nothing about it said *this is the heart of our operations.* It was just another room, except filled with computers and all sorts of fun gadgets.

Emma had gleaned from someone—she'd forgotten who—that they'd shackled Little John. The key would be in here somewhere, she just had to find it. *Aha!* Emma picked up the square-inch piece of silicone, as thin as paper and a little sticky, and slipped out of the room.

She had to go wide to avoid colliding with a little human, and then did a double take, stopping in her tracks to look at the young boy standing in the middle of the hallway. He was so sad, but he held her gaze with the confidence of someone much older. Emma crouched in front of him and met that wizened gaze, searching for what had snagged her. There was a hook in him somewhere.

No, there wasn't. Emma frowned, then smiled. His head was shiny.

Not as flawlessly as Little John's, but almost there. Even as she traced its contours with her thoughts, she felt him mending the cracks. "Little little John," she said.

He smiled at her.

Then her smile faded, and his did, too. The most powerful telepath she'd met in a long time was trapped in the body of a six-year-old boy. And he'd made himself inert. Emma didn't know how, but she knew why. "They won't understand," she warned, but he already knew this and she wouldn't try to persuade him otherwise. "Find me. Any time. Anywhere." When she was sure he'd caught her meaning, Emma reached out and hugged him gingerly.

As soon as she'd released him, he ran away. He might never be able to dismantle the shield he'd copied from Little John, but Emma knew he'd never again have another nightmare that wasn't his. No, the other telepaths wouldn't understand why he'd done it, not after spending years, decades learning and honing their own skills into something useful rather than scary. But she hoped they would accept him.

If they didn't, she sure as hell would. And then she'd have one more bone to pick with the man who touted peace and understanding.

The compound was being expanded again. At this rate, Sue would soon occupy half of the city. This wing wasn't anywhere near finished; the lights in the hallways were sparse, and the rooms were more like creepy, empty caverns. She didn't like this maze. Ghosts haunted the hallways here.

Shaking her head against their clutches, Emma picked up her step.

A sudden, eerie scrape of metal against a hard surface sounded like a skeleton dragging, and she almost ran the other way. It was coming for her. It would rip out her heart and wear her skin.

Emma shuddered, forcing breaths past the lump in her throat. When she felt brave again, she moved her feet to follow the sound. *Die head-on.* Life was too short to live in fear. Her toes dragged through the dust, and her T-shirt wasn't enough to stave off the artificial chill. She hugged herself, rubbed her arms for warmth, bit her lips to bring back some feeling. She'd almost chewed her mouth bloody by the time she found soldier boy sprawled out on the floor of the very back room.

There he lay, spread eagle in the middle, sliding his arms back and forth as if making an invisible snow angel. And there was the scraping sound: his cuffs dragging across the floor. Emma smiled in relief. "Soldier boy," she whispered, but he didn't hear her.

John grunted and slammed one of his cuffs against the floor. When he sat up, Emma noticed the dark bruises that marred his jaw. His lip was split, and a huge knot bulged on his temple. She was all ready to start ranting at him about that, but he spotted her at the same time.

"Emma." He shot to his feet in an instant, took a step, then pulled up short, hands fisting at his sides. How far could he go before the cuffs hurt him?

Emma stepped into the room and reached out her hand for his. John took it and pulled her roughly into his arms. Stunned, she just stood there for a moment while he muttered curses into her hair. "Are you okay?"

He was asking her? She wasn't the one who'd been beaten black and blue. His heartbeat thumped against her cheek, and she sighed. *Seashell.* "No foot chewing. I brought a key."

John laughed and, just as she started to get comfortable, pushed her away. His hands brushed back her hair, cupped her face, ran down her throat and arms, then back up to her face, and all the while the cutest frown furrowed his brow. "What happened? Did they hurt you?"

Emma shook her head, and there he went again, smashing her against his chest. This time, she hugged him in return, patting his back. "There, there, seashell."

"Tell me what happened."

Funny. No *give me the key,* or even *get me out of here.* "I'm cold," she answered.

He squeezed her tighter, rubbed her back. She was so tired. Her mind needed time off and she just couldn't shut it down long enough to rest. She hadn't had a good night's sleep in so long…

John jarred her, and Emma jerked. Had she just dozed off? With the way her eyes felt, dry and swollen, that's exactly what she'd done. How long? "What time is it?"

"Baby, you're asleep on your feet," he said, gray eyes worried.

Emma shrugged, held up the silicone key. When John proffered his arm, she twisted the cuff on his wrist to find the lockpad, then stuck the key onto it. The cuffs beeped and expanded to maximum capacity so he could pull his hands out. No muss, no fuss. The key only worked once, then dissolved.

John tossed the cuffs and tucked her to his side. "Come on, let's get you to bed."

"As long as we cuddle afterward."

They got turned around in the maze and had to backtrack a couple of times before they made it back to the main section. "How are you holding up?"

Emma yawned so hugely, her eyes closed. They wouldn't reopen when her mouth closed, either. She hummed in answer and dragged her feet where he led. That's why she didn't see.

When John stopped suddenly, Emma jarred halfway awake.

"Hi," she heard a familiar voice say, and her eyes snapped open just as the first punch landed.

~

John's head snapped back and forward again. The blow was nowhere near as bad as what he used to get from other Shadows, but it made him see red, and his brain automatically switched to live combat mode. He shoved Emma back, out of harm's way, and launched at the son of a bitch who'd sucker punched him.

Objective: Destroy the enemy.

Parameters: None.

Number of opponents: One combatant.

Not even a challenge. John grabbed hold, slammed his opponent into the wall and pinned him there to deliver a rapid one-two to the guy's left kidney before several sets of arms and hands dragged him off.

John twisted to ram his head into one's nose, freed an elbow and drove it into the other guy's shoulder, dislocating it. The third pointed a weapon at him. A snot-faced, wide-eyed kid, shaking from head to toe. John lunged for him.

The gun went off, but the charge missed John and seared a hole in the ceiling instead.

He wrenched the weapon away from the kid, disassembled it with the ease of an afterthought. The kid whimpered, and his hands shot up in surrender when John started for him. By then, the first guy had come back to his senses and jumped onto John's back. John reached over his shoulder, took hold of the guy's jacket, then bent double to flip him to the ground.

"Enough!"

Female voice. Too young to pose any threat, but the sheer authority behind her command countermanded John's overwhelming desire to drive his booted heel into his enemy's skull. He pulled back at the last second, stepped away, and turned to face the girl with Travis by her side.

Travis looked murderous, but he didn't make a move. Smart man. John would have made minced meat of him, given half a chance. He might still do it if the man kept looking at Emma like he was about to make a run for her to take her away. *Not a fucking chance, asshole. Not again.* John shifted to put himself between Emma and the rest of them.

The little girl next to Travis glared. Against her dark brown skin, her crystal green eyes looked almost inhuman. "Stand down," she ordered, and John automatically stepped his feet apart into a less threatening stance.

Ever the fucking soldier.

With an imperious finger pointed at him in warning, the girl came closer to check on the two he'd taken down. "You better hope there's no permanent damage done. I don't have time to deal with this crap right now." She wore a lab coat, her wild black curls held back by a wide headband, and for some reason, the guy whose nose John had broken looked relieved she was there. "Can you walk?" she asked him.

The man nodded.

"Go to the clinic. I'll be right there. Matt, stop whining. Help me with Andy."

While the kid hurried to help the guy with a dislocated shoulder to his feet, the sucker-puncher dragged himself up, winded and disheveled. He had to know he had no chance in hell of taking on John, but the look in his eye said he was eager to give it another go. "Give me one good reason why I shouldn't kill you right now," he said.

Big talk for such an incompetent man.

"Knock it off, Jeremy," the girl general snapped, "and I mean right now."

"Don't tell me what to do, Brain," he returned, staring John down.

"What part of *no fighting* do you not understand?" she demanded.

Jeremy was about to answer, when his gaze shifted beyond John.

John felt rather than heard Emma's approach and delighted in the rising panic on Jeremy's face as she flattened herself against John's back, and peeked out from under his arm. "Hi, bro," she mumbled, then hid her face against John's spine.

Bro?

Jeremy. As in Jeremy Calen.

To his right, Travis smirked with malicious glee as John mentally connect the dots.

Ah, shit.

– 36 –

The moment the door closed behind them, it began.

The yelling. Travis' head pounded already. He rubbed his temples, popped a cookie into his mouth. Emma was fast asleep on the couch, totally oblivious to the world at large. *Lucky her.*

"You realize this is getting us nowhere," Juliet said at a surprisingly mellow decibel level. She and Steven had slipped in to mediate before Travis could shut the door in their faces. The general consensus was that Jeremy would get himself killed if left unattended. Travis couldn't say he blamed him, though. If he hadn't been so focused on Emma back when they'd first found her, he would have tried to take Wayland's head off himself. And would have probably gotten himself killed just as quickly. "He's not backing down."

"*He* is standing right here," the soldier said.

Juliet blinked at him. "I know. Why do you think we're saying all of this out loud?" She turned back to Jeremy. "Point is, he's not telling us squat, so I say we go another route."

Travis snorted.

"You got something worthwhile to add to this discussion?" Juliet asked him.

Well, at least she hadn't called him an asshole. He stuffed another cookie into his mouth. "No'awal," he said around the bite, waving her on. "Wo on."

"Pig."

And there they went, shouting again.

They weren't catching on to the facts, here, so intent on taking Wayland down for messing with their Pixie that they couldn't see what was right in front of them. That girl, fast asleep on the couch, was the one weak spot Wayland had. He'd engaged Jeremy to protect her, not himself. Even now he stood in front of her, facing off with the rest of them like some self-appointed bodyguard. The fact that Travis didn't like it was irrelevant; he was a big enough person to realize they couldn't win this war without an ace up their sleeve, and right now, Wayland was all they had. So as long as the Shadow kept putting himself between Emma and a potential threat, Travis would tolerate his presence. Still wouldn't stop him from using it against Wayland, if necessary.

—*There's a computer behind you,*— Jeremy said without moving his mouth.

—*So?*—

—*Let's see what there is to know about this guy.*—

Emma mumbled in her sleep and everyone finally shut up for a minute, all eyes watching as Wayland tucked a blanket around her.

Travis curled his hands into fists, scowling at nothing in particular.

Worse, Jer noticed, and they engaged in a silent staring contest before Juliet's quiet voice broke the silence. "They will come for her again."

"Not just her," Wayland said. "All of you. You need to start preparing."

—*He's right,*— Travis told them.

—*The hell he is!*— Jeremy's powerful knee-jerk reaction pushed Travis back a step. He'd never known Jeremy to be such a hot-head, but then again, his sister had never been in so much trouble before.

—*I've seen what they can do,*— Travis tried again, hoping to make the man see reason.

Jeremy ignored him. Steven tapped his foot, itching to get at the computer.

Looking from the boy to the others in the room, Juliet's face pinched with worry. "Why don't you go put her to bed?" she offered in the general direction of Jeremy and the soldier. "Poor thing looks exhausted."

Jeremy stepped up before she'd finished. "*I'll* take her."

Too bad by then Wayland had already picked her up. "Try," he dared, staring Emma's brother down like he couldn't wait to go another round.

"Boys," Juliet warned, "don't make me tell on you."

Jeremy forced a feral smile. "You don't know where her room is. Let me show you."

When they walked out, Travis sighed. If they reached Emma's room without incident, he'd eat his shorts.

As soon as the door closed, Steven opened his mouth. "Are we actually saying we want to use him?" His way with words never ceased to amaze Travis.

"I don't know," Juliet said. "Maybe." Uncertainties weren't her thing; she hated not knowing all of the variables. Right now, they only knew John Wayland was a Shadow soldier who seemed to be impervious to telepathic probes. Nobody liked those facts, especially since it meant they couldn't verify anything he told them.

"We could always go it alone," Steven suggested.

"We could," Travis replied, turning to the computer console, "but I, for one, would like to live through the next year." Possible traitor status notwithstanding, the sad truth was, no one knew the Shadows better than one of their own. They didn't have to like it—Travis sure as hell didn't—but one way or another, they had to make use of him. It'd be plain stupid not to.

Juliet rubbed her temples. "Find anything?"

"Nothing recent. All I have so far is his birth record and some early school things. Oh. Oh, wait a minute…"

Steven and Juliet rushed over to see.

"Climb on my back, why don't you?"

They both took a step in retreat. A small one. "What did you find?"

Travis was quiet for a moment as he read through the report, scrolling too fast for Juliet to keep up. "Damn," he said. "I found a police report. Hold on. Wow." He whistled, spearing his fingers through his hair, tempted to feel a smidgen of sympathy for John Wayland. Or at least the boy he used to be.

"Speak," Juliet snapped.

"Hold on!" he growled. "The guy's got history, okay? And it's not pretty."

Juliet frowned and tried to push him aside so she could see better.

"What do you mean?"

"There was an incident twenty years ago on Colony 39."

Colonies that didn't even warrant a name were not nice places to live. Most had been set up in a rush with minimal prep, which meant the people there had to scramble to create enough of anything to sustain a population. These colonies tended to be overcrowded, poverty-stricken, and dangerous.

Steven shoved him aside. "Here, move over." Travis shrugged and let him at it. The boy was better at this stuff, anyway. "The police responded to what they called a noise complaint. Translation: someone was screaming bloody murder, and the neighbors freaked out."

"What did they find?"

"Bloody murder. This report is pretty damn comprehensive. Three officers were called to a ten-story building in the slums. The residents had already emptied and were standing around outside. The cops had to use riot gear to get through them into the building.

"They broke down the door and found a guy choking the life out of a seven-year-old boy while screaming in his face to"—Steven crooked his fingers in air quotes—"let him in. The mother was already dead, throat cut. Bled out all over the floor."

"Holy shit," Juliet whispered. At some point, she'd turned gray underneath her tan.

"Yeah," Travis said. Definitely not what he'd expected them to find.

Steven read the trailing end of the report. "He had a two-year-old sister. They found her... Oh, my God."

Juliet turned away. "I think I'm going to be sick."

"He couldn't get in." At the sound of Emma's voice, the three of them jumped. Red hair tousled, fully dressed but barefoot, she stood just outside the doorway, peering at them around the edge. "He wanted in, wanted control, but his wife had locked the door. So he beat at her to force her. But she didn't break. Little John doesn't know. They killed him so he wouldn't remember."

"Is it weird that what she just said almost makes sense to me?" Steven asked.

Juliet approached her slowly. "Pixie, where is Jeremy?"

—*Stop treating her like she's a wild animal,*— Travis snapped at her across a private channel.

Juliet flinched, glared back at him. *—I'm not!—*

—You're scared. You look scared, and she can see it.—

He'd caught that hurt look in Emma's eyes before she shrugged and peered down at the miniature tranquilizer gun in her hand. The one Juliet had insisted on bringing in case Wayland snapped again. "Sleeping," she told Juliet. "He was very sleepy."

Travis's mouth twitched. Served his ass right.

—You wouldn't be this cavalier if it had been you she'd knocked out with a tranq.—

—Obviously,— Travis retorted. *—I'd be fast asleep.—* He nudged her away to give Emma a celebratory one-armed hug. "Good job," he told her. "Where'd you stash the soldier?"

Emma looked up suddenly with a big, happy smile. "I like him."

Travis scowled. She couldn't know what she was saying.

Juliet crossed her arms. *—Didn't MacMurphy want you to stay away from her?—*

—I don't give a shit what he wants,— Travis replied, giving Steven a mindful, too, as he ushered Emma into the room. *—If you all weren't so busy pussyfooting around her, you might realize what Emma needs is for you to knock it the hell off.—*

At the console, Steven stopped typing to face them. *—Okay, dude, that's enough. I get that you have this whole love from afar thing going on, but it's starting to cloud your judgment. You were there last night. She's not stable. We don't know what will set her off. Keep pushing like you are, and you'll push her right off the cliff.—*

Emma huffed and shoved away from Travis. "Stop talking like I can't hear," she snapped. "I may not know what you're saying, but I know you're saying it."

Travis and Steven glared at each other.

"We're sorry, Pixie," Juliet said, not sounding the least bit contrite.

Emma ignored her and instead pointed at the console. "He couldn't get in. His wife locked the door. Only the kids had a key, and she locked them, too."

There was a moment of silence while they all absorbed what she said. Juliet all but radiated pity, which Travis couldn't stomach for another minute, so he blocked her out. Emma made sense. It just wasn't the kind they were used to. "Wayland inherited his mental shields from his mother?" he guessed.

"Oh!" Steven snapped his fingers. "*That's* what that meant?"

Emma frowned. "Not like brown hair. Second generation upgrade." She tilted her head at Steven. "Motherboard-anchored, not independent. Downloaded lock without the key. Little little John did it too, but different."

"Now you're talking my language," Steven said with a grin.

"Then please translate for the rest of us," Juliet asked sweetly.

"I'm guessing the daddy was a telepath, right?"

Pixie nodded.

"Abusive?"

Another nod.

"And somehow the wife learned to protect herself and her children. Daddy tried to push them, they wouldn't give, he went into a rage and killed them all."

"Amazing how you can say all that with a smile on your face."

Travis groaned. They really needed to start locking the door.

Wayland looked like his head would explode, but he wasn't looking at Steven, he was glaring at Travis, and the arm he had around Emma.

"Hey," Emma greeted with a smile, oblivious to the byplay. "We found you."

- 37 -

John's stomach twisted violently, trying to cast up what wasn't there, but he gritted his teeth and held steady. A small handful of random words strung together into his nightmare: *Daddy went into a rage and killed them all.*

The only thing that kept him on his feet was the sight of Travis' arm around Emma. Having been denied a go at the man who truly deserved his wrath, John focused his rage on the only available target. He'd so enjoy tearing that arm from Travis' body.

The guy must have sensed it; he let go of Emma and stepped a respectful distance away. Didn't calm John one bit.

Steven reached for the console to turn everything off.

"Don't!" John snapped, and both Travis and Steven flinched. From the corner of his eye, John saw Juliet trying to herd Emma away, but Emma wouldn't budge.

John's focus didn't stray from the console screen. It could be nothing. For all he knew, John Wayland wasn't even his real name. The Shadows might have planted those stories, or it could be someone else entirely. Didn't have to mean what he was afraid it meant. No reason not to step into the room and take a look. Except, his feet refused to move.

Emma waited patiently for him to make up his mind, completely oblivious to everyone else's discomfort.

Juliet made her escape first. "I think I should go check on Jeremy." She edged around John and out of the room.

"It was Calen's idea to look you up," Steven said.

"But I wholly supported it," Travis added.

"I don't care whose idea it was," John said. "I just want to know what you found."

Steven relaxed instantly. "Oh. Okay, then." He stepped away from the console and waved John in.

When John didn't move, Emma took his hand. "Don't worry, I've got you." Her steady gaze held his, anchoring him in the now. Without any words, she told him it would all be okay, no matter what. She knew what it was to have her whole self stripped away, and if she could fight through it to reclaim her life, John could do no less. "Time to get you back from the dead."

"You think that's me?"

"You are who you choose to be," she replied. "Shadows cut off your head, gave you wings in its place. Neither of them are the legs you stand on. You're still standing. You can fly. But can you see?"

"What's she talking about?" Steven stage-whispered.

Travis shoved at him.

A police report was open on the screen. If John just turned his head, he'd see it.

"Do you *want* to see?" Emma asked.

What he wanted was his white queen back. If he could just look at the chess piece, touch it, he'd know how much of this was real and how much was a cheat.

Emma squeezed his hand. She was still pale and thin, her hair wild around her face. Scuffed up and chipped, but still so damn strong and steady. The strongest person in the room, as far as John was concerned. He looked down at her soft hand tucked so trustingly into his. *Queen takes rook. Checkmate.*

He had to know.

Keeping hold of Emma's hand, he turned to the screen. He had to read the first few sentences several times before they started to make sense, and the more he read, the tighter his stomach clenched. The report had pictures and feeds from that night, so he played the first—a direct feed of the entire operation—and beheld his nightmares come to life.

The sounds of screaming carried loudly enough to be picked up by recorders even before the police broke down the door. Inside, the place was dark and dirty, with stained walls and torn furniture. There was blood on the floor, drag marks where someone had crawled, bleeding, from one room to another.

As the main feed played, snapshots from multiple perspectives separated into a virtual file. In a still of the kitchen where some kind of fight had taken place, John focused on the empty slot of a knife stand where the largest knife should have been.

The next set was of the nursery, a rickety pen with torn blankets. No blood, just a little girl on the floor, her head turned at an angle so awkward, her neck must have been snapped. She looked so still, so small in the middle of that mess.

Screaming on the main feed brought his attention back as the police barged down the hallway and into the bedroom, where a sweaty, crazy-eyed man shook a boy, yelling into his face. The police shouted at him to release the child, to stand back, but even John had trouble understanding them through the clamor. The man didn't notice, so lost in his rage, so focused on his son, he had no idea other people were in the room.

Finally a single shot rang out.

A clean hit, straight to the head. The man dropped the boy, and his disgusting girth tumbled to the floor, across his dead wife. After ascertaining the suspect showed no further life signs, inadvertently recording the man's brains leaking out from the hole in his head, the police officer in charge turned to the boy.

He was in shock, curled up on the floor, staring at his mother, wide eyes leaking tears, but he wasn't sobbing. His arms were black and blue, one visibly broken, and his face was red from having been struck again and again. John felt a relentless burn in his cheeks which no amount of tears could ever cool.

Suddenly, the boy scrambled forward and started shoving at the dead man, trying so hard to get him off his mother. The police moved the man's bulk so the boy could get to her. Scrawny, malnourished, he petted her hair, shook her shoulder, crying for her to open her eyes, to say something.

When he realized she wouldn't be waking up, the boy looked at the officer in charge. "Kill me, too," he said. "Please."

The feed stopped, freezing on the boy's grief-stricken face.

Same eyes, same mouth. His nose had grown since then, and his hair had darkened, but John knew exactly who he was looking at: himself.

He could feel the others watching him. Emma squeezed his hand. He was clutching hers too hard. John forced his fingers to uncurl and let her go. Then he brought up the PD search they'd hacked and typed in a query: Ivan Sergeyevich, Greenfield Commons.

The database gave him nothing.

Behind him, Travis cleared his throat. "Need some help?" He tried to sound casual, but John still heard pity in his tone. He steeled himself against telling Travis to take his fucking olive branch and shove it up his ass. Instead, John gave a tight nod and stepped aside.

Travis nudged Steven to take over. The boy read the query, then brought up several other searches and typed in string after string of incomprehensible code. John knew how to acquire names and accounts, mostly by hacking a terminal and searching its most recent recorded transactions, but what the teen did now was beyond him.

In a few minutes, Steven had several reports all open at the same time: the life and death of a priest-turned-orphanage school principal. Ivan was real, and so was Greenfield. Ivan's death hadn't been listed in the police records because it had never been investigated. His death certificate cited his cause of death as "natural." His heart had simply stopped; he'd supposedly died of old age.

"I don't get it. Is this significant in some way?"

"It is to me," John said.

"Check if there was an autopsy performed," Travis suggested.

Steven typed some more, and said, "No autopsy. They took blood samples as standard procedure, but tests came back clean."

"Show me."

Steven pulled up the report.

Travis read through it, squinting. "His oxygen levels were above average."

"He was poisoned," John said.

"Not necessarily," Travis replied. "A lot of things could account for this."

"Did the orphanage keep logs?" John asked Steven, stomach churning. They'd already proven one of his nightmares was real. What was a few more? The floodgates had been opened; he couldn't close them again. John dug his nails into his palm, focusing on the pain to keep himself grounded.

His Shadow training took over. When a situation's parameters changed, recalculations became necessary to compensate. John shoved his emotional maelstrom into the background and scrutinized the facts from a bird's eye view, a detached observer, nothing more.

His dreams weren't full sequences of events, only snapshots of the important ones. But his younger self had kept meticulous time—he'd counted the days after the incident with the bully, dreading with each passing hour the punishment he'd been sure to receive. If John saw the logs, he'd know if it had really happened.

"Let's see." Steven started typing, then scoffed. "You call this security? Don't make me laugh. Oh, come on, that wasn't even a challenge."

"Don't mind him, he does this a lot," Travis told him as Steven hacked into the orphanage records database, then narrowed the results down to seven days before and seven days after Ivan's date of death.

"Guide me, guru man," Steven said. "What am I looking for?"

"That, right there." John pointed out a date and Steven selected it, giving them all time to read through a series of events the record keeper had thought were significant. Grocery delivery, upcoming class schedule change due to a holiday, grants received, two children adopted out.

Nothing out of the ordinary, which, in and of itself, was a clue. That would have been the day he'd have beaten the class bully almost to death. "Can you cross-reference this with the infirmary records?"

"Piece of cake. Well, would you look at that."

The infirmary records showed no admittance for a boy named Caleb Frye, but it did show a change in his condition when he'd come out of a chemically induced coma four days later. Steven brought up his chart next. Caleb had a history of fights, several treatments of fractures and contusions. The chart even had an entry for a faked stomach flu when he'd tried to get out of finals one year.

No mention of his being admitted for long-term observation. That would have been a search trigger.

"Go back to the log and check for visitors."

"Okay… Nothing."

"Parking scans?"

"Nope. Might help me if I knew what I was looking for."

"A conversation Ivan Sergeyevich had with a tall man in a strange military uniform regarding the adoption of one John Wayland. He'd been denied the petition."

Steven clucked his tongue in thought, then said, "Orphanages do background checks, right?"

"I suppose."

He typed some more, talking to himself all the while. "The account had been shut down after his death, but not wiped. Let me see if I can… Okay. Here we go. Time stamp, check. Uh-huh, yep, here we go…"

"No, you have to go left," Emma suddenly said, and John looked over at her, surprised she was still there and completely absorbed in Steven's search.

"I'm in virtual land, girl," Steven retorted. "You'll have to be more specific on the directions."

With a huff, Emma pointed right in front of Steven's nose. "Linguistics fall short of their definition. We don't have the nomenclature to classify the species. You have to run a visual tracker through the trees."

Steven stared at her.

"What?" Emma said. "I'm not an idiot."

"I'm beginning to see that," the kid said and traded looks with Travis, then shook his head and faced the screen again. "Right, yeah. Have a gander and tell me if anyone looks familiar."

A whole lot of ID images scrolled across the screen—hundreds, if not thousands, of searches Ivan had done in the days before his death. "There! That one."

Steven paused the stream and brought up the search records. The sergeant major's unsmiling face filled the top left corner, while his personal history streamed down in neat, organized sections—his date and place of birth, schooling history, employment as a personal security specialist, a spouse of five years, and two young children, both killed in a transport collision. All fake.

Ivan must have realized it, too. The sergeant major wasn't a chameleon like the rest of them were trained to be; he was a soldier to the core, and it was obvious to anyone who looked at him.

"Wow," Steven said. "There isn't a single part of this that's real. Not even the picture. Look." He brought up the metadata for the image and stripped away the manipulations to recover the original. The generic background disappeared in lieu of the black and white backdrop every Shadow had on his ID record. Instead of the pale green shirt, the sergeant major wore his standard uniform with his rank emblazoned on one shoulder.

Son of a bitch. "The day he came in, I met him outside of Ivan's office…"

"Do you want to get out of here?"

John was so intimidated by the man, he couldn't do more than shake his head.

"Soon," the man said and walked away with the measured step of a trained soldier.

"Ivan wouldn't hear of letting me go with him. Not even after what I did. I know how the sergeant major works; he would have thrown everything at Ivan to get his way through the proper channels, but he wouldn't have stopped there." John stepped back, trying to distance himself from his own life, to no avail. "He came back, I know he did. Two days after Ivan died, a woman took over the orphanage, rescinded Ivan's decision, and approved the adoption." John had been packed up and carted off so fast, his head had spun. "Jesus, it all happened."

Exactly as his mind had preserved it in his dreams.

And no matter how many times Dr. Wen had zapped his brain, those memories had survived.

"Welcome back," Emma said, her smile sad.

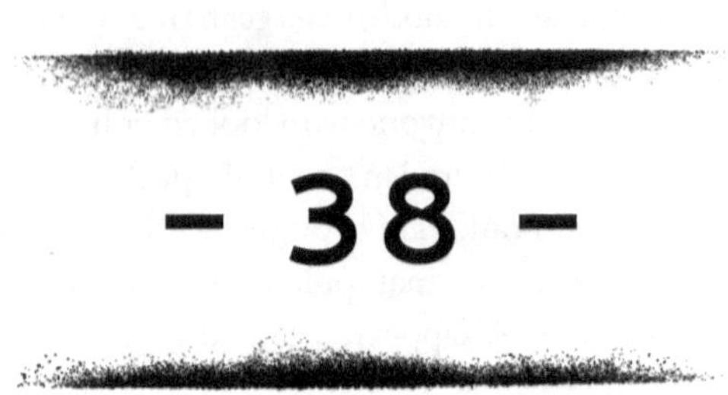

- 38 -

Back in his room, John slammed the door shut. Shivering as though with a fever, he sat down onto the bed and buried his face in his hands, bracing himself for hell.

It was one thing to relive his memories through nightmares he couldn't stop or control, something else to do it fully cognizant of what he was doing. But John needed to know. He let go of the rigid restraint he'd always imposed on his own mind and let the nightmares wash over him.

Just like that, he was seven years old again, terrified of his father and the nightly interrogations…

John sat across the rickety old table from a tall, bulky man past his prime, while his father stuffed his face with Mom's beef stew.

And the man stared. Cold eyes in a swarthy, sweaty face watched John. "You're lying to me," he said.

"I didn't say anything," John replied, ducking his head.

"Sweetheart, please," his mother said, trying to soothe the man. Her voice was brittle. She could see the explosion coming.

John's father slammed his meaty hand onto the table, rattling dishes and cutlery. "Shut your fucking mouth, Grace! Don't think I don't know about your little trip today."

"I… I went to the store."

"Lying!" He pushed to his feet, shoving the table into John so hard it pinned him to his chair and he couldn't breathe let alone move. "Don't

you fucking lie to me!"

"I'm not! I swear, I only went to the store."

His father grabbed a fistful of Grace's hair and yanked until she cried out. But she tried so hard not to weep. "Please," she whimpered. "You're scaring the boy."

He shoved her away. She reached out to catch herself, but the kitchen was too cramped and overstuffed, and she fumbled, knocking pots and pans off the counter before her head slammed into the corner.

"Mom!" John cried.

His father cuffed him hard enough to make his vision go dark. John would have fallen over, if not for the table pinning him in place. Then, without a word, the man sat back down to his plate. "Eat your goddamn dinner," he said as Grace struggled back to her feet.

With shaking hands, Grace washed her face, then rinsed a few plates before she came to John. No blood, but by morning there would be a massive lump on her temple. She gave him a quivery smile, stroked his hair and face. "Eat, baby boy, so you can grow up big and strong." Then a soft, secret thought whispered to him, —So no one will ever make you feel weak.—

"There, there, soldier boy."

John jerked away from the soothing hand. He stared down at Emma kneeling in front of him. She kept petting him, and he saw her blue puppy eyes begin to lose focus. "Hey, Emma."

She smiled. "Hey, Little John. Where'd you run off to?"

"Back in time for a bit."

"Did you see dinosaurs?"

He couldn't help but chuckle. "Just one."

Emma stroked his face, and his eyes closed. She had the softest hands. And lips. And damn, she tasted so good. "Emma?"

"Shh. Playing."

She pressed her lips to his again, teasing a little, and tempting a hell of a lot more than John was prepared for. He cupped her nape to gently push her away, but instead, ended up tangling his fingers through her silky hair. Emma rose up just a little, parted her lips, and slipped the tip of her tongue along the seam of his. John almost toppled over.

Oh, this was a bad, bad idea. "I don't think we should be doing this," he said, but already he was kissing her back.

"Stop thinking," she said and kissed him deeper. Her hands in his hair, her tongue in his mouth, John groaned and snatched her up from the floor. She braced her knees to either side of his hips, straddling him, and then her arms were around his neck, holding him so tightly, he couldn't help but reciprocate.

"Are you sure you know what you're doing?"

In response, she ground down on his lap. "I'm acquainted with the basics."

"Your brother—"

"Won't talk if he wants to stay awake. When he wakes up. But not for a while. Kiss!"

John laughed against her lips. "You tranqued your brother?"

"He was irritating me."

He caught her hands against him when she tried to pry his shirt loose. "Hold on. You're rushing. Shouldn't you make sure I'm ready first, before you just up and seduce me?"

Emma blinked, then dropped her chin to look down at his lap.

"Smart ass."

She pulled her hands free to resume assaulting his clothes. "Talk later. Kiss now?"

"Emma, wait."

She mewled, squirmed on his lap. "Stalling!"

He caught her hands reaching for his pants, and for a second, he had her palms pressed against his very eager cock. John groaned, squeezing his eyes shut against Emma's smile.

Can't do this. It's Emma! Even he wasn't that much of a bastard.

Then her hands pressed, kneaded, and she purred into his ear, "Want this. Give me."

And that small request nearly made John slip his leash. If he didn't know himself to be immune to telepaths, he'd think for sure she was manipulating him. But she couldn't, so how the hell was she doing this to him? Fifteen minutes ago, she was simply Emma Calen. Now, he couldn't remember why he shouldn't rip off her clothes and take what she offered.

John dropped his forehead to her shoulder. "You're killing me, here."

And because it *was* Emma Calen in his arms, he somehow dredged up enough will power to push her hands away. The little minx curled her fingers and scratched as she went, sending a shudder up his spine. "Emma," he growled. "I'm… trying to be… *Christ.*" She was moving again, her mouth now at his ear. "Is this punishment for what I did to you?"

Past. Present. Future. Her life. Not her life. Emma sitting in the training room, with Lucia and Rafe a wall over. So much love there. He looked at her, and she blushed; she touched him, and he purred. Didn't even know he was doing it. Love so intense, it saturated the air, muddled her head, and Emma felt antsy, out of breath. Overheated.

Walking the empty whisper halls, with no direction, and many at the same time. But she ended up where she always did: in front of one door and a room behind it, and a man inside that. Then she was there in front of him, kissing him. Just one kiss to brush away the sorrow and the pain she saw in his eyes. A man made of stone, steady and true, indestructible on the outside, dying on the inside.

So she kissed him back to life. Him. Her. Head spinning, she did it again. And then she was in his lap, with his arms around her so tight, she couldn't breathe. Didn't want to.

"…punishment for what I did to you?"

Emma stilled. *Where am I?* With Little John. Who really wasn't so little at all. *Where have I been?* In the training room. Dizzy with feelings that weren't her own but resonated on a level she hadn't known was there. It was… Emma didn't know what it was, but it made her desperate to see John.

Empty shell.

Seashell.

Where am I?

"Emma?"

With John. And he sounded like she was lost. Maybe she was. In a lot of things. But this didn't feel *lost*; it felt like the first step on the path back to herself. And it scared her. But this was soldier boy. She could feel him tense up, muscles quaking with strain.

Soldier boy, who stole me. Caged me. Saved me.

And he was still trying to save her. From herself.

Emma pulled back to meet his gaze, as lost as her own. "What time is it?" she whispered.

"You tell me."

No help from him. She had to figure this out for herself. With a nod, she closed her eyes and breathed.

Look inside. Find you.

She took the scary leap off the edge and into darkness. Past the bright rainbow of other people, through the warm, enveloping fog of Lucia and Rafe, and down into the core of her.

There, she found John. John bringing her food. John holding her in the night. John with his shiny head, and strong hands, and eyes deeper than the sea. John who spat in the face of the enemy for her. Always there with her, for her, when no one else was. Her John.

Lucia and Rafe may have pushed her out the door, but she'd come here on her own. Because she wanted him.

Emma opened her eyes and sighed. No more jumble, chaos, confusion, or otherness.

I am Emma. And I want John. It's me, not Lucia. And I want John.

But he still looked at pieces of her and not a solid whole.

Overstepped. On or off; no gradient. Emma didn't need one—things made sense in her head without it—but John was confused. *Not a no,* she told herself against the hurt. *Just not* yet. Swallowing past the lump in her throat, Emma twisted her wrists a little, asking for release.

John let her go. "Hi," he said. Did he see her now?

"Hi." She felt like a fool. She didn't like that feeling. Emma braced against his shoulders and pushed off.

"Hey," he said, hands on her waist to stop her. "You okay?"

Grateful that the dim lighting hid her blush, she nodded. *I forgot.* There were ways to do this. One thing after the other. She'd forgotten and jumped in with both feet, expecting him to follow, because he always did.

Not this time. This time, Emma was all on her own, treading water. About to drown.

He rubbed her sides. "Don't be hurt. You caught me off guard," he said, nuzzling her temple. "I had no idea you felt this way."

"Neither did I," she retorted.

He chuckled. "You sure you're okay?"

Emma shrugged. "Rejected."

John's fingers dug into her sides. He stared at her through burning eyes. "No."

She shrugged again. "Okay."

"You don't believe me? What do you think you're sitting on? I'm this close to shoving my hand down your pants, and the only reason I'm not is because I don't want to wake up to another one of your screaming fits in the middle of the night. Because of me this time."

That rant had started out so well, too! "Is it because I'm incomprehensible? Trust me, I make a lot of sense in my head." *It's the normal people who scare me,* she added to herself.

He thumped his forehead against hers. "It's because I'm having a bit of a hard time adjusting. A couple of days ago, you were my prisoner. Can you see how I might have moral issues with wanting you?"

Emma winced and pulled back, squinting at him. All true, but the words rang false. Her ears itched to hear the real reason she could sense hidden just beneath the surface. Soldier boy looked at her with eyes so clear, almost pleading but wanting something at the same time. There was something… She knew the concept, but what was the word? Had to be the right one.

Then, as if by magic, she read it in his expression. "Solder boy… are you a virgin?"

His eyes went wide. "What? No!"

Emma smiled to see his cheeks flush bright red. "Unspoiled flower."

"Don't be ridiculous. There are no virgins our age. And I'm—was—a soldier."

She nodded. "I know. They kept that leash so tight around your neck, I'm surprised your balls haven't fallen off completely."

He set her aside, shoved to his feet. "You're talking crazy again."

"Maybe," she allowed. "But I'm right, aren't I?"

"No," was his adamant response. "And don't go telling people I'm a virgin. Because I'm not."

Emma drew her knees up to rest her chin on them and watch him prowl the tiny room like a caged animal about to panic.

"I've had lots of sex. Tons. With lots of different women. Why are we even talking about this? It's insane—"

"You're rambling."

"—I'm not a virgin, dammit!"

"Okay," she said. He stared her down to drive his point home, so she nodded. "Not a virgin. Won't tell."

"There's nothing to tell!"

She bit her lip, nodded again.

John growled his frustration into his hands. "Nothing I say is making any difference whatsoever, is it?"

Emma shook her head.

"Great." He dropped back down next to her, burying his face in his palms.

She waited for him to start talking again. When he didn't, she said, "It wouldn't hurt, you know. Only girls hurt the first time."

John tensed like he'd just suppressed a shudder. "Can we talk about something else, please?"

"Okay. Like what?"

"Anything."

"Wanna know about my first time?"

"Anything besides *that*."

Definitely can't jump right in. "How about a date?"

John peeked at her from between his fingers. "What?"

"There's a movie theater, and the food's not bad. And there will be other people, so you won't be nervous. Oh! Rafe and Lucia can come with! And definitely no buzzing or white rooms. Not sure where I'll get flowers from, but I can think of something, and then we can sex!" Yes. Good plan. Best thing she'd come up with since forever. It would totally work.

Why wasn't he nodding along with her?

"Am I crazy again?"

His shoulders quivered in silent laughter. "If you are, then I must be, too, because that was the sweetest thing my ears have ever heard."

Emma squealed and ran for the door. "It's a date!" she said before she slammed it shut behind her. Now the only question was, which outfit would get her virgin out of his pants the fastest?

– 39 –

Only Travis came to train with her today. She had to be getting better; they were assigning fewer and fewer people to work on her brain. Emma laid down on the couch and sighed, preparing for another mind-fix session. She felt more together in her head already, but making sense there wasn't good enough if she still spoke nonsense. And Emma was eager to start making sense. Maybe then, more people would listen when she told them the coming darkness was so bright, it would shred their selves with its heat.

Big John had asked her to leave the battle room after she'd told them that. He didn't want her sitting in on their meetings anymore. Ever since he saw her dreams, the Special Unit was on official lockdown. In a matter of three days, telepaths everywhere had effectively withdrawn from the war-torn worlds, having gathered together in safe houses and gated communities to await news and instructions. Emma didn't know the details of everything going on out there, but it had to be bad for Big John to make that call. The only reason to gather was for them to hold stronger.

One man beside another made two. One telepath beside another could level a town. That was the true power of a telepath. On their own, each was strong in ways no one could see coming. Together, they had the potential to change the face of the human race. For no other reason than their combined abilities becoming stronger and growing exponentially by feeding off each other when they were all in close proximity. The weaknesses of one were not just compensated for, they were fixed by another. In a head-on assault, a wall of telepaths could never fall.

But such compensation came at a terrible price, and they would pay it, sooner or later.

The question was no longer *whether* they'd need to use their combined abilities, but *when*.

So bring on the sense, coach, because they needed to understand what they were up against, and no one was listening to Little John.

But Travis did nothing to initiate contact.

Emma craned her neck to look at him upside down. Travis sat in a chair by her head, just looking at her. So much like Big John—the same grave eyes, the same lines bracketing his mouth. Travis emulated their leader in every way, and one day he'd take over for him and be just as good a Big John. "Hi," she said. "I'm here."

He smiled just a little. "Hey, Pixie." His voice was weird.

Emma sat up and faced him. He'd changed little since she'd left; more grown up, stronger, but still Travis. Lost little Travis, all alone in the world.

He was one of the unlucky ones. Triggered in puberty, he'd thought he was losing his mind. His parents had taken him to psychiatrists, who'd pumped him full of drugs that had turned him into a brain-less, drooling mess. Then he'd chucked them and found his own street vendor. When Big John had found him, Travis had been skin and bones, living on the streets, going through horrible withdrawals because he couldn't afford to pay his dealer anymore. His family had forgotten him.

Travis leaned forward, braced his elbows on his knees. "How are you doing?"

People kept asking her that. Every day. But with Travis, it was different. He knew. Emma reached out to trace his eyebrow bisected by a thin scar. "Missed you," she said. Travis didn't hover. In fact, he hadn't even spoken to her since she'd been back. Avoiding her. But he was here now.

He smiled, and his eyes closed a little. "Missed you more." *So much…*

Emma caught that; a stray thought not imagined, but felt. Heartfelt. Travis had grown up good. After Big John had gotten him cleaned up and educated to catch up with the rest of them, he'd trained the boy into a man. A sentinel for Sue; the one they sent out when a telepath got out of hand, when they needed help, or needed to be disciplined.

He would have been the one cleaning up after her on Mars 2. Emma flinched and pulled back. They'd sent him.

Travis shook his head. "I volunteered," he said.

"Why?"

"Because it was you." He caught her face in his hands and touched his forehead to hers; as intimate a contact as a telepath could make. Brainpan to brainpan, he showed her. Everything.

The day they'd heard about the death on Mars 2 had been two days too late. Emma had been long gone by then, but Travis boarded the first shuttle out anyway. He'd been relentless, questioning everyone, day and night without cease, sussing out who knew what, who needed to forget what, which surveillance machines needed erasing. He'd wiped her off the face of that colony; nothing of her remained in The Madame. He'd looked in on Mary, then erased Emma from her memories so she wouldn't worry anymore, and gave her the peace Emma couldn't. He'd buried the police files, bribed soldiers, warped shuttle records to cover up her trail.

He'd done that instead of his job of searching for her in order to bring her in. He'd given her a head start because he—

Travis pulled back, leaving the thought unfinished. Emma peered into his eyes and found him lost; she'd left him. That hurt him the most. She'd had to. If she'd stayed, this place would have ruined her just like it was ruining so many others. He'd known she thrived on her own and loved every second of the life she'd made for herself before all of this had happened. Her happiness had made living here bearable. She'd needed to be away, and he'd needed her to be free, so he'd given her the only thing he could: a chance to live again.

The knowledge that the Shadows never would have found her if he'd only done his job and brought her back was destroying him.

Emma shook her head in denial.

It didn't change anything. Travis gave her a bitter half-smile. "I'm sorry." In his mind, she saw the sun—so far away, untouchable, but bright enough to illuminate the world and hot enough to warm him even from that distance. He loved that sun, even if he could never touch it. Even if it had left him, to go shine elsewhere.

"Travis—"

He stopped her from talking before she could stumble over the words. What could she say?

"I know," he said. "I just… I wanted to tell you I'm here for you. Any time, for anything. That's all." Then he walked out of the room.

Moments later, three teens came in, laughing at some joke they'd just shared. "Hey!" the girl greeted. Emma didn't know her name. "We're your designated brain rearrangers today. Just sit back and relax, and we'll have ya out of here in no time."

Emma looked her in the eye, but didn't say a word. Instead, she laid back down and closed her eyes, shutting out the world and losing herself in memories. She searched for Travis in her past and found countless hours spent playing video games and poking fun at news reporters, cheating on school tests and painting pictures in each other's minds.

She remembered the day she'd left for her new home on Torrey. Nell had thrown a party for her and Jeremy, and everyone had gathered in the dining room for a giant pink-and-green cake with no plates. Everyone, except Travis.

He'd found her afterwards, though, when it was just the two of them and a bowl of chips to cut the excess sugar from the cake. He'd hugged her off her feet, simply held her for a full minute—the first and last time he'd ever done such a thing. Then he'd set her on her feet and walked away.

Just as he'd done today.

She rewound that memory, placed herself in his tight embrace again, and relaxed into that feeling. But then her mind shifted and warped, and the arms around her grew stronger, bigger, while the man holding her grew taller, and she sighed, melting against him. Her Shadow Hawk. She laid her head onto his shoulder and blinked at Travis standing in the shadows a few feet away. *—Why did you* *make him take your place?—* she asked.

His smile was sad. *—I didn't. I just stepped back and let you choose where you wanted to be.—*

Little John rubbed his cheek against her hair.

—I think he's falling for you.—

"I think I'm falling for you," John echoed.

—Liar,— she accused. *—You can't know that. You can't read his mind any more than I can.—*

—Some things I don't need to spy out to see,— Travis replied. *—Most 'paths get so lost in thoughts, they don't look at what's right in front of them. You and I know better. Remember what I said. Any time. For anything. I'll always be there.—*

He was already fading from her consciousness. *—Goodbye,—* she whispered. More to herself than anything else.

– 40 –

Somewhere in the Tae Colony

The air stank of chemicals seeping out of the soil. Plants refused to grow; animals sickened within a year. But the ICG still deemed this colony an acceptable place for humans to live. Only the poorest of the poor did; those desperate enough to be swayed to their cause if need be.

Zayn had had the compound's interior retrofitted with air filtration systems and the best upgrades the rickety construction could support. Still a dump, but better than the outside, which was why he wanted Anna indoors as much as possible. Only now, he couldn't find her.

He'd been searching for the last two hours, and those who'd bothered to acknowledge him had no idea where she'd run off to. A heavy sense of foreboding made him go up to the roof. No one was allowed there. It wasn't structurally safe. Zayn mounted the stairs three at a time, then burst through the door.

The stench hit him hard, making his eyes water, but it was a minor inconvenience compared to the way his heart clenched to see Anna balanced on her toes at the very edge of the roof, arms spread out like angel wings, head tilted back to catch a rare, intermittent ray of blue sunshine. A strong breeze would send her plummeting twenty stories into the sinkhole behind the house.

Then she lifted her right foot.

"Nice day for a stroll," Zayn said evenly, reining in the terror that thrummed through him. The last thing he wanted to do was to startle her.

Anna peered over her shoulder and smiled brilliantly. Balancing on the ball of one foot, she pivoted to face him, arms wavering.

Zayn couldn't breathe. "That was lovely," he choked out, forcing a smile.

"Much obliged, ser," she said in an accent he'd never heard before. "I've been practicing all day. I call it *Flight of a Feather*."

"Feathers don't fly." He needed her away from that edge.

"No, I suppose they don't. But *Float of a Feather* doesn't have the same ring to it." Anna tilted her head, teetering off balance a little. "Drop of a feather, maybe? Drop of a hat. As in home is where you lay your. Hat, I mean."

"Anna, love, come here."

She grinned. "Why?"

Zayn swallowed with difficulty. "Because I missed you."

Her right foot touched down, but she was so close to the edge, she had to stand on tiptoe, heels kissing thin air. "I missed you, too."

Zayn stepped forward carefully.

"But unfortunately, you've been so busy with the universe. And now, I have a lot more practice to get in before suppertime." She raised her arms high, then bowed, sticking her backside out over the ledge in the process.

He saw it happen as if time had slowed to a crawl. Anna's heels lowered, seeking ground that wasn't there. She lost her balance, wobbled, reached out to brace herself, but had nothing to hold on to.

"Anna!" Zayn charged forward, caught her hand, snatched her away from the edge before she could tip over. He bodily hauled her back and didn't stop until he had her inside the stairwell, braced against a wall, with the roof door closed. Blood roared in his ears, and he couldn't take a deep enough breath, legs quivering so much he had to lean on her, sandwiching her between himself and the wall. "Christ, love, you're going to be the death of me."

"Zayn?" Her voice broke. "Zayn, what happened?"

"Shh, I've got you now." Gathering her up, he sat on the stairs with her, rocking them both. Two children lost in the dark. "You're all right.

Everything's okay now." He held her while she cried, again wishing he could get his hands on the butcher who'd poisoned her as a child and break every bone in his body.

Telepaths were not like other people; they were unique, their bodies different. Chem-treatments that kept others from becoming sick *caused* sickness in telepaths. The chemicals messed with their minds in the cruelest way possible—without a cure. The person Anna used to be was slowly dying every day, and Zayn could only watch it happen.

"I w-was in the bedroom," she sobbed. "I was just there!"

"I know, love. It's okay." He petted her hair, kissed away her tears. It broke him how much she hurt. Yet for all the pain she felt, at this very moment, she was his old Anna. She was with him in the now, for however long that might last, and he needed her to know. "I'll make this right, Annabel. I swear to you." He'd bring the chem-treatment industry down if it was the last thing he did. And if the ICG decided to fall, too, then so be it.

His com earpiece clicked with the signal for Luigi. Zayn touched it to answer. "What?"

"Michael is freaking. Shadows are on the move." Michael was a hybrid among them, part telepath and part seer; the counterweight to Anna's backsight. Though he and Anna were roughly the same age, Michael was still mostly lucid, and for whatever reason, somehow able to control the visions in his mind much better than Anna. They used to be friends, the three of them, until Michael looked at Anna with pity in his eyes. If not for Michael's gift of foresight, Zayn would have left him on Earth to rot like the rest of the Special Unit's rejects.

"Do we know where?"

"Hold."

In the moment of artificial silence, Zayn imagined Luigi crouching next to Michael on the floor. Michael would be delirious, shaking and sweating with the force of his visions. Sometimes the pain caused him to vomit or pass out. Sometimes both. Luigi had been assigned as Michael's companion, not to leave the seer's side for longer than an hour under any circumstances.

When Luigi came back, the news was surprising. "I got names. They're not local, but we can get a bead on them, easy. And get this:

they're all SU. This feels personal, chief. The Shadows never go after more than one target at a time."

Anna had quieted, breathing deep enough to tell him she'd be asleep soon, if she wasn't already.

"Orders?"

Zayn could only guess what might have incited the Shadows into an orchestrated attack. After all the death and destruction of the riots, he'd expected a show of force against the Evolutionaries, not the SU. The Shadows couldn't possibly have mistaken them; John MacMurphy was too much of a coward to make a public stand the way Zayn had. He'd never risk his precious chosen to protect petty ideals. No, Luigi was right. This felt very much personal.

"Zayn? You want us to give SU a head's up?"

He looked down at Anna. So innocent, so wholly trusting that he was good. Someone like her should never have to know the great sacrifices required for making the world a better place. And if he could help it, she never would. Annabel Lockhart would never know how callously she'd been dealt with by those she'd trusted most.

He issued the order for her.

"Do nothing."

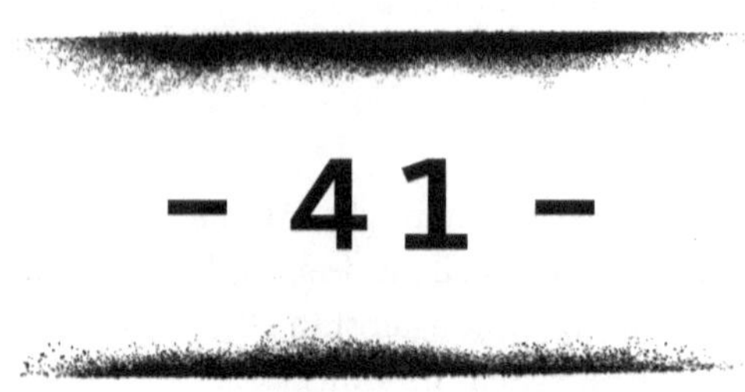

– 41 –

The movie started in an hour, which gave Emma twenty minutes to wash up, get dressed, find flowers, and go pick up her date. From the way Lucia watched her dash about her room, Emma figured she didn't look altogether sane, but there was method to her madness. When the rain of clothes had finally settled all over the floor and the bed, Emma could see patterns not visible when they'd all been folded up in a drawer.

That top with those shoes. But she needed a skirt. Men liked skirts. The shorter the better. Emma only had one, a bright green one that swished around her thighs, which made her look even paler than usual, but beggars couldn't be choosers.

There! All done. "How do I look?"

Lucia winced a smile, then tugged Emma's shirt off, turned it right side out before putting it back on her. She untucked the back hem of the skirt from Emma's panties, and untied the triple knot of her scarf belt, retying it instead into a neat little bow. "There, much better."

Emma nodded, then faced the mirror. "Augh!" She ruffled her hair. "I don't know what to do with this mess."

Lucia laughed. "It's not a mess. Here." She took some clippy thing and gathered Emma's hair low at her nape. By some mysterious process of twisting and tucking, Lucia had arranged the mass into a relaxed bun, leaving several strands loose to frame Emma's face. Standing back to admire her own handiwork, Lucia declared, "That boy won't know what hit him."

Emma frowned. "Do I know what I'm doing?"

"Which part, dear?" Lucia retorted. "The part where you're fraternizing with the enemy, or the part where you really can't wait to do it some more?"

Emma looked over her shoulder at her friend.

Lucia sighed. "I'm sorry, I didn't mean that. You have to trust your instincts. That's all any of us have to rely on. If your heart's telling you he's the one, then I'll stand behind you all the way."

"He saved me, Lucia," Emma whispered. "And he didn't even know he was doing it. I wouldn't have made it, if it weren't for him."

Lucia swallowed hard, but smiled, eyes glittering with tears. "Then I think it's time you went to pick up your date, don't you?"

Emma nodded and let Lucia walk her to the door.

Only to find Little John on the other side, looking as shocked as she felt. "What are you doing here?" she demanded.

"You look… wow."

"I was supposed to pick you up," Emma reminded him, scowling.

John dragged his gaze up from her legs to her face, then scowled back. "Girls get picked up. I'm not a girl."

"Okay, you're all set here, so I'm just going to go now," Lucia said. "Rafe and I will meet you there."

Neither of them registered her leaving.

"The da*tor* always picks up the da*tee*," Emma insisted.

John rolled his eyes. "We can either stand here talking about it, or you can put these in some water and come to the movies with me."

Little John disappeared behind a huge bouquet of flowers, and Emma gaped. "Where did you get these!" Gray Dublin wasn't called *gray* for the hell of it. Nothing grew in the city; fruits and vegetables had to be genetically manufactured, and flowers were imported to a handful of exclusive distributors who charged an arm and a leg for a single bloom. Soldier boy's bouquet would have cost several fortunes in import fees alone!

"Don't ask, and I won't have to tell you. God knows I don't want to think about it."

Emma gathered up the armful of roses and inhaled deeply of their fragrance. "Don't move," she said, carefully placing her treasure into an antique water pitcher and setting it onto the windowsill. She backed away slowly, and when she was certain it wouldn't topple over, Emma did a pirouette and launched herself at Little John, smashing an exuberant kiss against his mouth. "Thank you," she said.

Little John grinned. "You're welcome. Now, can we go?"

Emma nodded.

John regarded her legs wrapped around his waist and asked, "Do you want to walk, or shall I carry you?"

Emma considered her options for so long, he began to scowl. "I'll walk," she relented, hopping down to attach herself to his arm instead.

The movie theater was a relic from the past with authentic seats and carpeted walls, both forever imbued with the heavenly aroma of buttered popcorn. The screen was new, but the projector was ancient. It had to be, to play twentieth and twenty-first century masterpieces in all their glory. On the docket for date night was one of Emma's favorites: *The Princess Bride*. And just like in the olden times, before the movie played, the screen lit up with current events from around the Union.

The news wasn't good. As soon as the feeds rolled, Emma's elated mood evaporated. Cities were burning. People were dying. So much anger and hate—and it was everywhere! Why hadn't anyone told her? Why wasn't the SU doing anything! All of the other theater-goers just sat there, watching it play out, like just another movie, completely untouched by it. How could that be?

"These are pre-recorded," Jeremy said from behind her. She didn't know when he'd come in, but there he was. His voice was calm, but Emma knew better. He was tense in a way that had nothing to do with her having tranqued him the other day—he didn't like this any more than she did. "I've seen them live. I found this next bit particularly interesting. Watch the top left corner, second-floor balcony of the ICG building."

Emma blinked away frustrated tears to pay better attention, and her breath caught when she saw it. Next to her, John tensed. "Shadows."

Just like when Emma had been taken, a containment hover approached, only it didn't contain anyone. The energy field passed over the crowds on the ground, searing their brains and burning their bodies. Then the hover flew right over the ICG building, and three men in dark blue uniforms descended to the second-floor balcony, grabbed three of the panicked officials who were frantically waving for rescue. They never returned for the other two.

"What is this?"

"Griffith's end-game protocol," John said grimly, hand curled into a white-knuckled fist on the armrest. "He created the Shadows as a last resort, to protect against external threats. Now we know whom he wants to protect."

"And at what cost," Jeremy added. "Those men they left behind to die were strong opponents to Griffith's eugenics bills. They'll play it off and say they ran out of time, call it a great tragedy for the Union's governance. Blah. Blah. Blah. Call it whatever you want, this is nothing short of murder."

And Griffith's power grew by another little bit.

Emma shivered, hands shaking again, and that awful hum back in her mind. She couldn't get rid of it. Didn't matter that the theater was pitch-black, the projection lighting up the screen was bright enough that she might as well have been back in that white room. Griffith and his army of Shadows had destroyed her peace of mind, and she would never get it back. No matter how far she ran, or how many of them went down, there would always be another Griffith in the wings, ready to step in and take over. Evil like that was a plague the world would never be rid of.

She couldn't breathe.

With John intent on the scene playing out and her brother lost in his own grim thoughts, Emma was alone, faced with her own personal nightmare, and she couldn't breathe. Couldn't move. Couldn't—

The feed cut off and the news anchor returned, a symbol blinking in the corner to indicate it was a live broadcast. The anchor was a meticulously dressed young woman with her hair arranged to perfection and her makeup flawless. But her eyes were terror-stricken, and she was sweating. She didn't speak right away, glancing off to the side as if someone out there was directing her. "L-ladies and gentlemen, we have one more recording to show you tonight. There's been some debate as to its legitimacy, but the results of our testing conclude that it is, in fact, genuine. Please, take a look."

She moved off, and on the screen behind her, a strange symbol appeared. A two-leafed plant with roots in the shape of DNA strands. Emma frowned, panic giving way beneath the itch of a memory. She knew that symbol. Where did she know it from?

There was no music, no introduction. Just a man with a scar across his face coming to stand in front of the symbol.

Jeremy sat forward. "This is new."

The news studio erupted into noise and the feed was disrupted as people rushed in front of it, shouting, "Where's the Griffith feed? Get this off! Cut to commercial!"

"Jesus, this can't be real," Jeremy said. But it was too harsh to be anything else. This was really happening. Right now. Somewhere where no one could intervene. Whatever message Griffith had wanted to send, someone had replaced it with this.

Emma grabbed for John's hand, clutching it tight as a woman—the news anchor—screamed off-screen. Sounds of a scuffle were followed by the unmistakable zap of a pulse gun. Then the scarred man spoke, and Emma heard nothing but his voice.

"You wanted to know why we hide," he said. "We do not. We are being hidden from you. Right now, many people are paying a high price for your privilege of seeing this. They will be tortured, and they will be executed for disobeying Senator Griffith's directive to bury this recording. They took the risk anyway, because they believe in our cause: the future of our kind.

"You wanted to see the face behind the Evolutionaries. Here I am. I am you. *We* are you. Mothers, sons, brothers, sisters, children abused and forgotten, abandoned by those we relied on to take care of us. As you will be. Right now, Senator Griffith is unleashing his Shadow army to isolate his strongest supporters. The rest, he will leave to die. He has no interest in stopping the conflict. All he wants is to be the last man standing.

"*He* is not your problem. I am. Because I know something else that's being hidden from you. There are people out there strong enough to stop us—to stop all of this. But they refuse. Just like Griffith, they live their lives behind secrets and anonymity, turning away from your suffering. This message is for them. John MacMurphy, the Shadows are growing. They are coming for you, and they will have their due. But not before me."

The feed cut off, and the theater erupted with a hum of nervous noise. People talked, but they did nothing; they looked around for someone to tell them everything was under control, that their leader, the paragon of virtue they all looked up to and trusted implicitly, had a plan to deal with this. No one stood up to leave. It was unreal.

Watching them, John became aware of Emma's distress too late. She was hyperventilating, clutching his hand so tightly, her nails dug into his skin. Her eyes were wide, unblinking, focused on the screen as if at any second the enemy would jump out at her. "Emma—"

She cried out and bolted, clambering over startled people in their row to get to the exit.

John swore and went after her, aware of her brother doing the same. They clashed at the door, but John muscled through first and shoulder-checked Calen.

Emma hadn't gone far, turning frustrated circles in a corner to the side, beating at the walls.

"Emma?" John said. "Are you okay?"

She didn't answer, just threw herself at the wall again.

"Move," Calen snapped, trying to shove him aside to get to her, but John wouldn't let him. He had a bad feeling about this; Emma looked seconds away from another violent episode. Anything might set her off. His pulse raced, muscles tensed for battle, but that was the last thing Emma needed. *Breathe through it, Hawk. Throttle down.*

Easier thought than done.

"Out of my way!"

John shoved Calen back and ordered, "Stop. Give her a second."

Calen spat out a curse, but backed down.

"Emma," John said, voice low.

She stopped her panicked attack on the wall. Hugging herself, she sank to her haunches and huddled there.

"It's okay. You're safe. You're among friends, remember?"

"They didn't move," she whispered. "None of them. They just sat there and watched. How could they just watch?" She curled in on herself so tightly, her entire frame quivered, and it was killing John.

"It's only a recording," Calen said, as if that would make a difference. "He can't hurt us, you know that, right? We're safe here."

"I know him," she whispered.

"What?" John and Calen said at the same time.

Emma raised her teary eyes to her brother. "Don't you remember?"

John looked from her to Calen. "What's going on? What are you talking about?"

"The day MacMurphy came for us," she said, before a hard shudder raked through her, making her teeth chatter so hard she had to clench them together to make them stop.

John couldn't take any more of this. He pulled her to her feet and hugged her as tightly as he dared. "Easy, I've got you."

Emma twisted in his embrace to keep talking. "He was there, Jeremy. Don't you remember? He had a girl with him—blonde and pale, sickly. She used to dance around and talk to fairies."

Calen frowned. "I remember her," he said. "She was far gone, even then."

Emma nodded. "He was trying to get Big John to take her. That's how we got out of there—he distracted Big John, and we ran."

"And MacMurphy kept coming after us," Calen finished.

"And left the girl there," Emma added.

"Can't be the same guy," Calen said.

"He was so desperate to get her noticed." The unnerving back-and-forth between brother and sister wasn't quite a conversation, more like a continuous speech by two different people.

"Desperate people do strange things," John said, more for himself than anything.

Both siblings looked at him as if they'd just remembered he was still there. "We need to tell MacMurphy," Calen said.

"I'm pretty sure someone would have told him by now," John retorted.

"About the message, yes, but not about Scarface. If this is some sort of personal vendetta, then it won't stop at MacMurphy. We need to warn people."

"You need to prepare," John said. "You just met your other opponent in this battle. If these Evolutionaries and Shadows come at you at the same time, I don't care how strong you all are as telepaths, you *will* die. You need to scatter. All of you. Right now."

"You'd love that, wouldn't you?" Calen challenged. "Divide our ranks and make us easier to pick off. I bet that's just what Griffith's waiting for. You think you can play both sides against the middle?"

"Jeremy!"

"It's okay, Emma." John set her aside to face off with her brother. "You've got something to say to me?"

Calen looked about two seconds away from taking another swing, but he held back. "Emma, come on, let's go."

"She's not going anywhere without me."

"*You* are finished," Calen snarled. "Emma's going home, and if you so much as think about following us, I will kill you."

"You won't see them coming," John returned, deeming Calen's threat harmless. "Even if you do, there won't be anything you can do to keep them from taking her again—and believe me, they will. You can't keep her safe—"

"You have no idea the lengths I'll go to protect my sister—"

"—can't keep any of them safe, unless you *listen* to me—"

"—I *hope* they come, so I can watch them die trying—"

"—I'm the only one who knows how they operate. Like it or not, I'm all you've got, and Emma—"

"*You're the one who broke her!*"

The accusation echoed in a hallway gone dead silent. Those who'd come out to intervene all stopped in their tracks to stare. Lucia, Rafe, the Brain, and Travis front and center, leading the charge. They gaped at the sight of Jeremy Calen losing his shit.

"*You* took her. *You* locked her in that hellhole, and *you* stood there, day after day, watching her fall apart. *You* did that. She's so damaged, she can't even see you for what you really are. And it's all because of you! A brainwashed foot soldier who can't even remember how not to follow orders. And you come in here, telling us to trust you? The only reason I'm not frying every goddamn brain cell in your head is because *she* doesn't want me to, and even though I *know—I know—* you will betray her, there's nothing I can do to convince her, because *she believes* in you. Do you get that, you fucking troglodyte? Two hundred people in this place are all doing their damnedest to make her better, and we're all failing, because the damage you did can *never* be undone. You didn't just break her mind, you son of a bitch, you warped it. You made her into something she was never meant to be."

When Calen had finished, John couldn't tell whether he'd gone deaf or if everyone around him had gone mute. He couldn't hear anything beyond the ringing in his ears. His jaw clenched so hard, he couldn't open it enough to say anything, even if he knew what to say.

Then Emma brushed past him. "You shouldn't have come," she said to no one in particular.

Others parted to allow her passage as she ran off, and when Travis managed to tear his gaze from her retreating back to look at John and Calen's standoff, he directed equal measures of disgust and anger at both of them. "Before you get too comfortable on that high horse, Jer, you should know Emma had every opportunity to turn to you after Mars 2. You might want to ask yourself why she didn't."

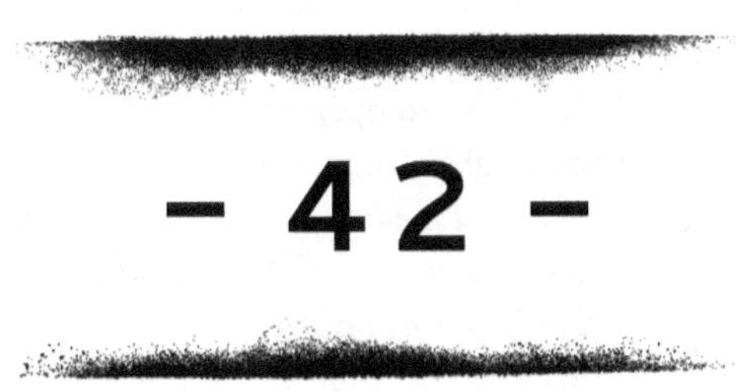

John left Travis to clean up the mess with Calen and the Evolutionaries. His ears burned with Calen's accusations, his steps wooden and unsteady as he went after Emma with no goddamn clue what to say to her. What *could* he say?

Christ, the look on her face.

She'd turned ashen, haunted blue eyes all but glowing. Whether or not she'd suspected what they all thought of her, hearing her own brother spell it out so callously must have shaken her in a bad way. And what Travis had said about her not seeking out Jeremy for help… John could guess why she hadn't. Why would she?

At her door, John hesitated. Inside, she was talking to herself again. Worse, her voice quivered. She'd run here to hide so no one would see her cry. John's hands fisted, itching to make her brother bleed.

Then another voice cut in on Emma's, and John frowned. *"Listen, honey, I love your brother more than all the snowflakes in the world, but even I have to admit he gets righteously stupid around damsels in distress. Let's not even talk about all the many times I wanted to kick his ass in the past. And, Pixie, it's ten times worse with you. He loves you. You're all the family he has left."*

"But what he said…"

"Yep, monumentally stupid. I'll bet he's wallowing in misery over it already." Good. He should. *"You have to remember he said it to hurt someone else, not you."*

"Doesn't make it better," Emma replied softly.

John wanted in there. This was worse than standing guard outside her cell; this door wasn't locked. He could walk in any time. But every time he tried to will his hand to open the door, it refused to move. Because Calen had been right. It *was* all his fault.

"Okay, new track. You want me to slap him upside the head for you? I'll even upgrade to claws if you want. One time offer."

Emma giggled wetly. "Tell me about Torrey."

She'd spoken of Torrey in her mindless ramblings before, having lived there with her brother before she ran away. John sorted through his mental list of places reported to have been irreparably damaged by the riots, but couldn't remember seeing Torrey on any of them before he'd left the base. The fact that she was talking to someone there was a good sign, at least.

"Still on lockdown. People were getting scared watching news about the war, and with the military calling the shots here, fights broke out, so the elders, in all their wisdom, decided to cut coms with outside worlds." Then how was she talking to Emma? *"Great way to make the good folks go kablooey. It ain't pretty, I'll tell you that. The Hunts were lucky to get out when they did. Amelia and her pet split the day soldiers arrived. Guess the new cat wasn't up for another revolution just yet. I should have gone with them."*

"Not without Jeremy."

"Yep, back to that stupid love thing. Life was so much simpler when I didn't give a damn."

Emma snorted. "And they say I'm delusional."

"Oh, honey, you are," came the mockingly sweet response, making Emma laugh. *"But that doesn't mean there's something wrong with you. You're not broken, just different. People can deal and accept, or they can go fuck themselves. Either way, it's not your problem to solve."*

"Is that the official Hellcat mandate?"

"Damn right it is! And when has that bitch ever been wrong?"

Emma sighed. "I do love you, Hailey."

"Ditto, kid. See you 'round."

A blooping noise signaled the end of their conversation, and John raised his hand to knock.

"Safe to come in," Emma called before his knuckles could connect.

Caught red-handed, John flushed and entered. "Hey."

"Hi."

"How are you feeling?"

"Like the lame dog no one has the heart to put down."

John winced. "Anything I can do to help? We could tranq your brother again and leave him up on the roof."

Emma smiled a little. "Itching powder in his shorts."

John grinned, warming to the subject. "Hair remover in his shampoo."

"Hemorrhoid cream in his mouthwash!"

"Self-tanner in the showerhead."

Emma laughed, momentarily forgetting her hurt.

"Tell me what you want," he said. "Anything in the world, just say the word."

Still smiling, she regarded John with a mysterious expression, then crooked her finger to beckon him closer.

Suddenly out of sorts, John took a step.

Her grin widened. "Closer."

He stepped up to the bed where she sat, and she pulled him down beside her. Pulse throbbing in his temples, he grabbed his knees in a white-knuckled hold and stared straight ahead.

"Truth now," Emma said softly. "Are you?"

"No," he replied hoarsely. "Not a virgin." Not technically, but the extent of his sexual experience could be counted on two fingers. A pathetic record. Sex he'd indulged in, purely to satisfy his curiosity. Hardly worth mentioning; his partners certainly never did. What he'd lacked in experience, he'd made up for as a byproduct of surveillance assignments, stalking subjects who'd turned out to have many and varied sexual tastes. Essentially, he'd learned the theory of technique by watching them fuck like bunnies, but never bothered to use it. Both times he'd sought sex, it had been for no reason beyond his own release, and he hadn't known or cared enough to bother with his partners', figuring they had to know better how to get themselves off.

In the end, the experience had left him disappointed and… homesick.

John didn't want that with Emma; she deserved so much more, everything he could give her. But what if he couldn't deliver?

What if he did, and it wasn't enough?

Emma gently pried one of his hands off his knee. "Nothing to it," she said, ducking under his arm so she could straddle his lap. "Think of it as a tactical assault." She put his hands on her thighs and rubbed them along the smooth length of skin to the swell of her buttocks.

His fingers tightened on reflex, arms flexing to bring the core of her harder against him, and he instantly shot hard. Suddenly, it was all he could do not to tear her clothes off.

No, nothing would ever be the same with Emma. She redefined the meaning of his universe. The very least he could do was return the favor and, Christ, he couldn't wait to do it. "Emma…"

She leaned in, pressed her lips to his in a soft kiss. "Are you with me?" she whispered.

His arms tightened around her, urging her closer. "Always," he said, then claimed her mouth. He kissed her like a desperate man seeking salvation, crushed her mouth open, demanding entrance, then tasted her, drank her in, stole her breath as if he had none of his own.

And Emma met him, stroke for stroke. She tangled her hand into his hair to keep him close, squeezed with her knees, pressed down on him, wanting more. Two unfinished halves seeking to be whole.

John clutched her shirt so hard, stitches popped. Emma couldn't let go long enough to shed it, so he did it for her, bunching the fabric up at her armpits. Then his hands were on her skin, rough with calluses, desperate with need, but gentled for her. He let her set the pace; he didn't push or demand more.

Emma broke away with a gasp of much needed air, quickly tugged her shirt and bra up over her head. His shirt followed right after, and then he gripped her ass and surged to his feet, taking her with him. Before she could wrap her legs around him, John dropped onto the bed with her, and elbowed himself up to peer into her eyes.

"Are you sure?" he asked.

"Are you?" she returned.

In seconds flat, he had her naked and pinned under him, and Emma strained to get closer, empty and aching for him. His hand caressed down the center of her chest, between her breasts and down to her belly button, then sideways to her hip, over her ass, and down the back of her thigh. He took hold of her calf just beneath the back of her knee and guided her leg around him. She arched up, aligning herself with his hard bulge behind the pants he hadn't dropped yet, and he thrust slowly against her, rubbing her just right, just enough to make her body sing and grow wet for him.

He lowered his face to hers, nose buried in her hair, and breathed in deep. "God, I love the way your hair smells."

It's what she imagined the shifters said to their mates, and she thrilled. "Take your pants off."

He stopped moving. "Keep talking like that and I won't last long enough to pull down the zipper."

Her sex squeezed on emptiness, and Emma mewled to be kept waiting. Before he could stop her, she reached between them and undid his pants, curled her fingers around his shaft to pull it out. He gasped and cursed, shuddered above her and stopped breathing, but he didn't spill yet. He was close, though, and Emma wanted to see him come. She squeezed him and gave a long, slow stroke up to the broad head.

John gritted his teeth, eyes squeezed shut, but when she circled the head with her thumb and brought it to her entrance, he opened them. "You won't break me," he said, a savage smile transforming his face into a delicious threat.

Emma smiled back and rubbed the head of him up and down over herself. "Challenge accepted." And she gasped when he moved his hips, bucking her grasp and sliding between her slick folds over her clit. She reached for him again, but he caught her hands and stretched her arms far up over her head. Keeping hold with one hand, he reached down with the other and resumed what she'd begun, using her own juices to slide his cock up and down over her, teasing at her entrance, pressing forward just enough to let her know he was there but not enough to penetrate.

It drove her wild. Emma was so close she could scream, and he kept her poised at the edge through the simple fact of his makeup: he was shielded. If he wasn't, the sensory back-and-forth would have made them both climax ten times over by now. This telepathic separation kept her firmly grounded in herself, focused not on his pleasure, but on her own. It heightened every sensation, intensified his every stroke, yet kept her from an orgasm until he chose to give it to her. And she couldn't make him go any faster.

Emma thrashed her head, pleaded, undulated her hips as much as his hold would allow. What had started out as a game to drive him crazy had quickly turned on her. So close. So. Damn. Close!

John leaned down and tongued her nipple. Emma arched off the bed. He did it again, and she bit her lip to keep from screaming, ever conscious of the compound full of telepaths milling outside the door—the door that wasn't locked. They could be interrupted at any moment and—

Oh, my God! John closed his lips around her nipple and sucked in rhythm to his thrusts.

Emma shattered, her core squeezing nothing, and she cursed him for it. But what came out of her mouth were two words. Just two. Words she'd never said to another man in her entire life; never thought she had it in her.

Those two words brought his head up, and she saw the fire they'd ignited. "Now you've done it," he said, and he surged up with one sure thrust and buried himself inside her to the hilt.

The orgasm just winding down exploded again all over her body, so intense, John would certainly feel it. He cursed and released her hands, circling his hips instead of pumping them as if he couldn't bear to let go of the feeling for even a single inch. And it kept going. On, and on…

…and on it went, squeezing him tighter than a fist. John didn't trust himself to move. Too much. Too damn good. This was Emma's pleasure, but somehow it was his, too. Her muscles contracted, and he felt it from the base of his spine, surging straight up to the top of his head, making him dizzy with it, hungry for more. He felt her coming back down to earth and couldn't wait to get her that high again.

Her hands were free and she stroked him all over, as if she couldn't decide where to touch first. She pulled him down lower until each of his thrusts rubbed her breasts over his chest, driving him mad. He wanted to feel all of her, every inch. Taste her everywhere.

When she fisted her hands in his hair and dragged him down for a scorching kiss, he almost lost it. His balls pulled tight to his body. Damn it, he wanted this to last!

He slid an arm underneath her hips and pulled her up, altered his angle and thrust harder, watching her eyes grow unfocused. She gasped, moaned, mouth opened, body tensed, and then she was coming again—hard.

And John couldn't hold back anymore. He surged into her, and sheer bliss washed over him, making him shudder.

In that instant, he felt the floodgates open.

Like a puzzle piece snapping into place, a single channel opened wide, and he split in two, everything doubling and multiplying. He saw Emma, but he saw himself, too; felt pleasure rock his frame, make him weak, but he also perceived the way he filled her, responded to the orgasm shivering through her, and his entire being permeated with a deep sense of satisfaction he'd never known, yet now, somehow, shared.

And it felt amazing.

John forgot to breathe while he stared into Emma's bright blue eyes, and knew she felt the same. Exactly the same, down to the last tremor. Because she was right there with him as the world tilted on its axis, and it was the longest, most powerful orgasm of his life.

But as it ebbed, the bright and shiny world slowly darkened and the connection closed. It left him gasping, alone in his head, watching the wonder in Emma's eyes fade into disappointment. Yeah, he was right there with her, too.

Her hands slid off him, her leg around him loosened, and John almost panicked. "Don't," he said, rolling over so they lay facing each other on their sides. He pulled her tight against him. "Don't let go." He was staring like an idiot, trying to see through her eyes, into her thoughts, but it didn't work.

Emma smiled a sad little smile. "It's gone." Pressing her forehead to his, she sighed and added, "But for a moment there, it was… beautiful."

And just like that, John Wayland understood the meaning of home.

Emma floated down a lazy pink river of gas, gazing at a green galaxy, when the dark matter around her started to vibrate with agitation. Dragged out of the first dream she'd had on her own since before she'd gotten taken, she opened her eyes, already frowning.

The room was dark, except for a small, artificial candle night light, and empty, except for soldier boy. "John?"

He didn't stir, limbs still and relaxed in sleep.

But he was having some kind of freak-out attack: his heart raced against her hand, and his breaths panted in short, rapid bursts that made even Emma feel lightheaded. Enough to wake anyone, or make them pass out, or something. But he wasn't waking, and he wasn't calming down.

Emma shook him. "John!"

Nothing.

"Lights," she commanded, then sat up to take a better look. His eyes darted behind his lids, and his mouth was set in a thin line, nostrils flaring, trying desperately to suck in more air. Emma shook him again. She punched him in the shoulder. She slapped his face.

Nothing.

"Damn your shiny head—wake up!"

He gave a small moan of distress, and Emma thought for one second she sensed a crack in his shield, but a split second later it was gone.

Should she call for help?

No. He wouldn't want others to know.

That left Emma.

She shrugged. Better than nothing.

Settling herself astride him, Emma laid her palms flat against the sides of his head and closed her eyes. Physical contact heightened a telepath's abilities, enabled them to see past basic shields. John's were anything but basic, but she had to try.

Emma traced along the surface of his shield, as shiny and solid as it had always been, searching for a way in. There wasn't one. But beneath her mental touch, it felt different somehow. Before, his shield had been like a smooth glass orb around his thoughts and feelings. Now it was just as smooth, but colder, more metallic. And metal was a conductor.

Emma turned her thought-self electric and zapped the shield with everything she had. She expected John to at least twitch, but he showed no reaction at all. *Shield must be grounded.* Like it had done with the wire cage in a scary white room, her command to wake up sizzled along the outside, but never burned through it.

She considered tossing water on him, but if hits, shakes, and slaps hadn't woken him up, then water didn't stand a chance. And with the rapid way he breathed, she might inadvertently cause him to drown. Heart beating too fast; it would sustain damage soon. He couldn't last much longer this way.

Frustrated and scared, Emma thumped against the shield, and heard the metal reverberate just the slightest bit. Like knocking on a massive bell.

Eyes snapping open, Emma came back to herself.

Current won't do it? Then here comes the battering ram.

She gathered everything she had behind her mental command and shoved it at his shiny metallic head with all of her telepathic might. —*WAKE UP!*—

GONG!

John sat up with a hoarse shout, throwing her off the bed.

Emma's ears were ringing so much, she saw stars, and John had to be worse. He'd been right beneath that giant bell. Feeling drunk and dizzy, she rose and went back to the bed, the entire world tipping and tilting around her so much, she almost banged her head against

John's as she sat down next to him.

His eyes were squeezed shut, and he clutched his ears hard enough to make the muscles in his arms bulge and twitch.

"Don't squish the bell," she said, words slurring. "If it's warped, it won't work next time." Her mouth flooded with saliva, and the pressure behind her eyes made them feel close to popping clean out of her head. Oh, this sucked so much galactic ass.

John tried to say something between huge gasps of air but it came out as a jumbled mess of syllables. And he was trying to say it very loudly. Ear ringing, definitely worse for him.

"I don't speak Yoda."

He glared and growled, "Learn."

Relief. She didn't break him. Good. "You're awake, aren't you?"

John looked around the room, breaths finally slowing a little. When he met her gaze again, he looked stunned. "I am."

She nodded. "You're welcome."

"How…" John winced and shook his head hard, finally letting go of his ears. "How did you do that?"

"I rang your bell."

He blinked, mouth twitching. "You what?"

Emma didn't seem to see any humor in that. "Why couldn't I wake you?" she demanded.

Shit. John swallowed. "Guess I just remembered." Hell of a wake-up call. John had completely forgotten about his treatments back at base. Now that the latest one had worn off, this could happen any time he closed his eyes to sleep. The prospect didn't exactly thrill him.

Emma untangled herself and sat at the other end of the bed, watching him expectantly.

John sighed. "It happens to me sometimes; I have a nightmare and my, uh, shield keeps me locked in until it plays itself out."

"How long does it last?"

"It depends." Hours. Sometimes he fell asleep straight into a memory, and woke up close to noon, drained psychologically and exhausted physically.

"How often?"

"It varies." In the beginning, it had happened nightly. He'd stopped sleeping all together to avoid the nightmares and only managed to make them into walking daydreams.

Emma scowled. "You're not talking."

"Won't do any good."

She gaped. "Won't do any—" Her mouth clamped shut, and she blushed. "A building full of mind-fixers, and it won't do any good?"

John shrugged. He'd already been checked out by an entire battalion of doctors, psychiatrists, PTSD specialists, and a slew of microbiologists, all trying to figure out what cocktail of sedatives and antidepressants might work best.

None of them had. His trauma was so deeply ingrained, no miracle of modern medicine could touch it. And with his particular talent of being inherently resistant to telepathic manipulation, no mind reader could, either.

But Emma had somehow managed it. She had reached him through that barrier and woken him from the midst of a night terror. Sure, she'd made his head pound like a son of a bitch, and for a while there he'd felt deaf and dumb, but he was awake. And as far as he could tell, he hadn't been under for more than an hour or two.

Emma shot off the bed and headed for the door, then changed her mind, came back, put on a shirt and some pants, and tossed his discarded clothes at him. John sighed and dressed, going along for the inevitable ride when she took him by the hand and dragged him out of the room.

The girl they called Brain was on call for the night shift when they barged into the clinic. Emma pulled John behind a curtained-off exam section and pushed him down onto the bed. "You sit," she ordered, then she turned to the Brain and shoved a hand-held scanner at her. "And you, fix him."

"He doesn't look broken."

"He's cracked. In the head."

The Brain snorted.

"Thanks for that," John muttered.

"Somebody mind telling me what's going on?"

Emma opened her mouth to answer, but John cut her off. "I'm

telling you, it won't do any good." It had taken Dr. Wen three years to calibrate his treatments to at least some effectiveness. Had John known he'd one day be cut loose and wind up on his own, he might have paid better attention, but for all he knew, Dr. Wen had used a mystical combination of fairy dust and solar flare radiation to treat him.

"Let me be the judge of that," the Brain replied. "I find it's more productive to know the variables and available resources before declaring whether something is possible or not."

John's eyes narrowed. "I'm not getting out of here until I talk, am I?"

Emma crossed her arms. "None of us are, so you might as well get to it."

The Brain turned on the scanner and put it to work, patiently waiting for him to speak up. With Emma tapping her foot at him, John stubbornly kept his mouth shut.

The Brain rolled her eyes. "Pixie, would you mind giving us a few minutes alone?"

Emma looked from her to John, then back. "I should stay."

"Go on," John said. "I'll wait here. You can bring me a cookie or something."

Still not looking totally convinced, Emma nodded. "Okay… Don't go anywhere."

"I won't. I promise."

After she left, the Brain plugged the scanner into a console and checked the readings on the screen. "You're patient with her."

"I have a lot to make up for."

"She likes you, you know."

"Yeah, God knows why, though."

"Oh, it's not that difficult to figure out. Hmm, this is interesting." Several scanner images cycled across the screen in quick succession, too fast for John to make anything out, but apparently it meant something to the child doctor. "There are faint marks on your sphenoid bones—that's roughly the area of your temples—consistent with electric charring."

"Figured there might be."

"Did you know there are also puncture marks?"

He frowned. "What?"

"And your myelin sheaths and meningeal envelope show slight traces of a very curious chemical compound." She typed in a series of commands. "Emma's right. You need to start talking."

"Why?"

"Because what I'm looking at here is consistent with the effects of an experimental form of EMC mind control."

"EMC?" *Mind control?*

"Electromagnetic-chemical. The take-no-prisoners kind. See, the way the brain and body work is more complicated than people like to think. It's not just neurons sending electrical impulses; that's only half of it.

"The other half is chemical signals. They work slower, but they're much more potent. With a concentrated electromagnetic pulse, EMP for short, you can disrupt the flow of electricity in the brain, which can cause any number of symptoms from mild disorientation, to memory loss, to loss of motor control, unconsciousness, even death. But because the neural pathways aren't fixed, they can rearrange themselves and compensate, heal the damaged parts of the brain.

"That's where the chemical part comes in. Once you disrupt a pathway, if you can somehow keep the neurons busy long enough, they'll lose the ability to reroute signals. You basically hardwire the brain so it won't do anything but what it's already doing; you won't learn anything new, won't develop new habits, won't question or doubt what you know."

Seeming to have shocked herself, the Brain sat and gaped at him. "It's the perfect way to create perfectly obedient soldiers. Of course, it has its drawbacks. Without the ability to change course, neural pathways wear out faster, leading to mental illness and deficiency later on in life, but I don't suppose that would be an issue, given the purpose a soldier serves."

A soldier follows orders. A warrior thinks for himself. Emma's words hammered at the inside of John's skull with a merciless pounding rhythm. How right she'd been.

"What are you saying?" he choked out.

"I don't know," she replied. "But I really, really hope I'm wrong."

— 44 —

When Emma returned, the Brain filled her in on what she'd found. The basics, anyway.

First order of business: John was now officially Dr. Jessica's patient. Despite assurances from both Emma and Jessica herself that Jessica was one of the best medical minds in the universe, John had to fight with himself not to make a mad run for it. Last thing he wanted was to end up as a ten-year-old kid's science experiment.

By the time she'd finished with him, Jessica was already deep in scientist mode, typing at the computer console. John's consent apparently didn't even merit an afterthought. Twice he got up to leave, and twice Jessica pulled herself out of her computer-induced trance to ask about his symptoms, forcing him to sit his ass back down and talk. Because, from what she'd told him, it was in his best interest to cooperate. The neural damage wasn't extensive, but it was there, and if he had any hope to stop it from spreading, Jessica was the one who held the key.

So he sat, and he talked. He told her about the day his father had lost his mind; about the nightmares, and how he couldn't stop or prevent them. She was unemotional as she listened, sporadically taking notes about this or that, asking follow-up questions to get the complete picture. The distance and lack of personal interest helped; he felt less like he was baring his soul and more like he was telling a story neither of them were a part of, which made it easier to say the words.

When he'd finished, Jessica put away her notes and sighed, looking him in the eye. "Here's the thing," she said, and John sat up, almost at attention. "The fact that you have impenetrable mental shields means you are a telepath of some kind, which means you are chem-resistant."

"And what does that mean?"

"It means I can help you."

"And how do I know you won't just keep doing what the Shadows did, try to control me for your own agenda?"

"One, because I don't have an agenda—I'm a kid, dude. World domination, not exactly high on my list of priorities at the moment. And two, because you really don't have another choice."

John believed her. "What do you propose?"

"I can flush the drugs out of your system, for one thing. It's a simple process of a detox tank for a day or so; you'll be submerged in an oxygen-rich solution, which will then be ionized to attract the chemicals and pull them out of you. The most uncomfortable part will be learning how to breathe liquid and not panic. But once that part is finished, I can generate a serum to repair the damage to your neurons and restore full functionality."

"Will it make me smarter?"

She grinned. "Let's just say it'll make you less dull. I'll set it up." She was already gathering tools for the procedure, eyes wide with excitement. "We'll have you back to normal in no time."

"Emma, maybe you should go back to your room."

Emma frowned. "Soldier boy?"

He took her hand and kissed her knuckles. "I'll be fine. Go on."

She didn't look happy about it, but she nodded anyway and walked out of the clinic, leaving him alone with Dr. Brain and her mad science experiment. An accoutrement of stuff was already piled up on the other exam table, and she was muttering what sounded like a list of supplies she still needed.

John pushed to his feet. "Thanks, Doc. I'll think about it."

Jessica chuckled as she dragged a loop of thick tubing out of storage. "What's there to think about? It's gotta be done. Might as well do it now, right?"

"To what end?" he asked softly.

Jessica did a double take, pausing with her arms full of equipment. "To what—haven't you heard what I said?"

Of course he had. Reading between the lines was a trick he'd only picked up recently from Emma, but it was turning out to be a useful skill. Jessica wasn't doing any of this for his benefit; for all her smarts, she was still a kid who'd just been presented with a cool new toy she couldn't wait to play with. Had there been any chance in hell of it making him better, John might have let her. But she'd just told him it wouldn't. In fact, it might even make him worse. John couldn't afford that kind of liability, not with the Shadows on the hunt.

Jessica must have read something in his expression; her enthusiasm cooled, and she let everything drop from her arms. "Listen," she said. "I know it's scary. What they did to you was so far beyond wrong, I'm going to have nightmares about it for months. And you're right to be nervous. I don't know how this will affect your neural pathways, but you have to try, don't you? Otherwise the Shadows have already won."

Too many big words and non-answers in that speech. "Will this restore all of my memories?"

"I don't know. Eventually, maybe."

"What about the memories I already have? Tactics, training, battle."

Her shoulders drooped. "I don't know that, either. Your neurons keep wanting to rewire back to the way they were, but it's possible that years of repetition will have burned all of that into your brain forever."

"And just as possible I might forget a huge chunk of it, if not everything."

She nodded.

"And if I forget where I am, what I'm doing here? If I get confused and break out to run back to them?"

She didn't have an answer.

"I could forget twenty years of my life and revert back to a terrified eight-year-old kid."

Jessica paled.

John sighed, disappointed. He'd been hoping she could at least offer some assurance, even if it was false. He was so damn tired of lost causes. "Like I said, Doc, I'll think about it."

Whenever he was in doubt or unsettled, John fell into his Shadow training. He became the soldier he'd been programmed to be. Instead of going back to his room, he marched directly to the gym and ran five two-mile circuits broken up by a series of push-ups, pull-ups, and crunches, one hundred each. But it did nothing to clear his head. He kept replaying the conversation he'd had with Jessica. All this time the Shadows had been spoon-fed a wariness of telepaths who could supposedly seize control of thoughts and destroy what it meant to be whoever a person was. And all this time, that was precisely what the base doctors and scientists had been doing.

John was no longer a Shadow. Chances were, once Jessica started treating him, he'd forget what it meant to be one in the first place. What would be left, if all his years of training were stripped away? Who the hell was he beneath it all? John had been a soldier for so long, he had no recollection of being anything else.

No, that wasn't true. He remembered being one other thing: a scared little boy hiding under the bed while his mother was being slaughtered. And the worst thing about it? The police reports Steven had found said he'd had a baby sister. John didn't remember her at all. Not when she was born, or what her name was, or even what she looked like. Nothing.

The thought he might have given up everything that mattered to become an artificial product of the Shadows made him trip over his own feet. The fact that he'd done it voluntarily, just to be rid of his nightmares, made him want to howl with rage.

By the time he'd dragged himself out of the gym and back to his room, it was late morning. His limbs ached with strain, and his hands were shakier than they'd ever been before. He took a quick shower, shaved, and dressed, all the time wondering what the hell he'd do next. If he left this place, he couldn't travel outside the city, let alone the planet, without stealing or manufacturing an identity.

If he stayed, a day might come when he'd look into the mirror and not recognize the face staring back at him. He wiped the mirror clean to look now.

His hair had grown, now more than three inches at its longest. The sergeant major would pitch a fit. Wet from the shower, it stuck out at odd angles in a crazed, disheveled look. His face was flushed from the heat, making his gray eyes stand out, red-rimmed and wild. Not eyes he would trust. John knew his nose and his mouth to be his own, but he'd never been one to stare at himself for any length of time. He recognized his overall features as he would a friend, or a favorite portrait, but nothing about them said, "Yes, that's me, and I know it."

When the mirror fogged up again, John was glad. He folded the towel neatly on the drying rack, tossed his dirty clothes down the laundry chute, aligned the toiletries into a neat row according to size and function, then turned off the light before stepping out into his room.

Emma sat on his bed, biting a nail. "Bad new first," she said.

He almost smiled. "She can't fix the nightmares." He believed that, at least, to be the truth, and as he said it, he was… glad. The nightmares might have been the bane of his existence, but they were irrevocably his; the one thing he could point to and claim as a part of his identity, which meant he had one. To him, this was a relief. But Emma looked close to tears.

"Hey," he said, crouching in front of her and bracketing her hips with his arms. "It's okay."

She slid off the bed and, threw her arms around him, squeezed tight.

John rubbed her back. "Emma, I'm fine."

"You're not!" she insisted. "I couldn't wake you!"

"Shh," he soothed. "Everything will be all right. You'll see. Maybe Jessica can work miracles."

Emma made an unflattering sound.

John grinned. "Or not. Then again, maybe you can."

Emma pulled back to stare at him.

"You got through to me, when nothing and no one could before. You woke me up."

"I rang your bell."

He laughed. "Yeah, you did." And she'd done it long before last night. Something about Emma had gotten through to him, since the first time he'd laid eyes on her. No one else had ever made him question his orders, let alone disobey them. Anyone else he would have let die in that white room. But not Emma. Somehow she'd made him see right from wrong, even while Dr. Wen had reinforced his conditioning. That had to mean something. It meant there was hope for him yet.

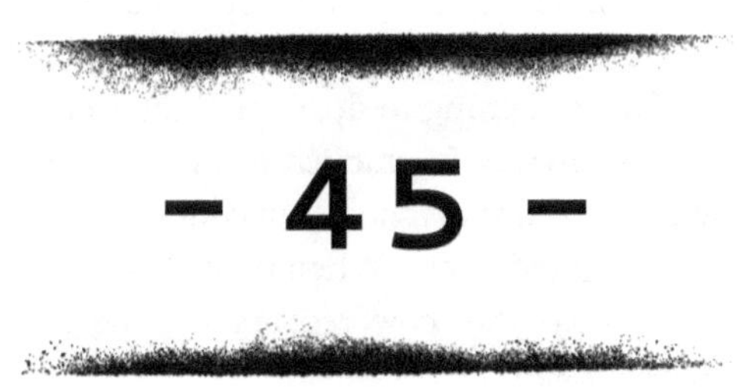

– 45 –

February 29, 3036 – Leap Day

Invisible Day. The day that didn't exist. The day the war really began.

It was a war no one but the combatants would ever know about, fought in secret places of nowhere and nothing, in between areas where no one bothered to look, if they even knew how.

At 10:27 in the morning, Gray Dublin time, the first report came in from Terranos, a far away colony of farmers and herders.

Three teachers in charge of educating a handful of children in negligibly small communities had disappeared in the night. No one had seen anything, heard anything, sensed anything. The only telepaths on an entire planet—gone. Swallowed up by shadows in the night.

Shadows couldn't have delivered their message any better than this: *We know who you are. We know where you hide. And when we come for you, no one will know, and no one will help you.*

Three teachers. Beautiful, learned minds who'd never harmed anyone, who'd only ever provided knowledge and stories and took care of young children while their parents worked.

The Special Unit was in mourning. Travis and a team of investigators were dispatched immediately; they left so quickly, Emma never got a chance to say goodbye.

She wanted to make something bleed.

Big John had put Little John in charge of combat training. Every day, groups of telepaths gathered to learn how to defend themselves from an attack. As if Shadows would stoop to hand-to-hand, when they could just blow a crater where the SU building used to be.

But it gave them something to do, something to focus on, other than fear. In theory, anyway. In practice, fear had become a phantom limb everyone tried so hard to ignore, but couldn't shake. When they smiled, their eyes wanted to cry. When they spoke, they whispered. And when they trained, they cowered, apologizing every time they managed to deliver a light tap.

And Emma was livid.

Little John led two daily sessions of combat training, morning and afternoon, and Emma was always in both, facing their guru with the group of telepaths, mirroring his stances and strikes, eager to get to the sparring part. She felt handicapped whenever he paired her with anyone other than him, having to hold back because her partners always did.

They didn't understand her, and trying to explain to them telepathically always made things worse. Although her thoughts were more structured now, they'd somehow settled on a different frequency from everyone else. If Emma opened up to them, they could communicate with her as they always had, but when Emma projected out to someone, they received a jumble of randomness, like a coded message without a key. She'd try to say something simple like *duck*, but what they heard was *swing left*. Not even the ones in charge of her therapy could explain why it happened, or how.

Even when she got better, she still got worse.

Toby was her sparring partner today; a scrawny sixteen-year-old kid with scared, buggy eyes and sweaty hands. In a fight, he was about as useful as a limp noodle. Emma punched Toby straight in the nose. Not a hard hit, but his head still snapped back and his eyes widened. Instead of hitting back, he retreated, so Emma punched again, this time at his jaw. The blow turned his head to the side, and his arms lowered for a moment in surprise. Bad! *You never drop your guard!* She punched his shoulder. "Arms up!"

And he did raise them. Over his face and head as he hunched down and blindly scrambled back into the next sparring pair's space.

Emma punched at his body instead. *Pow!* There went his left kidney. Toby wailed. *Pow!* There went his right. He stumbled sideways into Micah, tripped him, and Micah fell into Eliza and Jay, taking them down. Three of them out for the count, and all Toby's fault. She punched him straight in his solar plexus, and Toby's arms shot down to hug his midsection as he fought for breath, leaving his face unprotected. His knees wobbled, almost giving out as he desperately tried to get away from her. Tears welled in his eyes. How dare he cry!

Emma would have followed him, but Little John took hold of her arm to pull her back. She came around, swinging, but unlike Toby, John was ready. He ducked, then kicked her legs out from under her. One move, and Emma's back hit the mats. "Everyone take a break. Back here in thirty minutes," John ordered.

The others ran for the door as if a real Shadow chased them.

Then John turned on her. "What's the matter with you?"

Emma shoved to her feet, threw off her gloves. "I am pissed!"

"So you beat up on a defenseless kid?"

"Yes! No!" Words jumbled inside her. She tried so hard to come up with the right ones, her face flushed with heat and it only made everything worse. "Argh! I am so... angry!"

"Yes, I see that."

"Why aren't they?" she demanded, pointing at the door everyone had poured out of.

The tense set of John's shoulders relaxed a fraction. "They're scared."

"They don't get to be scared! Not when one of our own is locked in a white room somewhere, terrified out of their sanity! There's enough fear in us already; they don't get to add to it!"

John uncrossed his arms and reached for her. "Emma—"

"No!" She knocked his hands away. "Stop looking at me like I'm crazy again. You know I'm right."

He sighed as if she'd disappointed him. "You can't dictate someone else's emotions, Emma. The others aren't like you. They don't know what it's like..."

Emma laughed, a bitter sound that made John trail off. "Oh, they know," she said. Of course they knew. They were freaking telepaths. Each and every one of them, from the most senior instructor, down to the youngest baldy baby in the nursery, knew exactly what Emma had gone through. Knew so well, they might as well have been in there with her. "Of course they know," she snarled at John. And their awareness of every terrifying, humiliating detail made their inaction a betrayal not only of her, but also of everything the Special Unit stood for.

Telepaths were supposed to be a unified front; there was no *one* among them. No matter how far apart they were, they were together in this. How could the others not understand? Fear didn't just weaken one of them, it weakened them all, and how dare they do that! Somewhere out there, Matthew, Melody, and Maureen were still alive, locked away and petrified. Holding on, because in their heart of hearts they believed they would be rescued. They believed. As Emma had done. But they didn't have soldier boy to break them out of their cage. They only had the SU. Frightened little telepaths hiding in their little hole in the ground, shaking in the dark and watching for the Shadows to start moving.

Matthew, Melody, and Maureen. Emma repeated the names to herself, committing them to the heart of her memory and the memory of her heart. *Matthew, Melody, and Maureen.* M, M, M. Right in the middle of the alphabet. Teachers in the middle of their small, tightly-knit communities. The senator had vowed to strike at the heart of them, and he'd done precisely that.

And here they all were. Scared.

"Of course they know," she said again, voice barely above a whisper. Then she walked out of the training room, disgusted with everything and everyone in the whole damn compound. She ran out through the dorms, past the entry hall, deep into the unfinished wing, where she knew a single staircase led up.

She ran up. And up. All the way to the roof. At twenty stories, the building was a squat little thing in a forest of shiny high risers. Gray Dublin didn't have much color to it. There were only buildings here, and transports, and people. The occasional splash of green wasn't anything organic, but rather a holoscreen advertisement for some hot new gadget everyone had to have. Even the sky was gray, stagnant. Dead. People lived and worked here because they had to, not because they wanted to, and given a choice, most of them would likely be anywhere but here, which made Gray Dublin the perfect hiding place.

People didn't look for secrets here. They pretended not to see at all.

Surveying all of that glass and metal, Emma felt the gray cage close in on her. Her breaths came short, her hands shook, and her eyes stung with helpless tears. She lifted her face to the sky and screamed. And kept screaming, the wordless cry of a soul who'd come much too close to breaking. But she was stronger now and she would fight back. And anyone who heard her in that moment knew it, too.

Long after night had fallen and the city lights had blazed to life brighter than daylight in every direction, Emma returned to the compound. Dinner was a subdued affair with no conversation floating around the tables, only the sound of cutlery clicking and clanging against plates of food.

The moment he saw her in the doorway, Jeremy rose from his table across the room and left. He'd been avoiding her ever since his blowup outside the movie theater. In some part of her heart, Emma knew he was ashamed of himself and this was his chosen method of atonement. But he'd gone from one extreme to the other; from smothering the invalid, to abandoning her to do whatever she pleased. While Emma was grateful for the space and his tentative tolerance of her relationship with Little John, it still hurt when her own brother went out of his way to avoid her gaze.

He avoided her so well, in fact, she had yet to corner him long enough to fix what had broken between them, and the longer they went on this way, the more she worried the rift would be permanent.

Appetite ruined, Emma played with her food without eating it, sipped at her juice without tasting it, just waiting for a sufficient amount of time to pass so she could leave without offending. Before she left, she sought out Toby to apologize. He flinched when she touched him and he was as tense as a board the entire time she spoke. He said nothing in reply, an indication she'd messed up pretty bad. She'd have to make it up to him somehow.

Because people were giving her looks again, Emma retreated into her room to be alone. It wasn't a bad room, with a comfortable bed, a couple of cubbies for clothes, and fake windows which she'd programmed to show Torrey. She had a bathroom, too, and a TV with access to an immense database of entertainment. Not that Emma cared.

With the lights turned low, she sat on the bed and did nothing.

It was very quiet.

So quiet, she started nodding off, and when the knock came, it startled her so much, she fell off the bed and banged her elbow on the floor hard enough to make her arm go numb.

"Emma?"

She stilled at Little John's voice on the other side of the door. *Uh-oh.* Emma cautiously reached out to open it, hesitated, then shook her head at herself and grasped the handle. She opened the door a little, looking out to gauge his mood.

He sighed. "Are you okay?"

She didn't know what to say to that. "Are you still angry with me?" Her voice was hoarse from yelling, and she winced, making a mental note to get some tea with honey in the morning.

"Are you?" he countered.

Emma opened the door all the way to let him in. "All angried out for the moment. All everythinged out. I'm sorry I yelled at you. And my arm is tingly."

John frowned. "What?"

"Huh? Oh, I hit my elbow."

"Let me see."

"It's fine," she said, but pulled her sleeve up anyway to show him.

John turned her arm a little to inspect it. "You'll be fine," he said. "The elbow's the strongest point on your body. If you can use it, don't hesitate."

Emma rolled her eyes. "Yes, sensei."

He looked at her for a moment, then pulled her forward, wrapping her into his arms. "We'll find them, Emma."

She sighed and hugged him back, squeezing harder to demand he do the same. He did, and she relaxed a little. "Is that why you came?"

"That," he said, "and I couldn't sleep. Missed you."

She grinned. "Seashell got lonely?"

John chuckled. "Yeah."

"I was going to go to sleep." Strictly speaking, it wasn't a lie. Emma would have slept eventually, but her routine of falling asleep wasn't the same anymore. With John, she could close her eyes and drift off with ease, but on her own, her nerves got the best of her. Sometimes when it was too quiet, she still heard the humming, which always made her heart race so much she couldn't even will her eyes to close. When that happened, she usually stayed up until exhaustion took the choice away from her. At least being too tired to stay awake meant she was too tired to dream. A small solace, but an important one.

John pulled back to meet her gaze. "Will you let me stay?"

Emma heaved a great big sigh. "If you must."

John chuckled, brushing her hair back over one shoulder to press a kiss to the side of her neck. "That's very charitable of you."

She hummed with pleasure. "One does what one must for the greater good."

– 46 –

Emma was getting better at classifying her hallucinations. Though the edges of her vision were hazy, this one was definitely not a dream. She recognized the place as a part of town recently destroyed and abandoned after the riots, one just outside of Gray Dublin. The former hub of activity, a travel port and immigration center for this part of Earth was now in ruin, a great big pile of debris like an industrial junkyard.

The boy whose mind Emma occupied had to be new to the group. He still had the misguided sense of immortality all young people shared before reality ripped it out of them. To him, they were all heroes, saviors of humanity. His name might not get emblazoned on national monuments, but people would be talking about the Evolutionaries for centuries to come, and he was one of them.

He looked down at his precious cargo—a hovering gurney with a hard cover that concealed the girl inside. He'd been charged with keeping her safe. No one got to be this close to her anymore, not since that episode on the roof. Annabel was the only thing Zayn treasured, and he'd entrusted her to the boy. It was an honor, and a validation. To their scarred leader, the boy was a man.

Zayn. The scarred man's name is Zayn.

The boy looked up to him with a terrified sort of awe. To him, Zayn was a messiah, a prophet of the coming age, which would be reborn from the blood and ashes of the old. Only the righteous and the steadfast would live to see it.

"Coast is clear a few blocks ahead," Leanne murmured, "but beyond that, I hope you have a plan." Zayn could be frightening at times, but Leanne was just plain wrong. From what the boy could see, she didn't have any girly feelings; she was all about guns and fighting, and he was pretty sure if she ever smiled, hell would freeze over.

"We'll stop soon," Zayn replied. "Michael won't last much longer anyway, and I need to check on Anna."

"You think she's ready to wake up?"

Zayn's eye twitched. "I guess we'll find out," he replied grimly.

The beauty sleeps until her prince comes to awaken her.

The thought slipped past Emma's grasp and came out of the boy's mouth.

Everyone stopped in their tracks.

"What did you say?"

The boy looked down at the gurney again, frowning, confused. Where had that come from? He'd just been thinking about how messed up Michael looked, all green with bloodshot eyes, walking funny since the seizure. He'd wanted to tell them Michael would need to sit down soon, and instead…

"Repeat what you just said," Zayn ordered, face harsh, voice hard.

Emma pulled back and hid in a memory, peering out through a haze of ghosts at the scarred man who walked a dangerous edge, ready to snap.

The boy blinked. "What? I just said Michael needs to sit. Why are you looking at me like that?"

Michael chuckled, taking advantage of the pause to lean against the remains of a wall. "Looks like we've got company," he slurred, closing his eyes with a sigh.

"Fuck!" Leanne snapped. "I told you this was a shit idea. We should have stayed in Tae."

Zayn ignored them both and advanced on the boy, making him trip over his own feet in retreat. Cornered against a defunct holoscreen, the boy stared at his hero, wide-eyed. "Your name," Zayn demanded.

"V-Victor," the boy answered. "Severov. Victor Sever—"

"Not you," Zayn said. He leaned in close, staring into Victor's eyes, through them, and Emma shivered, feeling exposed. "Your name," he demanded again.

Emma pulled in on herself tighter. If she could have fled, she would have. But the boy's mind was a maze of corridors shifting frantically with fear. If she moved, she'd get swept up in the tide and lost. She might never wake up.

Denied an answer, Zayn pulled out a giant knife from behind his back and pressed the tip to Victor's cheek, just below his left eye, making him whimper. "I don't need to kill him to get you out," he said. "I can just gouge out his eyes."

"No!" Victor cried. "Please!"

"Tell me your name."

"I don't know what you're talking about!"

"Leanne, keep them moving, and be on the lookout."

"You heard the man, let's go!"

The company moved on, leaving Zayn alone with Victor and the puddle of piss growing at his feet. But with the knife pressed against his skin, the boy focused on it so hard, it centered his mind and calmed the storm. Mark of the truly brave. His body might shake, but his mind was sharp, ready to react.

"I'll ask you one last time."

Emma felt the blade press deeper, just nicking skin, and it brought her out in a rush. "Sleep doesn't help," she said out of Victor's mouth.

If possible, Zayn's anger intensified even more.

"You think she's calm when she sleeps, because you can't see inside her mind."

"I'm not hearing an answer to my question."

"Sleep doesn't help," she repeated, desperate to make him understand. Annabel hurt more than he could possibly imagine. Emma knew—she shared her pain. No one should have to hurt like that. "It makes things worse. It takes away her control, and she can't fight back." The boy supplied a detail she hadn't known, and she added, "Who was in that box before you put her in it? Were they hurt? Did they die? She's feeling it all, and she can't stop, because you locked her inside!"

The knife moved lower, scraping over Victor's cheek to just under his chin. "Goodbye."

"Wait! I can help! That's what you want, isn't it? To help her? It's what you've always wanted. You thought cornering MacMurphy would do

it, but you were in the wrong place at the wrong time. He was too busy trying to save me."

The pressure eased off, just a little, but Zayn's expression never changed. Emma figured this was as much of an opening as he would ever give, and she had to take it. She might never get another chance. No one would.

"Emma," she said. "My name is Emma Calen."

The knife lowered, and Zayn tilted his head. "Now what would you be doing in my company, little bird? Lose your way?"

"Yes," she said. "And ended up exactly where I need to be."

Zayn backed off and crossed his arms over his chest. "I'm listening."

So Emma talked.

~

It was dark when she opened her eyes. Fully awake, Emma listened to John's heartbeat for a moment, telling herself this wasn't the stupidest thing she'd ever done. Then she eased away and got out of bed.

One chance. One chance to make an enemy into an ally. She had to do this, and she had to do it alone.

John stirred. "Emma?"

"Shh," she soothed. "I just gotta pee."

He settled back in with a sigh, and Emma waited until his breathing evened in sleep. Hard day for all of them, but soldier boy had been going on three hours of sleep, total—if that—for almost a week. Even Shadows crashed eventually.

She tiptoed to the door and eased it open, careful not to let the hallway light touch his face. *I'll see you again,* she thought, knowing he couldn't hear, but hoping against hope he'd feel it. This wasn't goodbye, only see-you-later.

Sneaking past Jeremy's room, she entered the control room to make sure she wouldn't leave Sue wide open to attack when she walked out the door. Big John stored an arsenal of weapons in here ranging from harmless to deadly. Emma would have armed up with stun guns and tranqs if she thought it would do any good. Zayn wouldn't let her anywhere near Annabel with any of them, but to walk out without some way to defend herself wasn't an option.

Before moving on to the main corridor, Emma palmed a tranq dart—small enough to fit into her pocket, but more importantly, non-lethal. Good middle ground. Onward and upward.

Making it past the clinic was the hard part. The Brain never slept. Some glitch in her DNA made her the only human being Emma knew who could function without periodically shutting down. Like a dolphin, Jessica could go to half-power, which made her about as smart as everyone else, and that was her sleep cycle.

Luckily for Emma, the girl wasn't at her post. Snack run, probably. Emma ran for it, eyes on the prize. Almost out!

The door opened and she gasped, running right into Travis. He stumbled back with an *oomph* but managed to keep his footing so they didn't end up rolling on the ground. "Have to admit," he said, "I wasn't expecting this warm a welcome back."

"W-what are you doing here?" He was supposed to be on Terranos with the others.

"I live here," he said with a chuckle. But then he looked closer at her, and his easy grin faded. "Where are you off to?"

"Just out," she said.

He didn't buy it for a second. She could feel her own heartbeat echoed in his mind; he knew something was up. "Emma, you can't go out there alone. The soldiers are retreating to save their own asses. Two blocks from here, it's a war zone."

"I won't go far," she lied. "I just can't stay cooped up in here. The walls are too heavy."

Travis didn't budge. "Did you even tell your boyfriend you're leaving?"

Emma rolled her eyes. As if he'd have let her go. "He's asleep."

Travis shook his head. "I'm calling Jer."

"No! You can't!"

"Emma, you don't know what you're doing—"

"You promised me! Any time, for anything. I'm asking you now. Don't tell anyone you saw me. They can't know where I went."

His mouth hardened. "I can't. Ask me anything but to watch you walk out forever. I can't do it."

"*Please.*"

He muttered a curse. "Wait here. I'll just go grab some things and then we can go. Don't go anywhere until I get back."

I'll look for you in two hours, Zayn had said. *I better not see anyone else tagging along.*

Travis would die if he came with her. She couldn't allow that. As he moved to walk past her, Emma caught his arm, pulled him back and, rising on tiptoe, pressed her mouth to his. His shock rippled through her. *I'm sorry,* she thought, then jabbed the needle into his neck.

He broke away with a shout, but it was too late. The tranq worked fast; he wouldn't have time to send out a distress call. Emma caught him despite his weak efforts to brush her off, and she lowered him to the ground so he wouldn't hit his head, hating the utter betrayal in his eyes. "I'm sorry," she said. "I have to save them, and this is the only way. Forgive me."

"No…" His eyes closed.

Emma bit down on the inside of her cheek until she tasted blood. After making sure Travis was safely out of the way in case someone barged in, Emma walked out the door and didn't look back.

Travis hadn't lied. Not even a block away, battle sounds echoed through the night. Emma could smell burning chemicals and the garbage that hadn't been picked up in weeks. It had piled up everywhere, as far as the eye could see. Buildings were stained with graffiti and blood; broken glass crunched under her feet. It smelled like the wrong end of a sewage system, but at least these streets were empty.

She walked for at least a mile, hugging herself against the chill of early spring. When the fighting sounded too close, she veered off, hid low, and waited until it passed. She shivered, but not quite out of fear, only the anticipation of battle. *I've walked through the gauntlet already and I've survived. Nothing more can hurt me.*

But it would hurt the others. Big John was keeping everyone confined and hidden inside the Special Unit, but sooner or later the protections would fail. The building would get overwhelmed, and everyone inside would die. It sounded like the entire city was under relentless attack; the telepaths had nowhere else to run. Even if they did manage to follow an escape tunnel to the end, what then? What if there was nothing there? What if, by the time Big John sounded the alarm, all of their emergency transports and shuttles were gone?

Not on my watch. Not again. Emma refused to let another person get hurt, if she could do anything about it.

She came up on Tiger Square, the site of Tristan's showdown with the Blood Moons killer years ago. The massive statue still stood there, heavy paw poised to tear into an unseen enemy, face scrunched up into a fearsome snarl. In Emma's mind, that statue lived—it roared into the sky, daring fighters to encroach on its domain. Its eyes watched her circle the square, silently asking, *Do you dare?*

Do I have a choice? she replied.

There's always a choice, it said on the growl of a percussion grenade in the distance. *Choose to live, or choose to die.* With a metallic groan, its snarl stretched wider, its head canted lower, and the great beast stalked toward her, eyes taking on a reddish-orange glow of molten steel that slowly spread across its body along the stripes. The tiger was alive, burning in the night, a hell creature charring the ground beneath its paws. And it was coming for her.

Emma squeezed her eyes shut. *You're not real.* Statues didn't move. They didn't burn, and they sure as hell didn't talk. *Just a hallucination. Nothing more.*

Right, because that makes everything better.

It roared.

No, the crowd did. People scared out of their minds, grasping at straws to force the world to make sense; beating each other, killing each other, because they didn't know what else to do. *They* roared. They were getting closer.

Emma opened her eyes. The statue was back where it belonged, dark and unmoving. She breathed a small sigh of relief and quickened her step.

On the other side of the square, an unassuming black transport waited with the door open. Her chariot, just like he'd promised. It would be programmed to take her to Zayn. Then again, given his state of mind, it could just as easily have been programmed to explode as soon as she closed herself inside. The first test of trust was hers; she had to prove herself worthy before he let her anywhere near Annabel.

Emma circled the transport as she would a live trap before she ducked her head to look inside. Empty. A nav console glowed in the darkness, but there were no maps or directions, no ominous announcements of her impending death.

She climbed in. The door closed behind her, and the transport took off, slow and steady, easing quietly around the battle, keeping to the shadows where no one bothered to look. Emma gazed out the window, horrified by what her city had become. People had turned savage. They chased each other down, beating the weaker ones in a fit of mindless fury until a healthy body had been turned into minced meat. The riot soldier boy had plucked her out of had been nothing compared to this.

This was hell. Fires and brimstone, blood and guts, all swirling in a mad torrent of smoke and rage that seared her lungs, poisoned her mind, clouded her thoughts. She'd left the doors open for it to come right in.

Pressing her hands against her ears, Emma built her shields back up; brick by brick, layer by layer, she shut it all out.

Silence. The transport was soundproof.

Emma relaxed a fraction, just enough to slow her heart rate.

At some point, the feral shadows outside ran off, leaving nothing but fires burning in the streets. Then even those faded away to darkness on either side of her. The moon's outline glowed through the clouds. Had the sky been clear, it would have been filled with diamonds. Just like on Torrey. Her heart ached for home. She wished she could be back there, cocooned and oblivious, safe to live her life in the quiet village where everyone knew her name, and wild cats wore human skin.

Did it even exist anymore?

She didn't notice the transport stopping until a chill breeze sneaked in through the open door to wake her up and focus her back to the present. Emma stepped out and looked around. A dead zone of some kind. Charred ruins everywhere she looked. Not a single building had survived whole.

"Hello?" she called.

Someone whistled.

A light flickered in the distance, and she followed, feeling her way along the uneven ground, tripping more than once but somehow finding her balance again. When she'd gotten close enough to see the outline of a door beneath a collapsed roof, the light retreated. Emma hurried after it, down a concrete stairway, below ground to an abandoned tunnel. Debris had been pushed against the walls to clear a path, and small lights had been mounted to mark the way.

Emma felt herself approaching a group of people ahead. She counted them, twenty-seven in all. Enough to overwhelm her if she tried to look inside them.

Walking into a death trap.

Maybe. But it would be worth it if it helped someone in the end. Even if it was just one person.

At the end of the tunnel, they'd left the door ajar. Golden light spilled out, flickering like thousands of candle flames. Emma hesitated in front of it. Someone would have found Travis by now. John would have woken up and found her gone. There'd be panic in the SU—and damn it, why hadn't she thought to leave a note?

She pushed it all away. Trust. It was all about trust. She had to trust they wouldn't do anything stupid, and they had to trust her to be sane enough to take this on.

Am I?

Does it matter?

She opened the door and stepped into the chamber.

"Welcome," Zayn said. He had a knife in each hand, and Emma knew how fast those could fly.

She gulped. "Hi."

Zayn looked the girl up and down, unimpressed. She was short, skinny, with bright red hair falling around an innocent-looking face. "I thought you'd be older."

She shrugged. "I thought you'd be taller."

He almost chuckled. "Not lacking balls, I'll give you that. But how about brains? You come alone?"

She rolled her eyes at him. "Tick-tock," she said, tapping her wrist. "The clock strikes one, and this mouse is running down."

Right. Not so much with the brains, then. He'd heard the Shadows had done a number on her. She'd told him some pretty interesting stuff earlier through Victor, and not all of it had made sense. "Leave us," he told the others.

"Zayn—"

"I said go."

Leanne and the others retreated to an adjoining chamber, taking their time about it. He waited until he was sure only Leanne listened at the door, before he sheathed one of his knives and really looked at the girl in front of him. "Why are you here?"

"Uh… you told me to come."

Clever prevarication. "Why are you really here?"

"Because I might be the only one who knows what she's going through."

"Lie. Try again."

"It's not a lie!"

"It's not the only truth, either. Not even the most important one. Try again."

She took an angry step forward. "Every second you waste here, people hurt. In here. Out there."

"So you sacrifice yourself for them?"

"I do it for *me*!" she snapped, and her voice echoed in his head.

He let a blade fly, trimming a skein of her hair at her ear. She didn't notice.

"I want *my life* back. I want to sleep in my own bed and not be afraid that I'll wake up somewhere else. I want my family to be able to walk outside without worrying they'll get their heads shot off—"

"And you think you can make it better? You think one little girl will make a difference now?"

She drew her shoulders back, raised her chin. "That's up to you. Will I be enough for you to stop this?"

He gave her the answer she already knew. "No."

Emma Calen nodded. "Then it'll have to be Annabel."

He threw another knife.

She didn't flinch. How aware was she right now? Any sane person would be ducking for cover. Didn't matter how brave they were, self-preservation always won out over convictions—they twitched, they cowered, they ran to save their own skin when the tide turned.

But not Emma. She looked him dead in the eye as if she didn't see anything else. As if he hadn't just made her bleed.

Fascinating. Zayn eased another knife from its scabbard on his arm.

"You can't hurt me," she said. "The worst thing that could have happened to me, already did."

The knife wavered in his hand. He believed her. Shadows swirled in her bright blue eyes, memories of torment the likes of which he couldn't even imagine. Only another telepath would understand the full depth of what she'd been through, although Zayn read hints of it all over her face. He sheathed the knife.

"If you hurt her," he warned, "I will kill you. Slowly."

She shrugged, strolling past him to the door leading to Anna's chamber, as if he'd just offered her tea and cookies. "Died once already, and I'm still swimming. Kill me twice, shame on you."

Oh, this would be interesting.

– 47 –

Recon. John sat against the tree, ten feet from the edge of a dead-fall gorge in the company of six other Shadows-in-training, watching the facility in the valley below.

Fifteen hundred hours in a thirty-hour day cycle. None of them had slept last night, recording hover after hover fly in and unload enough supplies for a small army to survive for a year without ever coming out. John was beginning to feel the strain.

Someone shoved him. "Hey! Wake up." Sixteen years old, fresh out of a grueling, two-day survival exercise. None of them were at their fullest potential, but a Shadow never let physical weakness stand in the way of his mission.

"'m awake," he mumbled, shaking his head hard, which revived him for all of five seconds before his eyelids started to droop again. Weren't they done yet? They'd gotten what they'd come here to find and Finn had called it in. They should have been heading back to the retrieval point already.

Except the sergeant major had ordered them to stand by.

It's a test, he kept thinking over and over again. A Shadow never dropped his guard. To fall asleep on assignment meant death. John didn't know how long they'd have to keep at it, but he knew the first guy to nod off would be washing out of the unit.

Making sure to keep out of sight, John got up and stretched out muscles so sore he had to bite back a groan. "I'm going to do a perimeter check." If he walked, he wouldn't be tempted to relax. The pain would keep him awake.

"Roger," replied the unit leader, who looked more awake than all of them put together. John didn't know how he did it.

After checking his weapon, he ducked low and edged around to the ravine. As far as anyone knew, the continent was abandoned, but the Shadows' intel said military personnel were still present, with installations like the one they now monitored scattered everywhere. For all they knew, it could have been nothing more than training ground. But they'd made the lethal mistake of taking over a Shadow facility. An abandoned one, but that didn't matter. Used or not, Outpost Green 24 belonged to the Shadows, and for someone to toe in on their territory was an open invitation to war.

John walked a half-mile from their post, then got down onto his belly to crawl all the way to the edge of the cliff. Five hundred feet below, a river snaked through the gorge. Narrow, but deep enough to have powerful rip currents. Finn had scanned the section closest to the compound and found an outline of something mechanical hiding in its depths. Shape and size suggested a weaponized sub.

"Is not enough to look at surface."

John startled and scrambled sideways, away from Ivan lying in the grass next to him.

The old man smiled. "Most important thing always deep below."

John shook his head hard. Rubbed at his eyes.

Ivan disappeared. Nothing around him but empty ground, with no imprint of someone having lain there. You're hallucinating. Sleep deprivation, nothing more. He had to pull himself together.

From overhead, the old man spoke again. "Why you fight?"

John turned to his back, weapon raised to fire.

No one there.

He removed his finger from the trigger and let his head thump back. Watching the clouds, he counted to ten, then back to one, willing his heart rate to even out.

Between one blink and the next, Ivan stood over him with a quizzical expression. "You know it will solve nothing."

"I don't want to fight," he slurred, face heating with remembered

shame. "They make me. I just want to be left alone." The clouds turned brilliant shades of red-and-orange, lighting the sky on fire one moment, and the next, cooling it to a blue-gray like the ocean after a storm. Light haloed around the old priest, pale wings stretched out so far they blocked out the sky.

Ivan shook his head. "No one want to be alone."

"I do." The only time John knew peace was when he was alone; when no one was around to stare at him and whisper, when he didn't have to talk, and lie. He hadn't told anyone about his father, but they still knew. And they kept asking, and he kept having to lie. John was so sick of the lies.

Ivan's wings turned black, contorted into people. Dark uniforms, guns held to the side. "What the hell are you doing?" one of them demanded. No face, just a black mask that barely moved.

"There's a shitstorm raining down on us, and you're taking a nap? Get up!"

They hauled him to his feet, and the ground swayed beneath him. He couldn't find his bearings. When they let go, he careened to the side, slamming against a tree. His ass met the ground, and suddenly a chess board appeared in front of him. Ivan frowned at the queen in his hand. "Everyone always let royal lead the charge," he said and set her aside. "They forget the foot soldier is most dangerous. No one ever see him coming."

An explosion of fire and shards shattered the hallucination, and John gasped as his vision cleared. The cliff's edge five yards from him now had a massive crater that ended at his feet.

The two Shadows were gone.

Alarm spiked through him, and he beat at his head. "Wake up! Wake the fuck up, soldier!" His knees shook when he made it to his feet, but he pushed through the weakness, ran back to his post. His unit was under attack. They needed him to have their backs.

Hovers in the sky, shooting at each other and at the ground below. The air was thick with smoke and the reek of burning flesh. Two men down. How many left?

His com was silent. Must have gotten damaged in the explosion. He was running blind, adrift without orders.

This is a test. The sergeant major must have expected them to react better. Mission failed. But they were still trainees. The sergeant major would know they were cornered and send in reinforcements. He wouldn't just let his trainees get killed for no reason.

The post was empty. No sign of his unit. No reinforcements inbound.

"I told you," Ivan said. "No one want to be alone." His voice trailed off as the world around John sank into darkness.

~

Pain exploded in his cheek, and John reacted on instinct, striking out before he'd opened his eyes. He was cornered, surrounded. Four hostiles, combative. Unarmed. They all shouted at him in some foreign language. Didn't matter. They'd fucked with the wrong Shadow.

"Jesus Christ, wake the fuck up!"

John knew that voice. He shook his head, squinted at the faces around him.

Not a battlefield.

He was in his room at the Special Unit. Emma's brother was on the ground, three other guys stood back, hands up in surrender. John shook off the nightmare, braced himself against the nightstand. The solid wood beneath his palm grounded him. "What the hell is going on?"

Calen rubbed his jaw as the others helped him up. "Emma's gone. She took off, and tranqued Travis. He's still out for the count, and Emma's shielding. No one can get through to her."

"No…"

"She could be anywhere by now. How the hell did you not hear her leave?"

Emma gone. He remembered her getting up earlier, but he must have fallen asleep again, right into a memory. He wouldn't have heard an explosion directly outside his door.

She couldn't be out there on her own. She wasn't ready. They had to find her—fast.

John drew himself up, Shadow training kicking in with a vengeance. Questions shoved aside, fears ruthlessly stamped down, weakness brushed off in an instant. John marched out of the room and down the corridor.

Curious people filled the hallway, whispering to each other. He ignored them all.

The girl genius, Jessica, was tending to Travis in the clinic. She swiveled around, gasping at the sudden intrusion.

"How long until he wakes up?"

"Too long," she said, watching him warily. "I gave him a stimulant to speed things along, but I have to be careful with the dosage or it could stop his heart."

"Irrelevant. Wake him up. Now."

She shook her head, hugging the digital chart to her chest. "He's already been scanned. He doesn't know anything—"

"She wouldn't have let him in, anyway," Calen said behind him. "Emma is stubborn as hell. If she doesn't want to be found, she won't be."

"Where would she go?" John asked, recognizing his tone as the same one the sergeant major always used on uncooperative trainees. He pushed the thought aside.

"I don't know. A few months ago, I could have made an educated guess, but she's changed. I can't predict what she'll do. She might not even have been lucid."

"No, she was lucid," Jessica said, "that much I'm sure of. Travis wouldn't have had trouble restraining her if she'd been loopy. No, when she walked out, she knew exactly what she was doing, and why."

"Something must have set her off. What did you do, Wayland?"

He'd failed in the one mission he had: to keep Emma safe. "She was upset that nothing was being done about the missing telepaths," John said, thinking the problem through out loud.

"You think she might have gone after them on her own?" Jessica asked dubiously.

"Christ, I hope not," Calen said. "But I can't exactly put it past her."

John shook his head. "No, Emma might be reckless, but she's not suicidal."

"Well then, what else could it be? That's the only thing worth talking about. Besides, you know, Gray Dublin tearing itself apart."

John and Calen met eyes. "Not the only thing." There was one other. "Tell me you have facial recognition programs in this place."

"I can do you one better," Calen replied with grim determination, already on his way out the door. "We have an uplink to all of Gray Dublin's security feeds."

John followed, tossing back over his shoulder, "Wake him up, and tell the others to get ready. We'll need bodies on the ground to extract her."

"You don't even know where she is yet!" Jessica called after him.

John could only hope the Shadows didn't, either.

– 48 –

Emma was acutely aware of Zayn's knives behind her. Even though he kept a fair distance back, it felt like he was breathing down her neck, and she had to make a conscious effort to concentrate on the ground. One step after another, she entered the dim chamber, where a bunch of crates had been arranged into a barricade. Behind it, the gurney lay on the floor against the wall, top cover removed.

Annabel sat there, as frail as Emma remembered. She'd grown some, as they all had, but her frame was as delicate as a bird's. A strong breeze would knock her over. With her thin arms hugged around her middle, the girl rocked back and forth, shivering every so often. If Emma chanced a look into her mind right now, what would she feel? Bones breaking? Heart stopping in her chest? Only a special breed of telepath could interpret ghosts of memories, and, poor thing, Annabel was one of the unlucky few.

Emma approached carefully, quietly, then sat on the ground in front of Annabel and waited.

"Anna," Zayn said softly.

The girl flinched. Not a good sign. Emma glared at him over her shoulder.

He gritted his teeth, a jaw muscle twitching. Zayn wasn't angry; it pained him to see his girl this way. He didn't want to give up hope she could get better, but holding out was killing him. More than once he must have contemplated putting Annabel out of her misery. It would have been the humane thing to do. Put the lame horse out to pasture. But he loved her too much to be that selfless; having her with him, even broken, was better than not having her at all.

"Chem-treatments did this," he said.

Emma shook her head. "No, that's not what they do."

"Not to you, maybe."

"No, the chemicals might mess with her body, but not her mind. I—"

"She was perfect!" he snapped, and Emma hunched over, anticipating an attack. "Her parents had kept her safe for ten years, hiding her where the butchers couldn't touch her. And she was perfect. Smart, and funny, and so damn alive. The second they found her and injected her, she started to break down. Don't tell me it's not their fault."

Emma clenched her jaw and sat up straight. "We. Are. Immune. Telepathy is a symptom of chem-resistance. They could have shot her up ten times over and it would have had no effect on her."

"You're lying!"

Anna moaned in distress.

"Just because you don't want to hear it, doesn't make it untrue!" Emma retorted.

"I know what those treatments do. I've seen it."

"You saw what you wanted to see. You're fighting your own demons, not hers."

Zayn looked ready to tear her head off, clutched his knives so hard his hands shook. He couldn't even unclench his jaw enough to speak.

To diffuse the situation, Emma throttled back and softened her voice. "Have you ever met anyone else like Anna? Anyone with her kind of gift? I have. When you walk into a room, you see a room. When she walks in, she sees everyone who's ever been there. Everything that's ever happened. This… being in here, anywhere with a large population, is torture. No one's ever taught her how to shut it out, so she can't. For her, life is one violent mob after another, all fighting it out inside her mind, and there's nothing she can do about it. It overwhelms her, sweeps her up so fast, she's there one second and gone the next. You know this. You've seen it happen."

"Ghosts," Anna gasped. "So many… they're dead, but they won't sleep. They never sleep…"

Desperation was a dangerous thing, especially twined with anger. Zayn wanted so badly to hold on to his beliefs, because they gave him a clear enemy to fight. If he gave them up, there'd be nothing left but Anna, and he couldn't fight against that. Zayn couldn't help her if the only one who could make her better was Annabel herself.

"Maybe you should wait outside," Emma suggested.

Zayn gave her an ugly look and made himself comfortable against the barricade. Far enough for Emma to work, but close enough to kill her in a hurry should he deem it necessary. "You have ten minutes. Prove me wrong, and maybe I'll let you live."

Great. No pressure or anything!

Emma dismantled some of her shields, then reached out to Annabel, delivering a tentative brush against the girl's mind.

Annabel stopped rocking and raised her head to peer at Emma through skeins of tangled blonde hair. Her face was ravaged with pain not her own. "Hello," she whispered.

"Hello," Emma replied, uncertain what to do next. With her shields down, whispers leaked into her brain. The others in Zayn's company were very loud thinkers. Nervous ones, too. Except for one. Lying deep inside another chamber, away from lights that hurt his eyes and half asleep already, Michael hummed a tune inside his mind.

It was a fly trap for Emma and she was instantly drawn to the melody, drifting away toward him. His mind was unlike any telepath she'd met before, all numbers and complicated formulas with decision trees instead of symbols.

—*How do you do it?*— she asked him, fascinated beyond what was safe. She couldn't help herself. This man could see the future.

Rather than startle at the invasion, Michael twitched his mouth in a crooked smile. —*Most of the time it's a haystack of a lot of people making a lot of decisions about a lot of things, all at the same time. But sometimes, one particular decision... clicks. There's this path that appears in their mind that hasn't happened in the physical yet, but it will. The path is set, and it leads somewhere. Put enough of those together, and you can paint the future. A specific event that'll take place a week from now, a month from now, sometimes even a decade. Instant magic.*—

Emma frowned. —*But what if someone changes their mind at the last second?*—

His response was droll and more than a little condescending. —*I deal in conviction, toots, not wishy-washy daydreams. Once the mind is made up, you'd be surprised how difficult it is to change.*—

No, she knew that; people were who they were. They might pretend to be something different for a while, but sooner or later the truth always won out. Changing a life wasn't a matter of one choice; it was a matter of making that same choice continually, day after day, night after night. Definitely not for the faint of heart.

—*...for example,*— Michael was saying. She'd missed the first part of his speech. —*Senator Griffith has convinced himself that taking out Zayn will put an end to the revolution. He's combing every available record for him at this very moment. He'll find Zayn's father and his connection to the chem-treatment industry, and for a second he'll think maybe Zayn can be brought to heel. He'd make a powerful ally, and the senator can never have enough of those.*

—*But he's not the trusting type, and eventually he'll remember that. The senator will change his mind and content himself with his Shadows. He'll give them orders to kill on sight and, depending on how good his intel is, he'll find us either next week, or... in approximately twenty-five minutes.*—

Emma jerked, startled. The Shadows were coming? Why wasn't he telling anyone? Why was he being so calm? If these people were still here when the soldiers arrived, every last one of them would die. The Shadows didn't leave loose ends.

—*Griffith is only part of the equation,*— Michael said in answer to her spike in fear. —*The rest is up to you. You have a choice ahead of you. Won't be easy, but it'll determine how this all plays out. So what's it gonna be, chatterbox?*—

"What's the hold up?" Zayn demanded.

Annabel searched Emma's eyes for something, then she smiled. "Hello again." She reached out to Emma's face, and Emma jerked back.

Zayn was there in an instant. "Let her touch you," he ordered.

Emma shook her head. "Bad idea. Very, very bad idea. Did I mention that would be a bad idea?"

Annabel looked confused, couldn't understand why Emma would

refuse her. But how could she not?

"She needs to know you."

—*He's right,*— Michael said. —*Anna won't trust you, unless you let her in.*—

—*Is that my choice?*— Emma retorted. —*Let her in and watch her snap, or refuse and have Zayn kill me?*—

—*It's one of them.*—

Great.

"Hello?" Annabel queried. "Who's there?"

A knife glittered to Emma's right in a wordless warning. Emma licked her dry lips, nodded and, with a quick prayer that this was the right thing to do, she took Annabel's hand and pressed it to her head. Her scalp felt weird where Anna touched her; static electricity made her hair want to stand on end. Annabel slipped into Emma's mind and dissolved through the surface layers where communication happened, right past emotions, perceptions, and reactions, straight into memories. And she didn't look at them one at a time, either; she spread out and absorbed them all at the same time as if copying Emma's personality into herself. Everything that made Emma who she was and everything that had changed her into who she'd become, was now part of Annabel.

The girl pulled her hand away and swayed back. Her closed eyes darted left and right, but when she opened them again, Annabel smiled, head lolling as if she were drunk. "What did the sparrow say to the wall?" she asked, then giggled in delight at her own joke.

Zayn took a knee beside her. "Anna?"

She focused on him, and her entire face lit up with joy. "Soldier boy! Missed you, fella."

The barbed arrow of pain spearing through Emma's chest was his. She didn't know how he managed to keep upright.

—*He's had a lot of practice,*— Michael said.

"Hey," Zayn said. "How are you feeling?"

"I'm complexed with prose, but my muse is operational."

Emma intervened before Zayn could work himself into a rage again. "Annabel? Do you know where you are?"

She frowned. "I lost my seashell." And looking from Emma to

Zayn, so utterly helpless, she asked, "Do you know where it is?" More rocking ensued. "I lost it, and now I can't hear the ocean." Annabel moved back and forth, harder and faster, hands fisting in her hair, tugging hard. "Where is it!"

"Okay, my turn." Emma caught Annabel's face in her hands and speared into her mind.

As she drifted outside of herself, Michael's voice sounded her farewell. —*Here they come…*—

~

"Incoming!" Leanne shouted, and on the heels of her warning, panicked foot soldiers stampeded for the exit. "Shadows inbound. Ten minutes out. Get your girl and let's go!"

Zayn shook his head. "Can't move her." He'd heard enough about telepathic melds to recognize one. Whatever Emma had done with Annabel was on a level so deep, separating them could kill one, or both. He couldn't take the chance that it would be Anna.

"Did you hear what I said?" Leanne grabbed him by the arm. "We have to *move!*"

He shook her off. "Take the others. Get them out. I'm staying here."

Leanne's booted foot rammed into his shoulder, knocking him over. Zayn rolled to his feet and threw a knife, but she expected it and knocked it sideways. She didn't draw her weapon to kill; she was out for blood. They clashed in the middle of the room, punches flying. Zayn took a knee to his kidney three times before he broke free and pulled his spare boot knife.

Leanne raised her gun. "You started this, asshole! You really think I'm going to let you take the easy way out, now that you put everyone else at risk? They need their general, and you need to finish this. So you are going with me." She pointed the gun squarely at Anna's head. "Or I'm going to make this a very easy choice for you."

"Zayn," Michael said from the doorway. "It's time."

"They won't kill *her,*" Leanne grated. "She's a telepath, and she's with Emma. They'll take her, they'll torture her maybe, but they won't kill her."

"You'll still have a chance to get her back," Michael added, "but only if you move fast."

Leave her behind?

"Forty-seven different outcomes to this, my friend. Only two of them end well for Anna. You staying here with her isn't one of them."

Zayn couldn't tear his gaze away from Anna. She was so peaceful now, lost in some internal universe where he couldn't follow. Her lips formed silent words, and it killed him not to know what they were. *Had* he been chasing ghosts all this time? If Emma had spoken the truth, then everything was his fault. How many times had he dragged Anna through survivor shelters and slums, places crowded with disease and misery, because it was easiest to hide there?

What if he'd taken her somewhere else instead? A new place, a new house built on virgin ground. They could have made a life together, and she might have been safe.

"Seven minutes," Michael said.

"You knew about this," Zayn accused.

"Some," Michael admitted. "Just made a logical sort of sense that if Anna saw memories, it might not have been such a smart idea to take her to places with so many of 'em."

"And you said nothing."

"Would you have listened? You, with your higher calling to bring humanity back to its natural roots? You, who used us all to get your way? No, my conflicted friend, she was too valuable an advantage for you to give her up. She's the reason we ever got as far as we did; she was your weather vane. I just tried to minimize the damage."

Zayn released the breath he'd held and it turned into a helpless sob.

"Anna's exactly where she needs to be right now. And if you love her, you'll leave her there."

Anna hadn't moved since Emma had begun. Together, they sat in a trance, oblivious to the outside world. They'd never know the others had left. Anna would wake up in hell without him, and she'd never know he'd done it for her own good.

His throat tightened enough to choke him. Approaching carefully, Zayn laid a hand onto Anna's shoulder and kissed the crown of her head. "I will see you again," he whispered. "I swear to you." She'd never know another moment of fear. "Keep thinking of me, love, and I'll find you. Wherever you are."

A low rumble outside. A hover on approach. Shots being fired, and people shouting orders.

"Time to go," Leanne said, dragging him out the door.

With the first shudder of a percussion grenade, the candles went out, and Anna disappeared in the dark.

- 49 -

"We've got company!" Steven shouted from the controls. "Two hovers, the Shadow kind."

"I can't get through!" Calen said. "Travis, can you take them down?"

"Don't bother," John told them, taking over for the kid. "The hovers will be shielded. I need eyes on the ground. Whoever isn't watching the sky, I want you on the down-feeds."

"Got it," Jessica replied. "There's movement around the wreckage. Over twenty. What am I looking for?"

The hover shuddered, then banked hard left. People screamed. Those not strapped in went flying.

"Did we take a hit?"

"Negative," John said. *Not yet, anyway.* "They're targeting the runners. Travis! Where are we on locating Emma?"

The man shook his head. "There's too much interference. I can't find her."

"Calen?"

"I've got nothing. We need to get down there."

One Shadow hover fired another shot, and the remains of a warehouse exploded with enough force to push them higher up. "Not an option," John said.

Another shot, another building went up in flames. The repurposed containment hover had just enough cloaking power for it to blend in with the landscape if they flew low enough, but it couldn't shield against fire. John took them higher, risking the Shadows' crosshairs. It was either that, or have the chemical flames eat through the hull. They were running out of time, and this piece of shit wasn't equipped with weapons.

"Jessica, I need those scans!"

"Working on it! Heat sensors are giving me a shitload of white noise. Tracking heartbeats. Most of them are running *away* from the buildings. I've got three on the periphery, and something that could be an echo just outside my scope. Move us a hundred yards to the left."

She sat with her back to him. "Your left or mine?" he asked.

Jessica slapped his right shoulder. "That way."

He turned the hover starboard.

"Guys, one of the Shadow hovers is giving birth!"

John swore. If they were dropping soldiers below, then this was a retrieval operation, not a search and destroy. "What about the other one?"

"Uh..."

"Steven!"

The kid looked up and pointed forward. "They're coming right at us."

John yanked the controls hard left until they faced the other way.

"No!" Jessica shouted. "I almost had the echo. Go back!"

A volley of shots cut her off and sent them careening in the wrong direction. The hover hadn't been designed for the quick maneuvers John put it through; it fought him every step of the way, rattling like an old can of rocks. How long before it crapped out completely? If he didn't get them out of firing range soon, the Shadows would shoot them out of the sky.

"Where are the runners?"

"Shadows on the ground are herding them into a trap," Jessica said. "They're not scattering. I'm losing heartbeats, here."

A diversion. Had to be. The leader wouldn't let himself get cornered, which meant he'd be in the other group of three. There was a chance that Emma was with him. "I need coordinates for the outliers."

"Calculating."

"John, watch out!"

The warning came almost too late. John dived, but the shot, fired from the hover behind them, grazed their hull deep enough to damage structural integrity. Instruments sparked angrily, and one of Steven's screens burst into flames. Calen stumbled from his seat to put it out. "Damage report," John ordered.

"We lost navigation," Calen said.

"Top feed is down, too," Travis added, coughing out a lung. "We're flying blind."

"Brain! I need those outliers."

"Twenty-seven degrees left," she called back.

"We'll never make it," Steven said, looking up through the window, where the pursuing Shadow hover eased over them for a kill shot. No way to get out from under that.

Think, soldier!

Containment hover. Not armed. Limited maneuverability, outdated equipment and a compromised hull.

Containment hover…

John sucked in a sharp breath. He flipped an overhead switch and, by some divine magic, the containment field activated, dropping an electromagnetic curtain down to the ground.

The Shadows armed their big guns—pulse weapons anchored to the bottom of the hover that would send a laser charge straight down to incinerate anything and everything to a depth of two hundred yards.

"Hang on to something," John warned. "Steve, on my signal, turn off the levelers. Ready? Go!"

Steven flipped a switch, and the hover started to lose altitude. John yanked on the controls as hard as he could. The thrusters squealed. The hover turned on its side, then completely flipped over in a barrel roll. The containment field flared out and cut straight across the Shadow hover like a hot knife through butter. The force of its split sent the two halves spinning end over end in opposite directions, propelled by thrusters they could no longer control.

John didn't have time to savor their victory; the ground was coming at them—fast. He let the hover complete its roll, then pulled with all his might to engage the thrusters. "Steve! Levelers!"

The boy reached out to flip the switch back, but too much force acted against his body and he couldn't do it. He shouted and unbuckled himself, launching up from his seat to get to the controls.

Levelers engaged. The hover groaned as it thrust upward, and they gained altitude so quickly it made John lightheaded. Up and over the ruins of a warehouse, John eased off the controls and let the hover stabilize itself. "Everyone still alive?"

Jessica unbuckled and dropped out of her seat. "Steven's out. He landed hard. Still alive, but out for the count. He needs medical attention right away."

Shit. "Get him in a stable position. Travis, take over the controls. Calen, I need to know where the Shadows are."

A pause.

"Calen!"

"They're gone," he said. "The ground troops are gone. Just… disappeared. The other hover is retreating."

No, no, no! "Show me." John's monitor lit up with the feed. Sure enough, the remaining hover was hauling ass out of the hot zone. But they weren't retreating. Shadows didn't retreat until they'd finished their mission. Whatever they'd come here to get, they'd gotten it.

"Survivors on the ground," Travis said grimly. "Picking up three heartbeats. Sixty degrees to the right, two hundred yards ahead."

"Emma?" he asked, already knowing what the answer would be.

Travis shook his head. "No."

Keep it together. They won't kill her. Emma was the only telepath who'd survived long enough to get out of their containment and recover, and that alone made her an irreplaceable acquisition. They'd study her first, find out what had gotten broken and how it had been fixed. And that would give John enough time to find her and get her out.

The containment hover held together just long enough to land. As soon as its bottom touched solid ground, the computronics shut down with a deep groan and emergency lights flickered on only to go dark again the next second, leaving John and the SU team stranded in the middle of nowhere with nothing but static from the coms and dead silence outside.

"I'm not getting anything," Jessica reported. "They must have knocked out communications for this entire region."

"Try again," Travis ordered, mindlessly punching dead buttons and flipping inert switches. "There's got to be something. There always is. Radios. Personal coms—try everything!"

"I did," Jessica snapped. "We're stranded. No signal anywhere."

John took a deep breath, willing his muscles to unclench. His heartbeat hammered in his temples, raising ghosts in his mind. If he gave in to them, there'd be no coming back, and he'd lose Emma forever.

"Don't tell me that!" Travis speared his fingers through his hair. "There has to be something."

No.

"I have tranq darts and a couple of pea shooters," the girl retorted, too busy trying to wake Steven, who was still out cold. "Why don't you go up on the roof and shoot out a distress signal? See how far that gets you!"

Calen watched John, hard eyes colder than the arctic night, and John would bet his last marble that the world rarely got to see this side of the mind reader. Good. They'd need it.

John unsnapped his safety restraints and surged to his feet, grabbing the pea shooters out of Jessica's supply bag on his way out and tossing one to Calen. He snatched Travis by his collar and dragged him to the door. "Sorry to interrupt your squabbling, but we've got work to do."

The hover door didn't open so much as fall off its hinges. John jumped down, kicking up dust around his boots. Thick smoke obscured his view, and the reek of burning chemicals made his eyes water. Calen and Travis both coughed and squinted in vain through the clouds of ash to gain some sense of direction, but John knew exactly where they needed to go. The hover had overshot the trio of heartbeats and landed facing south. His target was holed up approximately two hundred eighteen yards, west-northwest. He checked his gun, then dug the toe of his boot into the dust to swivel around, and marched. Seven shots in the charge.

"What, are we walking back to SU now?" Travis called after him.

"SU is fifty miles that way," John said, pointing south. "Feel free to start walking. I'm going to go find myself an Evolutionary."

"We should be looking for the Shadows!" Travis snapped.

The man wasn't wrong, but John couldn't move forward without tying up a few loose ends. Three, to be exact. Emma had come here for a reason, and he wanted to know what it was; why she hadn't trusted anyone else to come with her. Why she would have snuck out of their bed in the middle of the night and left him behind.

And then he needed to make sure no one who'd had a hand in luring her here was left with a pulse.

"Calen, you getting anything?"

"A hum," he said. "Very faint, and very far ahead. They know we're coming."

"Then let's pick up the pace."

"Wait," Travis said. "The echo was that way."

"I don't care about echoes—"

"You should," he insisted. "Could have been Emma. She could still be there."

John stopped. "Do you sense her there?"

Travis shook his head.

"If she were knocked unconscious, there'd be nothing for us to sense," Calen offered. "Much as I hate the idea of splitting up, someone should go check it out."

John made his feet walk on. *Eyes on the prize, Hawk. You know what happened, and you know what needs to be done to rectify the situation.*

"Damn it, Wayland, stop!" Calen caught his arm.

John reacted on instinct; put the man on his back and the gun in his face. "Option A," he snarled, "Emma was targeted and picked up by the Shadows ten minutes ago. Option B: she's lying dead over there, beneath a mountain of debris that used to be a warehouse. You two want to waste her time? Go ahead. I'm going to find the fuckers who brought her out here, and I'm going to end them. Try to stop me again, and I swear to God, I will fucking lobotomize you."

"Wayland—"

There was a grunt and thud behind him, and then a new voice entered the conversation. "That's some big talk for a guy with two guns pointed at him."

Calen scowled at him. "Tried to warn you."

"Put your weapon down and stand up, slowly," the woman ordered.

John tossed the gun and hauled Calen to his feet. Not twelve yards away, Travis lay unconscious on the ground with a booted heel in the small of his back. The woman it belonged to motioned for John and Calen to put their backs against the nearest wall, and they obeyed, John sizing up his opponent. She showed no hesitation, no fear, no anger, no excitement; she was one hundred percent focused, and totally unemotional. She kept Travis immobile in case he came to before she was ready, and kept the rest of them in her sights, standing far enough that if either of them attempted to rush her, she'd drill them full of holes before they'd gone two steps. John had seen Shadows less competent than her. Impressive.

After ascertaining she had the situation under control, the woman gave the all-clear, and two men joined her out in the open. None of them had weathered the attack very well. The scarred man bled from a side wound, but he didn't seem overly concerned with it, hands flipping knives instead of staunching the flow. "My apologies for this, gentlemen. It's not the way I'd have preferred us to meet, but it was necessary. If I hadn't disarmed you, you'd have shot me on sight, and killed two innocents in the process."

John calculated the distance to his discarded weapon. He could make a dive for it, fire off a shot, if he moved fast—

"I wouldn't if I were you," said the other man in the company. He wasn't armed. In fact, he was barely able to stand on his feet, covered in dust, his bloodshot eyes focused on some point beyond John's head. "The odds of you grabbing that gun before Leanne shoots a hole through your chest where your heart should be are fifty million to one. Not worth it, I think." He smiled blankly, a sleepwalker caught awake. "This is trippy. It's like watching a ball bounce all over the place without seeing anything it hits."

"This is Michael," the scarred man introduced. "He knows things. You've already met my associate, Leanne—very handy with a weapon. Don't get on her bad side. Trust me. My name is Zayn. And this might be the first time I'm talking to a Shadow with no intention of killing him."

"Damn, man," Michael grumbled, "quit messing with his head. It's fucking up the timelines."

"Where's Emma?" Calen demanded.

"Contained," Zayn replied, and ice licked underneath John's skin. So the Shadows had gotten Emma after all. And the only way to contain a telepath was to put her in another cell unit like the one that had almost killed her. How long would she have this time? Days? Hours? His hands started to quiver and he balled them into fists.

"Well, that cleared the minefield," Michael retorted, shaking his head. "Why don't you let me handle this one?"

Zayn waved him on. "By all means." He stepped back and gingerly lowered himself down onto the remnants of a wall.

Michael stepped up to Calen, almost close enough for the man to do some damage. But Calen hesitated, and before John could do anything, Leanne snapped, "Line of fire!" and Michael shuffled three feet to the right, away from John.

"Right, sorry. Okay! Here's the deal: Seven clear timelines at this juncture. One"—he pointed to John—"you do something brave, Leanne kills you, and we lose our chance to get the girls back. Two"—he pointed to Calen—"*you* do something brave, Leanne kills you, which will set off a chain reaction of a lot of bad shit happening, and ultimately result in all of us six feet under or scattered light years outside the galaxy. Girls included. Three—"

"We get it," Calen snapped. "Get to the point."

"Uh, no, you don't," Michael returned. "And that *is* the point. I'm trying to explain to you how this thing needs to play out."

John took note of Michael's every little idiosyncrasy—the way he swayed on his feet, the way his gaze wandered, the way his pauses stretched out in casual speech. His hand twitched every so often, just like Emma's had in the beginning. Michael wasn't all together, which would give John the advantage in a physical altercation. But, like Emma, Michael had more to him than met the eye. John knew better now than to underestimate a telepath, no matter how out of it he seemed. He'd hear the man out, learn what he knew, and then form a strategy of his own.

Michael rubbed the back of his head. "Look, you lost someone to the dark side. So did we. It's imperative we get them back and do it in a way that won't give Griffith more ammunition against us. Note the *we* in that sentence." Calen opened his mouth to reply, but Michael shushed him. "Yeah, you do need us. We know where they were taken. We can get you there, and we can help you infiltrate the facility without detection."

"I can do all that myself," John said.

Michael considered that. "Yes," he agreed. "Odds of you getting inside the Shadow stronghold are one to one. Odds of you finding Emma and Annabel, three to one. Odds of all of you making it out alive, twenty-seven billion to one. Now ask me how I know that. Go ahead."

No one asked.

Michael shook his head in mock disappointment. "Griffith knows you'll come for her. He'll roll out the welcome mat and serve you tea and cookies. He *wants* you to come. You're an asset he can still use, and Emma's his insurance that you will do exactly what he says from now on, the moment he says it. You walk in there, you're not getting back out. Period."

"How do you know all this?" Calen asked.

"Finally!" Michael rubbed his hands together with glee, all but bouncing on his feet.

Zayn rolled his eyes. "You'll have to excuse him. It's not often he gets to do parlor tricks for entertainment."

Michael pointed at Zayn without looking. "You have no sense of humor. It's gonna get you killed one day." Then he sighed, "I gotta sit," and he sat down hard, head in his hands. He didn't move for so long, John figured he must have passed out.

Zayn snapped his fingers. "Leanne, I think we're good here. Go check on the others in the hover."

Jessica and Steven. They'd left them without any defense. John started forward, and almost in that same instant, Leanne fired her weapon, searing a ten-inch hole in the ground at his feet. "I knew you would do that," she said with a savage little smile. She gave Zayn one of her guns, then jogged off the way John's company had come. John gritted his teeth to stay put, watching Travis for signs of consciousness. Was he even still alive?

"Griffith is a chess player," Michael finally said, then droned on as if not completely aware of his own words. "He uses the Shadows like pawns to get what he wants, sometimes against each other. He's so used to thinking twenty moves ahead, he's forgotten about the poisoned pawn." With a deep inhale, he straightened and tipped his head up toward the sky. "Each Shadow is a piece of the whole, and none of them know the entire strategy. They don't even know enough to ask about the end game. That gives us an edge. As long as Griffith's match is against himself, we have a chance to make things right. The second he smells another player moving pieces around the board, we're all fucked."

"Translation?" John said.

"Griffith and Michael share a gift for calculating the future," Zayn supplied. "We know about him; he doesn't know about us. That gives us an advantage we can't afford to lose."

"Which means keeping me alive is going to be your number one priority," Michael added. "Even if it means your life."

"What happens if we lose that advantage?" Calen asked.

Michael looked toward the sky again, searching for the sun behind toxic clouds. "Griffith's army will wipe out every last telepath in existence. And then they'll go after the shifters." Calen sucked in a sharp breath, and Michael smiled tightly. "Yes, he knows about them. And Dr. Chase. He's had his eye on them for quite some time. Imagine what the Shadows could do if they could turn into completely different creatures with nothing more than a thought."

"Why the hell should we believe you?" Calen asked, but the quaver in his voice betrayed him. He'd lost his focus the second Michael had said *shifters*. What the hell was Calen hiding?

"We all have too much at stake here to risk fucking it up because of some misguided sense of pride or revenge," Zayn said, making Michael snort in derision. He ignored the interruption. "We're willing to put the past in the past and work together. Can't do this alone, and neither can you." He looked directly at John. "And every extra second we spend here, debating this, is a second less your Emma has left to live."

– 50 –

"What time is it?" the girl asked.

Annabel laughed.

Tick. Tock. Tick. Tock.

The clock face melted down the wall, smearing numbers all the way to the floor.

"Time, and time, and time again. And again. And all over again. What time is it? I might as well ask you your name and it would make as much sense." Annabel tilted her head. "What *is* your name?"

"Annabel," the girl answered. No, that wasn't right.

Tick. Tock. Tick. Tock...

She tried again, but her tongue had forgotten how to speak words. It stuck to the roof of her mouth, and her teeth clenched, lips pressing together. Her eyes widened with fear. Who was she? Where was she? What was this? *Get me out of here!* But where would she go?

Annabel smiled, her eyes blinking up instead of down. "There now, little sparrow. It's all right. You're in my world now. Soon, none of it will matter. Just like time."

Light flared in the darkness, then just as quickly dimmed again. But in the brief flash, the isolation lifted and the outside world appeared around them. Hard walls stained black and brown. Uneven floor covered with layers of dust and debris. Wooden crates stacked into a barricade.

But it was wrong; the colors were off, like a faded photograph.

Ghosts flitted around the room, oblivious to the intrusion. They were blurred, with unrecognizable faces, uttering words muffled beyond comprehension as they walked across the room, melting through her, picking up objects that only became visible when touched.

Another flare. More ghosts, fainter than the first ones. Quieter, too. Going about their business, independent of anything else.

"What is time?" Annabel asked.

Two ghosts intersected, then split into six new ones.

"It's irrelevant."

The six split again, and the girl without a name found herself crowded by people who'd died long ago, forever alive and preserved in the emotional imprint they'd left behind. So many of them… clones of themselves, each moment of their lives here compounded until she had no room left to breathe. Their thoughts blended into a beehive hum that sent a shudder through her frame, and the twitch in her pinky returned, reminding her of things she'd forgotten. Awful things. Terrible feelings. Not all of them her own. She couldn't tell the difference.

"It's an illusion," Annabel was saying. "It doesn't exist. Past, present, future… all lies. We define them, because if we didn't, everything else would stop making sense."

Three of the ghosts laughed, and the girl laughed with them. But standing by the door across the room, a young woman looked at them and cried. The girl felt her heartache. It warred with the others' mirth, and a wave of annoyance from yet another source mixed into the swirling broth of confusion, muddling things even more. The girl lost her train of thought, forgot she was speaking to someone. Words to a lullaby drifted across her tongue in a language she'd never heard before but understood all the same, and a sick child's sigh of relief made her skin ripple with goose flesh.

Before the verse had finished, a massive boom shook the shelter, and her heart hammered, breath locked in her chest. Don't make a sound! Turn off the lights! She choked on fear one instant, felt butterflies for her lover in the next.

Melancholy, anger, pain, despair, love, laughter, anxiety, terror, helplessness—it all crushed in at once. She couldn't pick and choose from among them; they had no order of precedence, no safety net, no off switch.

"Shhh…"

The girl pried her eyes open to gaze at the smiling creature before her.

"We are the construct of a universe which has no beginning, no end, and no limits." As Annabel spoke, a ghost of her split off to wander among the others. Another drifted in the opposite direction to huddle in the corner and rock back and forth as a third leaned toward the girl, almost nose to nose, staring into her mind as if it were her own personal treasure box to explore. With each part of herself Annabel let go, her form faded a fraction more, slowly becoming ghostly itself. "It has no rules, so why should we? Why bother fighting the current?" Another version split off, calling out for someone. Annabel frowned at it, then closed her eyes and breathed in deeply, drawing that version back into herself. Wearied from the effort, she sighed and looked at the girl once more, eyes bleak. "Why should I hold on, when I know I'll get swept away anyway?" The wandering version looked back at the original and whispered words barely audible through the roar of the past: *For him…* Annabel shook her head. "The harder I fight, the stronger the current becomes."

She was losing herself. Willingly. She'd held on so hard for so long… for him. But now she was tired, defeated, ready to let go. And if she did, the girl without a name would fade right along with her.

"W-what's my name?" the girl asked, desperate not to disappear. There were things she needed to do. Important things. Only… she couldn't remember what they were. And she had to. *Need to. Or die…*

Annabel's eyes crinkled with humor. "What, indeed, Pixie-Em-ma-Sparrowgirl?"

The girl swayed, felt others nearby. Not ghosts. Too solid and menacing to be ghosts. Alarm made her grasp frantically for something meaningful: a thought, a memory—anything! She needed out of this labyrinth.

"More importantly, why should it matter?"

"Because…"

Annabel raised an eyebrow.

"B-because… it does."

The creature so unconcerned with the raging chaos, so willing to let it consume her, waited patiently for the girl to finish. Another clone slipped free. Then one more. They linked hands and skipped away. A third rose on tiptoe and twirled a perfect pirouette through Annabel's fading body. She was almost gone already. And the girl couldn't fight against the current Annabel had created.

What had she been saying?

The scent of burning metal tickled her nose. People coming. Soldiers. Bad. Very bad. Hawks and Hounds; Shadows in the night, coming to snatch her back to that place… where…

What had she been saying?

"My name… matters. To someone else. It's precious. It means something."

Annabel blinked when yet another version of her flowed across the room. This time, her gaze snared on it, and the girl saw through her eyes, watched as the ghostly pale blonde tiptoed toward a man leaning against the crates, flipping knives in the air. He didn't see her, staring fixedly at the real Anna sitting on the floor. He didn't react when her ghost reached out to touch his face, or when she slipped her arms around his waist and laid her head on his shoulder. To him, she didn't exist, and when the ghost let go and turned away, her cheeks were wet with tears the real her could never shed.

"What does it mean?" Annabel asked, recovering the thread of conversation. But the girl could tell she wasn't really paying attention; she hurt too much. A pain she couldn't share with her scarred lover—he carried too much of his own already. Thought she didn't know. It would devastate him to learn otherwise, and he'd never forgive himself.

What does it mean, your name? The girl didn't know. A ghostly hand passed in front of her face, reaching for something that wasn't there. Beams of light speared the darkness, sweeping around, and she saw her Shadow on the wall behind Annabel. Her heart gave an extra thump. *Seashell…* "It means… love."

At her words, all of Annabel's ghosts stopped, as did everyone else in all of their various forms. Heartbeats synchronized into one steady rhythm: *Pix-ie-Em-ma-Spar-row-girl…*

I am not a Pixie anymore. She died. Killed by the Shadows. I am the construct of a universe which doesn't follow any rules. So I won't, either.

Emma met eyes with Annabel and grasped onto her thoughts, forcing them into the present. She wasn't kind and she wasn't gentle. They didn't have time to screw around anymore; too many lives were at stake, theirs among them. Annabel resisted, exhausted from her struggles, scared of what she'd be coming back to, but Emma refused to let her wriggle free. "No more hiding. You love your Zayn so much? Then fight for him! He needs you. You don't get to run away and pretend it's for his own good. Fight, damn it! Remember him!"

Harsh voices in the tunnels, sounding off, shouting orders. Coming for them.

"Come on, girl, wake the hell up!"

She was trying; Emma felt the effort Annabel put forth. She'd grasped onto the focus, one ghost among many, one memory moving forward, and she was following him back to the present, but not fast enough. They were running out of time.

"You can do this, Annabel. For Zayn."

Cruel fingers grabbed her hair, yanked her head to the side, then a syringe pierced her neck. Emma cried out, lost her grip on Annabel, felt her screaming in her mind, falling back into the chaos she'd almost escaped from. Emma reached for her again, but already the serum coursing through her veins had soaked into her brain. She swayed, seeking an anchor that wasn't there—chest so wide she could stretch her arms out all the way and still not touch its edges; arms so strong they could make Atlas swoon; eyes so deep they could pull her out of madness. *Seashell...*

But he wasn't there to catch her this time.

And so she fell.

Never forget, she said in one last desperate blast, hoping Annabel would hear. *Not him. Not ever...*

~

They called a truce. Not permanent, and sure as hell not easy, but John no longer had the luxury of self-reliance. If he wanted Emma back alive, he'd need Zayn and his Evolutionaries.

Unfortunately, MacMurphy didn't seem to share his conviction when they all showed up in the main hall of the Special Unit. The old man turned beet red, and not even all of his telepaths put together could calm him the hell down.

At the end of a long argument that almost ended with John's fist in MacMurphy's face, it was decided the Special Unit would evacuate. Permanently. Travis arranged for everyone to make it across the war-torn city of Gray Dublin to the shuttleport, and ensured everyone safe passage onto a shuttle off-world. Groups of no more than twelve telepaths each scattered across the galaxy, with only the clothes on their backs and enough money to start a new life elsewhere.

MacMurphy was the last one out the door, glaring back at Zayn and his people, who made themselves at home in the vacated facility. Scarface didn't help matters, either, smirking the whole time in a clear message that he knew exactly what he was walking into and would make excellent use of every piece of technology in this place to further his own ends.

Then MacMurphy was gone, leaving only those who'd be going after Emma and the missing telepaths with John. Eleven telepaths and the ragtag group Zayn had managed to scrape up from the bottom of the barrel. Too many for John's liking. They'd need to move fast to extract Emma and Annabel. Challenge enough for trained soldiers—which these people were not.

"All right. Let's get you into the detoxer," Jessica said tiredly, shuffling her feet to the clinic. She'd insisted on staying behind to "get the jarhead's neurons back in order." Even MacMurphy couldn't get her to leave, and she'd threatened irreparable harm to anyone who tried to force her out.

"We need to move," John said. "Emma won't have time for us to dick around." They should have gone straight to a shuttleport and off-world the minute Michael told them which of the dozen Shadow outposts they were headed for. Instead, they'd wasted air with this whole charade. He brushed past Jessica to the control room where he knew some weapons were still left. "I can handle this." He'd have to. Couldn't risk her treatment zapping all of his training out of his brain.

Jessica jogged to keep up with his stride. "It took six guys to wake you up last time you had a nightmare. You really want to do that again?"

"No, which is why I won't sleep." The fleeing telepaths had left one weapons locker untouched. John took out gun after gun, tossing them to the fighters lined up behind the gaping child genius.

Travis holstered his and said, "I've got a long-range shuttle on standby at the private 'port. The pilot's keeping her off the ground for us, but we need to move fast. This city's done for." When John tossed him another gun, he passed it to someone else, keeping the line moving down and out, back to the main door.

By the time he'd gotten to the last one, only Jessica and Calen remained. John held the gun out to the girl.

She didn't take it. "If you're going into this as a suicide mission, at least have the decency to leave the rest of us out of it," she said quietly, as if everyone and his brother didn't already know what she was thinking.

"I would, if you people stopped following me," he retorted, shoving the gun at her before he headed out after the rest of them.

"You think this is what she wants?" Jessica called after him. "For you to trade your life for hers?"

"Doesn't matter what I think, or what she wants. Keep stalling us, and pretty soon it won't matter what we do, either." Emma's clock was rapidly ticking down to zero. John didn't have time to waste on debate.

Back in the main hall, John rounded up the troops. "I move, you move," he ordered, then glared back at Jessica just catching up. "You got a problem with that, stay here."

She scowled, but didn't leave. "They'll need a medic."

"They'll need an undertaker," Michael retorted with an irreverent snort.

Zayn cuffed him.

John motioned for them to move out.

Midday in Gray Dublin, and the sky was black with smoke. Buildings burned; the streets were littered with bodies, not all of them dead. Every few steps, someone moaned or twitched in death spasms, and John sensed the telepaths struggle not to respond. He kept them moving. Nothing anyone could do for these people anymore.

The closer they got to the shuttleport, the worse things became.

A massive mob had gathered around the perimeter, screaming and fighting to get inside. They were held back by a twelve-foot-high fence, but that didn't stop them from trying to climb over. The air reeked of blood and too many humans, who fought like animals, tore into each other, beating down the weaker ones to use them as stepping stones for a better reach. From fifty yards away, John already knew only a barely defined mass of stomped human flesh remained at the bottom of that fence by now.

He stopped the group in the relative shelter of an overturned transport to scope out the situation. As Travis had said, the shuttle hovered out of reach of anyone who might try to commandeer it. The guards had all bailed, electronic security was minutes away from shutting down without anyone to manually correct for the overload, and John was up shit creek. He could shoot his way through the mob, but not with so many people in tow.

Travis and Calen came up to either side of him. "What do you think?" Travis asked.

"Nothing good," John replied, earning himself a scowl.

"I wasn't talking to you," Travis retorted, looking across to Calen. "Two ought to do it, right?"

Calen made a face as the mob rocked the fence to break it out of its moorings. "Emotions are too high. Three, just to be sure."

Travis waved over one of the others; a cherubic blonde with black-tattooed lips. "You ready for this, Kaylee?"

"Born ready."

The three of them stood in unison.

"What—get back down!" John growled, but they rounded the transport anyway, advancing on the mob with weapons holstered and hands empty.

John swore and shoved to his feet to follow.

Jessica hauled him back. "Stop," she ordered. "Just watch."

John swung his gaze to the triad who approached the vicious, bloodthirsty mob mired in mindless panic. The outliers saw them first. One broke off to come at them. Six others followed, all armed with pipes and bats, anything long and heavy to batter their way forward. John's hand clenched around the butt of his gun. They were going to get themselves killed!

"Keep watching," Jessica said.

The fighters came to within ten feet of the telepath triad and then simply… stopped, expressions blanked. After a moment, they veered sideways and ambled off in different directions as if they'd forgotten what they'd been about to do. And the triad kept moving forward.

By now, the rest of the telepaths were on their feet, slowly following the leaders out of hiding. Jessica urged John forward and, against his better judgment, he put one foot in front of the other, walking through the eeriest damn situation he'd ever been in. Because as Calen, Travis, and Kaylee advanced, the mob calmed from the outside in. Their deafening screams abated little by little, fighting stopped, and those at the back of the crowd retreated to give those by the fence room to move. Silence fell over the scene, broken only by the rumble of hundreds of bodies stepping aside as John and the telepaths passed.

"Would you look at that," Michael said, sounding far too pleased with himself.

"You going to tell me you didn't see that coming?" Zayn retorted.

"Sure I did. But it's one thing to imagine it, and another to see it in action."

"Calen, wanna tell me what the hell's going on?" John demanded, swinging his weapon back and forth in case someone broke through the mind control.

"One telepath alone can change a mind," Jessica said softly. "Two, standing together, can change a village."

"And three can rule the world," Michael added, casting John an amused look. "Seems Griffith wasn't being paranoid after all. How's that make you feel, soldier boy?"

John shut him out. *Focus on the mission.* Until they got Emma back, nothing else mattered.

The mob moved sixty yards away from the fence, not a step more. And they all just stood there, watching the telepaths operate the digital lock mechanism on the gate, causing John's nape to prickle with unease. This wasn't natural. Tension ran so high in all of them as they strained to break the mental hold, he knew two things as clear as day.

One: the manipulation wasn't a complete takeover. All of those people staring them down were fully aware they were being controlled, and they didn't like it. The second they broke free, they'd tear his little group limb from limb.

And two: that would happen sooner, rather than later. Whatever those three were doing to keep so many people at bay had to be taking a tremendous amount of energy and focus. Didn't take a telepath expert to realize there was a limit to how long they could keep it up.

"We're in!" Zayn announced as his people shoved aside dead bodies to pry open the gate. They ushered everyone through, John taking up the rear, then Travis slammed the gate shut and slumped down against it. As if he'd fired a starter pistol, the mob went mad, screamed bloody murder, and rushed the fence once again. John dragged Travis away from the gate, with a shouted, "Move!" and shoved him toward the shuttle.

He didn't unclench until they'd loaded everyone on board and the shuttle had taken off, breaking atmo in a matter of seconds.

Once they were on a stable trajectory, Jessica checked on the triad. She snapped her fingers in front of one, but watched the other two for a response. When she saw John looking, she said, "Yes, every telepath has this capability. No, not many would try. Stay connected too long, and you lose the ability to *dis*connect. You lose your sense of self. The longer you're there, the more alike you become, until you move as one, think as one, speak as one. For all intents and purposes, you cease to exist. It's... not pretty."

"Now, I'm gonna take a shot at what soldier boy's thinking over there," Michael said, sounding like he'd been huffing fumes for the last two hours. Hoarse-voiced, slurring, he pointed a limp finger at John. "You're thinkin' the same thing we were thinkin' the day MacMurphy came for his precious prodigy. They had the power to stop this all along. Before it even started. And at any of a million times since then. And they didn't. See"—the finger waved between himself, John, and then toward Zayn—"people like us're so used to the concept of *sacrifice*, we don't know another way to live, and we can't comprehend someone incapable of comprehending it." He shrugged. "I woulda picked a couple of the stronger ones and had them go at it. Zayn woulda just pointed to the first ones he saw. You probably would have marched them out there at gunpoint if you had to. But MacMurphy? He says 'Leave no man behind,' and he means it. Doesn't matter how fucked in the head they are, he's gonna take 'em in, bake a batch of cookies, and call 'em son." Michael tilted his head at Travis. "Ain't that right—son?"

Travis glared at the man through bloodshot eyes. Slumped over in his seat, he looked minutes away from passing out, but that jaw muscle kept twitching in defiance. If he wasn't half dead, and if they didn't need Michael's foresight, Travis would lay into the man without hesitation.

Michael grunted. "MacMurphy's what you'd call a collector. He's got this *gift*"—he said the word as anything but—"to see a person's potential. Loverboy here got picked 'cause of all the dirt and sediment that could be chiseled off. Like cleaning up an antique clay pot someone just dug out of the ground. Pet project for when work was slow. Not much good for anything 'cept credibility points. Emma? She's more like a gem. Always had that sparkle. But you cut some facets into her, and boy, does that girl shine."

He blinked slowly, then transferred his gaze to John. "Break a clay pot, and there are a hundred more to be dug up and cleaned off. A gem like that? You'd be lucky to find even one in a lifetime, but she'll shine you, bright as a star, no matter where you mount her. People like shiny things. They trust 'em. Follow 'em, even if maybe they don't think they should. Emma was MacMurphy's ace in the hole. Quirky little girl, so deep in the shadow of her"—he looked to Calen—"*remarkable* family, no one ever thought to wonder what she might do if given five minutes in a spotlight of her own. Except for MacMurphy. He had her slated to replace him one day, and for good reason. That girl could change the face of civilization if she set her fractured mind to it." He leaned back in his seat and closed his eyes. "I'd say that's worth killing for."

Within moments, he was asleep, leaving the shuttle in quiet turmoil.

"When we land," John said, hoping to distract Calen and Travis from trying to explode Michael's head with the power of their death stares, "the kid gloves come off. We don't know what we'll be walking into, so unless you're eager to get your head blown off, you do as I say, no argument."

None raised any objections.

"I'll need a team to stay with the shuttle, to be ready to fly. The rest of you will go after the hostages. Don't lag, don't veer off course. You go in, grab the targets, and haul ass back out."

"What about you?" Calen asked.

With the weight of Zayn's interest on him, John didn't give the man the satisfaction of seeing him hesitate. "I'm the distraction."

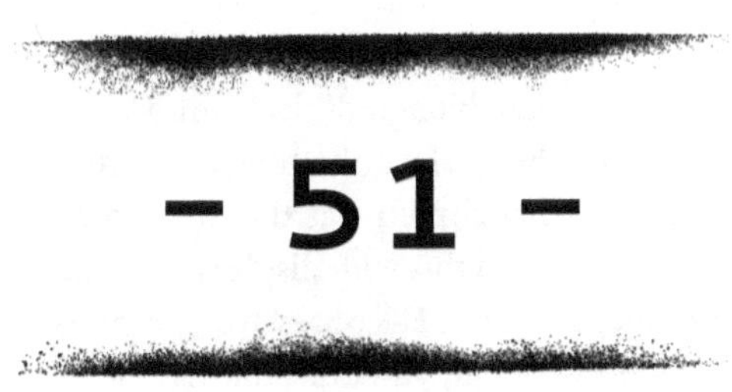

– 51 –

They'd covered her eyes and ears, tied her hands behind her back, and strapped her to a gurney. Emma wasn't supposed to know that. The tranq should have knocked her out cold, paused her frenetic thoughts. Just like last time.

Only it hadn't.

Emma wasn't awake, but neither was she asleep. Senses dulled, she drifted in and out of minds with no sense of direction, no control over where she'd end up, swept along one thought process to the next. Words were her trigger points, and names acted as beacons for their owners' minds. One in particular kept repeating: Sergeant Major. Time and again, Emma tried to follow it, but his mind was too far away to reach. For a long time, she kept hurling herself toward it, only to slingshot right back to the beginning. She was starting to feel like a yo-yo until… she stuck.

From inside a mind organized to a fault, she gazed out at her arch-nemesis: Senator Matthew Griffith, second son of a career politician and an all-around scumbag murderer.

"Where are they?" he asked.

"En route to us," Sergeant Major reported. "Asset is secured, plus what appears to be an additional telepath."

Griffith sat back and steepled his fingers. He'd heard something between the lines. "Damage?"

"Grade-X shuttle and half of its crew."

The senator didn't like that answer. "Explain."

Sergeant Major squared his shoulders. "Hawk," he said, with a side glance at the other man in the room. The Shadow stood by the door, wearing the same midnight blue-and-black uniform as John, the same Hawk insignia on his chest. The only thing distinguishing him from an army of clone-like henchmen was the missing pinky on his left hand. Sergeant Major noted this with displeasure as he did every time he dealt with Finnegan Rowe. His obsessive-compulsive attention to detail had labeled Rowe's injury an unfixable flaw. It irritated him that the senator had chosen this particular Hawk to join their meeting.

But, of course, the senator had his reasons. He always did.

"Sir, yessir!" Finn flipped open the cover on his wrist unit, then touched the face to activate a holographic recreation of the event. Only a partial construct; a time segment of seventy-eight seconds, in which the Shadow hover lined up with the containment unit below. The containment hover shuddered before it rolled over, its electromagnetic curtain slicing up. Suddenly the recording went wild, spinning end over end before it crashed some distance away and the feed was cut off.

When the replay ended, Griffith rubbed his chin thoughtfully. "ETA on asset delivery?"

"Sir!" Finn answered. "The shuttle is nine light years out. ETA seventeen hours and thirty-five minutes."

"And Wayland?"

"Unknown, sir."

"Find out."

"What's our plan of action?" Sergeant Major asked.

Emma didn't stick around to hear the answer. Something odd had flickered in Finn's expression, and she drifted over to him instead. His mind tasted like burned hair, his pathways all artificial constructs put together in unnatural ways. Where one thought wanted to lead to another, a wall appeared, redirecting elsewhere. By the time Emma had resurfaced, Finn was fighting a frown and she'd missed what the senator had said. Sergeant Major approved, though. He nodded and marched out, but not before casting an unspoken message at Finn: *Don't fuck this up.*

Left alone with his commander in chief, Finn stepped up to the senator's desk to wait with strained patience for the man to speak his orders.

He didn't. Enjoying the soldier's discomfort a little too much, the senator stared at him for long moments before he finally straightened in his seat and activated the desk screen to flip through files in digital holospace. Emma nudged Finn's motor functions to twitch his eyes down so she could better see what was happening.

Having selected two personnel files, the senator opened them side by side. Finnegan Rowe and John Wayland. Except for their names, pictures, and acquisition dates, the records were almost identical: starting at eighteen years of age, same timeline, same achievements, same skills, but for one small difference—John was incorruptible, and Finn wasn't.

The fact floated across Finn's mind as a side note to an otherwise ordinary service record. It didn't inspire any resentment, jealousy, or fear. To him, it was simply a genetic trait, like hair color or height.

In an army of people who feared telepaths so much they wanted to eradicate every last one, Finnegan Rowe stood apart. It intrigued Emma far more than Griffith's little speech about Finn being the best candidate to engage John when—*when*, not *if*—he arrived. She drifted deeper into his mind, followed the artificial pathways in a pointless cycle to nowhere and back, looking for some anchor. She didn't need much, just the smallest flaw in the design; a single instance in which the neural programming these men underwent on a regular basis was beginning to wear out. There was always at least one; a soul was too powerful to be suppressed completely. Sometimes, a simple memory or feeling was so persistent, it defied any attempt at manipulation.

Finn was no exception.

Deep inside his psyche, along a pathway dark from disuse, Emma felt a chink in the wall. While Griffith filled Finn's conscious mind with propaganda against tolerating dissent and assured him mercy would be allotted only if certain criteria were met, Emma probed at the weakness with smooth sweeps of her mental touch. With each pass, the wall became thinner, more brittle. Soon, she could sense something behind it, matching her like a reflection, wearing out a hole from the inside as she tried to dig through from the outside.

Almost through, Emma stopped. Her psychic fingers were a paper's width away from something powerful and intense on the other side, and if she allowed it to break through, as it clearly wanted to do, it would have an immediate effect on Finn. He'd remember, and he'd crack, right in front of the senator. Then he'd be sent directly to the treatment facility, and that opening she'd made would once again be sealed shut, worse than ever.

"I trust you understand the gravity of the situation," Griffith was saying. "We are at the most critical point in our campaign."

"Yes, sir," Finn replied, and the subconscious entity pressed on the remaining barrier, reached out from the darkness. It pulsated with the heat of intense emotion, but Emma couldn't yet identify what it was.

"Wayland could end our mission before it's finished. This cannot be allowed to happen."

"Understood." Steady pressure seared a hole through the barrier, and Finn's mind shuddered with a deep inhale.

Emma drew back, wary.

"He will try to sway you to his side. He will appeal to your camaraderie, loyalty of friendship, even your sense of justice. There can be no hesitation on your part. Wayland is no longer a Hawk."

The heat throbbed, tendrils of glowing red smoke curling outward to illuminate the pathway, and Emma's breath caught at the sight. Those pale, abandoned walls were smeared with drawings and symbols, like crude caveman markings that covered almost every available surface, as if he'd come here countless times before, searching for something. Searching for… it.

"I want your word that you can do what is being asked of you. Tell me now, and be certain. Because if not, then you are not the Hawk for this mission."

Emma felt Finn's heart hammering. He kept his breathing even, but as more of that light flooded the tunnel, the effort cost him and he paused for longer than he should have before giving the senator his answer. "It will be my pleasure." But the words sounded wooden, even to his own ears.

Emma hurried back to the forefront, already feeling herself fade away, while the thing she'd unleashed seeped out little by little, taking over the pathways. It wasn't happy with what it found. Anger, perhaps as old as the soldier himself, hammered at the artificial walls and demanded access into corners long sealed off. There would be no stopping it now. She could only hope Finn was strong enough to handle it.

Because it came with a name.

Riding on a powerful wave of emotional turmoil, the presence Finn had buried so deeply would no longer be denied. It swept Emma along without fanfare, taking over the soldier who even now struggled to keep his gaze fixed straight ahead as the senator narrowed his eyes in suspicion.

In a desperate bid to repair what she'd broken, Emma threw a barricade into its path—a thick glass wall to slow its progress and buy Finn a few precious seconds to compose himself. There'd be no mistaking it for a natural construct or the result of Shadow treatments; Finn would know someone had tampered with his mind, and perhaps even who. But at least for the moment, as Emma drifted out of his mind, his thoughts were once again under his conscious control. They just weren't hidden anymore.

As soon as she'd disconnected completely, Emma sank into a lazy pink river of peace. Not hers, though. Another mind, another place, somewhere in the vast infinity of space where booted footsteps drummed out a steady beat. She could tell time by them. They matched the rocking motion that sent butterflies fluttering through her belly. The urge to smile was suppressed by the tranq serum, but her host didn't care, blissfully unaware of Emma's presence in her thoughts, just one ghost among many. Nothing but silent specters, keeping to themselves.

The footsteps slowed, halting the river's current, and its pink water began to fade. Slowly at first, as if a great vat of milk had spilled into it, diluting the colorful purity. Then the swirls of white took on a glow so bright, it overpowered the need to sleep.

She remembered voices, and lives, and pain—so much of it, all at once, that she'd lost herself in the chaos. But it was all gone now. Like a bad dream, it had faded into the deep recesses of her mind, leaving her to drift back up to the surface, alone. *My name is Annabel,* she remembered. *I am twenty-five years old. I used to love to dance.* The details came back one at a time, slowly falling back into place, guided by the hum of a beehive.

She was smiling before she'd even opened her eyes, and when she did, nothing but a sea of bright white surrounded her. A blank slate in every possible sense. No ghosts, no memories soaking into the walls, no harsh words shouted at the ceiling, no thick blood pooling on the floor. Only clean, pure, nothing.

Before the door shut, booting Emma out, Annabel laughed, and she kept laughing with relief so deep it made her soul weep.

She didn't hear Emma screaming in terror just beyond that pure white wall.

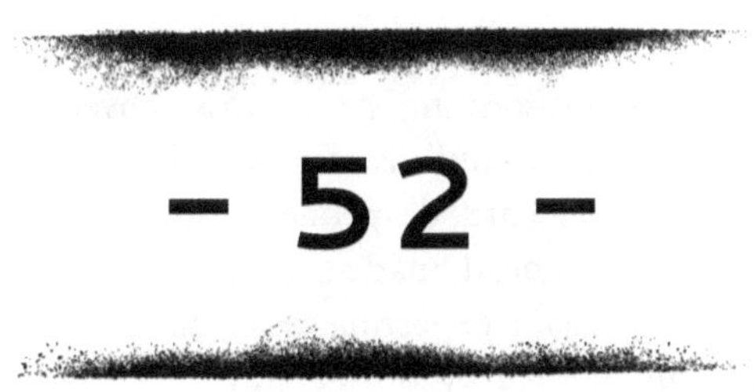

– 52 –

The shuttle flight lasted twenty-nine hours. It only took sixteen for John to start feeling the effects of sleep deprivation. While the others slept, he paced, reciting the Shadow code of conduct in his head to give his mind something to focus on. He fell into the old routine of marching footsteps, measured breathing, hands clenching and stretching out by his sides, and when his eyelids started to droop, he slapped himself hard across the face and shook it off. He stopped counting the times the sound woke one of the others into giving him strange looks before settling back to sleep.

Somewhere during the nineteenth hour, John started to lose time. One minute, he stood on the bridge, checking the flight conditions and reciting the tactical assault handbook; the next, he was in the cargo hold, a knife in his hand and his sleeve rolled up. The back of his forearm still had a neat ladder of faint scars. Last time he'd had to stay awake past seventy-two hours as a trainee, he'd resorted to cutting to mark the time. The cuts were shallow, just enough to stimulate pain receptors into waking him up.

"You going to keep this up much longer?"

John started, whirling on the intruder, charging on instinct before he could stop himself. The blade buried to the hilt in a man's chest, and John reeled back, staring at it. Blood soaked the deep gray T-shirt, trickled down the front of the man's cargo pants. When John forced his horrified gaze up to the man's face, it mocked him.

"Never did anything the easy way, did you?"

"Finn?"

The other Hawk flashed a quick grin, wholly unconcerned about the knife sticking out of his sternum. Arms crossed over his chest, Finn leaned against the shuttle's hull, as easy as could be. "'Sup."

John rubbed his face hard, desperate to rid himself of the hallucination. He shook his head, made a circuit to the door and back. When he looked up again, expecting to see the knife sticking out of a metal hull, Finn raised an eyebrow at him.

"You're not here. This isn't real," he informed the hallucination.

Finn shrugged. "So? Just makes me harder to get rid of." He shifted to push away from the wall, but the knife brought him up short. He was pinned. With both hands, Finn grabbed the handle and wrenched it out. Fresh blood poured from the wound. He looked down at it before giving John a wry smile. "Mother always said I was a goddamn bleeding heart."

John roared and punched the nearest wall with enough strength to send agony shooting through his wrist and elbow, all the way up to his shoulder. He ground his knuckles into the metal. *It's not real.* But when he looked up, Finn was leaning against the hull right next to him, blood dripping to the floor between his booted feet.

"Feel better?" the Hawk asked.

"What do you think?" John retorted.

"I think you're avoiding some pretty major issues here, is what I think."

John laughed bitterly. "There's a newsflash."

"Let's talk this through, shall we?" Finn was growing pale, shadows blooming beneath his eyes, but his face never registered an ounce of pain. Typical Hawk. Wouldn't drop his focus for something as inconsequential as a fatal stab wound. "What's your plan?"

"Don't have one." And even if he did, John wouldn't tell another Shadow, no matter how friendly they'd been in the past. John was now the enemy. Finn wouldn't hesitate to take him out if given half a chance, and John sure as hell wasn't planning to provide him one.

"Smart," Finn said dryly. "Walk into a military stronghold, half cocked, half dead, and emotionally compromised. Might as well take that knife and slit your own throat. Save everyone a lot of time."

John glared at the blade sticking out of the opposite wall. Not a speck of blood on it.

Meanwhile, Finn stood in a puddle of it, smacking his blue lips. "You got anything to drink in this place? I'm parched."

"You're a hallucination."

Finn rolled his eyes. "All right, Captain Obvious, listen up, 'cuz I don't have all day, here." His expression flickered like a faulty hologram, and suddenly his voice turned raw from smoke inhalation, his burned hand wrapped in shirt scraps, and they were hip-deep in a live weapon battle simulation on a mission to extract the sedated target alive and unharmed. "I've got fuck all for ammo."

"Two rounds left," John replied from memory. "You wanna go first, or should I?"

Finn scrutinized a pile of cargo boxes that looked more like a cement wall with bullet holes for hand- and footholds. "Target's just on the other side of that. Intel says they've got six guys on guard duty, eight more around the perimeter."

"And?"

"I'm thinkin'."

"Well, while you're doing that, how 'bout I just go retrieve the target on my own?"

Finn laughed, and an ugly, rattling cough shuddered his frame. "Funny guy. I say we call it."

"What—abort the mission?"

Finn lolled his head in a nod. "Last two Hawks against all them Hounds? Suicide."

"High priority target. Sergeant Major will castrate you for walking away."

Finn appeared to consider that. "Can live without my balls. Lacking a pulse, though? Kinda problematic."

Mud and grass kicked up around them; silent bullets exploded patches of earth into the air.

"Ah, shit! Incoming!" John rolled sideways to crawl across wide-open marshland. *A Hawk never abandons his mission.* One final push, and he hit the wall.

And it moved. Crates tumbled over him.

Marsh gone. Finn gone. No shots being fired. Just the silence of outer space and the whirring hum of the shuttle's artificial gravity generator.

A pointed cough brought his attention to the doorway, where Michael stood watching John like a dog who'd just gobbled up its own vomit. "Morning," he said. "When you're done playing pretend, we've got strategy to discuss."

John thumped his head back against one of the crates. "No."

"Excuse me?"

He pushed to his feet, retrieved his knife. He'd need to treat the blade before they landed. That would give him something to do. "You said Griffith can do what you do. The minute I form any kind of plan, he'll know. So whatever strategy you need to discuss, do it where I can't hear."

Michael stared at him for a moment, then scowled. "Sit," he ordered, and took a seat in the doorway so John couldn't leave.

"I just told you—"

"I heard you. But if all you idiots are gonna force me to be Obi Wan, then you're damn well gonna listen to what I gotta say. Now, sit your ass down."

"There's no shutting you up, is there?"

"Nope."

John rolled his eyes, dragged over a crate, and sat.

"You're going to die," Michael opened, and the strength of his conviction sent a chill down John's spine. "Forty-nine minutes after the shooting starts, and the Shadows turn on each other, you'll be dead where you stand. Or sit. Whatever. But see, I've got a problem with that, because your death changes the timeline into a branch of decisions that all end with a lot of people dying. Including me."

John stared, unable to think of anything to say in reply.

"I'll give you a minute to absorb this," Michael offered.

John had seen Michael's eyes roll back in his head more than once during the first part of this trip. Even now he looked like he wasn't playing with a full deck—and John was supposed to just take it all on faith that Michael might be right? There'd been a time, not that long ago, when John would have accepted it. After all, he'd been trained to take orders without question; a perfect soldier who never disobeyed. Until Emma. *A warrior thinks for himself,* she'd told him, staring straight into his eyes, desperate for him to wake up and see beyond the lies he'd been fed all of his life.

Wide awake now, he thought, wishing she was there with him. Real life situations, he could deal with. Figuring out what went on inside a telepath's brain was Emma's territory. *Question everything.* "What the hell makes you think I give a shit about anything you say to me?"

"Oh, I'm sorry. For a minute, there, I thought you wanted to live through this. Listen, buttercup, it's not exactly easy pulling this shit out of my ass, okay? I've got an aneurysm in my head the size of a marble. One more seizure and I'm done for. And the way this is shaping up, that means I probably won't last out the week. So what say we shelve the dick-swinging for another time, huh?"

"If you're so sick, why don't you go in for treatment? Why keep doing this?"

Michael rubbed the back of his neck. "Anna," he said, staring at the floor. "She and Zayn have saved my life more than a few times. I owe it to them to see this through."

"I believe you," John said, and meant it.

Michael nodded, still not meeting his gaze. "Then let's get down to business."

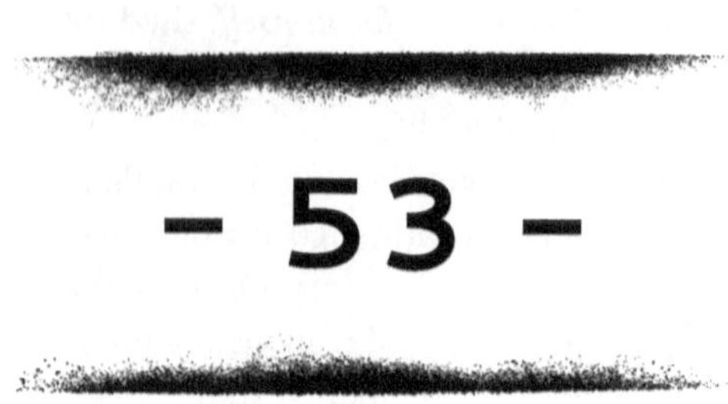

White on white. No break in the walls. No outline of a door. No mattress on the floor, or sink to run water. A bright white cage humming that maddening beehive hum that wouldn't let up, and Emma's neurons screamed. She tasted electricity on her tongue. Her eyes kept trying to roll back. Curled in a tight ball, she twitched, moaning, as tears pooled beneath her cheek.

I can't do this. Not again!

A spasm jerked her arms up, and she fisted her hands into her hair, tearing, screaming until she ran out of breath.

Then the silence crept in, sneaking up on her mind like a white hot laser beam erasing her brain. Subtle. Sound left, then her eyes started playing tricks on her; pale hands blending in with the sea of white until she couldn't see herself anymore. There one minute, gone the next. As if she didn't exist. And she didn't.

Tick. Tock. Tick. Tock.

With each click, more of her disappeared, and Emma couldn't stop it. The more she struggled, the faster she disintegrated. So she made herself lie still, skin crawling with a billion bees stinging their way inside through her skin. Shivering, twitching, chest unmoving without any need for air until some subconscious reflex made her lungs expand just enough for a fresh batch.

Tick. Tock. Tick. Tock.

"Hickory, dickory, dock," she whisper-sang to herself, just to hear something other than that hum. To know she was still there, still alive.

—*The mouse ran up the clock,*— a different voice sang back, and Emma firmed her chin to keep it from quivering. Hallucination. That didn't take long. Next would come seizures, and then farewell world. At this rate, even if someone were to come looking for her, they'd never make it in time. She'd be dead within hours.

So she might as well sing. "The clock struck one—"

—*The mouse ran down…*—

Emma blinked up at nothing. "Hello?"

Hummmmmmmm…

"The clock struck one, the—"

—*The mouse ran down…*—

Emma sat up. "Who's there!"

Hummmmmmmm…

"Answer me!"

Hummmmmmmmm…

"Hickory, dickory, dock."

—*Hickory, dickory, dock,*— that voice sang in a second round, and kept singing, beating her to the next line: —*The mouse ran up the clock.*—

"The mouse ran up the clock," Emma sang along, taking the first round on the third line: "The clock struck one—"

—*The mouse ran down,*— the voice finished, and together they sang the last "Hickory, dickory, dock."

Emma shoved to her feet, slapped her hands against the white wall. "Who's doing this!" That voice wasn't in her head; it was real—she knew it! An audio speaker had to have been built into the wall somewhere. She wasn't crazy! Running her hands over the smooth, unbroken white surface was like rubbing a static electricity generator. Emma felt the charge just short of zapping herself—an unpleasant crawling sensation against her palms—but she kept at it, tracing the walls one way and then back again.

Nothing.

Not a chink, not a crack, not even a seam anywhere.

She squeezed her temples hard. *I'm not crazy!* She had heard another voice in here. "Answer me! Please…"

Hummmmmmmm…

Emma sank to her knees, facing the wall, and hummed back, shuddering through that disquiet of matching frequencies. She kept humming—louder. If she was going to die, she'd do it on her terms. Head-on. Fighting back. She would not cower. *Louder!*

Her eyes rolled back, and she let them, embraced the vertigo as her body slumped to the floor; hardly felt the thud of her head hitting down. The silence that followed was far from absolute.

~

March 12, 3036 – Outpost Green 24

It would have to be here. The sergeant major would have to choose the one place guaranteed to wig John out. He looked out the shuttle window as they neared a landing spot and clutched the seat's arm-rests to keep his hands from shaking. Sleep deprivation didn't help. Every bird in the sky made him flinch in remembrance of the hovers dropping bombs on the Shadows below. Travis didn't dare fly them over the base, but John knew where it was: down in a valley, along the banks of a river deeper than it was wide. The crater would still be there, too, along with the ghosts of fallen trainees.

The shuttle jarred, and suddenly John's nose itched with chemical fumes. The floor turned black, corroding into a gaping chasm, while blood and charred flesh rained down around him.

He flinched, shook his head hard. *Only a memory.*

But one that was about to repeat itself.

"Hold on, I'm going to set this bird down," Travis announced. He'd chosen a clearing five miles away from the Shadow compound, as if that would make any damn difference. No doubt the Shadows had been tracking their flight path for hours; they had exactly zero-point-no chance of escaping detection. But John didn't have the mental stamina to argue that point with any of them. He had a hard enough time keeping his thoughts focused on the mission.

They will test you, Michael had told him. From the moment you step foot out of the shuttle, you will be off balance. And that's exactly what they want. Don't believe what you see. Don't listen to what they tell you. It's all for show. And beware the Hawk in the shadows.

Yeah, really fucking helpful.

Which Hawk? There'd been four others in John's unit alone. And what about the six hundred plus Hounds? What, they weren't a threat?

The more he thought about it, the less Michael's story added up. He'd given John a scenario and a series of decision trees, half of which were detailed enough to be realistic, the other half so vague they were completely useless. The ones that sounded like clairvoyant bullshit put him on guard the most. But no matter how convincing Michael had made himself sound, John still had a nagging suspicion at the back of his mind that this was all a setup. He didn't trust Michael, or Zayn, or the rest of them as far as he could throw this shuttle. They all had their own agenda and it didn't include John, Emma, or any of the other telepaths. Decades of training told him this would be a triage operation. If Zayn was only after his girl, then he and Michael could have walked in on their own, and walked back out without being detected. Yeah, apparently Michael was that good. They'd brought the rest along as cannon fodder; a distraction for some bigger play John couldn't predict. And he didn't like it.

The shuttle touched down with a bone-rattling thud. "Sorry!" the Evolutionary copilot said. "That was my fault."

John counted to ten and back before he unstrapped himself and pushed to his feet. The world did a sickening dip-and-whirl before he steadied himself enough to walk a straight line. Still felt like walking on a swaying boat, but he managed. More or less.

"Look at you." Zayn shook his head in a mixture of pity and mockery. "A sorrier sight I have yet to see."

"Looked in the mirror lately?" John retorted.

"What, this?" Zayn traced the scar on his face. "I consider it a beauty mark. Reminds me every day that people can't be trusted."

How ironic. "I'll remember that."

"Something's not right," Calen said, watching the control panel. "There's no movement outside. The area's deserted. Shouldn't it be crawling with soldiers?"

"Getting the same across brain waves," Travis added. "Nothing sentient for miles in any direction."

"So," Zayn said, summing up their situation, "either the Shadows have decided an unidentified shuttle landing in their backyard wasn't enough of a threat to address, or they've managed to learn to hide from you. Which version are we going with?"

Everyone, including his own people, ignored him. Instead, they all waited for John's orders. This wasn't what they'd been expecting. An army should have surrounded them by now, which would have given the telepaths plenty to do with keeping them back while the rest retrieved the POWs.

As far as John was concerned, his part of that plan hadn't changed. So, instead of wasting time on bullshit inspirational speeches, he slipped a couple of the smallest guns into his boots and walked out of the shuttle.

Green 24 had changed drastically. The grass was green, the sky blue, no battleships in the air, no plumes of thick black smoke or the smell of charred human remains. He'd walked this world an eager trainee the first time, ready to lay down his life for his unit, if need be. Now, he was a deserter, finally seeing the truth he'd been all-too eager to ignore before. And he had that much more to lose.

"Are we doing this, or what?" Calen asked, and John realized he must have been standing there for several minutes, just staring off into space. A rookie could have picked him off from a mile away, ten times over.

They hadn't. Which meant Michael was right. They wanted him alive.

"Change of plans," he said. "I want you to stay with the shuttle."

"The hell I—"

"That's an order."

"You're not in charge here!"

John turned on him, just managing to square his stance to conceal how unsteady he was. "The more of you that are together, the better chance you have of getting the hell out if this turns bad." Judging by his mental impairment and physical state, if John didn't get some shut-eye within the next five hours, his body would start shutting down. Hike five miles, infiltrate a top security military base, liberate prisoners, break out, and hike five miles back, possibly under heavy fire, all in under five hours? Piece of cake. "And by the way, if that happens, you haul ass out of atmo, STAT. You got me?"

Calen looked ready to deck him. "I am *not* leaving Emma behind."

John's vision clouded. Suddenly, he was on his haunches in front of Emma, who pleaded with him not to take her back to the Shadows. He shook off the vision and rubbed at his chest. It felt hollow. "That makes two of us. Travis, let's go."

John set the pace, while the others warily followed a dozen yards behind. He zoned out more often than not, and reached into his pocket on reflex, looking for the chess piece that wasn't there to ground him. More than anything, he wanted to look over and see Emma walking beside him, to take her hand and hear her prattle on in her nonsensical way. To just… have her there.

Won't be long now.

The first mile dragged on in a tense silence. After the second, the men at his back started to talk among themselves. John knew they were talking about him. In leaving Calen behind, he only had one ally left in the group, and even that was tentative at best in the "enemy of my enemy is my friend" sort of way. As Zayn and his people snickered and cracked jokes, Travis snapped at them to shut the hell up. It didn't work.

Somewhere past the third mile, the telepath separated himself to catch up with John. They hadn't seen a single soldier in all this time. John hadn't expected them to tip their hand so soon, but his entire body prickled with the sensation of dozens of eyes watching his every move. They would have surrounded the abandoned shuttle the moment he stepped out of sight. Hopefully Calen had the sense to keep watch and make sure they all got out before the Shadows made it impossible. They could still circle around to retrieve the rest of them at a different location, but only if the shuttle was still operational.

"…should be there when we get Emma."

"What?"

"I said you should be there to get her out."

"I have my job to do," John said, tensing his back against a shiver of dread. The first decision. According to Michael, this one would determine whether he lived or died. Son of a bitch hadn't said which was which.

"I need you in there with me!" Travis said. "You don't know what this will have done to her mind! Seeing someone who clearly shouldn't be there could cause a break with reality. Permanently."

"She's been through this before; she can handle it," John replied, trying to convince himself more than Travis. He'd love to open that door himself and bring her out. But that was exactly what the senator was expecting him to do. If he so much as looked in Emma's general direction, they'd both be worse than dead. He couldn't allow that. Emma's best chance of escape was if John distracted the Shadows enough for them to drop their guard, so Travis and the others could get to her. It killed him that Emma might see his absence as the final betrayal, but there was no other way.

Travis scoffed. "You are one heartless piece of shit asshole." With a challenging glare, he let John retake the lead. "I'll be sure to tell her that when I see her."

John unclenched his jaw long enough to say, "What makes you think she doesn't already know?"

For the last mile, everyone once more fell silent. They emerged from the sparse forest on the east side of the valley, a few dozen yards away from a switchback road leading to the compound. Two Hounds stood guard at the very edge, armed with rapid fire pulse guns, their heads covered by strange-looking white helmets. Apparently, the techs had managed to adapt the technology from the cells into smaller mediums. Now, they each had as impenetrable a skull as John, and the telepaths would be powerless against them. It gave John pause, but not for long.

As they drew nearer, tension from his team made the hair at his nape prickle, but John kept his gaze on the Hounds, not daring to signal weakness by checking on the others. As far as the Shadows were concerned, they'd known about this all along. John didn't attempt an attack, knowing full well the two Hounds were just an escort; a hundred more would be stationed around the area, weapons aimed to kill.

As they approached, one of the Hounds stepped up. "You come with us," he said, voice muffled by the helmet. How could he even see through it? The entire thing was like a swirling, unbroken shell that covered his whole head and face, a garish addition to the midnight blue-and-black uniforms the Shadows favored. Might as well have painted a great big bull's eye on their heads.

John looked over his shoulder. More Hounds grabbed hold of the others, pointing guns at their heads. He'd never even heard them approach. To their credit, no one in the company panicked, though fear shone through in several faces, including Travis'. He'd have figured out by now that, as long as those helmets remained in place, his telepathy was useless, and John could practically see the wheels turning in Travis' head to come up with a strategy to remove at least one of them.

The second choice—this one Travis'—would determine whether this fight lasted hours or seconds. John subtly shook his head in the negative. If Travis made a single move out of line, he wouldn't live long enough to finish the thought. The Shadows hadn't gotten as good as they were by being careless.

Travis looked ready to argue; his gaze flicked back and forth between the Hounds and the road he knew eventually led to Emma, seconds away from doing something stupid and getting them all killed in a hurry.

John couldn't do anything; they watched him too closely. This was Travis' decision. He faced the Hounds again. "Lead the way."

One did, pivoting on the ball of his foot to march down the road. The other waited for John to follow, then brought up the rear. The road was empty, and the compound gate stood wide open. Inside the perimeter wall, Shadow life went on as John remembered it. Supply convoys silently glided into warehouses, patrols walked the perimeter, Hounds and Hawks trained in the fields. The only difference was that now all of them wore those white helmets.

A commanding voice shouted orders through the audio system, and John's muscles twitched to obey. It pissed him off, and he gritted his teeth to check the impulse. But seeing the compound had another strange effect on him: he walked taller with surer steps, mind more focused, as if by walking through the gates, he'd left his lethargy behind, and his eyes scanned the facility's familiar layout with a clear objective. In the way of soldiers, this outpost was nearly identical to the one where John had spent most of his life, which meant the holding cells would be in the rear building next to the transport bay, with a fifty-yard perimeter of clearance in case of a security breach. Smaller than the others, no doubt. But unlike the one John had known, this one would be heavily guarded, now that a containment malfunction wasn't as big of a threat.

Exactly as expected.

The Hounds routed him past the barracks to command central. Two men stood at the main entrance, with two more on the inside and several more spaced at regular intervals down the hallways like a somber setup for a funeral procession.

So far, everything Michael had told him was spot on. But now John was coming up on a temporal blind spot where Michael had been unable—or unwilling—to tell him any details. *Beware the Hawk in the shadows* was all John had to go on. It would be a trap of some kind, and damn it, he should have paid better attention to counting the Shadows rather than brooding over lack of psychic intel. How many Hounds had he passed? Ten? Twelve? At least one of the men posted along the hallway had been a Hawk, but they all wore those white helmets, which meant identifying them was impossible.

"The commander in chief has requested to speak to you," said the Hound at his back as they stopped twenty feet from the end of the hallway, where one lone door was flanked by six more Shadows. They all trained their guns on him as the one at his back scanned him for weapons and removed the ones from John's boots. "You will not approach him, or speak unless spoken to. You remember the drill, don't you?"

"Memory serves." He'd barely finished speaking the words, when one of the Hounds discharged a sonic round, which struck John squarely in the middle like a full-body punch. He doubled over, fought for breath as the scent of blood wafted through his nostrils on each exhale. He wasn't coughing up a lung, so the damage was minor, but real nonetheless. His muscles locked, swaying him off balance as his diaphragm clenched in a painful spasm. John bit back the nausea easily enough, but forcing air back into his lungs proved a more painful undertaking.

"No speaking," the Hound repeated, then added a scornful shake of his head for good measure.

They were kind enough to open the door for him, and John straightened, pushed the discomfort to the back of his mind. One breath at a time, he mastered his body and walked through, turning right, down a short hallway that opened into the senator's spacious office. He turned left again to face the desk and the man in a pressed black suit who stood behind it with his back to him. Senator Griffith wasn't wearing a helmet, and the window he stared out of was actually a holoscreen. The entire space was a closed-in perimeter with one single way in or out; an area completely shielded from the outside world. The commander in chief had to be protected at all costs.

Beware the Hawk in the shadows…

The senator turned and smiled. "I simply had to be certain it was really you," he said. "Proceed."

John frowned.

The smallest hint of a noise made him turn around, but he wasn't fast enough. Finn already had his weapon raised level to John's forehead, and in a split second, the sonic round discharged. John hit the ground like a sack of potatoes. Lights out, good night, and good luck. At least he wouldn't have to be awake for the kill shot…

~

Sixteen Shadows surrounded their pathetic group, and those were just the ones Travis could see. They made no move to take them anywhere, hadn't even disarmed them. All of them still had their guns—or in Zayn's case, knives—and the Shadows just stood there, as if, even armed, the five of them posed no threat whatsoever. Yeah, Travis had to admit, to trained soldiers, they were less than piss in the wind.

Zayn and his men didn't seem at all concerned about their current predicament; they'd made themselves comfortable sitting or lying in the grass, watching the clouds float by. They all hummed some nonsensical tune in their minds, which pretty much guaranteed Travis wouldn't get anywhere trying to scan them. Too much of the same kind of noise confused the hell out of a telepath; someone would have taught them to do that. Travis glared at the self-proclaimed oracle, Michael, who sent him a wink, then closed his eyes and started snoring.

Zayn, sitting next to Michael, kept busy by flipping a weird-looking coin across his knuckles, staring off into space.

None of them were talking. That bothered Travis the most. The damn silence. He checked out and sought the shuttle in his mind. —*Everyone still alive?*— he asked Jessica.

She flinched at the initial connection, but recovered quickly. —*For the moment,*— she said, and allowed him a look through her eyes, through the shuttle window at the circle of Shadows standing shoulder to shoulder around them. A hundred of them, if not more, doing nothing; they didn't need a show of force greater than this. —*What do you make of it?*— she asked, worry crawling across the connection, making Travis stifle a shudder. Fifteen other people on that shuttle, seven of them Zayn's men and the rest scared-shitless telepaths—precisely what the Shadows wanted.

—*It's an intimidation tactic. Nothing more.*—

—*Obviously,*— Jeremy replied, joining in on the conversation. —*If they wanted to kill us, we'd already be dead. They hadn't even touched the shuttle; that, I can tell.*—

—*Can you get through to any of them?*—

Jeremy sent the telepathic equivalent of a wince. —*Not on my own. If Tristan and Dara were here, maybe. To one of them. If we were lucky. But check this out.*— Travis' vision clouded over, then he saw what Jeremy was looking at: five more Shadow soldiers along the tree line, spaced at regular intervals. Unlike those in a circle around their shuttle, these guys walked a set circuit, and from the tilt of their heads, they weren't watching the shuttle but the other Shadows, including each other.

—*Looks like they covered all their bases,*— Travis said, pushing aside the sensory share to look closer at the sixteen Shadows guarding him and the Evolutionaries. Just like back at the shuttle, more moved along the edge of the clearing, keeping an eye on things from a distance. —*My guess is they're the insurance, in case someone gets compromised.*—

—*Agreed,*— Jeremy said.

—*They would kill their own?*— Jessica asked in disbelief.

—*If it meant keeping the rest from getting corrupted? Hell yes.*—

—*What a charming bunch,*— she retorted. —*How long do you think they'll keep us here?*—

—As long as it takes for them to get what they want,— Jeremy replied grimly, and Travis couldn't disagree. *—They'll want to secure Wayland first. Once they have him, who knows?—*

Zayn checked his watch, clicked his tongue against his teeth, then went back to flipping that coin.

—Why wouldn't they have taken us to cells already?—

—Any number of reasons,— Travis replied. *—For one thing, they already have five in residence. Could be they're overbooked. For another, there's no better way to field test those helmets than with live subjects, which also goes to show us how immune they are to our weapons. An enemy who thinks he's defeated, already is.—*

Zayn checked his watch again, then tapped Michael awake. With a grunt, the oracle sat up, rubbed his face, and shook himself off. From the looks of it, he still had one foot in dreamland, but he smacked his lips and nodded to Zayn, who jerked his chin toward Travis. Michael rolled his eyes to which Zayn gave him a stern look, and the oracle scowled.

—Something's going on,— Travis reported to the others.

Everyone on the shuttle immediately sat up to attention, waiting for him to tell them more.

Only Travis had no idea what the hell was going on. One by one, the Evolutionaries subtly moved positions under the guise of stretches and scratches, until they each faced a different outward direction.

Some silent communiqué to Zayn was badly received, and the scarred leader irritably shoved at Michael.

Instantly, sixteen weapons raised, ready to fire. Not a single wielder said a word.

Michael cast Zayn a baleful look, then delivered a harsh mental rap against the inside of Travis' skull. Needles of pain stabbed out through his eyes as he answered the graceless demand for entry, opened a channel of communication, ready to turn Michael into a vegetable. Telepaths didn't do that to one another, let alone under these conditions.

But before he could do anything, Michael simply said, *—Ready on three... two... one...—*

Travis frowned at Zayn, who grinned back and raised the coin, compressing its middle.

A small spark accompanied a massive invisible energy pulse that swept over all of them, nearly bowling over the Shadows. They shouted and clutched their weird-looking helmets, struggling to get them off. Immediately, their minds, as well as those around the shuttle and countless others in the valley, popped up on Travis' telepathic grid.

"Go!" Michael shouted, and Travis didn't hesitate to throw a mental punch to follow the EMP blast. Twenty-seven Shadows dropped unconscious to the ground, while one hundred fifteen more kissed the dirt around the shuttle as Jeremy and Jessica followed his example.

That was as far as they could go. Incapacitating someone indefinitely took time, which none of them had. The Shadows were still alive and would wake up in a few minutes—

Or not, he amended as Zayn's people took up their weapons and went around shooting the passed-out guards in the head. One by one. Didn't even stumble. In under a minute, the clearing by the cliff was littered with dead Shadows, and Zayn's men ran out of the shuttle to do the same there.

—*What are they doing!*— Jessica screamed inside his mind.

—*We don't have a choice,*— Jeremy answered her for Travis' benefit. —*The shuttle's disabled. We can't take off, and if we let them live, they'll kill us all the minute they come to.*—

—*Welcome to war, Brain,*— Travis said, trying to sound brave, as his stomach did cartwheels.

He gritted his teeth against making a fool of himself as he leaned over a dead Shadow to relieve him of his weapon. Seemed the Evolutionaries already had their orders and, once re-armed with fresh guns, they all fell in step behind Zayn and Michael to head down the trail.

"Fourteen seconds," Michael announced.

Travis didn't know what would happen at the end of that time, but he wasn't about to wait there to find out. He followed the others down the incline, counting off the seconds in his mind. When he reached zero, Michael stopped, and everyone else stopped, too, waiting for him to give the all clear.

—*What's going on?*— Jeremy demanded. He could sense Travis' confusion.

—I'll let you know when I figure it out.—

—We're cleaning up here and heading your way. Don't do anything stupid before we get there, got it?—

Michael gave the signal, and the group moved on. "Twenty-seven seconds. Double time."

—Yeah, I'll be sure to do that,— Travis retorted.

At twenty-seven seconds exactly, they all stopped again, this time at the last turn before the main road heading toward the gate. Up ahead, people shouted; an organized panic had overtaken the Shadow compound once they realized their helmets were useless. Travis scanned forward, reading a whole lot of anger and confusion, but before he could zero in on anyone in particular, that damn rude rap again rattled his brain inside his skull. *"What!"* he snapped.

—You and me, bro. You ready?— Michael showed him a flash of what he expected Travis to do. Not a debilitating pulse like before, but a sustained sensory illusion to hide their presence. He wanted Travis to form a mental image of the compound, minus their group of five, and lay it over the minds of everyone in view of it. It wasn't easy, but it could be done. And if he could pull it off, unless someone literally ran into them, no one in the exercise yard would hear or see them walking right through their midst. Michael's job was to time their advance so they could avoid any direct contact.

Great plan. Except for one little problem. *—The buildings were shielded from the blast.—* All of the security feeds and recording devices were still fully functional. They might be able to avoid detection from the people in their line of sight, but they couldn't fool machines, and anyone watching the feeds would spot them immediately.

—True,— Michael replied. *—But to do anything about it, they'll need to come out and confront us. That'll be the first step to mutiny.—*

He was right. Any Shadows who stepped outside without one of those helmets would be instantly compromised. *—So, what if they have more of those things?—*

—That little gizmo Zayn is still molesting ain't exactly a one-off, if you know what I mean. Just needs time to recharge. Speaking of time, you have ten seconds left. You ready?—

Heart pounding, Travis wiped his sweaty palms across his thighs, and quickly pulled images from the soldiers' minds to form a map. It was like layering a multitude of photographs to form a bigger picture. Each man and woman had a different viewpoint, a different way of perceiving the compound. The images didn't align exactly, but the more Travis grabbed, the better it looked.

"Three seconds," Michael said, and Travis swore, rushing to finish a passable illusion.

They were already moving by the time he'd blanketed the soldiers with it. The image settled into place as the group passed the massive gates. The Shadows closest to them flocked to the manual overrides, bodily pushing the portal closed, while the sentries on top of the wall shouted intel, playing telephone to canvas the entire perimeter outside the compound.

For a split second, the fear of being locked in here made Travis' illusion waver, but he clenched his fists and held on. All of their lives depended on it, including those from the shuttle who were on their way there, led by Jeremy and Zayn's right-hand woman, Leanne.

Inside the compound, Shadows scrambled. More than half ran for the barracks and the armories, helmets discarded and pupils dilated with a fear they tried so hard to hide. Those in the field already armed with live weapons headed the other way, toward the wall to back up the sentries. With their coms disabled by the EMP blast, no one had any idea the enemy had already gotten inside.

They all reacted on instinct and years of training that told them to move a certain way, to think a certain way, to respond to a certain— ordinary—kind of threat. They'd climb the walls to look for a motley crew of untrained civilians walking up to the front gate. The thought that this was not the correct course of action was there in all of their minds, but it was the only course of action they'd been trained to carry out. Inaction, they all knew, got soldiers killed faster than the wrong response, eighty times out of a hundred.

Standard operating procedure at its finest: turning the bravest of the brave into the dumbest of the dumb. Travis could almost love them for that, and the smile he allowed made him more confident than he had any right to be. For the first time, he believed they could win this—not only the battle, but the entire war. If three telepaths could silence an angry mob, why couldn't four or five rule the world?

The thought appealed to him. So much so, in fact, that he almost ran into a Shadow headed for the barracks. Michael pulled him back just in time, and the soldier passed inches before his nose, almost tripping over his feet. Michael slapped Travis upside the head and shoved him forward again.

"Holding cells," Zayn demanded.

"Med bay," Michael countered.

Zayn turned on him, weapon raised. "Don't fucking test me. Where is she?"

They'd all stopped a hundred yards from the first building, in clear view of any number of security feeds. No one had come out to confront them yet, but they could already be on their way. They didn't have time for this!

Jeremy, keeping tabs on the situation through Travis, swore inside his mind. Travis, holding the illusion in place, couldn't do anything else telepathically. But the others could. They were scanning all of the Evolutionaries, and some of them had to be thinking about the plan and how fucked up it was going to get. It didn't bode well. Travis debated letting go of the illusion to intervene, but Jessica stopped him. —*Not yet,*— she said.

Michael faced off with Zayn for several seconds before he shook his head and sighed. "Smith, he just signed your death warrant."

Zayn advanced and pressed the barrel of his gun against Michael's forehead. "You said yourself I wouldn't need a seer to get myself out of this."

Michael smiled, a bit sadly. "I did say that, yeah. Didn't hear me mention anything about Anna, though, did you? Think I didn't see this coming? Seventy-six Shadows coming at us right now. Thirty more seconds and they'll start shooting. Smith takes a hit before you blast them. Ten seconds after that, Alec goes down and takes you with him. So you just keep on keeping on. I've got all day."

"Guys…" Travis warned, getting all kinds of red flag warnings from the others, going off in his head. They were running now, headed straight for the compound and standing out like bright red beacons in his mind. Something was wrong. Very, very wrong.

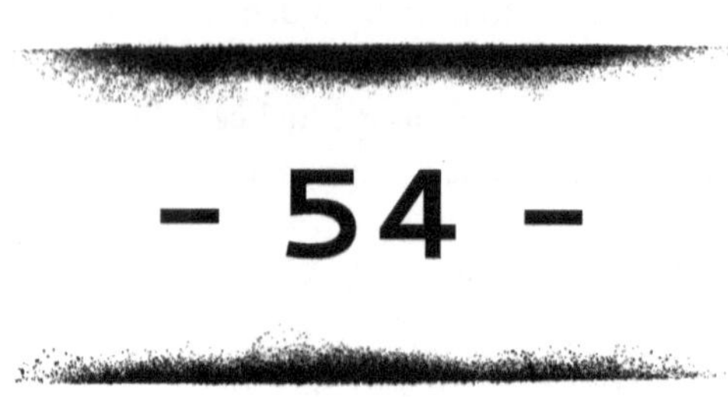

– 54 –

He wasn't dead. Not dead meant still in the fight. John pried open his swollen eyes. It took him a moment to get his bearings, another to stamp down his immediate panic. Finn had taken him to med bay. He was strapped in the chair with Dr. Wen at his instruments nearby, calibrating the machines to administer another treatment.

John yanked on the restraints in a futile attempt to break free. He couldn't.

Finn watched over the scene, hard-faced and unruffled, but he had his weapon in hand. He'd positioned himself to keep the door in his line of sight. Outside noises told John the perimeter had been breached. So much movement could only mean Shadows were scrambling to form a defensive line. Had the others gotten in already?

Can't rely on them, anyway. John was on his own.

"Finn," he said in greeting.

Trained not to engage with prisoners under any circumstances, the Hawk didn't reply.

"Got a favor to ask. Got some friends in trouble. Could use a hand getting them out. You mind?"

No response.

"Fair enough. How 'bout you just let me out of here and I'll do the rest?"

"Your protein levels are quite high," Dr. Wen said, looking over a series of brain scans. "You haven't been sleeping, have you?"

John ignored him. Just the sound of the doctor's voice raised his heart rate. That fucking butcher had created an army of thoughtless drones with his treatments. He'd raped their minds, warped them into something so unnatural it made John sick. And most of them, like him, had willingly submitted to having their brains fried and pumped full of chemicals, because they'd believed in the cause. They still did. "You have to know this isn't right," he tried again with Finn. "Think about your family out there. All the riots, the fighting… You think the senator gives a shit about any of them?"

Had that been a twitch?

John pushed, grasping at straws. "What about Laura?" He had no idea who the woman was, but Finn had called out her name in his sleep enough times that she must have meant something to him once.

The moment he said her name, Finn tightened his grip on his weapon.

Finally! "Is she still alive?" She could have been nothing more than a fond memory. "When was the last time you saw her?"

"The commander in chief has requested a full memory wipe," Dr. Wen said, not bothering to face either man as he spoke. "A radical approach, but orders is orders, as they say."

John's heart skipped a beat, then hammered so hard it rattled his rib cage. His dizziness doubled until his eyes tried to roll back, but he couldn't give up now. "Would Laura approve of this, you think? If she could see this place, what they did to you—to all of us—what would she say?"

A muscle twitched in the corner of Finn's eye, as if he'd just stifled a wince. Not enough. Unless John shook him to his very core, Finn wouldn't lift a finger, except to shut him up.

"How many times have they killed her in your mind already? With every treatment, she ceases to exist. And I know you keep looking for her. Is she there now? Do you have a fucking clue what I'm talking about?"

"How much longer?" Finn snapped.

"Won't be a minute," Dr. Wen replied calmly.

"All right, listen," John said, drawing on his last weapon as Dr. Wen engaged the chair mechanism to straighten it out into an inclined gurney. The delicate headband lowered, and John struggled to keep his voice even. "I didn't want to bring this up now, but you kind of owe me." He couldn't see Finn as Dr. Wen strapped his head down and placed the headband on. "First time we sparred. I could have killed you. Remember? That's what the sergeant major wanted. He ordered us to fight, and I knew if I landed just one blow to your head, you wouldn't get back up again. I could have done it! And we wouldn't be having this conversation now—"

Dr. Wen shoved a mouth guard into John's mouth. "Hush now. Everything will be all right. It's just a treatment to take your nightmares away."

John gripped the armrests so hard his arms shook. He couldn't move, couldn't even look off to the side to see if anything he'd said had had an impact on Finn. The Hawk made no sound, and with a sudden flood of desperation, John realized he cared whether he lived or died. More than anything, he *wanted* to see another sunrise, another glance at Emma's red hair blowing in the wind, even if only from a distance.

In his final moments before death, the man who used to be a boy eager for the end was frantic to live.

"In a few minutes, none of this will matter. Trust me. It's what's best for you."

John bit down hard on the mouthguard to stifle the scream building in his chest. He squeezed his stinging eyes shut and recalled the one memory he never wanted to lose again. *Emma. Emma. Emma,* he chanted in his mind, using every last instant he'd spent with her as a shield against what was to come. *Emma. Emma! EMMA!*

~

That name! *Goddamn that fucking name!*

Of all the things for Wayland to bring up.

Come on, Rowe...

Finn sucked in a sharp breath.

Rowe, Rowe, row your boat, gently down the stream...

She'd always been soft-voiced. Never had to make herself heard; people listened, all on their own. But her softest words she'd saved just for him.

If Miss Laura should command, life is what you dream.

Secret whispers in his mind, telling him truth from lie, keeping his thoughts safely his own.

Until she'd betrayed him.

You know better…

No!

Finn…

You're dead to me!

He remembered the look in her eyes when he'd told her he was joining an army. She'd never said a word, but her face… he might as well have killed her.

Christ, would he never be rid of that guilt?

What would Laura think of all this?

She'd hate him even more; she'd take that gun he'd given her for her sixteenth birthday, point it at his head, and pull the trigger.

And God help him, he'd let her.

This wasn't supposed to be his life. How had he let it come so far?

You never bothered to care.

Wen initiated the sequence, and Wayland went as stiff as a board, face contorted into a grotesque mask of pain. But he didn't make a sound. Full mental wipe. They'd reduce him to a vegetable, then rebuild him to suit their needs. No memories, no thoughts, no lingering doubts. Perfect soldier once again. And Finn would be next. Couldn't have Shadows knowing what really went on in that chair. Bad for morale.

Ten seconds.

Fifteen.

Thirty.

The cycle ended, and Wayland slumped, mouthguard hanging loose as his jaw drooped. Wen checked his vitals. Still alive, poor bastard. He'd be relearning to control his bowels for at least a week. "Heart beat steady," Wen reported. "Breathing normal, brain activity at minimal sentience…"

The doctor trailed off, and Finn frowned. "What is it?"

Wen leaned over Wayland. Against his better judgment, Finn edged toward the chair as Wen removed the mouthguard. Wayland's mouth twitched; he was trying to speak. Finn leaned even closer, and just barely caught the sound of Wayland's brainless whisper: "Emma… Emma… Emma…"

Finn reared back, stumbling over his own feet. "You said this would wipe him!"

Just like they'd wiped you? How eager were you to get rid of me?

Fuck you! You betrayed me!

Wen returned to the instruments. "It did! The procedure should be complete…"

That's horse shit, and you know it.

"How does the water fall… in the waterfall," Wayland mumbled, calling Wen a liar. "Hawk threw the hood… flew his master's hand… Warrior thinks… for himself…"

"Does that sound like a total wipe to you?" Finn demanded, hand clutching his weapon so hard, he had to make a conscious effort to relax his grip, or he'd end up shooting holes into the walls.

I betrayed you? that damn voice returned. *You were the one who walked away from me!*

I trusted you, and you spat in my face!

Horse shit! This time, it wasn't Laura's voice; it was his own. *She was the only one who ever told you the truth. And when she tried to warn you, you threw it all back in her face and walked away. You left her when she needed you the most.*

Wen shook his head. "I don't understand. He should be a vegetable."

Far from it. Wayland was shaking the treatment off, muttering nonsense that seemed to have some meaning to him, even as he drooled.

Seashells and waterfalls. Was he aware?

Are you, Finnegan Rowe?

Finn snapped his fingers in front of Wayland's face.

The former Hawk squeezed his eyes shut, then pried them open and turned his unfocused gaze to Finn. "Hawk," he said, "gotta shake that hood, man. Keeping you blind… You know better."

You know better, Laura echoed. *You always did. You chose to turn away.*

Shut up, I said!

But there was no keeping Laura quiet when she had something to say. *How can you possibly justify this?*

Finn mouthed the words as she said them. Sweet Laura McNally. Her words cut deeper than any blade.

Wen was going over his calibrations again, rattling off numbers and levels, affronted that someone had dared to resist his treatments. With his back to Wayland, he didn't see the former Hawk staring steadily at Finn. No accusations, no pleas, just a steady gaze filled with conviction.

It was more than Finn had.

This is wrong.

Can't be… It's my mission. The status quo must hold, or everything will fall apart—

But everything had already fallen apart. Every occupied world from here to clear across the galaxy was awash in blood; an endless massacre, with soldiers, civilians, and peacekeepers all succumbing to violence that spread like a disease from one world to the next. Not since the last great war had humanity seen so much death. The ICG had shattered; no one left to call the shots, except for Griffith and his chosen few, and a brainwashed army at his beck and call. Finn had no idea how the senator planned to shape the new order, and for the first time, that lack of certainty bothered him.

Was this the reason Wayland had deserted?

"Here we are," Wen said. "Maximum charge. That should do the trick."

"No, wait!" Finn shouted, but Wen had already initiated the sequence.

A terrible scream rent out of Wayland as his body arched, every muscle taut, restraints flexing to their breaking point, beginning to tear as he slowly died. But it was more than that; much worse than a simple death. The Hawk screamed as if his soul was being ripped to shreds, burning to cinder inside him. His body, rigid with electric spasms, shook as if he'd shatter at any moment. And still he screamed—an awful sound that horrified Finn beyond anything he'd witnessed before. The smell of charring hair permeated the air, just pungent enough to make a man retch, and Finn could do nothing but stand there and watch his once-friend disintegrate from the inside out.

~

Floating through an endless field of white, inside a void so complete nothing could exist within, Emma woke screaming as agony exploded like lightning inside her brain. Suddenly she was no longer in the white hell. She was everywhere, everyone, seeing, and hearing, and feeling everything on their minds. And through the endless blinding pain, she comprehended just one thing: something vital to her was dying.

~

They were only yards from the wall, with Calen holding the illusion and Kaylee retrieving access codes, when something happened inside the compound that turned their plan—and the world—on its head. To the last, every telepath in their company screamed and dropped where they stood, writhing on the ground.

And like flipping a switch, the soldiers manning the wall woke up to intruders at their gates, and opened fire.

Leanne cursed. "Cover!" she shouted, ducking down so those with shields could take the blasts while Leanne returned fire. "We need to move!"

But they couldn't, not with so many incapacitated. Might as well put on blindfolds and light cigarettes; the firing squad had unlimited ammo, and their group were all sitting ducks.

Because Zayn had fucked up.

Royally.

Their people inside were as good as dead. Leanne had to get the rest out of there. She hauled Calen to his feet. "Tam, take over! Bennet! Get 'em up! Now—we gotta move!"

Calen's eyes bled, and he couldn't walk a straight line without support, but he moved when Leanne did and they dragged themselves out of the direct line of fire, taking cover behind an outcropping. Shields were attached to rocks for more surface area, but it wouldn't last. The telepaths were their only way out of this now.

"Hey," she snapped at Calen and forced his chin up to look into his glazed eyes. "You with me?"

"I'm with everyone," he replied, and in the eeriest fucking display Leanne had ever seen, every single telepath spoke with him.

Leanne stifled a shudder. Michael had warned her about this. Of all the scenarios he'd foretold, this was the worst. Odds of survival were laughable, and if she couldn't get them separated, they were null. "Break off," she ordered.

"We are one," the telepaths intoned.

Out of time and options, Leanne punched him—hard.

All of them fell over.

But when Calen got up, the rest lagged behind. "Thanks," he said, speaking alone. "I needed that." Visibly shaken, he was nowhere near focused enough to move.

"We've got incoming!" Bennet shouted, turning his weapon up at the cliff.

Tam flanked him as a unit of Shadows all wearing shiny white helmets lined up at the edge of the outcropping.

And me without my EM pulser.

"Get your shit together," she told Calen and tore down a shield to hold over their heads. The force of each hit made her reel; they didn't strike the center, but aimed for the very edges, trying to knock her off balance. Leanne stubbornly dug in her heels and held steady, even as her arms went numb at the shoulders.

"I'm out!" Tam tossed her weapon, and the girl child called Jessica handed her another one.

Bennet gave a cry and fell. He didn't get up again. Hardy took his place, but a shot to his chest instantly took him out. Tam varied her aim to cover the hole in their defense until Natalie and Ulrich could plug it, but they were fast running out of able bodies.

"Any time you wanna weigh in here!" Leanne invited, staring hard at Calen before a lucky hit almost bowled her over. Shaking it off, she got her head back in the game and held steady, breathing slow and deep to keep her center.

She didn't see the telepaths exchange an uneasy glance, wasn't privy to the quiet debate going on inside their minds. But a minute later, she and the other Evolutionaries bore witness to the five-fingered hand of God reaching down through them to bitch-slap the whole damn battalion like a horde of motherfucking children.

Five telepaths stood up in unison and clasped hands in a circle, and for the ten seconds they stood utterly still, not a single shot touched them. The forward attack slowed, then stopped, and Tam along with the others turned their attention to the bigger threat up above. Every shot had to count, and they didn't miss many, but more Shadows kept coming, filling in the void, throwing their dead over the edge to make room. The bodies went splat when they hit the ground, each one making them all flinch.

Except for the five.

As one, the circle of telepaths looked up at the Shadows lining the cliff.

And as one, the soldiers along the perimeter wall turned their weapons up and slaughtered all of the high-ground troops. And they kept shooting while the remainder of their group struggled onto their feet, headed for the gate. It opened for them, and the Evolutionaries, flanked now by the surviving telepaths, walked straight into mayhem.

– 55 –

Travis hit the ground, and for one minute that seemed to stretch into hours, his brain roiled like a sparking mass of hell broth inside his skull. He heard nothing but a chorus of bone-chilling screams, saw nothing but a bunch of flashing lights as though his retinas had been burned. His shields tore apart, and for just a moment, his mind melded completely with the other telepaths, and in unison, they all echoed, "We are one…" Travis had just enough sense to be terrified.

Then something sharp bit into his shoulder, and he screamed, immediately coming back to himself as the hook dug deep and the man holding the handle dragged him across the grassy field. One of Zayn's men—Alec, was it? So he'd made it. Travis grabbed hold of Alec's wrist with his functioning hand. The man stopped, turned, and pulled the meat hook free of Travis' shoulder, then shoved a bandage stick into the wound. He twisted the end to break it off, and the material activated, expanding to staunch the flow of blood. Travis gritted his teeth against the pain. It was nothing now. He'd thank the guy, if he had voice enough to speak. Alec had saved him from a fate worse than death.

When he tried to get up, Alec shoved his booted foot against Travis' uninjured shoulder. "Stay down," he ordered, and for the first time, Travis looked around at the reigning chaos. Shadows had turned on one other, blank gazes seeing not comrades-in-arms, but enemies with weapons in hand. No one was spared—no one wanted to be; a

Hound would help another break free from a vicious attack, only to turn on him in the next instant.

"Oh, Christ," he whispered. "I know what this is…" The others had merged to gain control over the troops, and just like with the angry mob, they manipulated the Shadows, took them out as swiftly and as permanently as possible before exhaustion forced them to let go. This was the dark secret all telepaths carried in their minds. This was what the world would turn into, if the wrong people took charge, the reason they had so many strict rules and why death was the punishment for breaking them. In the end, Travis knew, not a single Shadow would be left standing. And the telepaths killing them would be no more.

Alec fired his weapon, his jaw working a piece of chewing gum the whole time. He shot only when a Shadow came too close, and otherwise saved his bullets. The others had scattered; Zayn had probably gone after Anna in the holding cells. He wouldn't bother with anyone else. Once Zayn had his, he'd disappear and leave the rest to rot. It would be up to Travis to get them out.

But where was Michael?

The oracle wasn't among the living, or among the dead on the ground. Travis recalled something about med bay, but why would Michael want to go there?

"Up you go," Alec said, hauling Travis to his feet.

"Where is everyone?"

"Where they need to be. Now move." He herded Travis in the direction of the holding cells. They ran low to the ground, skirting buildings to use solid walls as cover. Travis' gun was gone; Alec must have taken it from him when he'd run out of ammo. He didn't like his hands being so empty, but couldn't stop long enough to grab a replacement.

The perimeter around the holding unit swarmed with soldiers locked in hand-to-hand combat. Not a pulse gun in sight, but plenty of knives glinting in the sun. Trouble was, they'd all been trained the same way and now used the same techniques against one other, predicting each other's moves so well, no one was going down. The two of them were more likely to catch a stray hit here than when they'd stood in the middle of live weapons fire. How Zayn had managed to get through that gauntlet, Travis had no idea.

"Allow me," Alec said politely, taking point, and opening fire. He mowed down the closest Shadows, then punched a hole clean through their ranks. The survivors, sensing a better weapon within reach, all turned on the pair like crazed animals as they ran through. Alec grabbed Travis around the neck and hauled him in, turning in a circle to shoot down Shadows who'd gotten too close. He was still shooting as they reached the door, and when he ran out of rounds, he hurled the weapon at them and slammed the door shut in their faces. It locked automatically, an all-around seal they wouldn't be able to break with a tank.

Great. Now what?

An empty hallway stretched in front of them. It ended in a T at the far end; two paths that would branch out more, the deeper they went into the building. Travis picked up on a soft hum and immediately recalled the bright white beehive from Emma's memories. They were definitely in the right place, but from the size of it, there would be dozens of cells, each locked with a code of its own. That's what Michael had said—each cell was independent to preserve integrity.

"Time's wasting, Brainman. Let's go."

"Right." *Here goes a whole lot of nothing.*

~

The door opened then slammed shut, the sound reverberating through empty hallways. Zayn picked up his pace from a casual stroll to a slightly faster walk to duck out of sight. Damn! They'd gotten here faster than he'd anticipated. He checked his watch, then flipped the EM pulser in the air and caught it. *Heads or tails?* Heads, he announced himself and worked with Alec and the telepath to free the others before he got Anna; tails, he left them to their own devices and went after Anna directly.

Heads.

Fuck it. He went after Anna.

Michael had given him a mental map of counting footsteps, so like a blind man navigating familiar territory, Zayn counted off. The facility only had about twenty chambers, but they were spread so far apart, the empty hallways felt like an endless maze. No markers, no numbers, no exit signs. Hence the counting.

Zayn kept his strides fluid so his footsteps wouldn't echo. His ears felt stuffed with the sound of his own breathing. Palms sweating and mouth completely dry, but his heart beat in a calm, steady rhythm. This was a done deal. He'd take Anna, then slip out the other way to avoid the rest of the peanut gallery. There'd be a shuttle waiting for launch not far away—disabled, like all of the others thanks to Zayn's gizmo, but he had ways of getting stubborn machinery to work again. They'd be breaking atmo in minutes, and then, bye-bye Shadows, farewell SU, so long civilization as a whole. And good riddance to them all. From now on, it would be the Zayn and Anna show. Just the two of them in a small house on a virgin planet with plenty of greenery. As close to heaven as Zayn would ever get.

Three more long-legged strides brought him to her door—a heavy duty portal, locked and operated electronically. Using the EM pulser was out of the question; it would disable the door and seal her in. He pocketed the device and turned to the lock screen on the wall. They'd stepped up security for the new batch of telepaths; the holding units now had biometric security measures. Michael hadn't mentioned that.

Luckily for Zayn, he had one last trick up his sleeve, courtesy of an odd genetic quirk that had caused him to be born with no lines on his palms. No fingerprints, no handprints, nothing. Back in the day, Michael used to joke it meant Zayn had no future. Whatever. As far as mutations went, his was pretty damn useless, except for this.

Biometric scanners worked on two measures: the static resistance of human skin, which couldn't be replicated even with the most so-phisticated equipment, and the dermal map of swirls and lines that have identified individuals for centuries. Match the print, but not the resistance, and the lock wouldn't open. Match the resistance with a different print, and the lock wouldn't open. Match the resistance with no print at all? That's when the internal mechanism always lost its shit. It couldn't compute the possibility. Nothing human existed without some kind of identifying mark on the hand—or if they did, they were too few for the programmers to bother with. And the best part was that it registered as a runtime error rather than an entry attempt. Which meant Zayn could walk through vault doors like a ghost.

He placed his hand on the screen and pressed just short of cracking the glass. The mechanism gave a long, angry beep, and the screen turned red between his fingers. Exactly four-point-seven seconds later, the portal silently slid back into the wall. *Open sesame.*

And there she was.

Sitting against the far wall directly in front of the door, the only girl—the only anyone—he'd ever loved raised her blonde head and smiled so brightly, it outshone the stark white chamber. Zayn's heart gave an extra painful thump.

"You're here," she said, her gaze clear, steady on his face. She brimmed with happiness, so giddy Zayn could practically see her vibrating in excitement. And she was lucid. God, so fucking lucid. She was his Anna again, and for a minute, Zayn felt twelve years old, watching the enchanting little girl pirouette down the sidewalk. With a single wink, she'd stolen his heart right out of his chest. He would have died for her then and there if she'd asked. Still would.

Frozen, Zayn unstuck his tongue from the roof of his mouth to say something, anything. "Anna…"

Anna jumped up and launched herself at him, arms squeezing so hard around his neck it hurt. He didn't care; he grabbed her up and squeezed back just as hard, shuddering at how goddamn good it felt to have her back.

"This room is magic," she whispered. "There's no one else here. I want to stay forever."

And just like that, his joy shattered. "Anna, we have to leave."

She tensed, then pulled back to stare at him, and he couldn't for the life of him meet her crushed gaze. Straddling the threshold, with him on one side and her on the other, they kept the door from closing, but they couldn't stay there indefinitely. "Why?" she asked, genuinely perplexed.

"We can't stay, Anna."

"No, no, we can!" She smiled in encouragement as she disentangled herself and took his hands into hers to pull him forward. "We can stay here. Just the two of us. We could be happy, Zayn."

He shook his head, feet rooted to the spot. "I'll find us another place. Somewhere far away, with no ghosts. I promise. But we have to leave now."

Desperate, Anna tugged harder, eyes sheening with tears. "Don't make go back out there. I want to stay!"

His own eyes welled with regret so deep, it nearly crushed him. It would be a twenty-minute run to the shuttle, through a battlefield of the dead and dying, across an area saturated with violence and pain. And once they'd gotten through, a long haul flight off-world awaited them in a metal shell who knew how old, with memories and impressions soaked into every rivet and seal. He'd be taking her from heaven straight to hell again, and it would get a whole lot worse before it got any better. "We can't, sweetheart. We just can't."

"Please!" she cried, breaking his heart into a million pieces.

"I'm sorry, Anna."

Facing away from him, she stopped pulling. For a moment, she just stood there, head bowed, narrow shoulders rising and falling with shuddering breaths. He'd have dropped to his knees and slit his own throat if it would do any good. But even if the Shadows gave up and abandoned this place—unlikely—the entire stronghold was crumbling. Only a handful of buildings were shielded and still operational on the inside, and those wouldn't last very long. The moment he had Anna through that door, Zayn would deploy another EM pulse to destroy this place from the inside out. To make sure it could never be used again.

"I swear to you, on my life, I will find a good place for us to live," he said. "A brand new house, on a brand new world." His voice cracked as he spoke, but he didn't care. Zayn couldn't stand the sight of her so dejected, the feel of her hand limp in his, still tugging with a steady pressure to get free. He held on. They were so close to happy; he wasn't ready to let go. Not yet. *Not ever.* "You'd like that, wouldn't you? To have a home of your own, a dance studio outside, with a view of the beach. Just the two of us, Annabel. Just you and me. I promise."

She didn't reply. Damn it! He should have thought ahead. If he hadn't disabled all of the electronics, he could have stolen one of those helmets for her. Some might have survived the initial blast inside the shielded buildings, but even if they had, Zayn had no way of getting his hands on one now without going back through a whole lot of

Shadows. He'd never make it back here. "Please… please don't leave me now." He wouldn't survive.

After a long moment, with her head still bowed, Anna bobbed the smallest of nods. Not assent. Resignation.

Zayn tugged on her hand. "Come on, it's not far to the shuttle. I'm right here with you."

Anna shifted her foot the smallest bit, then slowly turned around. With her gaze fixed on the ground, her long tresses obscured her face and Zayn couldn't tell how she was doing, but didn't chance a pause now that she was moving forward. One small step after another, she shuffled into the doorway, and then beyond.

But as soon as her heels cleared the threshold, her head snapped up, eyes huge and trained on him. "I can't," she whimpered.

Anna is exactly where she needs to be right now, Michael had told him. *If you love her, you'll leave her there.*

Never!

"It's okay, Anna. I've got you. I'm right here."

A small, frantic moan escaped her. "No, you don't understand." Her gaze darted left, then right, and she flinched. Zayn watched helplessly as her eyes began to glaze over with the familiar blankness.

"No, no, no, Anna, stay with me, okay? Just walk. It's not far, I promise. You can do this—I'm right here!"

"I'm so sorry, Zayn…" Her words drew out like a record player running down, and she trailed off into a silent stupor.

"No! Anna!" Zayn shook her hard by the shoulders. He'd seen this happen before, too many times to count, but this time it was worse, underscored by a bone-deep fear that this was the one trip from which she wouldn't return. "Wake up! Look at me!"

Her brows drew together, lips firmed, and by some unfathomable feat of concentration, she managed to look at him, and see him. "I'm so sorry," she said again. "I'm not strong enough." Her fingers grasped the back of his neck, pulled him to her, and she touched her forehead to his.

Zayn closed his eyes, willing to open himself up and let her in. "Yes," he said. "Use me. Stay in my mind. I'll keep you safe."

But that's not what she wanted. When they connected, Anna opened the floodgates and buried him in a thousand lifetimes—years of happiness and joy, the intimacy of living in each other's pockets, alone. No intrusions, no interruptions, no ghosts to poison the moment; a life in which the tiniest whisper shuddered the world on its axis. Anna drowned him in love so deep, it left him breathless; in happiness so complete, it almost brought him to his knees.

"Yes," he said. "I'll give this to you. All of it. Forever." No matter what it took, Anna would have the life she'd always dreamed of. He gave the smallest tug to get her moving again.

Anna rooted her feet. The connection faltered, then broke apart on a tidal wave of sadness Zayn felt in his soul. He opened his eyes, searching her gaze for a reason. Her cheeks were wet, her smile unsteady. "I wish that were true. More than you could ever know." She moved so fast, his dazed mind couldn't catch up—her hand slipped down to his hip, and a blade sang out of its sheath, glinting light into his eyes for a split second before she buried it into her chest.

"*NO!*" someone screamed—a terrified, broken animal sound human vocal cords ought to be incapable of. Zayn caught Anna's hand around the handle too late, the blade already buried to the hilt. Her knees gave out and she sank to the floor, dragging him along. Shaking, he frantically brushed her long hair from her face. "Oh, God, Anna! What did you do?"

She stared him in the eye, stubbornly refusing to blink, and smiled. "I loved you. I did… I did…" Her eyelids drooped. She'd aimed her blow perfectly, just like he'd taught her; turned the blade sideways to slip between the ribs and straight into his soul. The damage was guaranteed to be fatal.

"No, no, no, no, Anna… Don't leave. *Anna!*"

"Goodbye…" Her whisper escaped on a sigh as she breathed her last, and her body, only moments ago so strong and full of life, so full of hope, went limp and heavy in his hold. For a moment, Zayn imagined her ghost standing in that white room beyond the open doorway, smiling at him, dancing; an angel forever free of her torments and happy at last. Then she faded away, and there was nothing.

In that quiet, empty hallway, kneeling in a pool of dark blood that no longer spread, the whole of Zayn's universe ceased to exist.

– 56 –

At the end of the cycle, the room plunged into silence, and Finn held his breath, waiting for Wayland to stir. He didn't. Seconds ticked by with no signs of life; the screens had all flat-lined, the delicate headband still smoking from overload.

"Huh," Wen said, mouth twitching in a curious smirk. "Didn't see that coming." He adjusted his glasses and studied the screens like a librarian searching for his favorite book.

Finn dragged in a breath, forced himself to blink.

Threat neutralized. Wayland was dead; a useless slab of meat strapped to that goddamn chair.

Finn couldn't swallow past the bitter taste in the back of his throat. Laura's voice had gone silent, leaving him alone in the tableau of the life he'd chosen. He was a Shadow Hawk, a reaper of the corrupt, not passing judgment, but carrying it out. His legacy to the world would be more of this: dead bodies lying on the ground, paving a path toward the unknown.

It didn't seem right, leaving Wayland like that. Traitor or not, he'd been a hell of a soldier—a friend. He deserved better.

Though Finn was well aware it wasn't his place, he shouldered his weapon and reached for Wayland's restraints. He had one wrist strap undone, when the door behind him burst open. Finn reacted on instinct, launching himself at the trio of men in the doorway. Two met him, while the third went after Wen. Finn engaged in hand-to-hand, his weapon still at his back; the two wouldn't allow him a split second to reach for it. They fought as if they'd choreographed the fight, ducking his swings, whaling blows he never saw coming. *Goddamn telepaths!*

One opponent caught him by his uniform collar. Finn threw him off, but the next thing he knew, he was ten pounds lighter and the guy had Finn's own weapon pointed at him.

As soon as he saw it, the other intruder backed off. "Thanks for your cooperation."

Finn charged at the gunman, who fired a round at his feet. "Easy," he said. "Don't wanna kill you. Will if you force me."

"Michael?" the other called.

The one who'd gone after Wen stood at the computers with the head medic on the floor at his feet. Hard to tell whether Wen was still alive. "Working here," Michael said. Didn't look like it, though; he just stood in front of the controls, staring off into space.

Suddenly he shuddered, blowing out a harsh breath as his knees buckled.

The others tensed, and Finn saw an opportunity to take them down, but for some reason his feet refused to move.

Be still, Laura's voice echoed inside his mind. *Be watchful.*

You're not here, Finn returned, his frame quivering with a sense of utter loss. *This isn't real.*

As if to soothe him, the memory of her smile sent warmth across his thoughts. *Real enough for now. A memory is sometimes the only thing you can trust.*

Michael straightened, breathing hard. "Bye, Anna. I'll see you in a bit." A handful of random words, but their impact was palpable—a eulogy he hadn't spoken to anyone present, judging by the stricken looks his comrades gave each other. Again, they tensed, an opening Finn should have exploited, but he couldn't. They stayed put, and so did he.

Michael shook himself off, then turned his attention back to the readouts. "Okey-dokey," he said with forced cheer. "Here we go!" He wriggled his fingers in the air, then started to push holographic buttons. The dead man's chair whirred as the mechanism reactivated and then Wayland's body jerked with a jolt of electricity to his back.

"Charge to two-fifty!" Michael yelled. "Clear!"

Another jolt.

Michael consulted the readouts. "Again. Clear!"

Finn watched the macabre scene with growing disgust, distracted enough to completely switch out of battle mode. Three enemy intruders, two of them armed, and he could do nothing but watch the maniac at the controls zap a dead body—apparently for the fun of it. *This is why telepaths need to die.*

Don't trust your eyes, Laura's voice whispered across his mind. *Nothing is as it seems.*

It was pretty fucking obvious *this* was!

Michael slowly turned, a mad scientist look in his eye. "Just call me Frankenstein. *Mwahahahaha!*"

Zap!

The screens flashed with a momentary heartbeat, and Finn's eyes widened with unexpected hope.

But in an instant, the screen flatlined again, and a deep sense of disappointment shocked Finn down to his core. Had he wanted Michael to succeed? To bring a traitor back to life? "Brain's fried," he said, to remind himself as much as to inform Michael. "Restarting the heart won't do jack." *Why the hell am I just standing here?* He was a fucking Hawk! He should have been able to handle three civilians, goddammit, even if they were mind readers. Had he trained his whole life for this moment, only to give up?

Michael backed away from the controls. "Yeah, you might have a point there. Ah, well." He shrugged, then typed in a new sequence of commands before stepping over Wen toward Wayland. "Lots of folks dying out there. 'Bout time, eh? Whole galaxy dripping blood, and the reapers all tucked away to wait it out. Wasn't right."

It's not right, Laura echoed.

As if he'd heard it, Michael raised an eyebrow at him. "You've got issues, man."

He had no idea.

"I do some," Michael said with a weak grin. "She's still alive, you know. Girl's a survivor. But she didn't learn that from you."

Finn barely stifled a shudder.

"No, you were too busy running away from life." Michael sucked in a sharp breath as the machinery whirred to life again, spun back around just as the chair delivered its charge. The screen beeped with another spike, one single heartbeat in the chest of a dead man, and in that exact moment, Michael whipped out an ancient-looking syringe and stabbed it into Wayland's chest. "Woo! Almost missed it."

Be watchful.

Finn's breath locked in his chest as he stared at the screen, the flat line mocking him. The others, too, seemed transfixed. Yet another perfect opportunity to strike, and Finn tensed to do just that, when he caught the barest hint of a mutter from Michael. Frowning, Finn leaned forward to hear better.

"...Dr. Chase. Come on, pretty lady, don't make me be wrong..." What the hell was he talking about?

Then something happened—small, subtle, like a static charge gathering in the air.

Finn dragged his gaze away from the screen to look at Wayland's face. The unmistakable pallor of death was... lifting. Wayland's cheeks darkened slightly, and then a bit more. His eyes darted briefly behind closed eyelids, yet his heart was still silent, his chest unmoving. The man was dead.

Wasn't he?

"Come oooon, Lady Luck," Michael said, louder this time. "Work your magic for me just one more time."

The holographic screen beeped with a heartbeat. Just one.

Then Wayland's chin twitched down a little, mouth opening as if he desperately needed air.

Finn's foot dragged forward to approach. Either the others were too stunned or no longer deemed him a threat, but no one attacked, all gazes rapt on the soldier strapped in the chair. Finn pressed his fingers to the inside of Wayland's wrist, which still retained the heat and vitality of life, but there was no perceptible...

Heartbeat!

The screen beeped again to confirm.

Pressing harder, Finn counted the seconds. At ten, there was another beat. At fifteen, another one. At eighteen, one more. Wayland wheezed in a short breath, then quickly exhaled, as if he lacked the strength to hold on to it.

Five more seconds. Another breath, stronger this time, as his heart beat out a sluggish, unsteady rhythm.

Holy fucking shit…

Finn stared at Michael who, despite the tense set of his mouth, managed a wry grin. "Told you. Frankenstein." But the statement held no arrogance, not even pride. Michael's eyes were haunted, sad, and Finn recalled the earlier eulogy to Anna. Could she have been the nameless female telepath they'd picked up with Emma Calen? They'd scanned her up and down, but the ICG registry had yielded no results as to her identity. Not even a birth certificate. Unlike Emma Calen, who at least had a rudimentary record of her existence, the blonde girl was a true ghost.

"What happens now?" Finn asked. Outside, the fighting was getting closer. Shadows were dying out there; he should be with them, doing his duty to fight the good fight.

Only he no longer knew what that was.

"You get to choose," Michael replied.

Finn frowned.

Michael's men brushed him aside to finish unstrapping Wayland, whose breaths labored, heart stuttering on the readouts. They disconnected him completely, leaving only the wheeze-and-rasp of air through his throat to indicate he was still holding on. The minions dragged him to the door, sharing his dead weight between them, as Finn stood dumbfounded across the chair from Michael.

No orders. No direction. His unit was destroying itself in a conflict that would spill into med bay any second. The moment it did, he'd get swept up along with the rest of them. Their minds had been taken over to turn them against each other, but for some reason, Finn had been left untouched. His thoughts were clear—confounded, but lucid—at least for the moment. But that would change the second he came into contact with another Shadow. Like an infectious disease, it would take him over, and he'd be lost in the battle until the telepaths decided to release him.

With a surety he had no basis for, Finn knew this as irrevocable truth. Michael's doing, no doubt. At the man's humble shrug, Finn realized Michael was already in his mind, showing him what was going on and what was about to happen. In precise, time-delineated chunks, he presented Finn with two futures.

In one, he accompanied Michael and the others as an escort to the nearest shuttle. It would mean opening fire on his own troops to protect the group. He'd then leave this planet with the enemy he'd fought against his entire adult life, forsake the Shadows to their doom, and start over on another world, somewhere far from here. A fresh start, from nothing.

In the other, he accompanied Michael and the others as an escort to the nearest shuttle. And no farther. Once that shuttle took off, he'd rejoin his troops and ride the telepathic storm until it petered out, leaving the survivors to pick up the pieces. He might make it, he might not. His choice.

But in both scenarios, the Shadows were finished. No more chain of command, unity shattered, leaving a handful of soldiers who knew nothing except how to kill. Those remaining would scatter—Michael made that very clear. No more mercy. They'd learned their lesson all too well. If the Shadows ever tried to rise again, they'd be ruthlessly hunted down.

Why me? he thought. Of all the Shadows, why leave him to this choice?

Michael smiled. "You're not the only one."

That revelation should have mollified him. Instead, it pissed him off beyond all reason. Because it meant they'd chosen. They'd scanned the soldiers' minds and decided who should and shouldn't be spared. "What the fuck gives you the right?" he growled, hands clenching with the need to crush Michael's throat to pulp.

As embattled Shadows crashed through the front door, Michael raised an eyebrow. "You did."

Bodies poured in, and the smell of death and charred flesh permeated the sterile air. Alarms went off with flashing lights and deafening sirens, indicating a biohazard containment breach. The sensory overload nearly brought Finn to his knees, but Michael's unflinching gaze held him immobile. One choice. One chance to get out, to turn things around… to make a new life.

He was being given a new beginning because someone, somewhere, had benevolently decided he was worth more alive than dead. Judgment passed.

Don't tell me you never expected that door to swing the other way, Laura's voice mocked.

And Finn hated that she was right.

As fucking always.

~

Alec had an ingenious way to open the cells.

Step one: Use a laser handgun to sear a hole through the outer wall coating above the lock screen. This had to be timed perfectly; too long, and the beam fried through the wires and killed the mechanism. They'd tested it on a couple of seemingly random cells to get the rhythm down, and Travis hoped to Christ there'd been no one inside. Short of a bomb, they were now locked down forever.

Step two: Sort through a whole mess of wires to find two specific ones while muttering incoherently. Of the fifty or so identical wires running vertically and horizontally in a damn intimidating grid, Alec had to find the one that kept the lock screen operational, and one that connected it to the Faraday cage around the cell and regulated the amount of electricity running the circuit. But again, with Michael's foresight and a whole lot of counting, Alec knew which ones they were. A handy talent, foresight. If only it didn't fry the brain so completely.

Step three: Yank said wires out, touch the live ends to the lock screen, and hope for the best. The timing had to be exact; they had only two seconds between cutting the power to the screen and the backup power activating to short circuit the mechanism into unlocking. It hadn't worked with the first one they'd tried. This time, Alec's hands shook the slightest bit when he pulled the wires down.

Zap!

The door opened.

Inside the cell was Matthew, a tall, lanky man in his late forties, glasses askew on his hawk-like nose. His long frame was tucked so tightly into a corner, they couldn't get him to his feet and had to drag him out. But the moment he crossed the threshold, Matthew sucked in a sharp breath and wailed, shaking uncontrollably. He latched on to Travis and wouldn't let go, while his mind washed over Travis' with a staggering amount of fear and chaos.

Matthew had only been in there for a few days, so only a fraction of his mania was due to the effects of telepathic repression. More than anything, Matthew was reacting to the isolation and sensory deprivation, the endless possibilities of tortures yet to come, and the knowledge that he might die before anyone staged a rescue attempt.

Not for the first time, rage set Travis' blood on fire for the *weeks* of torture Emma had gone through. The moment they'd found her, he'd known her mind might never again be set to rights after something like that. But Travis no longer cared. The fact she was still walking, talking, and comprehending—*coping*—was nothing short of a miracle, and one for which he wholeheartedly thanked the heavens. "Let's move," he ordered, refusing to let that miracle die.

He pried Matthew off, shared his weight with Alec as they moved on to the next cell. Not the adjacent one, however. Alec led them through the facility, following some sort of map of numbers; the man heard Michael's voice in his head, counting footsteps for him to where they needed to go. When Alec stopped and repeated their procedure to open the door, Travis held his breath, desperate to see Emma on the other side.

Instead, they found Maureen caught in a maddened fit, attacking the sheer white walls, screaming at them, clawing down their smooth surface until her fingernails tore off. The plump fifty-seven-year-old math teacher was mindless with a rage they couldn't calm; she fought them viciously as they dragged her out, and didn't stop screaming for a good long while, riling Matthew into hysterics, too.

"We need to move faster," Alec said.

No chance of that with two crazy people in tow, unless Travis could calm them somehow.

No. They were aware they'd been freed, and that would have to suffice. He had no idea what shape Emma would be in. She was most at risk of succumbing to the mental stress; he needed to save his focus for her.

"We can leave them here," Travis said. Maureen had run out of voice, mouth still open to scream, but nothing came out past a harsh wheeze. Without the noise irritant, Matthew finally began to calm. They'd be all right if left on their own, at least for a while.

Alec shrugged prosaically. "Not my monkeys, not my circus. Shuffle on, then."

Travis ruthlessly stamped down his guilt and shoved to his feet, shaking off Matthew's hold. Emma and Melody were still locked up somewhere, and they didn't have much time to get them out.

One more door. Laser surgery done. Wires out. *Zap!*

Melody. Twenty-year-old girl with her entire life ahead of her, laid out on the floor, unconscious. But her face was pinched with pain she couldn't block. If memory served, she'd taught preschool. Sweet-tempered creature. She'd spent her days teaching five children to read and write.

Travis balked at stepping into that beehive again. Every time he did, his brain vibrated inside his skull, on the brink of exploding. *How the hell could Emma have lasted as long as she had?* Dizziness overtook him as he leaned over Melody, but he locked his knees and scooped her up into his arms. Swaying on his feet, he brought the girl into the hall, then laid her on the floor. She sighed, her face relaxing in repose, but her eyes were still closed, her pulse erratic. She wouldn't wake.

Worried, Travis took a quick peek into her mind, and almost knocked himself out. Melody was stuck in some sort of drug-induced psychedelic nightmare of creepy clowns and talking rabbits. Whatever they'd used to knock her out, they'd seriously fucked up the dosage. Melody would need medical intervention, STAT, or she might not wake up again.

"Leaving this one behind, too?" Alec asked.

Travis' jaw clenched too hard to answer. He gave a curt nod and forced himself to look away.

Alec didn't. He gazed down at Melody a second longer, then shook his head. "Shame. This one's kind of cute."

"Let's move," Travis grated. Every second was one less Emma had to live.

Alec saluted, but didn't start walking right away. First, he reached down and pulled Melody's skirt lower over her legs to cover her. Then he nodded to Travis, and took off running down the hall.

Travis raced to keep up with him, blindly turning corners, heedless of what might be waiting beyond the bend. They ran a circuit so wide, Travis lost track of the turns; he had no idea where he was or where he'd left the others. Another twinge of guilt, another surge of adrenaline propelling him forward. To Emma.

Finally, they reached the last door, which stood alone in a long, empty hallway, as if even in this segregated building, she'd been sentenced to quarantine, just in case. Alec burned through the wall to expose the wires, then hesitated.

"What?"

"Just shut up for a minute," Alec snapped. "Fourteen or fifteen…? Seventy-two times five hundred and twelve… too many combinations. Fifteen, right? Yeah, gotta be." He counted out the fifteenth wire. Hesitated again. "No. Fourteen."

"Are you sure?"

Alec gulped. "Guess we'll find out." He gave a sharp yank on two wires that sparked angrily, indicating a much higher voltage than any of the others. When he touched them to the screen, it burst in an explosion of sparks and fire, knocking both men back. Neither heard the door open past the muted report of rapid gunfire.

– 57 –

Pain was her world: searing white agony zinged across her neural pathways, paralyzing her. Muscles locked, breath gone, heart seizing in her chest, Emma lay on the bright white floor, grinding her molars to dust. Her eyelids blinked uncontrollably, flashing her retinas with unbroken white. Visions of pain-stricken faces. More white. Bright blue sparks of lightning across a sheer-black sky, raining down blood. Blinding white.

What she wouldn't do for a single shadow.

Eyes welled, overflowed, blurring her vision with a sheen of red; bloody tears dripped onto the pristine white floor beneath her cheek, a miniscule dark stain that splashed and grew. Minute by minute, the edges of her memories softened, became more brittle, like sun-baked brick giving way to the relentless desert winds. Each puff of breeze carried a little more of her away, and she had no more strength to fight it.

Her soul was dying.

Burning, freezing, withering, Emma retreated inside herself, huddling beneath an unfamiliar shower as hot water cascaded over chilled flesh. She laughed in this strange world, talked to herself to reacquaint her mind with the sound of her own voice.

Just beyond the door, she knew, a Shadow loomed, waiting for her. It used to shield her, hide her from the blood-red searchlight of others of his kind. Hounds sniffing out her trail. Hawks swooping in to collect on a debt. Emma looked up, and the roof disappeared, giving her an unobstructed view of the sky and the blood moon hanging low, so big it could crush her.

Then it, too, disintegrated, blowing away like so much glitter on the wind.

The shower cooled, and she shivered.

That door…

At some point, she'd have to open it, face the soldier on the other side. Her heart leapt at the prospect, then gave an extra hard thump at remembrance. *My seashell is gone…*

Emma moaned. Squeezed her eyes shut against the truth. Curled in tighter and embraced the screaming agony. Maybe if there was enough of it, it would kill her faster.

But her mind refused to lie down and sleep forever. Self-preservation was an instinct she'd lost control over long ago, and it forced her mind into frantic spin cycles, hurling out desperate calls into the world, regardless of who might hear. Over and over, the telepathic distress call burst from her, only to be swallowed up by the insidious hum of her glowing prison. Not even a shard of an echo returned to her to let her know she, at least, still existed. There was nothing.

Until the door opened.

Emma heard the odd *swish* sound overlaying the beehive, and cracked open one eye. Before her, an exit from hell—a dark rectangle of an opening just big enough for her to pass through.

But on the other side of it, impossible sights.

People.

Not Shadows but normal people, dressed in dirty, torn clothes stained dark with blood. They dived for cover as the darkness flashed with streams of light. They spoke to each other, but Emma couldn't hear them past the hum.

She sighed. *Hallucination.*

A sudden shadow made her blink. She looked up, finding a familiar face over her, and she frowned, opened her mouth to speak, but couldn't find the right word. He had one. A word that belonged to him, alone. She knew it. Why couldn't she remember!

Why does it matter?

At that thought, Emma calmed. Only a cheat. He'd be gone soon, and then she'd be back in the beehive, all alone. Her eyelids drooped as she settled back to sleep. *Won't be long now.*

Past the ringing in her ears, she heard his voice in jumbled sounds that made no sense, but the tone reached her. His urgency, the strength of his grip digging into her arm, dragged her kicking and screaming back to him. He was shouting at her, face contorted in pain. He shook his head. Winced. Tried again.

Said her name.

"…can you hear me?"

Yes, she thought, somehow certain he'd hear her.

He didn't. "Emma!" She saw his heart breaking in his eyes as he cupped her face, pressed his forehead to hers. Contact.

Travis!

Emma reached out, fingers cramped into grotesque claws, and caught his wrist, held on for dear life.

Holding on.

Not a cheat.

He's real!

A desperate sob escaped her. "H-hel-lp… me…"

Faster than she could comprehend, Emma was up off the floor, jolting and swaying toward that rectangular darkness. As they neared that opening, the hum intensified, clawing at her mind and demanding she stay, refusing to let her go without a fight. It screamed across her thoughts like an enraged beast as they leapt out, and then… silence.

Heartbeat thudding in her ears, Emma blinked up at Travis still clutching her, and he grinned with so much relief. So much love. "I've got you," he said, his words reaching her slower than his lips formed them.

Emma smiled, despite the ache in her soul. There was a gaping hole where something important used to be. It was gone now. Never coming back again. Part of her had died, and she'd felt it tear out of her; even in the midst of hell, she'd felt it fade away. Travis was the only lifeline she had left. Seeing him, touching him, she held on to her heartbeat, but it wouldn't last. As soon as she remembered what she'd lost, she'd die again. Forever, this time.

Someone shouted a warning, and Travis looked away from her.

Emma frowned. What could have put that look on his face? She recognized it, but couldn't name it. Just as she'd heard those shouted words but couldn't decipher them.

She yelped when Travis jerked her around and bent his body to shield her. A great blow bowled him over on top of her, and he shuddered.

Zayn! Drop it!

Meaning returned, delayed.

I'll kill them all!

A small, broken sound eked past Emma's lips as she stared, uncomprehending, at Travis' still form. Shaking her head, she wriggled out from underneath him, turned him over and gathered him into her arms. There was a hole where something important used to be. It gaped open his chest, edges seared black, and the smell of burning flesh made her sick. His eyes were still open, staring hungrily at her, even as his mouth opened and closed, desperate for the breath he couldn't draw.

Footsteps approaching, sounds of fighting. Alarm. Danger! *Run away!*

She couldn't.

Still shaking her head in denial. Vision blurring. Chin wobbling too much to speak. *He is so scared.* She felt him in her mind reaching for the sun—for her—as darkness closed in around him.

Not knowing what else to do, Emma gathered him in and built him a meadow on the edge of a great lake, with puffy white clouds in the sky and sweet-smelling flowers all around. She hugged him close, told him everything would be all right, that he wasn't going anywhere. That she'd keep him safe right here. Forever.

His gaze calmed, mouth stretching into a small smile. With a sigh, Travis faded from her grasp, his body turning heavy in her arms.

The hot barrel of a pulse gun pressed to her temple. More words. Meaningless.

When the last of Travis had vanished from her mind, another gaping maw opened up inside her soul, and this time, there was no pushing it back. Its teeth ripped into her without mercy, a torture far beyond that of the white hell, and Emma threw her head back and screamed.

She *felt* the gunman drop to the ground, along with dozens more in this building alone. But it didn't stop there. As Emma's power flared out for only the second time in her entire life, she maintained just enough focus to channel it away from familiar minds. Her friends and allies stopped in their tracks, while hundreds of others outside fell to their knees, tearing at their hair, clawing at their eyes, locked in their own nightmares that wouldn't end.

They'd shown her no mercy; she spared none in return.

Grief so great it would kill her threaded across the visions, breaking hearts as her wrath broke minds. Completely. Irrevocably.

By the time she'd run out of breath, Emma was on her feet, mind fully open to the world—an exposed sore sowing agony wherever she went. Somehow, she moved, and somehow, others did, too. Within moments, she was out the door, and her mind refused to comprehend the sight before her. She didn't force it. Stepped over bodies and splashed through puddles of blood so thick, her feet stuck to the ground for the smallest instant. Emma walked among the dead and dying with a single target in mind.

He was shielded.

So were others. A group distinguished by the subtlest of hums moved from building to building, gathering survivors and shielding them, as well. *All the better to hear you.*

A stranger spoke to her. His pain dripped like sweat across her mind while he stayed at her back, weapon raised against any attackers. She didn't know him; didn't understand him. Didn't rightly give a fuck. He'd brought three telepaths out of holding, and for that, she'd chosen to spare his life. But that's all he'd get. And if he didn't stop kicking her heels as she walked, she'd reconsider her mercy in a hurry.

Three buildings down stood another shielded place that edged the river; some kind of last hold out against an enemy attack. Her prey was there, waiting for his convoy to take him off-world. He'd think himself so safe, surrounded by ten… fifteen armed guards, immune to her manipulation. The smile that stretched across her lips felt downright demonic. She veered and took off running toward that river.

The trailing gunman shouted and joined her in her pursuit, mind filled with alarm and anger. Something about another group elsewhere, with transport to safety. He should have been there with them, instead of here with her.

She spared him half a thought; a weak command to go join them, then, if he wanted to go so badly. Emma didn't need him. This hunt was hers. *When you set your hounds on something, make sure it can't fight back.* The senator's first mistake. His biggest one. Emma wasn't a soldier; she had no training and no experience beyond the few tricks she'd been taught.

But that was precisely what made her so dangerous. She had no intention to fight fair.

The gunman didn't leave. Something about timelines and decision trees. Whatever. Not far now.

Emma ducked close to a wall, slowed to approach the corner with caution. She sensed the hum of five sentries who'd be on guard for any threat.

Hand on her arm. With a snarl, she turned on the gunman, ready to blast him into catatonia. But he held up his hand, fingers splayed. Holding her gaze to get her attention, he folded his thumb inward. Then his index finger.

A countdown.

Three…

Two…

One…

Emma whirled and ran out, full-tilt, ducking her head at the last second to slam her body into one of the soldiers, and she knocked him on his ass. As he swung his weapon up, firing automatically, he mowed down two others. But he wasn't out cold. His blow knocked Emma back, and she knew if she hit the ground, he wouldn't let her up again. She rolled as she'd been taught, got her feet under her, and shoved up again.

But the stranger already had the soldier's gun, boot crushing a uniformed neck as he opened fire at the others. Within seconds, the area was secure, and he gave her a cocky grin. "You're welcome."

Emma nodded her thanks, but she was far from done. Something big stirred in the river beyond. Waves crashed against the banks as the level rose impossibly fast, until a great metal hull broke the surface.

A submarine.

Emma's eyes widened. If Griffith got on that thing before she got to him, he'd disappear forever. She ran for it, heedless of the ten other soldiers who were even now filing out of the building, guarding the senator from all sides. *Almost there! Almost!*

Hand on her arm again! Her momentum swung her around, fist already curled to knock her attacker's lights out, but he ducked under her swing, and hauled her into his chest, squeezing the breath out of her. Frantic thoughts mired with her own; words and names and feelings all jumbled into a world of pain.

Jeremy.

He was shaking, dampening her shoulder with his tears as he held her so tightly, her feet dangled off the ground. He spoke, and when his words failed to reach her, he opened his mind and showed her instead. Too much all at once; different versions of the past colliding, and for an instant, Emma panicked that she'd get lost in it all, like Anna had.

But her mind wasn't like Anna's, and Jeremy wasn't as frantic as his thought patterns seemed. The chaos he showed her had order and, second by second, the pieces fell into place to rebuild the past she'd lost. Her childhood. Her family. The Special Unit.

And then, finally, her soldier boy.

Something inside her broke as she saw him from a distance, being carried to a shuttle. She clawed at Jeremy's shoulders, desperate to escape the sight, but he wouldn't let her, made her watch as the vision zoomed in closer, closer—so close she could see his mouth moving with breath, the side of his neck fluttering with a heartbeat.

He was alive.

The submarine gave a great roar as its propellers engaged. The latch shut and locked, and water churned as the beast submerged. Gone. Along with the senator and what remained of his army.

Emma let them go. For now.

Because John was alive.

– 58 –

The drawback to fighting secret wars was that no one knew or cared when they ended. By the time the team had left Outpost Green 24, only a handful of Shadow soldiers remained, and those had scattered into the universal winds the moment they had the chance. With the biggest threat eliminated, things should have quickly returned to normal.

But they didn't.

The conflict had gone too far, gone on too long, and had nothing to do with Griffith or his secret machinations. After centuries of oppressive government control, the people had dropped their shackles at last, mindlessly purging eons of repressed anger onto the world at large.

It wasn't civil war anymore; not even war, in general. With no one left to rebel against, anarchy spread like a disease on each world, with vicious mob rule turning everyone into an enemy. The death toll, announced nightly on the news, was staggering—and it only continued to rise.

The Special Unit wasn't immune, either. Twenty-nine members had died in the Gray Dublin evacuation alone. Five hundred seven lost to violence on Earth, to say nothing of the other inhabited planets. Telepaths took shifts throughout the day, compiling death lists. Every new name was a friend, a lover, a relative. A kindred soul in an increasingly soulless world.

The siege of the Shadows had claimed too many. The survivors of Gray Dublin had been inconsolable at those losses, a tragedy only slightly lessened by the return of their three taken, then subsequently increased a hundredfold when gentle Maureen hanged herself in her room the first night back.

They couldn't take much more of this. If things kept going the way they were, humanity would destroy itself completely; a once mighty civilization would be reduced to dust and toxic fumes.

With the ICG dissolved to nothing, armed forces without directives, and peacekeepers mired in battles everywhere, there was no one left declare the war over. So it became a necessity for the previously independent Special Units on each world to unite under one Enclave, to at least attempt to save their own.

As the reports continued to pour in, with the death tolls rising endlessly, the twenty-three leaders of the new SUE were forced to acknowledge no one would be riding to their rescue. With heavy hearts, John MacMurphy and the other twenty-two came to a bitter unanimous decision: there was no other way, no end in sight, unless they came out of hiding and did what telepaths did best. But the cost would be immense; blood of their blood would need to be sacrificed to restore order among the civilized worlds.

Faced with the responsibility of choosing candidates, MacMurphy couldn't even bring himself to come up with the right words to explain. How was he supposed to tell the people he'd helped raise that, after so many dead, he'd need to add more? How could he ask for such a sacrifice, after he'd promised them all a better future among others of their kind?

Turned out, he didn't need to. Almost as soon as the SUE meeting adjourned, telepaths everywhere began stepping up to volunteer for the grim duty.

One telepath alone could change a mind.

Two, standing together, could change a village.

Could four or five break through an entire planet?

No one knew. What they were all painfully aware of was that the attempt alone would destroy all involved.

Like the heroes of Outpost Green 24, now irrevocably joined at the mind. They replied in unison when spoken to, but otherwise showed no signs of independent cognition. A true hive mind, dependent on each other for survival, incapable of separation. For now, they were kept sedated for their own safety and for the safety of others. But everyone, including the five, knew that one day they'd become too much of a threat and would need to be eliminated.

And that was the decision all one hundred twelve volunteers had made: to give their minds to save a planet, and eventually relinquish their lives for its continued existence. None would ever be recognized for their sacrifice; no one outside the Enclave could ever know the lengths to which they'd gone to save humanity from itself. To expose the extent of their manipulation would put every single telepath in the crosshairs for immediate extermination. After all, if they'd managed to control so many people once, what was to stop them from doing it again?

And so, tucked away in the only safe place left to them, John Mac-Murphy and his flock of telepaths watched the human race disintegrate, and planned to rebuild it once again. Hopefully, the right way this time.

– 59 –

April 1, 3036 – Torrey

"Pixie?"

Emma didn't respond. She never did anymore. No point. Not like anyone could make sense of what she had to say, and the wasted effort would only distract her from her vigil. But unlike so often before, this time, MacMurphy didn't sigh and walk away. A chair lightly thumping down behind her made her inwardly flinch, and she cursed herself, redoubling her concentration.

"Emma," MacMurphy tried again. "I know you can hear me. Can you please look at me?" His voice sounded strained, tired, and it set off subtle warnings in the back of her mind. But she didn't let go, pressing her forehead harder against the glass.

On the other side floated her soldier boy in a massive vertical tank filled with an oxygen-rich solution. Jessica had put him into a chemically induced coma. His heart beat, his lungs worked, but the brain monitors showed no sign of activity. For two weeks, he'd been in there, finally undergoing the detox Jessica had been pushing for. But after what they'd done to him at the Shadow outpost, the Brain herself didn't hold out much hope for his recovery.

Emma didn't care. She refused to give up on him. He was her anchor, the only one who made any sense. He'd come for her, and had paid a terrible price. They all had, but she couldn't shake the thought that John had borne the brunt of it. Because the Shadows had hated him the most. He'd broken rank, turned on them, beat them at their own game, and they couldn't let it stand. They'd destroyed him from within out of spite, to make an example of him, to show the world that no one opposed their might and lived to tell about it.

I did, she thought fiercely. *You didn't break me, and you won't break him. I won't let you.* The Shadows had taken far too much from her already. She would not hand over another piece of herself, if she could do anything to stop it. She'd fight for John, just like he'd fought for her, and she'd bring him out of this, come hell or high water.

For now, his body needed time to heal. But the Brain had said even if he regained consciousness after they took him off the meds, chances were he wouldn't remember anything at all—not his name, not his past, not how to walk, talk, or feed himself.

Emma had listened to the long list of things that had been damaged, and how they couldn't be repaired, and had internalized them as an ongoing to-do list. Every single one she'd find a way to mend, starting with his memory.

They thought she sat here with him, day and night, out of despair. They sensed her constantly reaching out to him and thought her mind was broken, that she didn't know any better, stuck on some futile spin cycle until she exhausted herself.

In truth, Emma knew exactly what she was doing. John wasn't merely unconscious; he was in a coma, the most inactive a mind ever got. Without any control whatsoever, his shields were vulnerable. She kept reaching out to him, not to communicate, but to wear down his shiny, impenetrable wall. If she could just get through it for a second...

MacMurphy sighed. "I have to go away for a while. We've set events in motion, and things will be changing soon, but there's... I left something undone, and I have to finish it. You'll need to keep an eye on things for me. Will you do that?"

More subtle warnings. She ought to ask him what he was up to.

Couldn't do it. John's shields were changing, losing some of their smoothness, and Emma was certain she was on to something. Like applying sandpaper to a piece of wood, she kept chafing at the barrier between them, determined to get through.

"Anyway, I just wanted to say goodbye."

Sadness.

MacMurphy never said "goodbye." He said "see you later." And if he didn't see you, he tracked your ass down.

But by the time Emma had made that connection and momentarily broke away from Little John, MacMurphy was gone. In his place sat Hailey, her white hair arranged in a messy ponytail at the top of her head. She read the news from around Torrey, and it took Emma a moment to tune in to her words.

"*...English Village officially emancipated from military control. Peace talks have yielded excellent results. Off-world troops have stood down from all further hostilities, and have agreed to restoration efforts in the village and surrounding fields in exchange for amnesty and asylum. Officials estimate that the majority of buildings damaged by the fire can be rebuilt and restored for habitation by the end of the month. While crop yields so far are a fraction of what they ought to be due to field contamination, our farmers say there is no reason to panic. The systems that have expedited produce growth at the birth of English Village thirty years ago are still operational despite lack of use, and will be implemented again to minimize distress this coming winter.*

"*Such inclusive collaboration between the local government and outside forces marks the first and only cooperative endeavor anywhere since the civil war began. This writer takes heart in the hope that it's a sign of coming relief to the terrible destruction felt all around the galaxy.*"

Hailey looked up as if she'd felt Emma staring, and for a moment, she simply stared back, until that irreverent smirk made her silver eyes sparkle again. "Things are looking up, eh? About time, too. Did you know the refugee shelters are overflowing? And I'm not just talking about this place."

With nowhere else to go, the Gray Dublin telepaths had made Hailey's lab their new home and center of operations. And since Torrey was by far the most peaceful place found anywhere anymore, word had reached the other worlds, and more telepaths and survivors kept pouring in, all hoping to start fresh and make a home here.

Only two problems with that. One: the facility hadn't been designed to house so many people. They'd converted convalescence rooms into dormitories, repurposed scientific equipment for off-world communication, and fought constantly for bathroom use. But making the best out of a bad situation still didn't make the situation any better. Even a community used to practically living in each other's minds reached its limits at living in each other's pockets.

And this coincided with the second problem: Hailey wasn't exactly known as a graceful hostess. After her genetic experimentation—on *herself*—Hailey was now only half human. The other half was a winter-loving, solitary apex predator who chafed something awful at having her territory invaded. This overcrowding drove her up the wall; she bristled constantly, snarled when people pressed in too close, and had begun to claw at those who dared to trespass on her alone time.

Nevertheless, they were all stuck here together. At least for the moment.

Hailey and the mind readers.

And the sole surviving Evolutionary, Alec, who was currently under house arrest, which didn't seem to bother him one bit while he followed the freshly recovered Melody around the facility like a pinned-on shadow.

The lab wasn't just a refuge, it was a field hospital for incoming wounded, of which there were legion. With Amelia and her husband struggling to make it back from wherever they'd gone, getting red-taped at each and every layover point, a week-long trip had stretched into three. And they'd be delayed even further. In the good doctor's absence, the telepaths were on their own, and the Brain had her hands full day and night with tending to as many people as she and her team could handle. By necessity, she'd become an expert at triage, and though she'd die before admitting it to anyone, Emma knew it took a terrible toll on the girl. She might have been an intellectual genius, but no one that young was ever prepared to make a life or death decision, let alone several throughout the day. The perpetual insomniac now cried herself into a two-hour nap every night, and no one but Emma ever heard the tears fall.

"Which reminds me," Hailey said. "I've been thinking. What if we usurped Hunt's castle? I know, it's nuts, but stay with me for a second here." She ticked off her reasons. "Hunt and his litter are gone. They might come back, they might not. And in the meantime, there's a big-ass stone fortress not ten miles away, going empty. It's a waste, if you ask me."

Despite the conflicts in the nearby village of Amberley, none of the troops had ever come close to Hunt's private land, let alone attempted to take the castle. Emma guessed it was probably for the same reason the telepaths hadn't: they knew whatever had built it was bigger and badder than what they could take on.

"It could work, right? And he wouldn't mind. He's all buddy-buddy with you people, anyway. And at least it would be *us*, not *them*." By *them*, she meant normal people—villagers, soldiers, and refugees who had no idea how special Hunt and his family were, and therefore couldn't use that knowledge against them.

Emma imagined the tiger man wouldn't be any happier about it than Hailey was at having *her* home invaded. But Hailey had a good point. The Hunts had disappeared, most likely forever, and Torrey had to move on without them.

Emma turned back to John and left Hailey to her own devices, but she heard the self-satisfaction in Hailey's voice when she said, "I knew you'd see things my way."

Hours later, Emma jerked up from her cramped position and realized with dismay that she'd fallen asleep at her post. No idea how much time she'd lost, or what she'd missed, but when she rolled her head on her shoulders to work out the kinks in her neck, she saw Jessica sitting on the floor beside the tank, gazing at John with hollow eyes. "I stopped the meds and the electric charge," the child genius whispered. "It's just him in there now."

"What time is it?" Emma asked, voice raw and quivering.

Guessing the real question behind her query, Jessica answered, "If he has any chance at all, we'll know in the next two to three hours."

Emma nodded and, sitting back in her chair, broke off all physical contact with the tank, clenching her hands together so hard they hurt. She didn't care. With Jessica sitting next to her, lost in her own thoughts, Emma watched her soldier boy breathe liquid, and waited.

Live, she silently willed. *Surviving isn't enough anymore. I need you to live!*

Unbidden, Annabel's ghostly voice returned from memory to echo through Emma's mind and, without meaning to, Emma voiced the words aloud. "We are the construct of a universe which has no beginning, no end, and no limits. It has no rules. So why should we?"

She sensed Jeremy's skepticism before he'd even stepped clear of the doorway, though he made no reply. Instead, he came in, sat down on Emma's other side, and pried her hands apart to take one into his, leaving her free hand empty, lacking anything to hold on to, until Hailey came back in and took it in both of hers. Moments later, Lucia appeared at her back, her hands on Emma's shoulder, followed by Rafe, mirroring her from the other side. When Nell limped inside, her leg still in a cast, a restless quiescence settled over them.

But the gathering wasn't over. One by one, the room filled with people—her friends, the only family she'd ever known, all quietly offering her the support Emma hadn't realized she'd so sorely needed. They didn't say a word the whole time. Their presence was enough. She wasn't alone. No more white walls caging her in, no invisible shield swallowing her voice. She felt warm, and loved, and protected, and none of it made a damn bit of difference to her fluttering heart. Nor did it make her breaths come any easier, or do anything to stem the flow of stinging tears as she watched the man inside the tank for any hint of movement.

Seconds turned into minutes. An hour gone, and still nothing.

Lucia gently raked her fingers through Emma's tangled hair. It'd used to soothe her to sleep back when she'd been a child, when she'd waited for her big brother to return from a long assignment. Now, her worry was deeper than the gesture could soothe, and Lucia's tension radiated through her with every move until Emma thought she'd burst out of her skin.

Two hours gone.

Time was running out. The longer John remained unconscious, the smaller his chances of making it through.

Desperate, Emma broke free to press her forehead back to the glass, palms flat on either side. The others muttered behind her. She shut them out, closed her eyes to better feel. All these years, nothing had ever been able to wake John up from a nightmare when it took him over.

Except for Emma.

I know what to do, she realized. *I've done it before.*

He'd only been asleep then, but his shields had been at their strongest. They felt different to her now. There was a chance.

Before she could reason herself out of the attempt, Emma gathered herself for a telepathic equivalent of a body punch. Had to get it right on the first try—all or nothing. Battering him repeatedly might do more harm than good.

Ready…

Not yet!

Give it all you've got.

Ready…

Almost…

Now!

Emma released the pulse with so much force, the others gave a cry of alarm. Jeremy shouted her name, shot to his feet, and wrapped his arms around her to pull her away, as Jessica rushed to the controls. They yelled, one over the other, with pain and confusion throbbing across Emma's telepathic channels. She still wasn't fully in control of her mind; they'd all felt the blow she'd meant to direct at John alone.

With Hailey writhing on the floor, mid-shift, and Jessica calling for sedatives, Emma watched John and gathered for another strike. *Can't give up. Just one more try…*

Suddenly, the tank erupted with frenzied movement, liquid churning, sloshing over the rim, soaking Jessica and Rafe.

They all froze.

"Get him out!" Emma screamed, fighting Jeremy to get free. "Drain the tank; you have to get him out!"

Jessica fumbled at the controls, too stunned to think clearly, while Rafe searched for the release valve. *Too damn slow!* Whether John remembered anything or not, he'd just woken up under water, liquid filling his lungs. He was panicking, heart rate spiking to dangerous levels.

Emma wriggled around in Jeremy's hold, grabbed the weapon he now carried strapped to his hip at all times, and fired two shots at the tank. Glass shattered and fluid exploded all over the room, depositing John on the floor at her feet. She threw the weapon aside, then dropped to her knees as his body convulsed to expel the liquid from his lungs. Shaking and curled up on his side, John tried to push himself up, but his hands kept slipping in puddles, eyes rolling back in his head. He stubbornly blinked against the impulse, fought to stay conscious.

"Soldier boy?" Emma gathered him into her lap, cupped his face, and looked down into his bloodshot eyes for any hint of recognition. "John! Can you hear me?"

Hacking coughs racked his frame, even after his lungs were empty. He wheezed, and Emma winced at the pained sound. "Get a blanket," she ordered.

As if she'd woken from her stupor, Jessica snapped to attention and sent the others scurrying to fetch her tools and supplies. The room emptied out in a hurry. Soon, everyone was gone, except for Jessica and Jeremy. A wet piece of torn cloth floated over to Emma, the only indication that a very cranky snow leopard Hailey now prowled the lab halls. Jeremy hadn't rushed out to corral her, so she wasn't out for blood. That was a relief, at least.

"John? Seashell…"

Jessica needed to get to him, to check his vitals and to see how much damage Emma's little stunt had caused. But Emma wouldn't let go of him, and as the others poured back in, assembling a stretcher and handing over supplies, John's arm curled around her hips, clutching so tight it hurt.

"John!" She shook his shoulder. If he felt anything, he gave no indication, but Emma somehow *sensed* his discomfort. He was cold, disoriented. The unfamiliar territory had put him in a panic, but even while he knew he should be doing something about it, he didn't know what. Light stabbed into his eyes, and he turned his face into Emma's midsection to hide from it. The small motion curled him tighter around her; a fetal position with her stuck in the middle. No one could pry him loose to get him on the gurney.

"We need to move him," Jessica said. "He's already bordering on hypothermia. The shock to his system could make his heart arrest—"

Emma shushed them all and waved them back. They blasted her

with indignation and concern, but they did back away.

In a softer tone, trying like hell to calm herself down, Emma spoke to her Shadow Hawk. "Soldier boy, can you hear me?"

His shields were still solid; she couldn't see through them, but somehow, he projected outward, and his answer was… chaotic, confusing. All emotion, no coherent thought; just impressions of too many things wrong. He knew he'd lost time, and not knowing how much terrified him. Knew he was supposed to do something important, but couldn't remember what. Knew he was chin-deep in a life-or-death situation, but couldn't piece together why or what threat he was supposed to guard against.

Guard. Because he had something to protect.

Something important, and beautiful, and delicate. Something that made him feel ashamed.

Emma stroked his wet hair. "You're safe," she said, and his shivers translated to her until she couldn't keep her hand steady. "No one's going to hurt you."

Sound against her belly. John was trying to speak.

Desperate for anything, Emma leaned down to hear better. "What was that?"

He tilted his head just enough to make himself heard. "H-how does the… water. Fall. In the waterfall?"

Her happy cry carried far and wide, startling everyone within earshot. Emma didn't care. John was alive; her anchor was back! His mind would take time to heal, of course, but by all that was holy, he *would* heal. Emma would make sure of that.

For now, he was with her, and that was all that mattered.

They were safe, and together, and these days, that was more than anyone could hope for.

"I've got you," she said, "and I'm not letting you go again."

When he gave her a squeeze in answer, Emma knew they'd make it, just fine.

– 60 –

Senator Matthew Griffith didn't like surprises. He liked them even less when they didn't work to his favor. That annoying little precog prick was lucky he'd died of an aneurysm during the siege on Green 24. Otherwise, Griffith would hunt him down and skin him alive, strip by strip. How dare he interfere with his plans!

This defeat set him back *years*! Now, not only did he have to babysit a bunch of whiny politicians—who should have been installed into an alternate housing facility and out of Griffith's hair while he restructured a new governing body—he also needed to rebuild an entire Shadow unit from the ground up!

Well, almost from the ground up.

He smiled grimly at his e-pad's readout. Seventy-two Hounds and three Hawks had survived the attack on Green 24. Most of them had been away on assignment at the time. He would simply redistribute them among the other nineteen units scattered across the galaxy until the construction of Outpost Red 3 was completed.

Let MacMurphy and his savants celebrate their little victory; let them throw their own into the fire like they'd been doing. So far, six planets had declared peace and were beginning work on reconstruction, all in a matter of weeks? Ha! Over a dozen more were still mired in death. Sooner or later, the telepaths would get tired of dying for the effort, especially with Griffith's Shadows swooping in to rile the people up again.

He'd strike just when things seemed to be on the verge of stabilizing, and he'd do it as many times as necessary for MacMurphy to get the point.

Shadows might die, but they never lost.

The last laugh would still belong to Griffith.

Last door at the end of the hallway was his office, where a Hound waited to report on the progress of outpost Red 3. Last week, ground had been broken, and if Griffith's calculations were correct, the main facility should have been completed, with the barracks nearly so. Any luck, and the supply line would keep functioning without disruption for another month. After that, Red 3 would be complete, and the Shadows could begin recruiting. Already he had several possible candidates in mind. The war had created an awful lot of orphans with a grudge. What sort of person would he be, if he didn't help them channel that rage into a productive endeavor?

Which reminded him, he'd need to contact the House of Holy Mercy about that woman, Laura McNally. Griffith slammed the door behind him, mood fouling. Talk about a thorn in his side. "Report," he ordered, not bothering to spare the Hound a glance. Just to stand in the presence of their commander in chief was privilege enough. Shadows shouldn't be given too much slack on the leash; they might decide to demand more.

"Hello, Matthew."

Griffith whirled around. No. Impossible! "How did you find me?"

John MacMurphy unfolded from his seat, slowly straightening to his full height of several inches taller than Griffith. MacMurphy had changed little in the last twenty years; his hair had grayed and his face was now creased with fine lines, but he still carried that same pride in the square set of his shoulders and the stubborn tilt of his chin. "Turns out, that 'little precog prick' had one last ace up his sleeve."

Griffith shook his head, and kept shaking it as he backed away, putting the desk between himself and his lifelong enemy. His heel caught on the foot of his chair, and he sat down hard. "No, this is a trick. You're not really here; you're messing with my head!" Just like when they were young. Always with the pranks, and the jokes, and the rooting out of his secrets until Griffith had learned to anticipate MacMurphy's moves, to prepare himself to misdirect him before he decided to provoke.

"How do you suppose I'm doing that? This entire building is shielded." MacMurphy approached the desk, placed his hands onto the polished surface to lean into Griffith. "You and I have a score to settle."

No, no, no! This didn't compute! MacMurphy was supposed to be on Torrey, hip deep in telepath casualties! He'd been monitoring the numbers, and their dead were in the thousands—they should have been chasing their tails to regroup, not mounting an offensive!

MacMurphy smiled at Griffith's unease. "You'll be wanting to push that alarm button now." Then he raised an eyebrow. "On second thought, don't bother. It's been disabled, along with all coms in this part of the building. Your soldiers have orders to stand guard outside and not enter under any circumstance until you tell them. Which you won't."

Griffith steepled his fingers to hide their sudden nervous quiver. *Bluster. Stall for time.* He always came out on top in situations like this. It was his gift. "So what now? We duke it out, man to man? Like in the old days?" MacMurphy would strike first where he thought Griffith was most vulnerable: in his sense of entitlement. He'd make Griffith believe he wasn't worthy, that everything he'd done had been for nothing, a waste of time and resources. He'd make Griffith feel the size of an insect, then crush him with a few choice words. But Griffith could stall the inevitable. He'd only need a few seconds to get his backup com out of his pocket and—

MacMurphy chuckled. "What do you know about the old days?"

Griffith frowned. "What do you mean?"

MacMurphy stared him down, a steady gaze that pierced through the shield of a nonsensical rhyme, around the blocks he'd erected to protect his ego, straight to the heart of Griffith. Looking into those unflinching eyes, Griffith *felt* his past change. MacMurphy trolled through his memories, altering details here and there, and subtly shifting the core of what made Griffith who he was, warping not what he'd accomplished, but what he remembered and had forgotten. Little by little, his memory of John J. MacMurphy faded away, as if the two of them had never met.

When MacMurphy's telepathic presence retreated, taking with it even the unease at his physical presence in his office, Griffith was left facing an impertinent idiot who'd somehow gotten in without an appointment, and his cheek twitched angrily. "What do you want, Mr. MacMurphy? I don't have all day."

"I'm here to give you the status report you requested."

Had he? Oh, yes. He'd been waiting for news. Hadn't realized it would be delivered in person. He'd have been much happier with a written report, but at least this way, Griffith could better discern if the man was lying to him. "Well? Get on with it, then!"

"You'll be happy to know the SUE is making excellent progress on reconstitution. Initial feedback is positive, and losses have been minimal so far." His voice lowered to add, "Of course, even the smallest loss is a grievous one."

Griffith hummed in agreement. "Yes, lamentable. Go on." He didn't bother to fabricate sincerity; his mind had better things to do. If the numbers added up, by year's end, society would be at peace once again, mourning their dead, but building forward instead of fighting back. Somehow, that made him feel... dissatisfied.

"Once our work is finished, we'll be disbanding the SUE back into individual chapters. The governance of society will return to the municipal level and build from there. Just like old times."

"Old times, yes." The words brought up resentment so deep, it left a bad taste in the back of Griffith's mouth, but he couldn't seem to recall why. Something to do with... Oh, who the hell cared?

"Emma Calen will take over the Torrey Unit in my place. She doesn't know it yet, but she'll step in naturally when I don't come back. The others trust her; she'll do well by them."

Griffith slammed his heel down on the plush carpet. Another miscalculation. The Calen girl should have been his! *Mustn't let him see a weakness, or he'll pounce.* The thought welled up out of nowhere and disappeared again in the next instant. "Anything else? I'm a very busy man, Mr. MacMurphy. Let's hurry this up, shall we?"

MacMurphy shrugged. "As you wish. I only have one last message to impart."

All at once, Griffith's vision hazed over with black, startling him, and he let out an undignified shriek. He blindly groped for a com as, deep in the darkness, images began to form—a quaint little town like something out of ancient times, for which his mind supplied a name: Torrey. The vision zoomed down from above and into the streets where people milled, smiling at each other and stopping to hold conversations as if no one had anywhere important to be. A message seemed to be stamped across the background. Not spelled out in words, but implied with a feeling: *You didn't break us, and you never will.*

Before he could dwell on what that could possibly mean, Griffith zoomed through the streets and across a sprawling field to a castle—a real castle! Inside the courtyard, dozens of children played. Like a ghost, Griffith faded through them to enter the main hall where adults went about their daily work, and a little girl with wild hair and wearing a lab coat gave orders to her waiting team. When they dispersed, Griffith followed one of them into a different room, this one with a balcony overlooking the lake. A smaller group sat around in a circle, smiling and laughing, as if they heard something Griffith couldn't. Another message there: *We thrive together, and we always have.*

The bad feeling in the pit of his stomach worsened. His hands shook, and he felt afraid, as if this was all just a show to distract him while something feral snuck up behind his back. Yet he couldn't look away; the vision forced itself on him, and whisked him away to a nursery, then gone again to a library of old paper books. And again, to a kitchen with a wood-burning stove, a tower looking out over the landscape, and down to a dungeon with its maze of computers and holographic screens. Up and down, sideways and forwards, then back again, and 'round and 'round until Griffith couldn't tell which way his feet pointed anymore.

Finally, the vortex spat him out into the gardens to hover over a particular pair, who lay together on a blanket in the tall grass, the woman's red hair haloed around her head, the man sifting his fingers through it. They talked in utter gibberish; familiar words strung together in ways that made absolutely no sense to Griffith, but the two of them seemed to understand each other just fine.

"W-what is this?" His voice didn't sound like it belonged to him. Surely, he'd never emitted such a pathetic sound! Senator Griffith didn't whimper!

The redheaded woman laughed, but stopped when the man didn't laugh with her. She gazed into his face, and her expression softened, her eyes burning with liquid heat. "I love you, seashell," she said.

The man's shoulders rose and fell in a great, heavy sigh, as if her words had affected him beyond what he could bear. "Forever and infinity, Pixie-girl."

"This is the fruit of your labors," MacMurphy replied, his voice sounding so very far away.

Was it? No, it couldn't be. If he'd been working for this, then why did he feel such crushing defeat? Why was he so enraged? "What have you done to me? *Guards!*"

"You always thought you knew me so well, that you could predict every move I made." Griffith swiveled his head to follow the source of that voice from one side to the other, while the vision of the two lovers embracing in the sun mocked him. No matter how hard he tried, he couldn't get rid of it. "There is one secret I never told you, old friend. Because if you'd known, you'd have never stopped looking over your shoulder. Always so curious about my core ability; always trying to ferret it out so you could plug it into your equations. You're about to have a taste of it, firsthand."

"St-stop this," Griffith wheezed, and he swiped his arm sideways, knocking himself out of his chair. "Guards!" he wailed, crawling away as the lovers in his mind began to undress each other.

"They can't help you anymore," MacMurphy whispered right at his ear.

Griffith struck out at thin air.

The edges of the vision began to fade. "For all you've taken from us, I'll deprive you of everything you have. Your words, first. So no matter how hard you try, you'll never be able to speak another order again. Not even to save your own life."

As if on command, Griffith's tongue stuck to the roof of his mouth. He moaned and forced his mouth to open wide, but even when he moved his tongue, the instinctive knowledge of *how* to speak eluded him. His call for help eked out as an animalistic cry, unstructured, wordless, and as he scrambled for a way to form the letters with his hands, he discovered they'd forgotten, as well.

"Next, your sight, so all you'll ever have are memories of what you think the world looks like."

His vision went dark, remnants of the lovers' tryst floating like photo negatives across his mind for a moment before they faded into nothing. Fear gripped him so tight he couldn't breathe. He couldn't recall the room's layout, or what his attacker looked like, or even what *he* looked like! And he couldn't form into words how much that terrified him. But he still understood MacMurphy speak. At least he still had that.

"And one last thing," MacMurphy said. "But before I take it away, I want you to know why I'm not killing you right now."

Griffith whimpered, crawling backwards until his head hit a wall. His shaking hands traced it to a corner, and he pressed himself into it as that terrible voice followed, close enough to murmur evil straight into his ear.

"Death is too merciful a sentence for you," it said with the calmness of a reaper. "A thousand torturous deaths would never be sufficient punishment for all the evil you've sown into this world. I can't undo any of it, but I sure as hell can make you pay. Someone you would have destroyed taught me that."

I would have remade the world from its ashes! he screamed inside his mind. His voice boomed there, but the powerful sound transformed into a choked squeak when it slipped past his numb lips.

"You see… well, I suppose you don't. But do know that this thing I'm doing to you can never be reversed. New eyes will never bring back your sight. No amount of therapy will ever restore your ability to communicate. And once I take away your hearing, no surgery will ever give it back to you. Because your eyes and ears still work, I'm simply preventing your brain from deciphering what they take in. Likewise, your brain can still understand language, it just can't project it. By any method known to man."

This can't be happening. It's only a nightmare! He'd had them often enough in the past, but his thrashing heart had always woken him up, back into the safety of his own bed, with a contingent of armed guards standing between him and the boogeyman.

Why wasn't he waking up?

Wake up!

"This is your punishment, Senator Matthew Griffith, the great and terrible commander in chief of the most fearsome army ever trained. I'll reduce you to a deaf, blind, and dumb pile of useless shit. For the rest of your pathetic life, you'll be a prisoner in your own mind, and it won't matter how much you scream. No one will ever help you."

Sounds in the room. A swish of fabric, footsteps on the polished floor, walking away. Griffith desperately clung to those sounds. The door had to be somewhere in that direction. If he could just get to it, call for help out in the hallway…

The door opened. "Goodbye, old friend. I won't see you again."

Two more footsteps, then the door clicked shut.

And Senator Matthew Griffith, the great and terrible commander in chief of the most fearsome army ever trained, never heard his own scream tear out of the terrified kernel of his soul.

The End

ALIANNE DONNELLY is an avid lover of stories of all kinds. Raised on a healthy diet of fairy tales in a place where they almost seemed real, she grew into a writer who seeks magic in the modern age and enjoys sharing a little bit of it with the world through every story she writes. Her books span the spectrum from fantasy to science fiction with varying degrees of romance sprinkled throughout. Alianne now lives in California, where she spends her free time reading, writing, and daydreaming. For more books, news, and updates, visit aliannedonnelly.com.